THE
FASHION
DESIGNER

THE
FASHION
DESIGNER

NANCY MOSER

SHILOH RUN PRESS
An Imprint of Barbour Publishing, Inc.

Print ISBN 978-1-68322-601-7

eBook Editions:
Adobe Digital Edition (.epub) 978-1-68322-809-7
Kindle and MobiPocket Edition (.prc) 978-1-68322-810-3

This book is a work of fiction. Names, characters, places, and incidents are either products of the author's imagination or used fictitiously. Any similarity to actual people, organizations, and/or events is purely coincidental.

Cover Design: Faceout Studio, www.faceoutstudio.com

Published in association with the Books & Such Literary Management, Janet Kobobel Grant, 52 Mission Circle, Suite 122, PMB 170, Santa Rosa, California 95409-5370, www.booksandsuch.com

Published by Shiloh Run Press, an imprint of Barbour Publishing, Inc., 1810 Barbour Drive, Uhrichsville, Ohio 44683, www.shilohrunpress.com

Our mission is to inspire the world with the life-changing message of the Bible.

ecpa Member of the
Evangelical Christian
Publishers Association

Printed in the United States of America.

DEDICATION

To my family
who taught me that
dreams can come true
with faith, hope, and hard work

**

"Be strong and do the work."
1 CHRONICLES 28:10 NIV

CHAPTER ONE

Late August 1912
New York City

Annie Culver tidied her work table for the last time. She set her ruler and French curve to the side and placed her scissors, tablet, and pencil in a drawer. These tools of her trade had become extensions of herself, a way to transfer a fashion idea into a dress pattern that could be used by home sewers across the world. Idea to pattern to finished product.

I've come so far. Am I a fool for leaving it all behind?

"Get a move on, Annie." Her friend and coworker Maude Nascato stood at the door of the workroom. "Risk not, want not."

Maude's strange phrase snapped Annie out of her reverie. "What does that mean?"

Maude pinned a straw hat onto her black upswept hair. "Whatever it needs to mean to warm your cold feet." She paused and gave the room one last look. "Our quitting is a good thing, Annie. As Mark Twain said, 'I was seldom able to see an opportunity until it had ceased to be one.' We've seen the opportunity. We're walking through this door and into a new adventure."

"But is the opportunity a wise choice?"

Maude released an exasperated sigh, strode to the table, took Annie by the arm, and marched her out of the workroom. "Courageous people don't look back."

"I don't feel courageous. I feel nauseous."

Maude laughed. "I'm afraid it goes with the territory."

They met Annie's husband, Sean, on the sidewalk outside. He too worked for Butterick Pattern Company but was staying in his position. Someone had to pay the rent.

He studied her face. "It will be all right, Annie-girl."

"You promise?"

Maude started walking, leading the way to a celebration commemorating their momentous decision. "I am compelled to quote another author. John Galsworthy has pinned Annie to a tree with this quote." She took a fresh breath before saying, "A worrier is 'one who is always building dungeons in the air.'" She put a period on the phrase with a sharp nod.

Annie took offense. "Do you have any more quotations to toss at me?"

"Not at the moment."

"What a relief. But to your complaints about my worrying, how can I not worry, Maude? How can you two be so calm? This is an enormous step we're taking. We have no idea if our new business will succeed. And if it doesn't, I'm not the only one out of a job, but you and Edna too. She's worked at Macy's for decades and is quitting because of some harebrained idea I came up with. What if we fail?"

Maude stopped walking and faced her. "What if that building there suddenly falls to the ground in front of us? What if that motor car jumps the curb and runs us down? What if—?"

Sean stopped her tirade. "Your examples are overly dramatic."

She shrugged. " 'Twas all I could come up with on short notice." She slipped her hand around Annie's arm. "There are worries big and small all around us. Some we can deal with directly, and some we can't."

"I know you," Sean said, taking Annie's other arm. "You've never let circumstances stop you. You won't let anything get in your way."

Annie tried to embrace their confidence, yet the worry remained.

❦

"Welcome, fellow rebels!" Edna Holmquist greeted her friends as they entered the flat she shared with Maude.

"I prefer the term 'brave soldiers,'" Maude said.

Annie spotted Sean's parents—her in-laws of nearly four months—and hoped the terminology wouldn't make things worse, for his father had vociferously argued against their plan. Annie kissed her mother-in-law, Vesta, on the cheek. "It's not as sensational as they imply." She turned to Edna. "How was your last day at Macy's?"

"Poignant." She sighed dramatically.

"How many sewing machines have you sold over twenty-two years?" Maude asked.

"One thousand two hundred twelve."

Annie laughed. "You kept track?"

"My sales book kept track."

"Pfft." Richard Culver returned to the sofa. "It's ridiculous to discard perfectly good jobs to pursue an idiotic folly."

"Hello to you too, Father," Sean said. He kissed his mother's cheek, and they shared a look of commiseration.

"I believe in you," Vesta said. "I am thrilled with the notion that you three ladies will be starting your own fashion company."

"The *notion*," Richard said. "Not reality."

Edna offered him a sandwich from a tray. "It is a reality, Mr. Culver," she said. "We have financial backing, creative energy, and a fire in our bellies."

"It's a fool's errand, doomed to failure." He looked askance at the ham-and-cheese sandwich, took one, then set it on his plate on the end table beside him.

Annie was not going to let him squelch their joy, yet she wasn't comfortable enough with the family dynamics to stand up to him. From what she'd learned from Sean and Vesta, their lifetime quest was to keep Richard on an even keel. It was the best anyone could ask for, as the man never seemed happy. Except perhaps when he was making money in his general store in Brooklyn. Though even then, profits were never high enough, employees lazy, and the preferences of customers, woefully fickle.

Annie had a choice to make. She could let Richard's negativity squelch their celebration—and feed into her own worries—or choose to be enthusiastic and encouraging.

She owed it to her friends to choose the latter.

Famished, she took a large bite of her sandwich. "Edna, these hit the spot." When she was finished with the bite, she said, "I know the risk we are all taking and thank you for it. Beyond the unknowns, I am chuffed to bits about our new venture." She took up a glass of lemonade and held it high. "To New York City's newest, most brilliant, and most smashing fashion house!"

"Hear, hear!"

Everyone toasted except for Richard, but Annie refused to let him drown the moment. She was done with him.

"When is our meeting at the Sampsons' tomorrow?" Edna asked, as she sat and ate her own sandwich.

"Ten o'clock," Maude said. "Have we decided on a name for our company yet?"

"I vote for Annie's Dresses," Edna said.

"I second that name," Vesta said. "You should get the credit, Annie, for if it wasn't for—"

Richard pointed to the seat beside him. "Shush, woman. You are not a part of this. Sit."

Annie despaired the look of hurt resignation on Vesta's face. But she knew a way to brighten it. She took Sean's hand and gave him a look. "Yes?" she whispered.

He drew her hand to his lips. "We have something else to celebrate besides the start of a new business—the real reason we asked you here tonight." He looked to Annie.

"We are also starting a new family." She scanned the faces of their audience.

Vesta jumped from her seat. "A baby?"

Annie nodded and felt tears fill her eyes. "It's due in February."

She was embraced by all—as was Sean.

Richard remained noticeably seated. Finally, all eyes turned to him.

"Father? Will you congratulate us?"

"We will be grandparents, Richard. Isn't it grand?"

He took a sip of lemonade then set the glass down. "You two certainly move quickly."

Annie felt a wave of disappointment. Couldn't he be happy for them?

Sean put an arm around her waist. "After nearly being on the *Titanic*, we realize life is short."

Maude nodded. "The three of us had an amazing time in Paris getting ideas for Butterick at the fashion shows, but all would have been for naught if we hadn't missed our train to Cherbourg."

Annie finished the scenario. "Which caused us to miss the sailing."

"God saved you," Edna said.

Vesta's eyes turned misty. "Saved you, and saved your future together. I'm so pleased with your happy news."

Sean kissed Annie's cheek. "Our close call is why we married soon after we got home from Europe."

"We did not expect a child so quickly," Annie admitted. "But we are not in control of such things. God is."

"Tell Him to slow down," Richard muttered.

"Richard!" Vesta said.

Annie heard Sean's breath hasten. How dare his father mar this special moment? "We will not ask God to slow down," she said. "The Almighty is never late and never early, and we are very willing to accept His perfect timing."

"Indeed we are," Maude said. "A marriage and a new life came out of our close call, and so did the business."

Edna lifted her glass. "To God's perfect timing!"

Hear, hear.

CHAPTER TWO

T hey live *here*?" Maude asked as they stood in front of 451 Madison Avenue.

"In that wing," Annie said, pointing to the four-story brick-and-stone wing to the right of an outdoor atrium.

"There are four other smaller townhouses in the rest of the building," Sean added, pointing around the horseshoe-shaped structure. "But wait until you see the inside of the Sampsons'. Theirs is enormous, and everything is covered in gilt, marble, marquetry, and—"

"Marquetry?" Edna asked.

"Tiny pieces of wood inlaid together to make a design," Annie said. "Macy's had some boxes with marquetry for sale. I saw an inlaid table too."

Edna stared at the building. The flowers in her wide-brimmed hat shuddered in the breeze. "Boxes are one thing, I just never thought it would be used in a house. Mansion. Manor. Whatever it is."

They walked through an ornate wrought-iron gate, and Maude led the way to a double-entry door. "No stopping now. We need to go into whatever-it-is in order to fulfill our fashion destiny."

"Whatever *it* is," Annie said under her breath. For though she tried to exhibit an air of confidence about their future, she knew Mrs. Sampson better than anyone, and knew her to be zealous to the point of folly and fickle to the point of frustration—everyone else's but usually not her own. Her thought process was unique and often unfathomable.

It's unfathomable that she believes I can be a viable fashion designer.

"Annie? Are you coming?" Sean asked.

She was so glad it was Saturday and he could come with them. Annie shifted her portfolio of fashion designs under the other arm and pretended she was brave. She rang the bell.

They were shown inside by a butler. He motioned them to the right, down a wide hallway leading to the drawing room. "The Sampsons will be with you shortly."

Annie was glad for the delay as it would give her friends time to absorb the opulence around them.

Maude gazed at the hall floor. "Look at this tile. There must be thousands of pieces put together to create the design." With a hand to hold her hat, she looked up. "And look at the ceiling. Are those tiles too?"

They all looked up at the barrel vaults that interconnected above them. They were replete with intricate patterns like the floor.

"All that detail for a hallway," Maude whispered.

"The drawing room is even fancier. Follow me."

Annie's sense of purpose intensified when she reminded herself she'd been in the drawing room before, during her first meeting with the Sampsons the previous autumn. She and Sean had also experienced the vast dining room that evening. Those facts spurred her confidence—to a small degree.

Once through the drawing room doors, the newcomers gasped—with good reason. The room was enormous, with marble walls and columns. The ceiling was coffered and covered in gilt. Painted murals divided windows on three sides. The fourth side sported two fireplaces flanking the entrance where they stood.

Annie pointed to the elaborate floor. "See, Edna? Marquetry."

"I hate to step on it."

"Who knows how to create such things?" Maude asked.

"Who has the money to pay for the labor of it?" Sean said.

"The Sampsons do, and—" Annie heard footsteps echo in the long hall. "Shh."

They all faced the door, ready to greet their host and hostess.

Mrs. Sampson swept in, the ruffles on her dress waving like lavender flags of chiffon. She immediately did a twirl. "You like?"

Actually. . . "Is it new?"

"Brand. I had my dressmaker whip it up for our time in Newport this summer." She executed another twirl. "It portrays the essence of graceful motion, don't you think?"

The essence of flaunting too many flourishes. "It does move well," Annie said diplomatically.

"The color is beautiful," Edna managed.

"The chiffon is feminine," Maude added.

Mrs. Sampson stopped her preening. "*Is* beautiful and *does* move, as if you are finding it difficult to find something nice to say about it?"

Oh dear.

"I meant no offense," Maude said. "I meant to say that fabric that is sheer and flowy—in general and in respect to your specific dress—is—"

Luckily Mr. Sampson intervened. "Why don't we sit and work out the details of our joint venture?"

"I've been stewing about it all summer," Mrs. Sampson added.

Mr. Sampson winked at her. "And if you know Eleanor, you know she can only stew so long before she spills the pot."

As they were shown to some chairs, Annie and Maude exchanged a look of relief at getting through their awkward faux pas. It would not bode well to be on tenterhooks before the main discussion began—a life-changing discussion.

Sean helped Mr. Sampson draw some other chairs closer together, creating an intimate circle in the huge space, a circle suitable for conversation.

Mrs. Sampson arranged the myriad of ruffles on her lap and over the arms of the chair. Only when she was finished did she speak. "Well then."

Her words were met with silence. Finally Annie said, "Where do we begin?"

"With a soiree, of course."

"A what?" Sean asked.

Mr. Sampson interpreted. "A party. Eleanor loves parties."

"I do. I happen to be quite good at giving them."

"And attending them," he said.

"That too." She drew in a deep breath as though fueling her next words. "The plan is for you to sew up a dozen dresses and have a fashion soiree right here, with the who's who of New York City in attendance. In fact, I will ask their daughters to be the models. The whole of society will be so awed by your designs that they will order them in copious amounts and—"

Annie lifted a hand, stopping her words. "I thought our customers were working women."

"Everyday women," Maude said.

Edna nodded and pointed to Annie's portfolio. "Annie's already drawn up some designs that we think—"

Annie began to reach for it, but Mrs. Sampson stopped her with a hand.

"Not yet." Her face had grown stern. "I believe we need to remedy this misconception between us."

It was more than a mere misconception. It was the essence of their business.

Sean sat forward in his chair. "Remember when we spoke about the business on the voyage home from the Paris fashion shows?"

Mr. Sampson let out a breath. "After we all narrowly missed the *Titanic*."

Annie shivered at the memory. "I will never forget when our captain told us the news of its sinking—while we were still out on the ocean."

Maude scoffed. "I still hold it against him that he said everyone was saved, when clearly they were not."

"Now, now, Miss Nascato," Mr. Sampson said. "False information is rampant in times of great tragedy."

Maude sighed. "I still miss Madame."

Annie nodded. Although the rest of them on the Paris junket had been delayed—and therefore saved—their superior, Madame Le Fleur, had found a way to make the train. And the boarding. She had perished in the icy waters of the North Atlantic.

Mr. Sampson's wife put a hand on his arm. "We were saved for this. I know it."

Annie was glad to get back to the subject at hand. "I agree with you. But as Sean pointed out, our initial idea was to provide functional, comfortable, and stylish clothing for the masses."

"Not the elite," Maude added.

Mrs. Sampson played with the draping on her sleeve. "Yes, I suppose that was the original intent, but I've had second thoughts, more grandiose thoughts."

Annie's stomach grabbed. "But that's why you two invited me here for that first meeting when I was working at Butterick. You were against the ridiculous fashion of the hobble skirt and other designs that constricted women's movement and ignored their needs. You were a proponent of function over fad."

"That is true," Mr. Sampson said—mostly to his wife. "That *was* our initial focus, Eleanor. Perhaps you've strayed a bit off the mark."

She sprang to her feet. "Off the mark? I have found the mark, and it is a bull's-eye! If Eleanor's Couture is going to be a success—"

"Eleanor's Couture?" Annie's throat was dry.

"Well yes. I *am* at the epicenter of this business." She stared at Annie. "Am I not?"

Maude answered for them. "If you will excuse me, I thought Annie was the epicenter. If not for her, none of us would be here."

"If not for our money, none of you could afford to be here."

Her words skittered across the marquetry and landed in the space between them.

"My sweet. . .you are too blunt."

Mrs. Sampson turned to her husband. "I speak the truth, Harold. Are we not the ones at risk here? Who knows how much this endeavor will cost us?"

Mr. Sampson offered a sheepish smile. "Forgive my wife's frank nature. But you must admit the extent of the financial risk is unknown."

"That it is," Sean said. "And we appreciate your backing and support."

Annie had to speak her mind. "With all respect, we are also risking much. Edna, Maude, and I have quit our jobs to fully and wholeheartedly pursue this venture."

The Sampsons blinked, as if they hadn't thought of this point.

Mr. Sampson broke the silence. "All the more reason for our support."

Annie felt her heart race. Her legs twitched, longing to stride out of the room, out of the whatever-it-was, and return home. Perhaps it wasn't too late to get their jobs back.

Sean must have sensed the direction of her thoughts, for he touched a calming hand to her knee. "The main issue seems to be the identification of our customers."

"Ordinary women," Maude said.

"Wealthy women," Mrs. Sampson said. "Focusing on them will be the surest way to gain a profit."

"That could be true," Sean said. "And we all want the business to be successful. As Annie stated, the ladies have given up their livelihood betting on it. But there is more than profit involved. There is purpose."

"A purpose we all share," Annie said. She wished her heart would stop pounding because she knew her voice would too strongly reflect her emotions. This was business. She needed to approach it like a businesswoman. *Please, God, help me say the right thing*. She managed a smile. "Perhaps we can compromise."

"That is always a wise suggestion," Mr. Sampson said. "Continue."

"Perhaps we can create the twelve dresses and have your party."

"Soiree."

Annie let it go. "It *would* be a good way to gain the opinions of fashionable women. And the orders that are generated can keep the company afloat at the beginning and give us time to create a full line for a less-gentrified customer."

Mrs. Sampson readjusted her flounces. "It's possible. You've brought sketches?"

❦

The four friends entered Sean and Annie's flat with a communal sigh as though they'd been waiting to be in a familiar place before taking a full breath.

"I'm exhausted," Edna said.

Maude threw her plumed hat on the table, where it was saved from the floor by Sean's coffee cup. "Sorry," she said, moving it. "And I agree. Maybe that's why none of us have talked since we left the Sampsons'."

Annie removed her hatpins, stuck them in the brim of her hat, and hung it on the coat rack. "My mind is a muddle."

"A middling, mauling muddle." Maude took a seat at the table.

Before sitting across from Maude, Sean hung his derby next to Annie's hat and removed his suit jacket against the heat. Edna sat on the window seat and set her hat beside her.

Their hats off signaled they were in for the long haul.

"Muddled minds or no, it's time to talk this through," Edna said.

"Eleanor's Couture," Maude said.

They groaned.

"It's so hoity-toity," Edna said.

"As I told her, not what we had in mind at all," Annie said.

"We should have had a name ready," Sean said.

"It certainly would *not* have had 'couture' in it," Maude said.

"Better late than never; perhaps we need to offer Eleanor an alternative." Annie strolled to the window. The street below teemed with everyday women going about the business of living. She sat beside Edna. "Let's share some words to describe our customer and what they want out of clothing in general."

A stream of words were tossed into the air between them: *comfort, ease, style, affordability.*

"How about calling it Budget Fashion?" Edna asked.

Annie shook her head vehemently. "We want to offer clothes they can afford on a budget, but we want the name to sound more lofty. Inspiring."

"Shoestring Fashion," Maude offered. "Clothes for You. Cheap Clothes."

Annie was glad she winked.

Sean pointed to a Sears catalog nearby. "People can buy reasonably priced clothes from Sears."

"Or Macy's," Edna said. "What makes our clothes different?"

Annie pressed her fingers to her forehead—which was beginning to throb. "If my thoughts were a muddle before, they are now a seething storm."

Edna put a hand on her knee. "Let's set the name aside for now. We have work to do. Twelve dresses to sew for Mrs. Sampson's soiree." She pointed to Annie's portfolio near the door. "Get out the sketches and let's talk about the changes she wanted."

The sketches were set on the table and the four of them gathered close. Annie sighed deeply. "She ruined them."

They all nodded.

Annie continued. "She took the simplicity of my designs and spoiled them with fancy froufrou." Each design now sported extra flounces, flowers, and frills. "Either you can't see the design for the ornament, or she's designed another ridiculous ruffle rumpus like the dress she was wearing."

"Who does she think she is?" Maude said.

"She's the money," Sean said.

"Who are we?" Edna asked.

Annie had thought about this. "You are the sewing expertise, Maude has the patternmaking skill, Sean is the salesman, and I—"

"You are the creative talent."

"We all are. Together we make a whole."

"Mrs. Sampson is more than the money. She's a charlatan," Maude said.

"Too harsh, Maude," Annie said.

"Harsh is as harsh does. She's a hypocrite, luring us into a business with talk of function, comfort, and innovation that will free women's movement, when what she really wants is a vehicle to keep fashion as fussy as it's always been."

Edna opened another subject. "And I do not want to have our sewing workshop in that library of theirs. Yes, the space is plentiful, but the walls are

18

paneled and dark, and the room smelled of dusty books."

"And ancient history," Maude added.

Annie looked around their small flat. "We agreed that we would sew in our flats at first. We could use Edna's larger dining table to cut the fabric."

"But didn't we also decide we will need to hire seamstresses to help? I don't want workers in my house," Edna said. "I suppose I'll do so if I need to, but if this business takes off as we hope, we need a place of business where we can all work together in one space."

Sean clapped his hands once. "I've got it."

"What?"

"An apartment upstairs is empty. The Delgados moved out last week."

Annie jumped ahead. "It's larger than this one. It has two bedrooms. We could rent it."

"With what money?" Edna asked.

"I'll get Mr. Sampson to pay for it," Sean said. "As a businessman he will understand the need for a proper work space—away from his home."

Annie remembered their tour of the Sampsons' library. Although Eleanor had been passionate about using the space, Mr. Sampson had seemed hesitant. He'd said little, and his face had pulled in resignation more than approval. "Talk to him, Sean. And will you talk to the landlord too?"

"Consider it done. In fact, I'll go speak with Mr. Collins right now. I saw him outside."

He left them staring at the designs. "So are we going to sew these dresses like Mrs. Sampson wants?" Edna asked.

The decision was enormous. Yet Annie couldn't see any way out. In one meeting their plans had been fully appropriated, pinched, nicked, and stolen. "We have no choice. If not for Eleanor none of us would be here, discussing—"

"Exactly. If not for her we'd still be working at our fairly well-paying jobs." Maude shook her head. "The Sampsons led us round the flagpole but forgot which flag to raise."

Annie had no defense and felt the pull of guilt. If not for *her*. . .

Edna touched her arm. "Let's do what Eleanor asked. Who knows? Maybe we'll get orders for a thousand dresses."

"A thousand?" Maude said. "We can't handle that many!"

Annie laughed. "We are never satisfied, are we, ladies?"

"But what if—?"

She raised a hand, stopping Maude's words. "Let's deal with the problems at hand. We need a workshop—which Sean is trying to procure. Meanwhile, we have the designs and a venue in which to show them. So let's sew."

⬥

Maude looked at her list of fabrics and supplies. "I know we can get everything we need retail, but we need to open a wholesale account."

"With whom?" Annie asked.

"I've got some connections," Maude said, her eyes on the list. "I'll see what I can do."

"Until then, I'm sure I could get a discount at Macy's," Edna said. "For supplies, and for two more sewing machines—or more."

"They'll do that? Even though you quit?"

"Velma will do me the favor—us the favor. I know she will."

Velma MacDonald had been Annie's boss in the Macy's sewing department. She'd remained a good friend, even after Annie left to work for Butterick.

Sean came back to the apartment, his face glowing. "I got it!"

"The flat?" Annie asked.

"For how much?" Maude asked.

He hooked his thumbs in his vest. "For the same price as this apartment."

"How did you manage that?" Annie asked. "It's much bigger."

"I promised Mr. Collins you'd make his wife and his daughters a dress. Gratis."

"How many daughters?"

"Three."

Four dresses to make. . . Annie had an awful thought. "This isn't four dresses a month, is it?"

"No, no," Sean said. "Four dresses total."

"That's not overwhelming," Edna said.

Annie kissed Sean's cheek. "Thank you. You have helped tick one box."

"Out of many to be ticked," Maude said.

"One at a time." He pointed to Maude's list. "What's next?"

Annie took a fresh breath. "This is such a fifteen-puzzle."

Everyone looked at her. "What are you talking about?"

"Americans don't say that?"

"Obviously not," Maude said.

Annie thought a moment, trying to find a way to explain it. "Fifteen-puzzle is a game with cubes that have numbers on them. They have to be arranged in a square so that each line adds up to fifteen."

"Sounds challenging," Edna said. "But what does a game have to do with our situation?"

"It's so difficult and confusing to solve that if something is called a fifteen-puzzle it means it's difficult."

"Why didn't you say so?" Maude said. "Okay, partners. Let's get this fifteen-puzzle in order."

CHAPTER THREE

There we are," Edna said as she set the third sewing machine in place. "It took more than a week, but we are officially ready to sew."

Annie scanned their new workshop. The two bedrooms of the flat were set up with the machines—Edna's brought over from across the street and two others she purchased at a discounted price from Macy's. The main room contained a large table to use for cutting.

Edna finished arranging the last two spools of thread on a pegged rack on a wall. "We are as ready as we can be."

"As soon as the fabric arrives," Annie pointed out. She glanced out the window. "Maude has been gone an extraordinary length of time."

They all turned toward the door when they heard heavy footfalls on the steep stair leading to the third floor.

"Help!" came a cry.

Annie was the first to burst into the hall. Maude stood on the stairs, juggling two long rolls of fabric. One slid out of her grasp and tumbled down the stairs to the floor below. "I almost made it," she said.

Annie gathered the roll from her arms, and Edna recovered the fallen bolt.

A winded Maude entered the workshop. "There's more coming. I paid the driver to help with the rest."

The fabrics were taken into the main room and placed on the large cutting table. All were tied with string. Annie cut one roll free, letting yards and yards of sea-green batiste flow free. "Maude, this is lovely."

"I told you I'd choose well—following your extensive directions of course."

"How many more rolls are there?" Edna asked.

"Ten. Twelve all told. A different fabric for each of the twelve dresses."

Annie considered the cost. "Each roll has how many yards on it?"

"It depends on the fabric. Forty to sixty."

Edna fingered a mauve silk. "You have enough here for dozens of dresses. Couldn't you get cut yardage?"

"For twice the price." Maude removed her hat and hung it on a wall hook. "Aren't we trying to sell more of the same dress once Mrs. Sampson's friends see them?"

Edna nodded, but her hand was at her mouth. "It's just a lot of money up-front."

Annie put an arm around her shoulder. "That it is. Such is the cost of starting a new business."

"It's the Sampsons' money," Maude said.

Annie objected to her flippancy. "That doesn't mean we shouldn't be wise and frugal when we can be."

Maude pushed a stray hair off her forehead. "I assure you I could have spent us into tremendous debt."

"We thank you for your restraint," Annie said.

The driver began to carry in the other ten rolls. Maude tipped the man.

The twelve rolls on the table complemented each other—by design. Since they were all going to be shown at the Sampsons' during a single party, Annie thought it would be visually pleasing to present a unified ambiance of autumn greens, blues, coppers, and ivories.

"When are the models arriving for measurements?" Edna asked.

"They should have been here by now." There was a knock on the door. Annie opened it with a welcome. "Come right in, miss—"

It wasn't a miss but a boy. "This here's for you," he said, handing Annie a note.

She read it and sighed. "The two friends of Mrs. Sampson who were in charge of gathering *their* friends to be models send their regrets. They can't come today—or model at all."

"None of them?" Maude said.

"Apparently not."

"So much for Mrs. Sampson's influence." Edna sank into a chair. "Without models we have no measurements, without measurements we can't make the clothes, and without clothes we have no soiree."

Annie took it a step further. "Without a soiree we have no business."

"We're stuck," Maude said. "A cart without a horse."

"A chicken without an egg."

"A—"

"Don't be so morose." Annie was rather surprised *she* was the hopeful one. "This isn't the end, but merely a bump in the road. Since Eleanor's models bowed out, we get our own."

"Where?"

Annie pointed to the open windows. "There. Listen. Our models are all around us."

Edna and Maude joined her at the window. Mothers called to children, working girls hurried to and fro, and women sold their goods from pushcarts.

"Some of them are almost pretty, but most are quite ordinary," Maude said.

"Mrs. Sampson's customers should be looking at the dresses, not the women wearing them."

"Or caring about which wealthy family they represent."

Maude bumped into Annie's shoulder and whispered, "I will not have Mrs. Doonsbury wearing one of our creations. She has absolutely no waist, and her bosoms sag toward her toes."

It was a rude—though accurate—assessment of the woman who ran the butcher shop nearby. "We can be a bit picky, but not too," Annie said. "Could we ask Mildred and Velma from Macy's? And perhaps Suzanne and Dora from Butterick?"

"And your friends Iris and Jane from the Tuttles' bakery," Edna added.

"Iris is about to give birth. But perhaps Jane."

"And seven other girls right here in the neighborhood. Most will think it's a lark to wear such pretty clothes."

"That's the spirit. Let's gather some models."

"Perhaps if they agree, we could take their measurements right then and there," Maude suggested. "That way I could start making the patterns."

"Sean and I are due for a visit to the Tuttles anyway," Annie said.

"There's no time like the present," Edna said.

Maude took up her hat. "I agree. You head to the Tuttles' this evening, and Edna and I shall gather some models of our own."

❧

The heady aroma of fresh bread greeted Annie and Sean as they entered the Tuttle bakery.

Upon seeing them, Mrs. Tuttle squealed and rushed around the counter to give Annie a hug. "It's been far too long, girlie." Then she held Annie at arm's length and studied her. "*Tá tú ag iompar clainne.*"

"What?"

"Yer expecting, ain't ye?"

"I'm impressed," Sean said.

"So it's true?"

"It's true," Annie said. "How did you guess?"

"After having five of my own, I have a sixth sense about it. You're looking rather peaked and worried." She touched Annie's chin. "That means you're having a girl." She winked at Sean. "That all right by you?"

"I am fine with either gender," Sean said. He turned to Annie. "Peaked? Are you feeling all right?"

"I'm fine. Really."

"If a mother-to-be is glowing, it's a boy. If they look haggard, it's a girl. If you'd like to do the ring test, I could tell for sure."

"The ring test?"

"You give me a strand of your hair and I attach a ring to it. Then you lie down and I dangle the ring over the baby. If it starts to make a circle it's a boy; if it swings side to side, it's a girl."

"Who thinks of these things?" Sean asked.

"Wise people with years of experience," Mrs. Tuttle said.

Annie remained skeptical. "So the ring correctly predicted the gender of all five of your children?"

"Three out of five." Mrs. Tuttle shrugged and their attention was drawn to Jane coming forward from the rear of the bakery, wiping her hands from washing pots and pans. At the sight of them, the girl beamed.

"How nice to see you!" Jane gave Annie an embrace. Then out of habit she put her raw hands behind her back. While staying with the Tuttles, Annie had taken over Jane's washing chores for a short while until she was hired at Macy's. She knew the backbreaking endless work of it.

Mr. Tuttle finished helping a customer then locked up for the night. He handed Annie and Sean two rolls. "Last o' the day."

"Come sit," Mrs. Tuttle said. "You can eat, and we can have a visit." While Mr. Tuttle started covering the leftover loaves, the rest of them moved to the back of the narrow shop and sat at a table.

"Where is Iris?" Annie asked. "How is she faring?"

"Well enough, though she's down to the wire. It will be any day now."

"That's why she's upstairs helping with the children and not down here," Jane said. "She's getting so big it's not proper for her—"

"Jane!" her stepmother said. "We don't say such things."

Jane reddened. "But it's true. You yourself said Iris shouldn't be out where customers could see her once she couldn't hide it anymore. Annie understands. And she's like family."

Am I going to have to hide away too? "Thank you for the sentiment, Jane. Indeed, you are all like family to me. If not for you taking us in after we ran away from service. . ."

Jane nodded. "We still miss Danny."

Mrs. Tuttle crossed herself. "To think he would have been the uncle to Iris's babe."

Annie welcomed the comfort of Sean's touch to her arm. Being in this place, among these people, with the aroma of bread in the air, made her remember what life was like just a short year ago. She, Iris, and Danny had cut and run from their jobs as servants, impulsively giving up the known and venturing into the unknown of the city, hoping for a better life—or at least a more exciting one. Two girls of nineteen and seventeen, and a boy of twelve.

But the exhilaration of freedom waned quickly when their money was stolen, followed by the ache of growling stomachs and weary bodies. They'd huddled in an alley that first night, second-guessing their decision. The Tuttles took pity on them, gave them a roof over their heads, food in their bellies, and jobs to earn their keep. The entire family was the salt of the earth. And the butter and the sweet.

"In October it will be a year since Danny's death," Jane said quietly.

Annie remembered the day when Gramps had brought Danny's body back in the wagon. He'd been killed by a man who'd been obsessed with Annie, killed for standing up to him, all four-foot eight, eighty pounds of Danny against a man with evil in his heart.

Mrs. Tuttle put a hand on Annie's. "He'd be ever so pleased with your new one on the way, as well as his sister's. Remember what he always said?"

Together the three women repeated Danny's wisdom, "Make the most of today!"

Annie could still hear his voice and see the dimples of his smile and the twinkle in his eyes.

Sean brought them out of their melancholy. "He'd be proud of all of you."

Mrs. Tuttle slapped her hands on the table. "That, he would be. He was always the encourager, bless his soul."

Speaking of encouragement. . . Annie turned to Jane. "Actually, other than a visit, I have come to ask Jane a favor."

"Me?"

"You. Specifically you." She was glad to give Jane some special attention as the girl received too little of it. "My friends and I are starting a fashion design business, and we are having a fancy party to show off our dresses. We need models to wear them. We wondered if you would be interested."

"Me?"

"Yes, you," Annie said. "Would you like to take a go at it?"

"Would it take her away from work?" Mr. Tuttle called from the counter.

"It would be in the evening. October the first."

Jane bit her lip, but there was a flash of pleasure in her eyes. "I would love to." She looked to her parents. "Could I?"

Annie was ready to argue if they said no. Jane was a wallflower because she never got out. Her entire world revolved around family and the bakery. Although she was not the prettiest of girls, Annie expected there was an inner beauty that could be tapped.

Mr. and Mrs. Tuttle exchanged a long look. Finally he nodded. "If it doesn't interfere with yer work."

Jane jumped to her feet, nearly toppling her chair. "When? How?"

Annie laughed. "I'm glad you're excited."

"What about me?" Mrs. Tuttle stood tall and smoothed her hands over her sturdy torso. "I'd like to wear a pretty dress too."

Annie wasn't sure what to say. Mrs. Tuttle wasn't stout, but she had a mature figure, far from lean. And yet. . .she represented an enormous segment of women.

Annie looked to Sean and could tell he was considering it. "We *are* designing for all women," he said.

"Indeed we are," Annie said. "Yes, I think you would make a delightful model."

Mrs. Tuttle turned toward her husband. "Hear that, hubby? I's going to be a fancy model."

"Hmph," he said. "Model, maybe, fancy, never."

Instead of taking offense, Mrs. Tuttle laughed. "Don't mind him. And he's right. What happens next?"

"We are starting to sew the dresses, so what I need are some measurements." She drew a measuring tape from her reticule, along with a small piece of paper and a pencil. "Perhaps we could step into the storeroom?"

Just then Iris appeared from upstairs. She *was* enormous, her hand supporting her belly as she walked. Her attire was almost comical, as she wore a skirt pulled up under her bosom, making the front of it ride high enough to see her ankles. Her blouse—that Annie recognized—was only buttoned halfway down, the splayed ends tucked under the skirt. She wore an apron over the whole of the ensemble, a white flag that did nothing to enhance her condition, but rather drew attention like a banner marking a spot.

Annie rushed to greet her, their embrace awkward.

"Sorry, I can't give you a proper hug," Iris said.

Mrs. Tuttle stepped forward. "Annie's expecting her own."

Iris's eyes grew wide. "I'm so happy for you! And you, Sean. Congratulations."

"Where is Thomas?" Annie asked.

"He's out delivering with Gramps."

There was a series of thuds from the flat above, causing them all to look upward. Then a cry.

"That would be little Joe," Iris said.

"You're still caring for the five of them?" Annie asked.

"It's not so bad. The older two will be in school soon. Though it is odd that all five will be the aunts and uncles of our baby, when they are but babes themselves."

So it was with mixed families. Mr. Tuttle had lost his first wife—the mother of Thomas and Jane. So there were at least ten years between the two of them and their five half-siblings.

"I needs to sit."

Annie led Iris to a chair where she sank down with difficulty. *So this is how I'll be. . .*

Iris adjusted her makeshift maternity clothes around her middle. "Sorry for the way I look. It's mighty hard finding something to wear anymore. I look like I'm trying to cover a barrel with a napkin." She nodded to Annie's middle. "At least you're in the early part of it."

For now.

"Tell me all the news of your life," Iris said.

While Sean and Annie told her about the business, the inkling of a new idea skittered through Annie's thoughts. It was an idea so preposterous that she couldn't let it land and take root without letting some time pass.

That time came a little while later, after she'd taken the measurements of Mrs. Tuttle and Jane, and said her goodbyes.

She and Sean rode the streetcar home. "You're quiet, which either means you're angry or planning something."

"The latter. Maybe."

"What?"

Her thoughts were in the early stages that she normally wouldn't share until they were more fully formed, and yet, perhaps they shouldn't be formed. If so it was best to put an end to them sooner rather than later.

"Did you notice Iris's awful clothes?"

"I felt sorry for her. She's obviously very uncomfortable."

"She is. But it's more than her physical discomfort that I found alarming. It was the shame she felt regarding her appearance."

"You are going to be in her condition in a few months."

Annie hesitated. She didn't want to be rude, but. . . "I don't want to look like her. Surely there are maternity garments that can fit a woman's changing figure."

"Are there?"

"I honestly don't know. Even if there are, I was thinking that maybe we should add a few such outfits to our line."

He scoffed. "Not only are you asking ordinary women to be your models—including the rotund Mrs. Tuttle, but now you are going to show up at the soiree with a model wearing maternity garb?"

"Well, yes. Why not?"

"Did you ask Iris if she would model? She can barely walk."

"The model can't be Iris. She's due any day. But I'm sure we could find some woman in the neighborhood to do the honor. Or maybe. . .maybe I could model whatever we come up with."

Sean removed his derby, ran a hand through his hair, and sighed. "When do you plan to tell the Sampsons about all this?"

NANCY MOSER

"Never?"

"Surely you jest."

"That's too long?"

"You're going to surprise Eleanor? That will not go over well."

Annie looked out the window as they passed ordinary women, the women she wanted to dress. "If I tell her, she'll try to stop us."

"Probably."

"I don't want to be stopped. This new idea feels right. God opened this door. It's our responsibility to walk through it."

"That's what you said about our initial affiliation with the Sampsons. *That* was a door we walked through. So is this another door? Is it God's door? Or Annie's?"

Once again she took solace in the view.

CHAPTER FOUR

Sean entered their flat while Annie was at the table, sketching. "I'll be right with—"

But then a smell assailed her, forcing her to turn to him. "You smell like fish."

He held a package wrapped in newspaper. "With good reason. I bring you dinner."

She breathed in and out a few times to gauge the thought of it against her sometimes queasy stomach and was relieved to find no adverse reaction. "Thank you for that. I do need to eat. But let me finish this design first."

He put the fish in the ice box and pulled two potatoes from his pockets, along with a cone of green beans.

She pointed at the beans. "Let me nibble."

He handed her the newspaper cone and she pinched off the end of a bean and began to eat it. But then her attention was drawn to an advertisement.

She dumped the green beans on the table.

"What are you doing?" Sean asked.

She unfolded the cone, smoothed the paper, and read the advertisement aloud. " 'Maternity Corsets. Lane Bryant is the largest house in the world selling maternity apparel daily to thousands of expectant mothers.'"

He looked over her shoulder. "There's a picture of a woman wearing a corset. In a newspaper. I'm shocked they allow it."

"So am I, but the point is, they did. And the larger point is that I need to go to this Lane Bryant and see what they are offering in maternity clothes before I create clothes for our line."

"Where is the store?"

She looked at the ad. "Twenty-five West Thirty-Eighth Street. I think that's close to Fifth."

"Not too far. Do you want me to come with you?"

31

She shook her head adamantly. "A man in a maternity shop? I think not."

"I agree. Go tomorrow and take Maude along."

It was agreed.

~~~

Annie looked down at the noted address then at the nine-story building in front of her. "Twenty-five West Thirty-Eighth Street. This is it."

Maude nudged her. "You could just read the sign above the door."

And there it was. LANE BRYANT. Annie put a hand to her midsection. "Why is my stomach tight with nervous knots?"

"I have no idea. As far as anyone inside knows, we are just shoppers. You *are* expecting, you know."

"But I would like to meet Lane Bryant. The courage she showed by placing an advertisement for corsets. . ."

"Lane might be a man."

Annie shook her head adamantly. "A man would never think of creating maternity wear. Lane has to be a woman."

Maude shrugged. "She might not even be here."

It was true. And yet, Annie had a feeling she *would* meet Lane Bryant, and a deeper feeling that it would be an important meeting. If Maude had asked her to dissect her feelings, she would have been at a loss, but that didn't make them any less real.

"Let's go." She took Maude's arm, but Maude seemed to be looking toward a woman with a blue hat going into a brownstone a half-block away.

"Do you see someone you know?"

"No," Maude said quickly. "Not at all. Let's go in."

Once inside the shop, Annie was immediately impressed by the beautiful clothes on display. She fingered a luscious crepe.

"May I help you ladies?" a clerk asked.

"I—we—were wondering if Mrs. Bryant was here."

"Mrs. Malsin, you mean," the woman said.

"I'm sorry, I thought—"

A thirtysomething woman stepped toward them. "There's no reason for you to think otherwise," the woman said. "I am Lena Bryant Malsin. And you are?"

"Annie Culver. And this is Maude Nascato."

"Nice to meet you. What has brought you into Lane Bryant this day?"

Maude quickly said, "She's expecting."

Mrs. Malsin beamed. "Then you've come to the right place."

Although Annie was eager to see the fashion, she didn't want to proceed under false pretenses. "I am indeed with child, and yet, I am also here for another reason." She noticed some customers listening in. "Can we talk somewhere private, please?"

"About what, may I ask?"

"About fashion."

The woman's wariness turned to pleasure. "I can think of no better subject. Come with me."

They were led to a small table and chairs in the back of the store. Mrs. Malsin moved some fabric swatches aside. "Please. Have a seat."

Once they were settled, Annie began. "Miss Nascato and I are starting our own line of women's fashion."

"Congratulations. Who is your customer?"

Such a direct question. Annie suddenly found it hard to pinpoint.

Maude intervened. "We're not sure as yet. We are presently working on designs that will be showcased at a fashion soiree at Mrs. Harold Sampson's home next month."

Mrs. Malsin nodded once. "For the upper crust then."

"Yes. And no," Annie said.

"You must be more definitive, Mrs. Culver. That is one of the keys to success: define your customer then design for *them*."

"I fear that's the root of it," Annie said. "Although we have the backing of Mrs. Sampson, and though our current designs are being made in silk and organza—as she requested—I am not sure she and I—"

"We. Not sure that she and we," Maude corrected.

Annie took a fresh breath. "I'm torn between designing the clothes she wants us to design and designing the clothes *we* want to design."

"Mrs. Sampson is our investor," Maude said.

Mrs. Malsin chuckled. "You do need that. After my first husband passed away, I sewed lingerie for wealthy women in my flat, with my baby son playing nearby. My customers were well-off."

Annie pointed to the front of the store. "But your prices seem reasonable."

"My customers *were* well-off."

"How did you transition from those women to the masses?"

Mrs. Malsin sat back in her chair, smiling. "You're asking for my story?"

"I guess we are," Annie said. "If you're willing to share it."

Mrs. Malsin motioned to a clerk walking by. "Could you please bring us some tea, Beatrice?"

"That is kind of you," Annie said. "We didn't mean to impose."

"No one feels imposed upon when given the opportunity to talk about themselves. Let's see. . .I suppose I should start from the beginning because this store is rooted in that first voyage across the sea from Lithuania. My sister had come before me and lived here. I came alone a few years later. I was only sixteen. My mother had died soon after I was born. We were raised by our grandparents."

"I am an immigrant too," Annie said. "Just a year ago. From England."

Mrs. Malsin spread her arms. "And now look at us. Two entrepreneurs, proving that the American Dream is alive and well."

More for you than me. Though hopefully someday. . .

She continued her story. "When I arrived, I discovered my family had arranged for me to marry someone."

"Mr. Bryant?"

"No, no. Another man whose family had tried to buy my hand by paying my passage. But I refused."

"I'm sure he didn't take that well."

She shrugged. "If he felt duped, so did I. I quickly put the situation behind me. I didn't know a word of English. My sister worked in a garment factory and helped me get a job there. I earned one dollar a week, but within a few years I had learned English and was skilled enough to earn fifteen."

"Good for you," Maude said.

"Yes, it was good for me. All the hard work in the factory taught me what I needed to know to get where I am today."

"Every experience has a purpose," Annie said, almost to herself.

"I agree. Nothing is wasted."

"Did Mr. Bryant also work at the factory?"

"Oh no. He was a jeweler. He was from Russia and was older than I." Her face softened with memories. "A year after meeting we were married, and ten months later, our son, Raphael, was born." Her face clouded. "But David died six months after that, of tuberculosis."

"I'm so sorry."

"I was a twenty-year-old widow with a baby. I had little money. I couldn't work at the factory because I had Raphael."

"What did you do?"

"I pawned the diamond earrings David had given me as a wedding present and used the money to buy a sewing machine. I moved into an apartment with my sister, and we sewed clothes for women. We began to specialize in wedding dresses and fancy lingerie."

Tea was brought, and Mrs. Malsin poured. She held a cup beneath her chin as if drinking in the aroma. "I remember Raphael sitting on my lap while I sewed. . ."

Annie could imagine holding her own child in such a way.

"We did well enough that we opened a store on Fifth Avenue, living in the back. One day a customer came in, bemoaning the fact that she was expecting and had nothing suitable to wear in public. I made her a dress and sold it to her for eighteen dollars. That was the start of it, this business of mine."

"You filled a need."

She nodded once. "Society was squeamish about seeing pregnant women. It was quite ridiculous. Is ridiculous."

"You were Lena Bryant," Maude pointed out. "Why is the store called Lane Bryant?"

"Because I made a mistake and was too nervous to correct it." She raised a hand, stopping their questions. "My sister married and her husband loaned me three hundred dollars to expand the store. When I was making out the deposit slip to open a bank account, I was so nervous that my signature was wobbly and looked like Lane instead of Lena. When the bank officer opened the account for Lane Bryant, I wasn't courageous enough to argue."

"I believe you were plenty courageous," Annie said.

"*Are* plenty courageous," Maude said. "I saw your advertisement in the newspaper."

"Now *that* was a struggle. My husband, Albert, finally got the *New York Herald* to run an advertisement showcasing maternity clothes. We sold out that same day."

"So there *is* a need."

"A great one." Mrs. Malsin put a hand to her midsection. "Soon I will be wearing some of my own designs again."

"You are—?"

"I am."

"Your second?"

She laughed. "My fourth."

Suddenly Annie felt better about being a working mother. If Mrs. Malsin could do it with four, certainly she could handle one.

"Where do you manufacture your dresses?" Maude asked.

Mrs. Malsin pointed upward. "There are nine floors here. The bottom two are showrooms, and the rest are offices and workrooms."

"Now that would be a dream come true," Annie said.

Mrs. Malsin sipped her tea. "What is your situation now?"

Both Maude and Annie snickered. "We just rented a space in the building where my husband and I live. We have three sewing machines." She realized how paltry their situation was compared to the establishment that was Lane Bryant. "It's not much but—"

"It is a promising start." She set her teacup down. "Would you like to look at the clothes?"

"Yes, please."

Mrs. Malsin led them through the racks on the first floor, explaining how elastic bands were the key, along with empire waistlines. "See the accordion pleats in the skirt? They allow for a woman's natural expansion. Why don't you try this one on?"

Annie had never tried on a ready-made dress. She was led to a fitting room. A woman named Mary stepped in with her, ready to assist with the undressing and dressing. As the woman unbuttoned the back of Annie's dress, Annie laughed.

"Does madam find something amusing?"

"Very much so," Annie said, "for I used to be a maid, helping my mistress get dressed."

"My, my," Mary said. "I overheard you talking about having your own design business. That is quite a step up from where you started."

"Yes, it is."

"Who is your customer?"

Again, the question. "I thought I knew but was lured in a different direction. Now I'm confused."

Mary helped her step out of her dress and into the maternity gown. "Find a niche. That's what Mrs. Malsin has done. She's always talking about finding a need and filling it."

"Wise advice." Annie put her arms through the sleeves and Mary buttoned the back of it. Annie lifted up the overskirt to see the accordion pleated underskirt, attached to an elastic band. She looked at her profile in the mirror. "Although my condition isn't obvious as yet, I can see how this would expand with my waistline."

"It looks very pretty on you, Mrs. Culver. The aqua hue compliments your brunette coloring."

Maude called from outside the room. "Come out so I can admire you."

Annie obliged, turning in a full circle, making the skirt billow.

"Very nice," Maude said. "Let me look at the construction." Maude's hand crept toward Annie's midsection where the outer and under skirt met.

But when Annie saw Mrs. Malsin watching, she pushed Maude's hand away and said to her, "I promise if we offer maternity clothes they will be of our design, not copied."

"There is always room for competition, Mrs. Culver. It is the American way. But. . .many of our designs are patented. The corset for one."

"I have no wish to design corsets. But I *am* interested in one—for myself."

Another clerk approached Mrs. Malsin with a question, and after a short discussion, she said, "Forgive me, but I must attend to something. Mary, would you take the ladies up to two and show them the corsets? And if Mrs. Culver is interested in a purchase, give her a twenty-percent discount."

"That is very generous," Annie said.

They took an elevator to the second floor, which was filled with corsets, undergarments, nightgowns, and wrappers. Annie reluctantly reminded herself that, being jobless, they lived on a tight budget.

"Ooh," Maude said, taking a luscious pink wrapper from the rack. "The lace is delectable."

And frivolous. The dressing gown was something her mistresses, Lady Newley and her daughter Henrietta, would wear. Or Mrs. Sampson.

"Here is the corset," Mary said, showing it on a mannequin. "See how it rises a bit high in the back, to right below the shoulder blades, and angles lower in front."

Annie studied it. "The front panels expand?"

"They do. The back support and lower frontal support prove beneficial to mother and child."

Maude looked skeptical. "It may be the best maternity corset in the world, but it seems a bit wrong to constrict a woman's body in any way during a time that is already uncomfortable."

"How many children do you have?" Mary asked.

Maude reddened. "None." She opened her mouth to say more then closed it. "None."

Annie chastened herself. What had she been thinking, inviting Maude to come to a maternity store when she was unable to conceive? Although she couldn't say anything in front of Mary, she would try to make amends once they were alone.

For now it was best to hurry along her purchases of the dress and the corset.

Mrs. Malsin saw them to the door. "It was a pleasure speaking with you ladies. Please stay in touch, and feel free to contact me if I can be of any assistance."

Annie was touched. "I do believe you have changed our lives today."

"You overstate."

"I do not," Annie said.

"She does not," Maude said.

Annie and Maude caught a streetcar to head back to the workshop. Once they were seated, Annie said, "I want to apologize for dragging you along on this outing."

"Apologize? It was extremely interesting. I truly think we could offer some—"

"I mean, because it involved maternity items. I didn't mean to pour salt into your wound."

Maude slipped her arm through Annie's. "The world is full of babies, expectant mothers, and women with husbands. I will not experience any of those milestones, but if I ran from all evidence of them, I would have to lock myself away in some convent. It is *not* my choice that I cannot conceive, but it *is* my choice that I will not marry and subject a man to a childless future. I have learned to be content with what I *do* have." She squeezed Annie's arm. "I have the best friend in the entire world, a job that challenges me and allows me to be creative, a place to live with Edna, breath in my lungs, and beating in my heart. God is good, all the time."

Annie's throat tightened. "You are so brave, and your faith so strong. You humble me."

"Good."

CHAPTER FIVE

Edna looked over the maternity design. "Mrs. Sampson will have a conniption when she realizes one of the designs is for an expectant mother."

Annie studied the sketch that included the elastic band idea taken from Mrs. Malsin's design, but she planned to use a challis instead of the accordion pleats—the latter being much more expensive to produce. The challis would drape nicely and be soft to the touch. And not heavy. Above all, Annie wanted the maternity dress to be easy to wear.

"Do you want me to go ahead and make a pattern for it?" Maude asked.

Before Annie could answer, she heard her name being called from the hallway outside the workshop. "Annie? Annie Culver. Where are you?"

Eleanor Sampson.

Annie slipped the design out of sight and opened the door to greet their patron. "You found us."

Eleanor put a hand to her heaving chest. "Two flights. I am quite out of breath. Get me a chair before I pour into a puddle."

Edna took a pile of drawings off a chair just in time.

"Much better," she said when seated. Then she motioned to a man dressed in a chauffeur's uniform who accompanied her. "Davis, set the satchel on the table."

The man did as he was told then stepped back. "Would you like me to wait, ma'am?"

"Up here, no. Attend to the automobile. I shan't be long."

When the man was gone, Eleanor pointed at the satchel, grinning. "I've brought you some treasures."

Annie and Maude exchanged a wary look. "Sounds intriguing."

"They are beyond intriguing; they are stunning."

"They?"

Suddenly finding her strength, Eleanor stood and opened the satchel. She removed an assortment of trims, wound on cardboard. One was heavily encrusted with gold beads, while another came in the form of a knotted fringe. There was also an assortment of beaded appliques in bright colors, and finally an enormous length of wide Chantilly lace suitable for a dainty lawn dress of years past. She set them on the table reverently then stepped back to admire them. "Aren't they amazing?"

"They're lovely," Annie said—and she wasn't lying. But they also had nothing whatsoever to do with each other. It was a potpourri of adornments.

"You don't expect us to use them on the dresses, do you?" Maude said.

"Of course I do. They are handcrafted."

"Which means they're expensive?" Edna said.

"Of course they're expensive." Eleanor took up a floral shaped applique made of red and silver beads and placed it against Annie's right shoulder. "See how much it adds to any design?"

Annie gently pushed her hands away. "We can't use them."

"Why not?"

"We need trims we can buy in bulk. We wish to mass produce our clothes. Hand-beaded trims are out of the question."

Eleanor shut the satchel with a click. "Let me worry about that."

"But—"

"My friends expect the best from me, and I intend to give it to them."

But it's not about showing off for your friends, it's about business.

Eleanor strolled to a mannequin that was dressed in a dress of burnt orange. She fingered the fabric. "This isn't silk."

"No, it is not. It's rayon."

"I've never heard of it."

"It's a fairly new fabric." Annie stopped before adding the words, "Less expensive."

Eleanor gave it a wary look then moved on. "We are on track for my soiree?"

"We are. With a lot of hard work." Annie felt compelled to tell her about the ordinary women who would be the models. "I have found enough models."

"I heard that Anabelle Klingerhorn bowed out. She has always been a flighty, fickle girl."

"Her friends declined too."

A groove formed between Eleanor's eyebrows. "I. . .that's disturbing. I thought it was settled."

"It is. We found replacements."

She let out a breath. "That's a relief."

"Actually, when the daughters of your friends bowed out, I had an interesting idea about the model situation. I thought—"

Eleanor waved her off. "It is handled?"

"Well, yes."

"Good. Enjoy the trims. I really must go. We are having dinner with the Belmonts, and I must get ready. Alva detests guests who are late." She kissed Annie on both cheeks and was gone.

The three women stood in stunned silence. "What just happened?" Edna asked.

Annie fingered the three-inch band of breaded trim. "We can't use this."

"Can't use any of them," Maude said.

"What is she thinking?" Edna asked with a sigh.

"She is thinking she wants to show off to her friends by making the dresses more flamboyant." Annie sat on the window seat and rubbed her forehead. "We have a little over three weeks until the show. We don't need this complication."

Edna sat and put an arm around her. "We're all exhausted; you more than any because you're overseeing every aspect of the designs."

"And there's two of you," Maude added.

Annie put a hand on her abdomen. "I know I need to slow down, but how can I?"

"Let's start fresh tomorrow." Edna took Annie's hand and extended her other hand to Maude. She bowed her head. "Dear Father, once again we are a three-strand cord that cannot be broken. Replace our exhaustion with your stamina, our confusion with your clarity. Guide us so this opportunity plays out exactly as You planned."

Annie appreciated the prayer, but when she opened her eyes she immediately saw the trim. "But what do we do with. . .that?"

Edna pulled her to standing. "Nothing today. Everyone needs to go home, have a nice evening, a good rest, and start again tomorrow."

"But—"

Edna shoved her toward the door. "Go on now. Maude and I will finish up here."

It felt good to have someone else make a decision.

≈

Glittery trimmings wove through Annie's fitful sleep, tying themselves in knots, growing into a giant heap upon the work table that made its legs buckle.

She startled awake just in time.

Next to her, Sean opened one eye then turned over and went back to sleep.

There was no more sleep for Annie. The tendrils of the dream lingered, and she knew the only way to be rid of it was to get up and go to work.

She quickly dressed and quietly slipped out of their flat with only the slightest click of the latch. She tiptoed up one flight and entered the workshop at the top of the stairs. She turned on the lights and faced the table—which had *not* buckled. She touched the stack of trims which were each neatly wound. The angst of her dream faded as reality fell into place.

Yet the reality was, trims or no trims, there was an enormous amount of work to do.

Annie became so engrossed in the sewing that she was shocked to look up and see the first glimmer of day outside the window. She looked at the clock on the wall. It was half past five. She needed to hurry downstairs and slip into bed before Sean awakened and scolded her.

She turned off the lights and hurried into the hall. In her haste she caught the hem of her skirt in the door. She yanked on it once, then twice with extra force.

As it loosed itself, she lost her footing on the landing and. . .

Fell. Toppled. Rolled to the bottom of the stairs, landing in a heap amid her echoing scream.

She lay still as the pain took her captive. Which hurt most? Her ankle, her forehead, her shoulder? Or her side?

"The baby!" She covered the growing child with protective hands. The fear of harm overshadowed the sting or throbbing of any other injury.

She heard voices. And doors. Their neighbor, Mr. Ruffalo, rushed to her side. He turned to his wife, "Get Sean!"

There was no need, for Sean had also heard Annie's fall. He ran to her

42

side, taking over. "Are you hurt?"

"I—I don't know. The baby. . ."

Sean turned to the Ruffalos. "Run and get Dr. Grant!"

Luckily, a doctor lived in the next building. Mrs. Ruffalo rushed off to fetch him.

"Help me sit up," Annie said.

"Should you?" Sean asked.

She wasn't sure, but as more neighbors came out to see the cause of the clatter, she made a choice. "I can't very well stay here. Help me inside."

She began to stand, but Sean would have none of it. With Mr. Ruffalo's help, he took her into his arms and carried her to their sofa.

Mr. Ruffalo pointed at Annie's head. "You're bleeding."

"Get a towel." Sean pointed to a dish towel nearby. Mr. Ruffalo handed it to him, and Sean folded it into a compress he gingerly pressed against the back of her head. "Breathe deeply." He touched her cheek then bowed his head. "Father, please help Annie and the baby be all right."

"Amen to that," Mr. Ruffalo said.

Annie added her own prayers and closed her eyes, grimacing against the pain. *Please, God, please God. . .*

She heard the two men talk, then silence. Annie opened an eye and saw that their door was closed against the curious. She and Sean were alone.

"Is the doctor coming?"

"Any minute," Sean said. "What happened?"

Annie didn't have time to explain, as the door opened and Dr. Grant entered. Sean relinquished his spot, and the doctor pulled a chair close to the sofa. "What happened?"

"I fell down the stairs."

He opened his bag and removed a stethoscope. "What were you doing out at this early hour?"

"I'd like to know that too," Sean said.

"I was in our workshop upstairs. Sewing."

"You were what?" Sean asked.

Dr. Grant shushed him and listened to her heart.

"The baby," Annie said. "I worry about the baby."

He glanced at her abdomen. "You're four months, yes?"

She nodded. He had been the doctor who confirmed her pregnancy.

He shook his head. "It's too soon for me to hear its heartbeat." He positioned his hands above her midsection then hesitated. "May I?"

"Please."

He gently pressed against her abdomen. "Does this hurt?"

"No."

He prodded a bit more, and she was relieved to feel no pain.

Then he sat back. "Where do you hurt?"

Upon her explanation, he examined her side, her shoulder, and her ankle—which was swollen, and moved her joints to check for breaks. He asked Sean to bring a bowl of water and cleaned the cut on Annie's forehead and applied a bandage.

"You are lucky to have no broken bones."

"And the baby?"

"We won't know for sure, but since you feel no pain there..."

A wave of relief swept over her. "Thank You, Lord." She began to sit up but he gently pushed her back.

"There will be none of that."

"None of what?"

"Getting out of bed. Not for at least a week."

"But I have work to do! There's a fashion soiree and—"

The doctor put the stethoscope in his medical bag then leveled her with a look. "You just fell down a flight of stairs, young lady. You are carrying a child. That is your work for the next five months."

"Five months?"

"I'm not saying you can't ever return to your sewing, but I do forbid you from even visiting your workshop for an entire week."

"I'm being held prisoner."

"You're being held accountable to your child and to common sense." He took her hand in his. "Mrs. Culver. Annie. All who know you admire your spunk, your creativity, and your drive. But you must get your priorities in proper order and take care of yourself and the child. If your health fails, none of the rest matters. Understand?"

Sean nodded emphatically, also waiting for her answer.

She looked into his eyes, and then into Dr. Grant's, and knew she was beaten. But more than beaten, she knew they were right. "I understand."

"And...?"

"And I agree to your conditions."

"Excellent." He handed her a small bottle of pills. "Here is some aspirin for the pain. You may take two pills every four hours. I will stop by this evening to check on you. And know that I will come at any time if you feel any unusual pain or cramping." He wrote a number down and handed it to Sean. "During the day this is my office telephone. Or if it's after hours, run next door and get me."

After the doctor left, Sean sat beside Annie and stroked her hair. "My darling Annie-girl. Why were you working in the middle of the night?"

"I couldn't sleep."

"Not being able to sleep is one thing, but going to work is another. You wouldn't condone Maude or Edna working in the wee hours of the morning."

He was right. "But we have so much to do."

"Then the others will have to step up and work harder. You've taken on a disproportionate amount of the responsibility. It's time to share the burden."

There was a knock on the door, but it immediately opened. Edna and Maude streamed in, their hair still mussed from sleep.

"We heard you fell?"

"Heard from whom?"

Edna waved the question away. "The neighborhood grapevine travels quickly."

"Whatever were you doing in the workshop?" Maude asked.

Annie found her explanation more embarrassing than courageous.

Maude put her hands on her hips. "You don't trust us."

"Of course I do."

"Your actions prove otherwise."

She changed the subject. "Would you make some tea, please?"

"No, you don't, chickie. You are not getting off that easily," Maude said. "You thought extraordinary measures were needed to finish the work, and you were just the one to do it."

"I was trying to help."

Edna took her hand. "Maude, shush now. You are being far too hard on our Annie. We know her heart was in the right place."

"Even if her common sense was absent."

Edna flashed Maude a look. "The point is this: I am certain God has given us the abilities and the time to achieve good results. Extra hours may be required, but not at the expense of our health. Or the baby's health." She glanced at Annie's midsection. "The doctor said all is well?"

"As much as can be known. Yes."

Edna glanced heavenward. "Thank You for that, dear Lord."

"But the doctor said she is not to work for a week," Sean said.

Annie saw the smallest flash of panic spark between her friends. Then Edna repeated, "A week?"

Annie explained. "I am supposed to rest. But I know I will go barmy here with nothing to do."

Edna touched the bandage on her forehead then looked at Maude. "We will do the work. Another seamstress is starting today so there are now two of them, plus the two of us."

Maude stared toward the door, and Annie could tell something was bothering her.

"Maude?"

"I know you're not to work, but one issue remains unsettled: what should we do with all those gaudy trims Mrs. Sampson brought over?"

"Ignore them."

"Really?"

Annie cemented her decision with a nod. "They aren't suitable."

Maude let out a breath. "I agree."

"Mrs. Sampson will *not* agree," Edna said.

"I'll deal with her." Annie exuded more confidence than she felt.

"Enough of that." Edna pointed toward their flat across the street. "We'll go get properly dressed and come back with some tea, rolls, and jam. And a few hard-boiled eggs. You must eat."

Annie squeezed her hand. "You are the best of friends. And I do trust you to accomplish the work."

The women left, and Annie could hear their footfalls on the stairs.

"I'm proud of you for relinquishing control so graciously," Sean said.

"It was an act," Annie said.

"You aren't relinquishing control?"

"I have to. But that doesn't mean I like it."

⁂

After eating breakfast Sean helped Annie get to bed. Her body ached from the fall, and her head hurt. She needed sleep, not just from the shortness of her night but from a deeper need to heal.

When she awakened, she saw a note on Sean's pillow saying he'd gone out on an errand. He would return soon. At the bottom of his note was a verse: "Be still, and know that I am God."

She lay on her back, feeling thankful for his care *and* his wisdom. She put her hands on her abdomen. "Please be all right, little one. I am sorry for putting you through such a jostling." She looked to the ceiling. "Please, Father, don't punish our child for my mistake."

She smoothed the covers and set her arms upon them. It was then she was confronted by something foreign: solitude and stillness. She'd been alone up in the workshop, but she had been busy. To be still and cognizant of that stillness was disconcerting.

Her breathing slowed, and she felt her muscles relax. Her mind drifted from the here and now to the past.

Her life had always been filled with the busyness of necessity. She'd been raised in the countryside of England where there were always chores to be done, and had moved to Crompton Hall as an under-housemaid when she was fourteen. In that position she was up before the dawn, lighting fires in the grates, making beds, cleaning bathrooms, the work never ceasing. She did not return to her tiny bedroom until long after dark, when she fell into bed for a few hours' sleep before the cycle began again.

Last year, she'd come to New York City with Lady Newley and Miss Henrietta and had shared a room at their relative's mansion with Iris, an American maid. Iris and her brother Danny—the hall boy—had been her coconspirators, leaving service behind, diving into the ocean of the big city. They'd been taken in by the loving Tuttle family, helping in their bakery and sleeping in the storeroom amid the sugar and flour.

Annie smiled when she remembered their desire to better themselves. Her thoughts darkened at the memory of Danny being killed soon after, but brightened at the knowledge that Iris had married Thomas Tuttle and they would soon have a child.

Working at Macy's and then Butterick, moving in with Edna, marrying Sean, going into business with the Sampsons. . .each portion of her life was filled with decisions and movement, never-ceasing, relentless.

Until now.

She picked up Sean's note and read the verse aloud. " 'Be still and know that

I am God.'" She laughed. "You have me right where You want me, don't You?"

Suddenly, she felt the oddest flutter in her abdomen, as though a butterfly was moving about on the inside. She held her breath and waited to feel it again.

And there it was!

"Is that you, little one?" she whispered.

But she knew it was more than the child.

It was God.

⁂

Annie was awakened by the sound of the door opening. Then hushed whispers.

"Sean?" She sat up in bed then immediately remembered feeling the baby move. "Sean, come in here, I have something exciting to—"

Sean appeared in the doorway, but he was not alone.

"Vesta!"

His mother rushed to her side, leaning over to give her a hug. "You gave us a scare, my dear. How are you feeling?"

"I'm feeling better. In fact. . ." She hesitated then decided the time was perfect. "I felt the baby move!"

Sean sat beside her, taking her hand. "How do you know?"

"I just do. It was like a butterfly's wings from the inside."

"That's it!" Vesta said. "That's how it feels at first."

Sean touched her abdomen. "Can I feel it?"

"Not for a while," Vesta said. "But eventually you will feel the kick and even see an elbow move from side to side."

Sean's eyes grew large. "Really?"

"Don't look so terrified. It's a miraculous thing."

Annie nodded. "It's a miraculous thing to feel the baby move now, after the fall. I was so afraid. . ."

"God is good," Vesta said. "And you will be well soon."

"I know it," Annie said. "With all certainty."

"Until then," Sean said, "I have brought Mother to help in the workshop, or with anything you need down here."

Annie remembered Vesta's enthusiasm for their project but also her husband forbidding her from being a part of it. "What does Richard say about it?"

Vesta stood and straightened her shoulders. "We didn't ask him."

"You didn't?"

She looked to her son for support. "We told him about your fall and that my services were needed."

"He could not object," Sean said. "I think we shocked him into submission by *not* asking."

Vesta chuckled. "You should have seen the look on his face when I left with Sean."

"He will get over it."

She nodded, making wisps of gray hair dance around her face. "I plan to come every day to help in whatever capacity is needed."

Annie extended her hands. "You are both a godsend."

"I even commandeered Father's driver to bring us here today," Sean said.

"And he will pick me up to take me home at six each evening," Vesta said.

Annie was overcome with relief. Vesta was a willing set of hands. That she had an interest in fashion was a blessed bounty. On their first meeting she had intimated that before her marriage to Richard she had wanted to design clothes. Now was her chance.

"Come, Mother," Sean said. "Let me show you the workshop."

Vesta kissed Annie's cheek. "Never fear, Vesta is here!"

⁂

Returning home at the end of her first day at work, Vesta smiled when her butler opened the front door before she reached it. "How do you do that, Baines?" she asked. "I have never had to wait a single moment on the stoop because you always open the door at just the right moment."

"That is my intent, Mrs. Culver."

She took out a hatpin, removed her hat, and stuck the pin in the band. She gave it to him and peered into the parlor. "Has Mr. Culver arrived home yet?" She sincerely hoped he had not.

"He is in his study, ma'am. He requested that you join him as soon as you returned."

Drat.

"How was your day, ma'am?"

"Delightful."

"And Miss Annie? Is she recovering?"

"I believe she is. It's kind of you to ask."

49

He gave her a bow and left her alone in the foyer. Richard wanted to see her. If only she could go out and *not* come in at all. Yet she knew if she came home at seven or eleven, he *would* have his say. Richard was not a man who would be denied.

The negative train of her thoughts shocked her. She loved her husband. The highlight of her day was when he returned from the store.

That used to be the highlight of my day. Before today, before the door of the world opened and I stepped through.

"Vesta?"

She stepped to the right enough to see down the hallway that led to his office. Richard stood outside the doorway, summoning her.

Don't be so dramatic. He's calling you, asking for you, saying your name, not summoning you.

"Vesta," he said again, his voice stern. "Come here."

The image of her own father came to mind, and the many times she had responded to his demands with *Yes, Father*. But she quickly—and wisely—adapted her response. "Yes, Richard."

He disappeared into the study, and she reminded herself to breathe as she entered the room. She applied the smile she had perfected after decades of marriage. "How was your day, dear?"

"Sit."

Good dog. She sat, trying without success to act nonchalant. She'd never been good at it. Her face reflected her emotions and thoughts like a finely polished mirror.

"I never expected you to be gone all day."

"I was needed."

He blinked, as if remembering the reason for her absence. "How is Annie?"

"She must rest—for many days. Doctor's orders." And since she knew he would never ask, "The baby seems fine too."

"Capital. I still don't understand why she was at that dratted workshop of theirs at such an hour."

"Because it is a workshop. Because there is work to do. There are many days when you go into the store early and return home late—because there is much work to do."

"Yes, but..."

Vesta bravely finished his sentence. "But she's a woman."

"Well yes. This whole women's rights brouhaha is absurd. Women voting? Women in the workplace? I went to the bank today and there were women tellers, and the president's secretary has been replaced with a woman."

Vesta exaggerated a gasp. "How shocking!"

He stopped stroking his mustache. "It is highly disconcerting."

"Yes, dear." Suddenly, a thought burst into Vesta's mind, and she found herself speaking it aloud. "Women have always worked."

"In the home."

"And in the fields. And factories. And in shops. *You* have a female employee. Mrs. Burroughs has worked for you for ten years."

"The sister of my bookkeeper. The result of a favor given. An exception, not the rule."

"Your loss."

"What did you say?"

Vesta's throat grew tight. "I admire the working girls of today. They have ambition. They have. . .gumption."

"They are taking jobs away from men."

"There is plenty of work to go around."

"Hmm."

She took his response as a victory. "Annie wishes to design for working women."

"Don't encourage her."

"That's rude, Richard. Don't those women deserve to look nice and wear functional clothes that are comfortable enough *to* work in?"

He moved a piece of paper close and picked up a pen. "I liked bustles."

"Why?"

"They were. . .interesting. All those flounces and drapery."

Vesta wasn't sure which point to address first, the fact Richard had an opinion about fashion or the absurdity of his preference. "Bustles made sitting awkward. And the weight of them, pulling back. . ."

He shrugged. "I stand by my opinion."

And I stand by mine. She stood. "I'm going to dress for dinner now."

"You're not going tomorrow."

It was not a question. "Yes, I am. Annie is still confined to bed."

"But I need you here."

"To do what?"

"To do. . .what you normally do."

"And what is that?" He looked flummoxed, and she realized he had no idea how she spent her days—not that there was much depth to them now that the children were grown. She got to the crux of it. "I am bored here, Richard. Sean and Sybil are grown, with lives of their own. The household runs without me. And you will not let me work at the store."

He shook his head adamantly. "Totally unacceptable."

"Why is that? Sean and Annie worked together."

"It's. . .unconventional."

"Only for our set."

"The women in our set do not work outside the home."

"And I guarantee they are as bored as I."

"They—they are involved in charity work."

"As am I."

He made a face. "Which charity?"

She was hurt that he was unaware of her good deeds. "I help raise funds for the foundling home, the city mission, and the veterans' home. I even volunteer occasionally."

His eyebrows rose. "You actually. . .go there?"

"In person." She leaned toward him and said, as if in confidence, "I've even held a foundling child in my arms, served a meal to a homeless man, and had a chat with a veteran who was missing a leg."

His lips moved as though he wanted to say something. Yet all he managed was, "Well then. Good for you." He set his pen aside and took up a cigar, snipped the end, and lit it. Acrid smoke wafted toward her nostrils.

"You know I dislike that smell," she said.

"I will see you at dinner then."

She was being dismissed. Summoned and dismissed. How pitiful.

CHAPTER SIX

Vesta knocked and entered Annie's apartment without waiting for a response. She carried a dress draped over her arm, along with a needle, thread, and scissors.

"Annie, you're out of bed," she said. "Should you be out of bed?"

"I have moved from the bed to the sofa. I am not running wild or jumping up and down but am sitting quietly in a new setting." Annie fingered the necktie of her dressing gown to make her next point. "And see? As usual I am not even fully dressed. Does that appease your concern?"

"I'm not sure. For the past three days you've cajoled us into bringing you handwork to pass the time. I don't want you to overwork."

Annie scoffed. "There is little risk of that. And a person can only sleep so much and only read so many books."

"Did you enjoy *Sense and Sensibility?*"

"Very much, though I have decided I much prefer to live out my own drama—which will commence tomorrow when I am set free of my confinement."

"The doctor has given permission?"

Annie nodded. "But actually, it has been the baby and its increased flutterings that convinced us I am recovered."

"We thank God for that." Vesta considered the room's light. "Do you want to move to the window seat to see better?"

"A good idea."

Vesta arranged a backrest of pillows and drew a kitchen chair close to act as a table for the supplies. "There. Can I get you anything else?"

"I am fully equipped. Stop in later and tell me how the day progresses."

Annie was left to her work—which she usually tackled immediately.

Yet today. . . the hem was forgotten as she paused to look down upon the teeming street below. Although she'd observed the scene often, the number of times she had done so with full eyes and comprehension could be counted upon a single finger, a finger symbolizing her viewing on this day, as if seeing it for the very first time.

Below her, dozens of men and women went about their days. The sight of them made her happy, and she found herself uttering a prayer, "Lord, bless them."

You bless them.

She blinked at the thought. How could *she* bless them?

Look. Watch. See.

She watched wives, mothers, and women moving from errands to home, or to their jobs in stores, offices, and factories. The image of Mrs. Sampson's fancy trims flashed into her thoughts but was quickly discarded. She knew she'd made the right decision to deny the woman's request.

And yet. . .there was more to deny.

Watching the real women, living real lives, needing real clothes, caused an idea to fully form. *This is my customer, has always been my customer.*

She sat back and blinked. "Then why did I let myself be tempted to sew otherwise?"

Maude came into the flat. Annie had been so focused she had not even heard a knock.

"I brought you another hem to sew—if you have—"

Annie turned to face her. "We're doing it all wrong."

"Doing what wrong?"

"We're designing clothing for Eleanor's Couture. Minus the fancy trims but still Eleanor's fancified designs."

"I don't understand."

"We are not designing *our* clothes."

Maude looked confused. "It's not what we intended or wanted, but we agreed to Eleanor's demands because she is our financial support. Plus, it's a way to gain opinions about our designs from women who wear nice fashion."

"What does it matter if Eleanor's wealthy friends like our designs? They aren't our customer." She pointed out the window. "*They* are."

Maude took a seat beside her. "What's gotten into you?"

"Sense. And a sensibility to all the ordinary woman out there who need to move freely and comfortably, who deserve comfort *and* feeling pretty in the process."

Maude put a hand on Annie's forehead. "You don't feel feverish."

"I am perfectly well."

"Perfectly daft to even think of changing direction at this late date."

Was she daft? Annie closed her eyes and prayed aloud, "Oh, Lord. Show us the way we should go."

I will. Trust me.

She held her breath a moment, embracing the affirmation. Then she looked at Maude. "We're supposed to trust Him."

"And you know this how?"

He just told me. Annie stood and took Maude's hand. "Because we should always trust Him. Let's go to the workshop."

"But you're supposed to rest."

"Rest time is over. Now is the time for action."

Maude forced Annie to slow down on the stairs, or she would have attempted to take them two at a time. Together they burst into the workshop.

"Annie!" Vesta said. "You're not to be back until tomorrow."

"What I have to say can't wait." She saw the two seamstresses sewing in the other room. "Stop the work! Stop all the work."

"What's gotten into you?" Edna asked.

"God and good sense."

"What?" Vesta asked.

Maude shook her head, but she was smiling. "Trust her," she said. "It's for your own good."

Annie's heart beat harder. She had everyone's attention. What she would say next would affect all of them. *Lord? Yes?*

She waited to feel a check in her spirit, but feeling none, continued. "We're starting over."

"Starting what over?"

"Everything." She saw her old portfolio leaning against the floor by the window and put it on the cutting table. She dug through the pages and took out her initial designs. "These. These are the dresses we are to make."

"But Mrs. Sampson changed those original designs, making them elaborate and showy for her friends."

"Her friends are not our customer."

Edna put a calming hand on hers. "But Annie. The Sampsons have financed us. If we don't give them what they want, they will pull their support. We will have nothing."

"We've had nothing before." Her words sounded strong, yet her stomach clenched. "In truth, I think we need to break from the Sampsons altogether. It's not fair to give Eleanor fashion that doesn't suit *her* vision."

She saw Edna and Maude exchange a look. Maude spoke for them. "We quit our positions in order to do *this*. And now without financial support *this* is at risk of ever being successful."

Annie shook her head. "*This* is not what we wanted to do. *This* is not even what Mrs. Sampson assigned me to do. She befriended me because she saw a fiery passion for good fashion design, not fad or frippery. I've lost that fire just as she has lost her focus. We must get it back."

Everyone took a fresh breath. The air tingled between them.

"We need to talk to Mrs. Sampson then," Maude said. "It's only right we tell her."

Annie hated the mere thought of it. "As soon as Sean gets home from work, he and I will go see them so we waste no more time on this wrong road."

"Are you sure we can wait until then?" Vesta asked. "I could go with you. Now."

Annie considered her words and agreed. "Are you sure?"

"If you do all the talking, I can certainly be there for support. I hate to waste an afternoon working on the wrong designs."

Annie smiled. She had never felt closer to her mother-in-law. Her friend.

Edna shook her head. "I should insist that you return to bed, but I know you won't rest. Not when your fire is aflaming."

Annie kissed her cheek then looked at the others. "I will do right by all of you. I promise."

"Go ahead and do right, but. . ." Maude pointed at her dressing gown. "I suggest you get dressed first."

Annie felt herself redden. She hadn't even realized she'd left the flat in her dressing gown, with her hair cascading upon her shoulders like a girl. "I have one favor to ask of all of you."

"It appears your wish is our command," Edna said.

"Pray for us as we see the Sampsons. Pray God gives me the right words. Pray Mrs. Sampson is merciful."

⟶∞⟵

The baby did not cause the flutterings in Annie's midsection. They were the result of her overanimated nerves. A hundred questions and scenarios rushed through her mind, making her heart overbeat and her legs wobble.

"Please hold onto me," Annie said as she and Vesta stood at the front door of the Sampsons' mansion.

"Are you all right?"

"I will be. Once this is over."

Vesta nodded and looked at the grand entrance. "This is a gorgeous home. Enormous."

"Don't be intimidated," Annie said, ringing the bell. *The Sampsons are intimidating enough.*

The butler answered. "Mrs. Culver. Good morning."

"Good morning. Is Mrs. Sampson available?" Annie asked. "I know we come unannounced, but it's important."

"Unfortunately, she is not to home."

"Oh." Annie felt deflated.

"But Mr. Sampson is here."

Actually. . .perhaps that would be better. "Yes. Please. May we see him?"

They were led into the drawing room. Annie remembered the last time she'd been in this room, the day everything changed when Mrs. Sampson mentioned Eleanor's Couture. Today, everything would change again. Why was change so frightening? And exciting?

Mr. Sampson entered and they both stood. "How nice to see you, Annie." He looked at Vesta.

"I would like to introduce you to my mother-in-law, the other Mrs. Culver. Vesta, this is Mr. Sampson."

"How nice to meet you," she said.

"Charmed." He gave her a wink. "Please take a seat."

As soon as he sat down, his pug dog jumped up on his lap and received a scratch behind the ears. He scanned their faces. "Something is wrong?"

"Not wrong," Annie began.

"Not wrong at all," Vesta said.

The dog stared at them with large eyes as if daring them to upset its master.

"I can tell something is weighing on your minds. Tell me."

Annie looked to Vesta, who nodded. "I think it's best—and easiest—if I get right to the point."

"Always a good decision."

"We are changing the fashion designs."

"For the better I hope?"

"Definitely. In fact, since they aren't what we originally talked about at our last meeting we think it's only fair to you and Mrs. Sampson that we call off the soiree."

His face clouded. "That's not possible. This party has become her sole focus." He shook his head. "Sole focus."

"But what if the designs don't please her anymore? They are far less elaborate than the dresses she expects."

He was silent a moment. Then he sighed. "I fully admit that the entire enterprise has gotten out of hand. I should have stopped her the first time she uttered the words 'Eleanor's Couture.' This excessive ornamentation is not the 'function over fad' we talked about when we met you a year ago."

"No, it's not." Annie felt the beginnings of relief wash over her. And yet Mr. Sampson's acknowledgment did not remove the problem.

"Alas, I have tried to speak to her about it," Mr. Sampson said. "But when she is on a mission it's like talking to a fidgety, willful dog who yaps incessantly, is determined to bite the table legs, and won't eat dinner unless it's freshly ground lamb." He lifted the dog's chin and looked it in the eye.

"It sounds like you speak from specific experience," Vesta said. "What's her name?"

"Penelope."

"She's quiet *now*."

"Because she's satiated and full and I let her have her way."

"As you wish to let your wife have her way?" Annie said.

"I believe there is no choice in that. Or rather no choice I can live with."

"So you wish to continue with the soiree, no matter how the fashions have evolved?" Annie asked.

He touched her hand. "We've come too far to stop. I trust you, Annie. You are a businesswoman. My wife is a dreamer. Do what you have to do, show the fashion you feel you must show, and. . .and. . ."

"And?"

"I will be here to pick up the pieces if things go awry." He stood, their audience over.

Although she knew it wasn't proper, Annie drew him into an embrace. "Thank you. For all you've done and for all you are about to do."

"Yes, well. . . I think we'll all breathe easier when this event is over."

⌘

Upon arriving back at the workshop, Annie and Vesta told the others about the conversation with the Sampsons. Yet that was not the most important topic.

Annie had a new idea that even Vesta didn't know about.

"I'm calling all the models in for a meeting this evening at seven."

"Why?" Edna asked. "They've already had a fitting."

"Because I want to pluck their brains." That didn't sound right.

"Pick their brains?" Maude offered.

"That's it. If we are designing for the working woman, we need to find out what they want, what their employers will allow, and what they would like to wear outside of work. I'll call Mrs. Tuttle and Jane, and—"

"The rest are at their jobs," Maude pointed out. "I'll call Suzanne and Dora at Butterick."

"I'll call Velma and Mildred at Macy's," Edna said.

Annie thought about the neighbor ladies. "I don't think they all have access to a telephone. I'll have to bring around notes or see them in person."

"No you won't," Vesta said. "I will bring around any notes. Just tell me where they live." She took hold of Annie's shoulders and led her to a chair. "Your idea is a good one. But let us do the legwork. You mustn't overtax yourself."

"Baby comes first," Edna said.

It was hard to let others do things for her, but they were right.

⌘

"You what?" Sean said.

"Vesta and I went to see the Sampsons."

"You're supposed to be resting."

"The doctor said I could go back to work tomorrow. It's just a day early."

Sean shook his head and sat beside her at the table. "Tell me what happened that spurred a meeting with them."

Annie shared all the details, ending with, "It was God's doing that Eleanor wasn't at home."

"I agree. You would not have received the same reception if your news had been shared directly with her."

She knew what he said was the truth. "Mr. Sampson is a gem."

"And a very patient, indulgent husband."

Annie reached for his hand across the table. "I feel so much better to have told him about it ahead of time."

"It was the right thing to do."

"We can now proceed with a clear conscience."

"You realize by your revelation you've just created more work for everyone. And I assume you need more practical fabrics than the silks and chiffons you previously purchased."

"Yes, on all accounts. But oddly the right work feels like less work."

"You will not *over*work," Sean said, squeezing her hand. "You must promise me that."

"I've learned my lesson. As Edna said, God has equipped us for the work to be done in the given amount of time. I trust Him."

"As do I."

"I finally feel as though God has me where He wants me, Sean."

He smiled and drew her hand to his lips.

Annie had another thought. "But. . .do you realize I might not have come to this God-place if I hadn't overworked, fallen down the stairs, and been made a prisoner, forced to slow down?"

He chuckled. "Next time, get His message without the tumble, all right?"

"I will do my best."

❧

The models came to the workshop at seven. The sewers, Gert and Ginny, stayed late to be a part of it. Annie had called Mrs. Tuttle and asked if they could bring some tea cakes or cookies along to supply sweets for the women's trouble.

During the rest of the afternoon, Annie had come up with some questions she wanted to put before the group. She hoped much would be gained by an open discussion. This would not be a test. There were no wrong answers.

As seven o'clock approached, the women streamed in, filling the workshop to overflowing. The addition of the tea cakes was a grand idea, and the plate was quickly emptied.

Then it was time. Annie asked them to take what seats there were—four ladies managed to squeeze onto the window seat amid much giggling. Gert and Ginny stood in the doorway of their sewing room. Annie stood before the group and began.

"Thank you so much for taking time out of your busy day to come here."

"I'll always come if you serve those cakes again."

"Thank you," Mrs. Tuttle said. "There's more where those came from."

Since everyone was certainly tired from a long day, Annie chose to get to the point. "The reason we have called you here is because you are all experts."

"In what?" Mrs. Tuttle asked.

"In living your lives."

"We can't argue with you there."

"We"—Annie point at Edna, Maude, and Vesta—"wish to design fashion for working women, mothers, wives, daughters. . .*you*. But first, we want to know what you would like in your clothes."

Maude stepped forward. "If you could design your perfect dress, what would it be like?"

The ladies thought a moment, but only a moment, for almost immediately the ideas flowed out of them, making Vesta—who had been assigned to take notes—struggle to keep up.

"I don't want it dragging on the ground. What a mess," Ginny said.

"I want sleeves that are loose enough that I can fully move in 'em," Gert added.

"But not too loose so they get in the way," said Betsy, a typist.

"I do like the recent style that has the waistline up higher, under the bust. It hides me big belly better," Mrs. Tuttle said.

They all laughed, but there were many nods.

"I like flowy fabrics but not too fancy."

"I need simple dresses I can wear to work in place of the usual dark skirt and white blouse that are so boring."

"Right," Betsy said. "Besides, I don't want to look like everyone else."

Annie interjected. "Your bosses will allow you to wear something beyond the office uniform?"

Betsy looked to the others. "I think they would. If the dresses were smart."

"I don't want the neckline too low," Mrs. Tuttle said. "I have to bend over and pick up children umpteen times a day. I can't have my bosoms showing."

"But not too high. I want necklines that are flattering."

"That suggest our assets without revealing them."

This generated a giggle.

"Actually," said Suzanne with a mischievous grin, "I'd like to wear pants like men. Do you realize how freeing it would be?"

"That's not going to happen," Mildred said.

"I don't want to look like a man. Men's and women's fashion should be different," another woman said. "Since we are different."

"If we wore pants, what would we do with our drawers? We couldn't tuck them in."

"Go without, I guess," said Dora.

They all laughed. "I refuse," Mildred added.

Annie needed to get them back on track. "What about colors? Prints?"

Velma from the Macy's sewing department raised a hand. "I'd love to have a dress with a pretty print, but I don't see many of those fabrics even available."

"Would you like prints?" Annie asked again.

"I'm not sure," Mrs. Trainer said. She was a mother of four from the neighborhood. "My husband will only let me have three dresses. One for Sundays and parties, and two others for every day. Solids are more versatile."

"As Velma said, we don't offer many patterned yard goods at Macy's," Mildred said. "Perhaps a stripe or two. Or maybe a small floral print."

That was true. In fact, Annie couldn't remember selling any fabrics with a printed design. "Do the rest of you agree about prints?"

They all nodded.

"I can dress up an ensemble with a hat or a necklace," Dora said. "My grandmother left me a gorgeous filigreed necklace with a green stone."

"An emerald?"

"Probably not. But it's pretty."

The talk of accessories made Annie ask, "What about hats?"

They all scoffed, and Suzanne spoke for all of them by saying, "We have no need for ostrich plumes or the ridiculous wide brims we see posh ladies wearing. I saw one that had a bow the size of a small child on its brim."

More laughter.

"Then what kind of hats do you like?" Edna asked.

"None would be good."

"None?"

"They're a bother unless it's cold out."

"And no corsets either."

Surprisingly, this came from Jane.

"I'm sorry," she said as she noticed she'd gained everyone's full attention. "I shouldn't have—"

"No," Dora said. "You are absolutely right. We all agree. Our lives would be ever so much easier—"

"And more comfortable."

"—if we didn't have to cinch ourselves in."

Mrs. Tuttle put her hands on her midsection and moaned. "When I take it off at the end of the day it's like I'm being let out of a trap." At their laughter she added. "Who's kidding who anyway? Look at me. I'm a baker. I like to eat. No one is ever going to think of me as a skinny-minny even if I wore a hundred corsets."

Annie agreed with all of them, and yet. . . "I'm not sure we can address the fashion of undergarments. That's an entirely different industry. But we can design dresses that are more comfortable and better suited to your needs."

"What about trim and embellishments?" Maude asked.

"Not too much," Maybelle said. "I want to show off the flowers I sell, not me dress."

"Lace is too fancy for every day. But I like that braid stuff," said Gloria, a woman who worked in a printing company. "Sticks up a bit? It's kind of fancy, yet not?"

"Soutache trim?"

"That's it. I like that."

Annie had another question. "How much are you willing to pay for a new dress?"

Since she worked at Macy's, it wasn't surprising Mildred answered first. "Dresses at Macy's vary, but the ones they make special, just for the store, sell for $5 to $10. But most women still have them made to their measurements and those are a little more."

"I can order a dress made to my size from Sears for $5 to $8," Jane said.

Velma offered the view of the home seamstress. "By the time a woman buys a pattern, fabric, and notions, she probably spends $3 to $5 on a dress."

"But that's the home sewer," Mrs. Dietrich said. "I don't have a sewing machine, wouldn't know how to use it, and don't have time because I work the pushcart six days a week." Her cart sold pots and pans and other tin items.

"Your dresses are better than Macy's," Suzanne said to Annie.

"I hope so."

"So you could charge a bit more."

"But not too much more."

Suddenly, there was silence. "Anything else you'd like us to know?" Annie asked.

A few of the neighbor women exchanged looks. Mrs. Trainer spoke for them. "We just want you to know that we support what you're doing. You've made us feel real special."

The ladies left, the door was closed behind them, and the four friends stood in the empty room and offered a communal sigh.

"That was enlightening," Vesta said. She held out her notes. "I tried to get it all down."

Maude sat on a stool by the cutting table. "They confirm what you said this morning, Annie. We've gotten off track doing things Mrs. Sampson's way."

"But no more," Edna said. "Right? We really are returning to our original inspiration?"

"We are," Annie said. "God willing."

CHAPTER SEVEN

Today was the day. What the ladies had accomplished in less than three weeks was close to impossible, and yet they had done it. They had started over, creating twelve dresses out of sensible but pretty fabrics that reflected their own design sense *and* fulfilled the needs and desires of their customers.

Annie awakened early, her stomach in knots. Moments later, she felt Sean's hand upon her shoulder.

"It will all work out beautifully, Annie-girl," he whispered.

She turned over in the bed to face him. "Everything is riding on this."

He touched her cheek tenderly. "Not everything."

She took a fresh breath. "You're right. Success or failure will not change *us*."

"Not a bit." He took her hands in his, their physical link filling the space between them. "Either way there will be challenges, yet our love is a bond that can't be broken. Ever."

She was glad for his words. She needed to hear them. "Ever," she repeated.

◈

Sean hired a wagon to carry the dresses and accessories, to make sure they arrived safely at the Sampsons'. Annie, Vesta, Edna, and Maude took the streetcar. They brought with them five models from the neighborhood. One of them had never been on a streetcar and held onto Annie's arm in terror. Maybelle was a street vendor who sold single flower blooms, two for a penny, that she gathered from the droppings of the floral store down the street.

"It will be fine, Maybelle," Annie said. "You're perfectly safe."

"I never been this far away from home. What country are we in now?"

Was she serious? "We're still in the United States. We're still in New York City."

Maybelle looked out the window. "The streets are so wide, the buildings so grand. Do kings and queens live here?"

Kings and queens of commerce. . .

"There are no kings and queens in America, silly," said Betsy, who worked as a typist in a solicitor's office.

"I take the streetcar every day to work at the printer's," Gloria said.

Mrs. Trainer shook her head. "With four young'uns, we stay pretty close to home."

Mrs. Dietrich agreed. "I have to live close or I wouldn't get my pushcart home each evening. Though the mister and I do take the streetcar to see a musicale time and again."

"With costumes and everything?" Maybelle asked.

"With costumes and everything."

As the ladies discussed musicales and plays, Annie worried—a small bit—about their reaction to the Sampson mansion. Would Maybelle be so awestruck she couldn't model? Had using ordinary women been a mistake?

Finally they reached their stop and disembarked. The plan was to meet the other models on the steps of St. Patrick's, just across from the mansion: Jane and Mrs. Tuttle from the bakery, Velma and Mildred from Macy's, and Dora and Suzanne from Butterick. The twelfth model would be Annie, wearing a maternity dress.

The Sampsons didn't know she was expecting.

There was a lot they didn't know.

Annie was relieved to see her six friends had already arrived. She could always count on them.

"Are you ready?" Jane asked Annie.

"Are *you* ready?" Jane was a shy one. Would she be able to pass among the guests with ease?

Mrs. Tuttle slapped Jane lovingly on the back. "She's ready, and so am I." She put a hand to her hair. "I spent extra time on my hair. I heard it called a French roll. Do you like it?"

"It's smooth and sleek. Well done."

"I saw it in a magazine. Iris helped pin it up."

"How is she faring?"

"The doctor says she's due any day. I gave me husband strict instructions to come get me if she goes into labor."

Annie was taken aback with images of Mr. Tuttle, with his stubbly face and brusque ways, breaking into the soiree, calling his wife and daughter home. She hoped the baby would wait until it was over—and immediately felt selfish for the thought.

It was time to go in.

But first. . .

"Can we have a prayer before we proceed?" Annie asked.

The women gathered close at the foot of the grand cathedral. Many held hands. Annie wasn't used to praying aloud, but found the words. "Lord, be with us today. Help us all do our best, and show us Your will. Amen."

Maude took over. "Come on, ladies! Let's put on a show!"

<hr />

They were all led to the upstairs library to get dressed. It was ironic that this was the same room the Sampsons had wanted them to use for the workshop. Annie couldn't imagine sewing under Eleanor's thumb. If they'd done that, she never would have fallen down the stairs and never would have come to her senses about the fashion they were offering the world.

The models got dressed, but every time the door opened, Annie's stomach flipped.

Vesta noticed. "You're watching the door as if expecting a monster to enter."

"Not a monster. Mrs. Sampson."

Vesta slipped her hand around Annie's arm. "Perhaps it would be better if she saw the fashion now and not for the first time, during the fashion show."

"I'm torn about that. Today she's in her element, entertaining her friends as the perfect hostess. If she sees beforehand that the dresses are back to my original designs, I'm afraid she'll be so upset that her party will be ruined."

"But if she doesn't know until the models walk into the room. . ."

Annie bit her lip, still staring at the door. "Am I being a coward?"

"I am not one to speak to anyone about courage."

"But you *have* been courageous, coming to work every day despite Richard's objections. I'm very proud—"

"He still thinks you need help because of the fall."

The fall was weeks ago. "He doesn't know you're helping with the actual cutting and sewing?"

She sighed and shook her head. "So you see, I cannot judge anyone regarding courage."

"And the truth shall make you free."

Drat. To remember *that* truth at this particular time. . .

But there was no denying it. "I need to tell Eleanor. Now," Annie said. *Before I get into my dress.* "It's the right thing to do."

Vesta gave her a hug. "Good luck, my brave Annie."

Annie didn't feel brave. Not at all.

❦

Annie spotted Eleanor making the finishing touches on a large flower arrangement. *Please, Father. Help me.*

Eleanor looked up, clapped her hands together, and drew Annie into an embrace. "Are you ready?"

"Nearly. How about you?"

"My guests will arrive any minute."

"How many are you expecting?"

"Twenty-two, though I received word that Mrs. Wallace has been under the weather, so may not make it."

"With or without her, that is a commendable gathering."

"If each woman orders one dress. . .do you have seamstresses ready to handle the business?"

Twenty-two dresses? Annie was surprised by the thought. She assumed once Eleanor's wealthy friends saw the simplified dresses, modeled by ordinary women of all shapes and sizes, there would be *no* sales. "I–I'm sure we can handle the orders."

"Of course you can," Eleanor said as she squeezed Annie's hand.

Annie remembered why she had sought her out. "Would you like to see the dresses ahead of time? We have made some changes. . ."

"I think that would be a marvelous. Let's go—"

The chimes on the front door echoed.

"Oh dear, there is no time. My guests are arriving. I will see the dresses soon enough." She scurried off to greet her guests.

Crisis averted.

Or merely delayed?

❦

Annie quickly dressed, and the models got in line. Annie checked each dress, each hat, each bit of simple jewelry or reticule.

Mrs. Tuttle pinched her cheek. "Take a breath, girlie."

Annie did so then saw that Jane was nearly white with fright. "You'll do fine, Jane. Don't be nervous. All you have to do is stroll around the room and let the ladies see the dress."

"What if they ask questions?"

"Try to answer them. Or look for Vesta, Edna, Maude, or me. We will be nearby to help." She let go of her own nerves to ease her friend's. "You look lovely. I'm so very glad you could help us today."

Jane's cheeks blushed. "I feel lovely—or as lovely as I *can* feel."

Annie touched her chin. "Smile and enjoy yourself."

"I will try."

That's all any of them could do. For Annie was in the same position, modeling her maternity design. She was pleased to know that she needed it. Her regular clothes were too tight. It was exciting to finally see evidence of their blessing.

Sean came close and whispered, "Say something to all the models. Encourage them."

He was right. Annie stepped back so she could see the lot of them. "Ladies, may I have your attention for just a moment?" They quieted and looked in her direction. "You all know what to do. Smile and stroll and—"

"Sell," Maude added.

In that regard, Maude was more hopeful than Annie, but she said, "You will do the latter by doing the former. Enjoy yourselves and be yourselves. We all appreciate your participation."

Mr. Sampson appeared at the door. "It's time."

Annie nodded and turned back to the women. "Take a deep breath, and let's begin."

∽◌∾

The ladies of New York society were seated around the drawing room, half on either side of the middle door. They were dressed in lovely afternoon dresses, with large hats adorned with feathers, flowers, and bows. And a bird. One particular hat sported a bluebird with overly large eyes.

Eleanor made a nice speech at the beginning, introducing Eleanor's Couture. She mentioned Annie by name and gave her credit as the designer, but it was obviously *her* show. Finally she spread her arms to make her final pronouncement. "I give to you, Eleanor's Couture."

Annie chose to be the first into the room, the general leading the charge. Or. . .the sacrificial lamb? As soon as she entered, Eleanor gave her a once-over look, her eyes wide. She quickly recovered and rushed to her side. "This is Annie Culver, the designer."

There was another smattering of applause.

Annie took advantage of their attention. "Thank you for your interest in our fashion. Today you will see a cross-section of ensembles that offer comfort, fashion, and frugality."

The last word raised a few eyebrows.

Annie continued. "I am wearing an ensemble for the woman who is expecting." She looked right at Eleanor. "As I am. It offers ease of wear, as well as modesty, allowing the mother-to-be to appear in public while she awaits the happy event."

There were murmurs behind fans and closed hands, but no one looked truly appalled.

Eleanor was clearly surprised but remained silent, so Annie swept a hand toward the models, inviting them into the room. "Special guests, I ask you to enjoy the new wave of American fashion."

Annie strolled the perimeter of the room, and through glances, saw that the models were doing the same. She spotted Jane smiling as her dress was examined. Mrs. Tuttle made another group of women laugh.

"Mrs. Culver," one guest said. "Let me see your dress, please."

Annie moved close. The woman's eyes were on the skirt of the garment. "Does it. . .expand?"

"It does," Annie said. "There is elastic at the top of the underskirt that allows you to make adjustments for comfort. And the overskirt is full enough to provide modesty."

The woman—whose hair was the most brilliant copper—looked up at Annie furtively then lowered her voice. "My old clothes no longer fit, and Mother says I will need to stay at home for the coming months, and. . ." She glanced at the older woman sitting nearby, who was speaking to a friend about Maybelle's dress. "I will go nutters if I stay inside so long. And honestly, I'm getting quite uncomfortable."

Annie smiled. "Have you heard of the store, Lane Bryant?"

The whisper continued. "Is that the shop that sells those corsets. . . ?"

"It is. Although we have this one dress in our line, Lane Bryant specializes in maternity wear. The store is just west of Fifth Avenue at 25 West Thirty-Eighth Street. Tell them Annie Culver sent you."

"That's nice of you to lead me to your competitor."

"You have a need. I cannot ignore it."

The woman gave Annie a genuine smile. "I will not forget this, Mrs. Culver."

Annie moved on, around the room. Many of the ladies seemed embarrassed at her condition and barely gave the dress a glance, but that was understandable. The joy of helping the copper-haired woman kept her going.

The room was alive with conversation, and the customers drank champagne and nibbled on caviar and *petit fours*. Eleanor was in her element, like a theatrical diva accepting adulation.

Yet Annie was savvy in her widespread observations, for though the guests were polite and even asked the occasional question, she overheard many comments such as, "They are far too simple," "Where is the embellishment?" "A dress suitable for staying at home but far too plain to wear in any sort of company," "Who are these models? That one woman is as portly as I." And more than once, "I have a dressmaker I trust. Why should I change my loyalty and risk using an unknown designer?"

She'd expected as much and was not totally disappointed, for their comments reinforced the knowledge that their customers were ordinary woman. And yet, what would Eleanor's reaction be when she overheard such opinions?

Perhaps she wouldn't. It would be gauche for the guests to speak badly of the affair to the hostess. And they did seem to be enjoying themselves. The models too, for each one was smiling as they made the rounds. And Edna, Maude, and Vesta seemed happy answering questions.

Annie made the circuit once but could do no more. Her ankle throbbed, and a sudden weariness fell over her like a shroud. She made eye contact with Sean, who stood at the doorway with Mr. Sampson, and he immediately rushed toward her.

"Are you all right?"

"I need to sit."

Mr. Sampson drew a chair close. "Can I get you anything?"

"I'll be fine." She wanted to lie down but instead put on a smile.

"I believe the event is a success," Mr. Sampson said.

On the surface perhaps...

Eleanor fluttered over, her face beaming. "The ladies love the dresses."

"I'm glad," Sean said.

She turned so her back was facing the guests and spoke confidentially. "Though Annie, what you did with the designs was shocking. Where are the trims I gave you? If I'm not mistaken, these are your original designs."

"They are," Annie said. "The ornamentation you so generously shared just didn't seem to suit—"

"Eleanor?" called a guest. "Come tell us about your upcoming trip to Chicago."

"You're going to Chicago?" Annie asked before Eleanor was lost to another conversation.

"Tomorrow," Mr. Sampson said. "Didn't you tell them, my sweet?"

"Oh dear," Eleanor said. "With all the preparations, I did not." She touched Annie's shoulder. "I'm sure you are far more capable than I of taking the orders and seeing them fulfilled. We are only gone a week, just a quick visit to Harold's brother for his birthday. We're taking the train. I will telephone every day to check on orders."

"You will not," Mr. Sampson said.

"Why not?"

"Because this trip is about family, not business. Annie and Sean can handle the orders here, and thus you will have a marvelous surprise when we get home."

She sighed dramatically but gave her husband a smile. "I hate when you make me wait."

"Delay is not denial, my sweet." He turned to Annie and Sean. "Do not worry about the expense for more fabrics and supplies. I have deposited the sum of two hundred dollars into an account for you, to use in our absence."

"Thank you," Sean said.

Annie was shocked. "That is very generous."

"I must see to my guests," Eleanor said. "Harold, come say hello to Alva. She was asking after you."

Annie was glad to be alone with Sean. "They speak of orders."

"I know. You didn't think the guests would like the dresses, and yet they—"

"They don't."

"What? They seem to. Look at them."

"I overheard some discouraging comments." She shared them with Sean.

"So they're not going to place any orders."

"Not a one. Beyond not liking the designs, they don't wish to change dressmakers."

"You're more than a dressmaker. And we want to mass produce these dresses."

"Which is another reason why our vision and the vision of Eleanor's Couture is not a good match."

"Did you expect it to turn out like this?"

Annie wasn't sure what she expected. "Mr. Sampson agrees with us. He knows Eleanor has lost track of her initial idea amid her desire to make a name for herself. Remember how he said he'd be here to pick up the pieces?"

"We're depending on it."

◦◦◦

The streetcar ride back to their neighborhood was a raucous one. The models were giddy with the excitement of the day.

"I loved the fancy ladies giving me attention."

"To walk among the gilt of those rooms. . .it was like being in a palace."

"One women said I was beautiful."

"One asked if I modeled regularly," Maybelle said. "I told her I sold blooms on the street, and she didn't believe me."

Annie was happy for their experience and relieved that none seemed to have heard the disparaging remarks.

By the silence of Edna, Maude, and Vesta, it appeared they *had* heard some of it. But now was not the time for that discussion. Annie was thrilled to have provided the models a day they would remember forever.

When they arrived home, Annie invited her friends to their flat to review and discuss the day. Hopefully Sean would show up soon, returning all the dresses to the workshop.

All fell upon the chairs with an *oomph*.

"We did it!" Vesta said.

"That we did," Maude said.

"I'm glad it's over," Edna said.

Annie couldn't help but notice that they all were skirting the truth of it. Perhaps they were being polite?

"We will not get any orders," she finally said.

The ladies exchanged a look and nodded.

"What did you overhear?" Annie asked.

They each repeated comments that mirrored the ones Annie had heard.

"At least they were polite about it," Edna said. "The models thought it was a grand success."

"I am thankful for that," Maude said.

Vesta rubbed the back of her neck. "Mrs. Sampson seemed pleased."

"After her initial shock," Maude said. "I thought she was going to faint away when you came out and explained your maternity dress."

"The highlight for me was when a young woman—who herself was with child—was interested in my dress. She'd been told she would have to stay at home for the coming months."

"We have one sale!" Maude said.

"Perhaps. Though actually, I sent her to Lane Bryant's."

"Why did you do that?" Maude asked.

"Because they have dresses ready for her to buy. They have corsets too. She needed help now, not in a few weeks or whatever time it will take for us to make her a dress."

"With the soiree done, what do we do now?" Edna asked.

"What if there truly are no orders?" Vesta asked.

They shared a moment of silence.

There was a knock on the door and Maude answered it. "Maybelle."

"Excuse me, Miss Nascato." She looked past her to the room. "I don't mean to disturb."

"Come in, dear," Edna said.

The girl stepped inside. "I wanted to thank you for the wonderful time today."

"We thank you," Annie said. "You did a fine job of it."

"I loved wearing such a nice dress. I ain't had a new one in ages." She touched her faded brown skirt. "This one was my sister's before she outgrew it."

Annie felt badly. Maybe they should have offered to let the models keep their dresses.

"The thing is, I was wondering how much the dress I wore would cost if I wanted to buy it for meself. That same sister is getting married come Christmas, and I would like to look pretty for the wedding."

Annie was negligent in not knowing for sure. They'd talked about prices—if they could buy in bulk and make the dresses in some semblance of mass production. But without knowing how today would go, without knowing how many dresses they should make, they hadn't come to any firm price per piece.

"Two dollars," Maude said. She looked to the others. "Wasn't that the price we chose?"

Annie thought fast, for she knew they would *not* be selling this dress for that price. "It's a special price for you, Maybelle, since you helped us by being a model. A deeply discounted price."

"I—I think I can affords that. Can I pay you fifty cents now and the rest in a week or two?"

"That sounds perfect," Edna said.

Annie heard noise in the hall and Sean's voice. The dresses were back. "Just a minute and we'll get it for you."

"I'll do it," Edna said.

They heard some discussion and feet upon the stairs going up another floor to the workshop.

In minutes, Edna returned, carrying Maybelle's dress. "Here it is."

Maybelle took possession as though it were made of the finest silk. "I will treasure it forever and ever. Thank you."

"Thank you, Maybelle," Maude said. "For you are our first customer."

Maybelle bounced twice on her toes and left with her dress.

"That is one happy girl," Vesta said.

"Which is why we do what we do," Edna said.

"I'm not keen on losing one of our samples," Annie said. "But you were right to make it a price she could afford, Maude."

"You know what this proves, don't you?" Maude asked. "Maybelle is our customer. Not those rich ladies at the soiree."

"It's as we thought," Vesta said.

"So now what?" Edna asked.

"Now we wait for the orders."

"Or the lack of orders."

"That will determine our next step."

"How long do we wait?" Maude asked.

"I don't know," Annie said. "How long?"

"A week at most."

"You're assuming the ladies will make a quick decision about ordering or not?" Annie asked.

"I assume they've already made their decision *not* to order," Maude said.

Annie tried to think of the next logical step but hated the uncertainty. "Until we see what's going to happen, there *is* work to do. The landlord needs to be paid. We agreed to make each of his daughters and his wife a dress."

"And we need to replace Maybelle's dress," Maude said.

"The workshop is in disarray from the frenzy of the past few weeks," Edna said. "I want to get it well organized."

"I'll help," Vesta said.

Annie felt so blessed to have these women who willingly did whatever work needed to be done. "Thank you for all you do and are about to do, ladies."

"We have no slackers here," Maude said. "If Eleanor's friends order, fine. If they don't, that's fine too. I will not sit around and do nothing."

"I agree," Vesta said.

"As do I," Edna said.

It was unanimous.

CHAPTER EIGHT

It had been a week. No orders. Not a one.

Yet they had three sales: Maybelle, Mrs. Tuttle, and Jane had purchased the dresses they'd modeled.

Everything pointed away from the concept of Eleanor's Couture, meaning it was time for a meeting with the Sampsons who were back from Chicago.

Sean had offered to take off work to accompany Annie, but she declined. This was her Waterloo, her battle to be fought.

She stood at the front door of the mansion, her stomach dancing with nerves. "God, help me," she said under her breath.

The door opened, and Annie was led into the drawing room for the scheduled meeting.

The Sampsons were waiting for her.

"How nice to see you," Eleanor said, kissing her cheeks. "Come have some tea."

They exchanged niceties, and Annie asked after their Chicago trip while the tea was poured and served. The warmth soothed Annie's stomach. A little.

"Now then," Eleanor said. "I've been made to wait long enough. Tell us the happy news about the orders flowing in."

Annie took a strengthening breath. "There are no orders."

"No orders?"

Mr. Sampson set down his cup. "Surely someone. . . . The dresses were very pretty."

"Actually, we *have* sold three dresses."

"But you said there were no orders."

"We sold three dresses to the models who wore them."

"That's not right! They can't have them."

"They paid for them." *Paid a little.*

Eleanor blinked too often. "This can't be. I imagined dozens of orders." She shook her head, uncomprehending. "And there will be. My friends *will* order. The soiree was a huge success. They told me as much."

Mr. Sampson looked at his lap, a hint that he knew the truth. "Your party was lovely, my sweet, and you were the perfect hostess."

Her gaze whipped toward him. "It was and I was, and so. . ." She looked at Annie. "If there are no orders it is because of the dresses. If you'd implemented my embellishments and used the expensive trim I purchased, we wouldn't be having this conversation."

Perhaps she's right.

"And those models. They were *not* elegant at all. I heard that one young girl say she sold flowers on the street."

"Maybelle," Annie said. "She is one of the women who purchased her dress."

Eleanor threw her arms in the air. "So we sell to a street vendor but not to the women who are the core of New York society?"

It was time for the full truth of it. "That's right."

Eleanor stood and paced in front of a fireplace. "This is totally unacceptable. This is not what I had in mind for Eleanor's Couture. You've humiliated me."

Annie felt the full weight of remorse. "That, I did not intend. But I simply could not create the fancy dresses you wanted. That's not what I signed on for. That's not why you asked me to partner with you. Remember 'function over fad'?"

"She's right." Mr. Sampson patted the arm of Eleanor's chair, urging her to return.

She sat with full reluctance bordering on a pout. "My party was *not* a failure."

"No, it was not. But there was a mismatch between the fashion and the customer."

"My friends simply need more time to place their orders."

Annie didn't want to be cruel, yet she didn't want Eleanor to base her future on false facts.

Luckily, Mr. Sampson did it for her. "I heard comments during the party," he said.

"Comments? You haven't told me about any comments."

"I didn't wish to crush your dreams."

Her eyes widened. "Crush?"

Annie hated to witness Eleanor's pain. "I'm very sorry."

Eleanor stood again, waving away their words. "This can't be." But then she settled in front of the fireplace and faced them. "Tell me. Tell me what was said. I need to hear it."

Annie looked to Mr. Sampson. He would know how much to say.

He cleared his throat. "The ladies commented that the dresses were pretty but too simple for their needs." He hurried on to add, "I feared there would be no orders, which is why I forbid you calling from Chicago. If you'd known about this earlier, you never would have been able to enjoy our time with family."

"You babied me."

"I protected you."

Eleanor leveled Annie with a look. "If you had created the dresses I had in mind. . ."

Annie returned to her original argument. "But those wouldn't be the dresses we talked about. Those wouldn't be the dresses that sparked our collaboration."

"Some collaboration. You did what *you* wanted to do."

Ouch. "You're right. But I based my decisions on our initial vision. Our target customer was a working woman, providing them fashion that was pretty but functional. At a reasonable price."

Annie watched Eleanor's face and saw her mind at work. It was fascinating to see her eyes flit about then finally calm. Eventually, she nodded. Once.

"You are right."

"I am? I mean, you agree?"

Eleanor held out her hand to her husband. "Oh, Harold. Why did you let me flutter away with Eleanor's Couture?"

He stood and took her hands in his. "I couldn't stop you. You know that's true."

She nodded. "I made a fool of myself."

"You gave your friends the chance to see new fashion. I know they enjoyed the party."

"I cringe when I think what they are saying in private." She sighed deeply.

"But alas, it is what it is."

"That's a commendable attitude, my sweet." He kissed her forehead.

After a moment's pause, Eleanor broke away from his touch and stood alone in front of Annie. "I admit my fault in this, my wild hare. But I'm afraid I can't continue to be a part of—of whatever you're doing with the fashion, Annie."

What did she mean?

Annie asked the question aloud. "What are you saying?"

"I no longer wish to be a part of our collaboration. Keep whatever money we've given you, but there will be no more funds."

Even though she'd recognized this possibility, to have it fully happen. . . "But—"

Eleanor's declaration seemed to sap all her energy. She turned back to her husband and fell into his arms.

"There, there, sweet wife. It's over now." He cocked his head toward the door, indicating Annie should leave.

Somehow she did. Somehow she walked through the gates of the mansion. Somehow she crossed the street, and somehow Annie sat upon the steps of St. Patrick's.

Words demanded release. "They can't do that!"

Three pigeons flew away.

They could do it, and they did do it.

And it was Annie's fault.

⁂

"So that's where we stand." Annie looked around the workshop, as though gauging the power of her story.

"Well then," Edna said with a sigh.

"Well then." Vesta's thoughts scurried wildly. When there had been no orders, when Annie had gone to the Sampsons to tell them the bad news, Vesta had prepared herself for some sort of repercussion. She'd been around businessmen her entire life. With failure came harsh consequences.

Or new opportunities. Since she'd privately predicted the Sampsons might financially bow out, she'd come up with her own solution. Her heart began to beat faster, but before she could say anything. . .

Maude stood with a flurry of waving hands. "Come now, ladies. Don't you understand the essence of Annie's words?"

"I do," Edna said. "We have no more money coming in."

Maude waved the phrase away with a hand. "No, no—"

"Don't ignore it," Edna said. "It's an enormous point."

"It is. But not the most important one."

Edna sat back, crossing her arms. "Enlighten us."

"The point is," Maude said, looking at each in turn, "we are now free."

"Nothing's free," Edna said, shaking her head.

"*We* are free to become the business *we* want to be."

Annie's face softened with relief, and she pulled Maude into an embrace. "I knew I could count on you to see the silver lining."

"Silver," Edna huffed. "That's what we need."

Vesta raised a finger, needing to know one more thing. "Is Mrs. Sampson going to continue with Eleanor's Couture on her own?"

"I don't think so," Annie said.

"She must have been crushed."

"Gutted," Annie said. "But her husband is there to help her through it. He saw the writing on the wall even before the soiree. He'll be there for her, no matter what."

Vesta smoothed the fabric of her skirt against her legs. "I envy her that."

Annie put a hand on Vesta's arm. "Is Richard giving you trouble?"

She avoided Annie's gaze. "He still doesn't understand what good I do here."

All the ladies piped up with words of affirmation.

Affirmation. What an extraordinary phenomenon. "You're very kind."

"You're very needed here. We could not have done this without you."

"Sean could talk to him," Annie said. "You should have told us he was making things difficult."

He makes all things difficult.

It was time for her idea. "Actually. . ." Vesta straightened her shoulders. "I *would* like Sean to talk to him but about something else."

"What else?" Annie asked.

"Money. My money, to be exact."

"You have money?" Maude asked.

Vesta nodded. "My grandparents left me an inheritance. A fairly sizeable sum, if I remember correctly."

Annie's face looked hopeful. "Do you think Richard will fund our business?"

"No."

"No?"

She loved being able to say what came next. "*I* will fund our business. It's my inheritance. It's my money. You and Sean take me home tonight, and together we'll speak to Richard."

There were hugs all around.

It felt wonderful to be able to finally contribute something tangible to the cause.

☙

After Sean got home from work and was filled in on the day's drama, he, Annie, and Vesta left for the Culver residence in Brooklyn. Their mood was hopeful as they traveled over the Brooklyn Bridge under the cover of many prayers.

"I remember the first time you and I crossed this bridge," Annie said, pointing to the walking level above the level that carried carts and automobiles across. She pointed toward the East River flowing under them. "We spoke of our dreams on that walk."

"I remember," he said. "It was New Year's Day, this very year."

She shook her head. "That is hard to fathom. So much has happened in 1912."

"What did you dream about?" Vesta asked.

Annie put a hand to her chest. "On my part? Not much. At least not at the time. I am a woman of facts, and the fact was, I came to America as a maid, ran away from service, found a job at Macy's—"

"Met me."

"Met you and let you lure me to Butterick, where I met the Sampsons."

"It was like you were given stepping stones."

It was an apt way to put it. "From there I went to Paris and became engaged." She kissed Sean's cheek. "I was saved from being on the *Titanic* and decided to take a chance on becoming a fashion designer." She looked at Sean. "A step which is now in jeopardy."

He shook his head.

"Don't shake your head. Everything I said was true."

"I'm not challenging the facts but the dream."

"Ah yes," Annie said. "You are the true dreamer."

"What are your dreams, Sean?" his mother asked.

"I dream of knowing I made a difference. I dream of knowing there is a definite reason I was born, a reason I exist now—not a hundred years from now. I dream of knowing that a portion of God's greater plan gets fulfilled through me."

"Your selfless dreams shamed me then, as they shame me now."

"That was never my intent." He pulled her hand around his arm, and she felt his warmth through her jacket. "I merely wanted—and want—you to see with a larger scope. Think beyond our jobs—which may or may not have much to do with our true purposes. Our lives can touch people. That is why we all exist."

Vesta smiled lovingly at him. "I am so proud to be your mother."

Annie saw him blush. "And I am so proud to be your wife." She kissed his cheek and remembered one last thing. "You said that God made us different, you and I. You fantasize and I organize."

"And together we make a whole."

"I envy you both," Vesta said. "It's like you were meant for each other. Unfortunately. . ." She shook her head. "Never mind."

"No, Vesta," Annie said, for she could tell that something significant was on her mind. "Finish your sentence. 'Unfortunately. . .'"

Vesta hesitated. "I shouldn't."

"You should," Sean said. "Tell us."

She continued five full steps before she relented. "Unfortunately, Richard and I do not share an intertwined connection like you do. He is what he is, and I am what I am, and rarely do we meet. Never, actually."

"Surely that's not true," Annie said.

Oddly, it was Sean who answered. "Surely, I believe it is." He relinquished Annie's arm to take his mother's. "I know you have not had an easy life with him—that Father causes tension where we all would prefer peace."

There were tears in her eyes as she looked up at him. "Somehow it comforts me to know that you've noticed. I've often felt quite alone."

"Forgive me for noticing but not acting," Sean said. "When I was younger I didn't think it was my place, and when I was on my own, I became absorbed in my own life." He swallowed hard. "And—and I left you to deal with him alone. I'm so sorry, Mother. I abandoned you."

She patted his arm. "Don't be silly. You grew up. You set off on your own path, just as you should have. Part of it is my own fault. I avoid conflict at all costs. I should have been stronger, should have stood up to him."

"Perhaps," Sean said.

Vesta looked at him, surprised. But then she nodded. "It is nice to have this sort of conversation, as adults. You are a fine man, Sean. A fine son."

He lifted her hand and kissed it. "And I could not ask for a finer mother."

Annie was moved by their connection. She'd never felt any type of closeness with her own parents. Disdain, anger, and control had ruled. There'd been no love—especially after her brother Alfie had died. Through it all Annie had been forced to think in terms of survival. Facts took precedent over emotion.

Sean broke through her memories with a glance. Then he told Vesta, "You are not alone anymore, Mother. For Annie and I are with you."

"Absolutely," Annie said with complete sincerity. She shoved aside the memories of her own family's lack of love and embraced the chance to love her mother-in-law. It was as though she'd been given a second chance.

Another second chance.

Reaching Brooklyn, they turned toward the Culver home.

Toward another person who was ruled by facts: Richard.

⌒⌒

When the three of them arrived at the Culver home, Richard was not yet home from work. It was probably for the best, for it gave Vesta time to tell the cook there were two more for dinner and time for her to do some digging, as she tried to find the papers regarding her inheritance.

Unfortunately, she believed they were somewhere in Richard's desk, in his study, which was his private domain—with Vesta emphasizing the word *private*.

That being the case, Annie was nervous that the three of them would be caught snooping.

She checked the clock on the mantel. "What time did you say he usually arrives home?"

"Six thirty."

"It's six twenty-eight now."

Sean closed a drawer and stepped toward the door. "We'll have to have the conversation without the papers, Mother. We don't want to risk—"

"Risk what, may I ask?"

His father stood in the doorway.

They all froze. Vesta held a stack of papers. "Richard."

"Vesta." He nodded to the other two. "What, may I ask are the three of you doing in my study?"

Vesta let out a small whimper. But to her credit, she stood tall and held the papers to her chest. "I was looking for the papers regarding my inheritance."

"Why?"

"Because. . .because. . ."

Sean came to her rescue. "Because the fashion event at the Sampsons did not go as well as we'd hoped."

"Our ties have been cut," Annie said. "They are no longer our patrons."

"Which led me to offer the money from my inheritance," Vesta said. "I believe in their business. I see it firsthand, every day. I want to help it succeed."

Richard crossed the room, took the papers from his wife, returned them to a drawer, and shut it with a decided click. "No."

"What do you mean?" Vesta asked.

"No, we will not give money to further fund this failure."

"It's not a failure, Father. We simply had a different vision for the business. The Sampsons wanted to cater to their wealthy friends. And we want to create clothes for the masses."

"Who have no money to pay for them."

Annie took offense. "We will price the dresses so they are affordable."

"Garnering little profit." He shook his head and sat at his desk. "As a businessman myself, it would seem the Sampsons have the better take on the situation. If you must design clothes, design them for people who can pay for them."

Sean stepped toward the edge of the desk. "But also as a businessman, and as the owner of a dry goods store, I know *your* customers are not wealthy but are ordinary people with modest incomes."

"I am providing goods that people need to survive. Not dresses that are. . .frivolous."

"Our clothes are not frivolous," Annie said. "That is why they will sell. They are fashionable but functional. And frugal."

"Cheap."

"No, Richard," Vesta said. "Now you're being rude."

"And you weren't rude, rifling through the personal items in my private study?"

Could they come out and begin again?

"We apologize for that," Vesta said.

"As you should." He took a cigar from an oak humidor and lit it, tainting the air with its foul odor. "If the failure of your fashion event isn't a sign from God to stop this foolishness, I don't know what is."

"It's a sign we need to go back to what we originally planned," Annie said. "Mrs. Sampson was the one who led us astray. We let her, because she and Mr. Sampson *were* the money. But we quickly came to see that we needed to return to our initial vision." She thought for a short moment about telling him of her revelation at the window but decided that as a facts man, he would not respond well to any talk about feeling God's direction.

"I'm asking you to trust us, Richard," Vesta said, taking a spot at the other corner of his desk. "The three of us have worked long and hard on this business. Yes, God closed a door with the Sampsons but—"

"To be precise, I closed the door on them before the fashion show," Annie said. The astonished look on Richard's face made her wish she'd not been so forthcoming.

"In what way?"

"I chose to stick with our initial plan and didn't bow to Mrs. Sampson's lofty aspirations."

"A stupid mistake," Richard said. "Wealthy women spend money."

"It was a necessary decision," Sean said. "But yes, a decision that has caused us to need funds. I really wish you'd back us, Father."

"No."

Vesta pointed to the drawer. "Which is why I have offered to use my inheritance money."

He leveled her with a look. "*Your* inheritance money?"

Vesta swallowed. "The money my grandparents left me."

Richard puffed on the cigar, sat back, and sent smoke rings through the air between them. "You have no money, my dear."

"Of course I do," Vesta said. "They left me nearly ten thousand dollars."

"Which transferred to me, as your husband—by law—as soon as we married. What was yours became mine."

"You could let her have it, Father."

"I could. But I will not."

Vesta's voice broke. "I don't care about the law."

"I do."

Silence settled around them like a fog. Vesta looked at Richard, and Richard looked at Vesta—who was the first to look away.

"If you'll excuse me." She ran out of the room.

Annie ran after her. She heard Vesta's footfalls on the stairs then a door closing. Annie followed her upstairs. She knocked. "May I come in?"

"Are you alone?"

"Yes."

"Come then."

Annie found Vesta sitting on a bed, her shoulders slumped, a handkerchief dabbing her eyes.

"He's insufferable."

Annie sat beside her. "He certainly could have been nicer about it."

"I always thought that money was mine."

"You didn't know about the law?"

"Perhaps I did, at one time." She blew her nose. "It's totally unfair. I have a notion to join a group of very vociferous women and march for our rights." She scoffed. "As if I have any." She turned to Annie. "I'm so sorry. I really wanted to give you that money."

"I know you did. And we both appreciate the generous offer, more than you know."

"Some good it did."

Annie put her arm around Vesta. "We'll find another way."

"What way?"

"I don't know."

Vesta took a breath then nodded. "God's way. Surely He has an answer."

Annie was depending on it.

❧

Vesta lay on the bed and waited for Richard to come to her bedroom to check on her. Yet as the mantel clock chimed the new hour, she awakened to the knowledge he wasn't coming. That it had taken her so long to come to that realization indicated the depth of her mental agitation. He never sought her out after an argument, never consoled, never apologized. Why would she expect this time to be different?

Because he didn't just hurt me, he hurt Annie and Sean.

Vesta had never shown interest in the money inherited from her grandparents. Until now. Until it could be used to fulfill a dream.

She hadn't had to. For in truth, Richard was an able provider. She wanted for nothing.

That wasn't true. She wanted for nothing of a material nature. Their home was comfortable yet stately. She had enough servants at her beck and call to cover every task. She wore beautiful clothes and ate delicious meals.

And yet. . .

With Sean and Sybil grown and gone, she was lonely. Richard's focus had been, and would always be, on the store. A few years ago, when she had been brave enough to complain about the time he spent there, he'd aptly pointed out that without his hard work they could not afford the life they lived.

But what kind of life *was* that?

Vesta sat up in bed, adjusting the pillows behind her. She leaned into their softness and adjusted them again to give her more support.

Support. That's what she needed. Not just physical support but mental, emotional, and even spiritual encouragement. When was the last time she'd spoken to Richard about faith or prayer? It was disturbing to think back a month, a year, a decade, and realize they had last shared their faith when they were Sean's age, when *they* were the ones starting a business and were in need of divine guidance and provision. With success had come spiritual apathy, or if not complete apathy, a passivity that bordered on taking God for granted. And—dare she say it—a certain level of expectedness and entitlement, as though they deserved their many blessings.

The insight propelled her off the bed and to her knees. "I'm so sorry we have taken Your many gifts as if they are our due. As if they are *our* doing. I am ashamed. Thank You for all You have done for us. Be with Annie and Sean as they seek Your guidance and help. Help me help them. And help. . ." She hesitated, for stating her need so blatantly was difficult. But since God already knew what was in her heart and mind she might as well say it aloud. "And help Richard and I mend our marriage. I have been living blindly in an opaque bubble, moving from day to day with little purpose to benefit myself or others. I have let him bully me beyond submissiveness, to the point of oppression, because I am too weak or lazy to stand up for myself. Please help me do what You want me to do. Give me the strength—"

There was a knock on the door. Vesta scrambled to her feet and smoothed her dress. Had Richard actually come to see her? "Yes?"

But it was only her maid. "Mr. Culver says it's time for dinner. But he wishes to see you in his study first."

"Thank you, Lola. I will be down presently."

"Do you wish to change for dinner?"

"Not tonight." *He will take me as I am.*

She glanced in the mirror, smoothed her hair, took a deep breath, and went downstairs to meet with her husband. Along the way she tried to collect her thoughts but found them tumbling down the stairs around her.

For the first time in her life, Vesta did not knock on the doorjamb before entering Richard's lair but simply walked in. She meant it as a show of strength, but upon seeing his raised eyebrows at her action, she immediately wished she could back out and come in again.

"Are you fully composed yet?" he asked.

His words rubbed her wrong for they implied no compassionate interest, only annoyance. "I am here, aren't I?"

His other eyebrow rose. "Shall the church bells chime in celebration?"

She did not respond.

"You should not have run to your room like a petulant child who didn't get her way."

All the revelation she'd received between the running away and this moment of standing before him dissipated in a breath. "I—I was disappointed I couldn't help Annie and Sean."

He shook his head. "I will not rehash an old discussion. Their business is foolhardy—as shown by the loss of their patron and their desperate need for more funding."

She took a step toward his desk. "They had a misstep at the beginning, but now I feel they are truly—"

"You feel?" He snickered. "What do you know of business and fashion design?"

She was taken aback but only for a moment. She pointed in the direction of their store. "Did I not help birth our store from nothing? Was I not by your side stocking shelves, serving customers, making decisions?"

"It was necessary at the beginning."

"I would go there now, every day with you. I am willing to help."

"I do not need your help."

The way he said it implied her help held no value whatsoever. "I have skills."

"You do."

A question surged. "Name one."

"What?"

"Name one of my skills." *I dare you.*

He stood and turned off his desk lamp. "Another childish response." He took on a child's whine. " 'Tell me I'm pretty, Daddy. Tell me, tell me, please, please?' "

The breath went out of her. "Your mocking wounds me."

"As your actions wound me." He moved toward the door. "Come now. You've already scared Sean and Annie away from joining us for dinner. And you know how I hate cold food."

"Cold should know cold."

He stopped beside her. "What did you say?"

The words came out before she could stop them. "You are a cold man, Richard. You have no feeling at all. You are cruel and spiteful and have no compassion for what others need."

He glared down at her. "Watch yourself, Vesta."

She stepped back and tried to keep her chin strong. "The children need our help. We have the means to give it. If they fail, so what? We will have helped them do their very best to achieve their dreams. By doing nothing, we doom their dream to failure."

He pointed at her. "*You* know nothing of business, logic, and money matters."

"As you know nothing of love, encouragement, and everything that really matters."

His face darkened, and his features contorted in a way she had never witnessed. With a swell of motion, he grabbed hold of her arm and dragged her out of the study, through the foyer, and up the stairs.

"Stop it, Richard! Let go of me!"

She nearly faltered on a step, tripping on her skirt, but his grip was so strong he yanked her through it, propelled her to the landing, and shoved her into her bedroom where she fell to the floor in a heap. He snatched the key that stood on the bureau and pointed it at her. "You will stay here until you come to your senses."

With that, he slammed the door. She heard the key in the lock.

"No!" She ran to the door and found her fears confirmed. She was locked in.

Vesta beat her hands against the door. "Let me out! Richard! You can't do this!"

But he could do that. He had done that.

Her legs gave out beneath her and Vesta fell into a puddle of tears.

❧

"I still can't believe. . . Your father is the most insufferable, stubborn, mean—"

Home from Brooklyn, Sean closed the door of their flat behind them. "Agreed. On all counts. But keep your voice down. We don't need the neighbors to know our business."

Annie fell upon the window seat. "What business?" she huffed.

Sean sat beside her. "What were my mother's words regarding the matter?"

She forced her thoughts to return to their time in Brooklyn. "God will have an answer."

"He will."

"When, Sean? When?"

"When it's time."

"We don't have time. We have the two hundred dollars the Sampsons gave us, but that will only take us so far. I'm not sure where to go from this point. We'd hoped for orders. At least a few."

"But we didn't truly expect them." Sean put a hand on her knee. "You made the clothes you wanted to make but presented them to the wrong customers. The consequences are not a total surprise."

Annie didn't like Sean's choice of the word *consequences*, though she couldn't argue it. "I should have thought of a more concrete plan of what to do in the aftermath of the soiree."

He laughed. "I am quite certain the words *aftermath* and *soiree* have never been used in the same sentence."

"Bully for me."

He took her hand. "It comes down to this, Annie-girl: we have to work hard and do our part, and trust God to do His."

Good words. A fine sentiment. But she had doubts. "If that's so, I ask Him to work quickly. Please."

Sean pointed upward.

Annie looked up and repeated her words as a prayer. "Work quickly, Father? Please?"

CHAPTER NINE

Before Sean left for a Butterick sales call, he and the partners met in the workshop to hear more bad news. Annie wondered if they'd ever again meet for a happy announcement.

"So, it's a no," Edna said, from the window seat. "No money from your father."

"None," Sean said.

Maude adjusted a hairpin and sat beside Edna. "But Vesta said she had an inheritance. She had money."

"Which became my father's money when they married."

"That's absurd," Maude said.

Annie shrugged. "It is. But it's the law."

"Where *is* your mother?" Edna asked. "Do you think she's all right? She's usually here by now."

Annie had wondered the same thing and turned to Sean. "I hate to imagine it, but do you think your father has forbidden her from coming anymore?"

"No, he wouldn't. . .I'm sure. . ." He hesitated then took a fresh breath. "I'm not sure. It's possible."

Annie had a horrible thought. "He's never been violent toward her, has he?"

Sean opened his mouth to answer then closed it. "Nothing extreme."

"Extreme according to whom?" Maude asked.

"He doesn't hit her, if that's what you're suggesting." His face changed. "In fact, I don't remember ever seeing him touch her in any way."

"Oh dear," Annie said. "*No* touch could be as hurtful as a slap."

Edna nodded. "Every time my Ernie passed me, he'd reach out and touch my arm, my shoulder. . ." Her face turned wistful. "My cheek."

Sean put his hand on the back of Annie's neck, making her ever so glad he wasn't like his father.

"So," Maude said, "what totally unacceptable punishment do you think your father is subjecting your mother to, as we speak?"

Sean turned his wedding band around on his finger. "I've lived away from home a long time, but I imagine he's making her suffer his silence, while she desperately tries to make his world perfect to win back his affection."

Maude scoffed. "Such as it is."

Annie could see the pain and worry on his face. "Can you postpone your sales call until this afternoon and go check on her?"

He bit his lip then stood. "I can. And perhaps I should."

Maude stood. "I'll go with you. I'd love to give that nasty man a what-for."

Edna pulled her back to sitting. "We will stay here and follow you over the bridge with prayer."

❧

While waiting to hear about Vesta, the ladies needed to focus on work. There were dresses to sew, a business to build.

Maude, Annie, and Edna stood around the cutting table. It was time to talk patternmaking. This was Maude's turn to shine.

"I think our best course of action is making every dress in a large variety of sizes."

"So no custom-made dresses," Edna clarified.

"We can offer alterations but that's all. The customers can try on the clothes right there in our shop."

"Shop?" Annie said. "Now we need a shop?"

"We do."

This new burden was heavy. "How are we going to afford a shop?"

Maude hesitated before answering. "I don't know."

Annie bit her lip and stared ahead at nothing, her mind spinning with the logistics. She'd been so proud that they'd opened their own workshop. Now they needed a store that would need to be manned with clerks? Have displays and stock?

"Annie?"

She returned to the moment. "Isn't there some other way we can get the clothes to our customers?"

"No," Maude said plainly. "Maybelle and all the other working women on this street, and in the entire city of New York, are not used to going to a dressmaker or a workshop to have their clothes custom-made. They go to a department store or order from Sears Roebuck."

"Most dresses are still made-to-order," Edna pointed out.

Maude rolled a tape measure around her hand. "I propose we offer women a ready-made dress. Immediately. Like Lane Bryant does."

Annie nodded. "I bought my first maternity dress there, right off the hanger."

"This changes everything," Edna said. "We buy other items and take them home the same day. Why not designer dresses?"

Maude clapped. "And so it will be! I will work on making patterns for all sizes of women—from Maybelle to Mrs. Tuttle. And then Ginny, Gert, and Edna will sew them."

Annie retrieved a new Sears catalog and paged to the dress section. "Here are the sizes they offer: thirty-two to forty-one inch bust, twenty-three to thirty-inch waist, and thirty-seven to forty-three inch length of skirt."

"But they can make special orders, yes?" Maude said.

"Yes." She looked at the page again. "For twenty percent more, and they take an additional ten to fourteen days' time."

"If we truly want to be a ready-made shop, we need to offer more sizes than Sears," Edna said.

"I agree."

"But all variations of those sizes? That's. . ." Edna counted on her fingers then gave up. "There are too many combinations of bust, waist, and length for us to handle."

"We could use the standardized sizes for Butterick patterns as another guide," Maude suggested.

Annie thought of another solution. "We have the measurements of our models, which represent a good cross section of customers. Perhaps hone it down to eight sizes?"

"Eight sizes times twelve designs equals ninety-six dresses," Edna said. "Is that enough to open a shop?"

"I could design more variety," Annie said.

Maude shook her head. "Twelve designs is plenty to start, though I think we need two of each size."

"That's 192 dresses," Annie said.

Maude let out a dramatic expulsion of air. "I think we also need to offer some basic dark skirts and pretty blouses for those women who need a uniform look for their jobs."

Annie disagreed and pointed to the catalog. "Women can get those pieces in a catalog."

"Or at Macy's," Edna said. "As I said, Macy's manufactures their own limited line."

"I think we need to focus on dresses," Annie said. "Not fancy, but not a waist and skirt a woman could buy elsewhere."

"Agreed," Maude and Edna said at the same time.

Annie felt a stirring inside and put a hand to her midsection.

"Annie? Are you all right?" Edna asked. "Is it the baby?"

Annie laughed aloud. "Not this time. This time I think it's a life of another kind. For a new idea has been born."

⸗⸗⸗

Vesta sat on the window seat in her room and watched Richard leave for the store. *He's leaving without letting me out?*

She banged against the window to get his attention like a moth trying to get free. She opened the sash and called out to him. "Richard? Let me out!"

He merely shook his head and got in the car Baines had brought around. It drove away.

Leaving her a prisoner.

She heard the key in the lock. Lola entered, carrying a breakfast tray. "Good morning, ma'am."

It was the same greeting she received every morning. As though this morning were no different than any other?

"I'm not hungry."

"You barely ate anything from the dinner tray, ma'am. You need to eat."

I need to get out of here! With that goal in mind. . . "I will eat. Later. But for now, help me dress."

As they went about the process of her morning toilette, Vesta tried to develop a plan. Last night she'd asked Lola multiple times to leave the door unlocked, or to be a conspirator in setting her free, but the threat of her master's wrath was enough to keep Lola's loyalties grounded with Richard.

Vesta had to do this on her own.

The first step was one of preparation. When the opportunity *did* come to escape—as she prayed it would—Vesta would be dressed and ready to flee.

Vesta heard a vehicle stop in front of the house. She ran to the window and gasped when she saw Sean alight. She called out the window, "Sean! Up here!"

He stopped on the walkway to the house and peered up at her. "Hello, Mother. I've come to see why you didn't come to work today."

Vesta glanced left and right, checking for the proximity of neighborhood ears. She motioned him closer. He stood beneath her window. "Your father has locked me in my room."

"What?"

"Locked. He has forbidden me from leaving."

"He can't do that."

"He did that. But he's at work. Come in and insist that Baines or Lola let you in to talk to me."

He strode toward the door, a man on a mission. His knock was strong and insistent. She heard Baines greet him. "Let me see my mother. Immediately."

The door closed, and the sound moved from the exterior to inside the house. Vesta ran to the bedroom door, her ear against it, listening.

There was some argument but then she heard Sean's feet on the stairs. The door unlocked, and she fell into his arms, clinging to him. "I'm so glad you came! You've saved me!"

Sean glanced toward the stairwell then put a finger to his lips, quieting her. He came into the room and closed the door behind. He took both her hands in his and whispered, "Tell me what's going on."

She told him the entire story that spanned the time he and Annie left the day before, to her own revelation of their unappreciative faith, to her argument with Richard and her captivity.

"He's gone wonkers," Sean said.

"I pushed him."

"He needed to be pushed." He paced back and forth near the door. "I knew he was obstinate and set in his ways, but I never thought he was cruel."

There are many forms of cruelty. "I need to get out of here," she said. "Completely. Out of the house."

Sean let out a breath. "That's serious business."

Vesta had second thoughts. "Is it too much?"

"We need to think this through." He led her to a settee where they both sat in silence, collecting their thoughts. "If I lock you back in here, what happens when he comes home after work this evening? Will he let you out?"

"I would hope so. Yet. . .I have never seen him so angry. The frenzy of his expression frightened me. And he has never manhandled me as he did, dragging me up the stairs like that." She rubbed her sore arm. She'd noticed bruises but didn't dare tell Sean about it.

"What happens if he finds you gone?"

Vesta's first thought brought pleasure, but she quickly brushed it away.

"You smiled."

He'd caught her. "It *would* give me some satisfaction to know that I had escaped his prison."

"He'll be even angrier."

"But I won't be here to see it." The thought gave her strength. Yet. . . "One enormous question looms: where will I go?"

"You will come live with us."

She'd hoped he would say that. "There is no extra room in your apartment."

"We will make room for you. And then you will be free to help us with our work. We all missed you. That is why I am here. To fetch you back again."

"What about Baines and Lola? I don't want them to lose their jobs over this."

Sean hesitated. "I will send them on errands. When they return, we will be gone."

"Gone," she repeated.

"Where is a carpetbag?"

She pulled it out from under the bed. "It's packed and ready to go."

He put his hand on the door. "Are you sure about this?"

Her stomach grabbed, but she said, "I am."

"I'll be back. Be ready to go."

Ready to go. Her heart beat in her throat but did not incapacitate her. Instead she felt a wave of courage. She sat on the bed beside the carpetbag and willed her racing heart to calm. "Peace, Father. Give me courage and peace."

Not ten minutes later, Sean returned. "Come!" he whispered.

He took the bag and closed the door behind them. Then they scurried down the stairs, gathered her coat and a hat, and ran out the front door to a waiting cab. Only when they were on their way did Vesta risk speaking.

"How did you get rid of Baines and Lola?"

"I told Baines that you had requested a special tonic and some headache medicine from the apothecary. I sent Lola along because she knows which ones you prefer."

"They were not suspicious?"

"I believe they were. But they also seemed glad to have a reason to be gone, an excuse they might tell Father when he returns."

"So they know you're letting me out?"

"Baines thanked me for being a good son."

She linked her arm in his and kissed his cheek. "You are the best son. And I thank God for you."

Annie looked at the clock on the wall. Surely Sean and Vesta should be back by now. Surely Richard wouldn't give them any trouble about it.

Surely he might.

Suddenly, the door to the workshop opened and Sean stepped in. "Surprise!"

Vesta came in after him.

The ladies swarmed around her, asking questions.

"Let her talk," Sean said.

They backed away, and Annie could see that her mother-in-law's eyes were puffy, her face haggard, even when she managed to smile.

"I'm so glad you're here," Annie said.

"I'm so glad to be here." Vesta took Sean's hand. "Thank you, son, for saving me."

"Saving you?" Edna asked.

"Did Richard hurt you?" Maude asked. "Because if he did. . ."

Vesta began to shake her head then nodded. "He locked me in my room."

"He can't do that! You're his wife. You're a grown woman," Maude said.

"He did it anyway," Sean said. "The servants had been ordered not to let her out while Father was at work. But I managed to sneak her away." He nodded toward the hall. "We packed a bag for her. She will live with us."

Annie was taken aback but recovered quickly. She would do anything for Vesta.

"Just temporarily," Vesta said, looking at her. "I can sleep on your sofa."

"Or I can," Sean said.

Vesta shook her head vehemently. "I will not come between a husband and wife. *I* will sleep on the sofa."

"What's Richard going to do when he comes home and finds you gone?" Maude asked.

"Come after me," Vesta said with a shiver. "Or perhaps not. I've made it clear where my loyalties lie." She touched Sean's cheek then looked at the ladies. "Working with all of you has awakened a new life within me."

Edna and Maude took turns giving Vesta a hug.

Annie was last and held on to her longer than necessary. She whispered in her ear, "I'm so glad you got away."

"Me too," Vesta whispered.

"Well then," Maude said. "You've come at just the right time. In your short absence we've made some heady decisions, and there is much work to do. More work to do."

"Tell us," Vesta said, turning to the cutting table. "Then put me on it."

Maude and Annie described their plan of offering sized, ready-made dresses in a shop.

"A storefront. On the street," Sean said, with doubt in his voice.

"Exactly."

"And how will we pay—?"

There was a knock on the door. Annie opened it to see the elder Mr. Tuttle—Gramps—from the bakery. Her thoughts raced to Iris.

"Has she had the baby?"

"Just did. I've been sent to fetch you."

Annie grabbed her hat then remembered the all-important question. "Boy or girl?"

"Girl."

"What's her name?"

"I'll let Iris tell you."

"Are mother and baby doing well?" Sean asked.

"Well enough. Come now, Annie. They're waiting."

At the last minute, Annie remembered the layette she'd made for the baby. And then Edna remembered the dresses that Mrs. Tuttle and Jane had worn at the soiree—and had purchased.

Annie left with full arms and a fuller heart.

Thomas answered the door to their flat, which was across from the Tuttle bakery. "Annie."

She drew him into an embrace. "Congratulations, new papa."

"Thank you. But it's Iris who did the work of it. Go on in. She's eager to see you."

Annie removed her hat and set the dresses aside. She entered the bedroom and saw Iris sleeping with a swaddled baby in her arms. She began to tiptoe out when Iris stopped her.

"Annie! Come in. I'm just dozing." She looked down at her child and touched her cheek. "Isn't she beautiful?"

Annie sat on the side of the bed and cupped the baby's head in her palm. "She's absolutely lovely. What's her name?"

"Danielle Ann Tuttle."

Annie's chest grew tight, and she was barely able to speak. "After Danny."

"And you." Iris took her hand. "I would not be here—we would not be here—if not for you. I'd probably still be working at the Friesens', scrubbing floors and cleaning the grates."

But Danny would *be here—be alive—if not for me urging all of us to leave service.*

Annie swiped a tear from her eye. "May I hold her?"

"Of course."

The baby was so light, like holding a bundle of air. The child immediately adjusted to Annie's arms.

"Soon you'll be holding your own babe."

Danielle squeaked, so Annie bobbed her up and down, quieting her. A question surfaced. "Was it. . .hard?"

"Giving birth?" Iris laughed. "I've never felt such pain in my entire life."

Annie sat again. "That's what I fear. The pain."

"I did too. And I won't sugarcoat it, pretending it was easy in any way. It was hard. It was labor."

It was funny how Annie had never thought of the full meaning of that word. The implications.

"If I can do it, you can." She nodded toward her daughter. "The pain was bad, but it was worth it."

"Of course," Annie said, running a finger along the baby's cheek.

"She's God's blessing, and I'd go through it again in a minute for her sake."

Annie laughed. "Wait a few years."

"Aye. That might be a good idea." She took the baby back. "Ain't it odd, Annie? We're becoming mothers now, when just last year we were runaways from service."

"Until Thomas wooed you and won your heart."

"The Tuttles won my heart. But. . .Thomas liked you better. At first."

Annie shook her head. "He never *liked* me. I was simply more his age."

"I'm glad you got the job at Macy's."

Annie didn't see the connection. "Why?"

"Because it took you away during the day, leaving me at the Tuttles with Thomas."

Annie laughed. "I'm glad it worked out for you."

"For both of us, eh?"

"For both of us."

❧

Jane and Mrs. Tuttle held their dresses against themselves. Jane spun around. "Oh, Annie. It's so beautiful. Thank you."

"Ahem."

Jane looked at her father, who said, "Who paid for them?"

"You did." She ran to him and kissed his cheek. "Thank you, Papa."

"Wife?" He tapped his other cheek.

Mrs. Tuttle kissed it—and gave it a pinch. "Thank you, m'love."

He pinched her bottom.

"We are going to be the toast of the neighborhood. Everyone's going to want one of your dresses, Annie."

Jane cocked her head. "Those ladies at the fancy party. . .did they want them too?"

"Did you get many orders from them?" Mrs. Tuttle asked.

Annie was tired of detailing their failure. "We've changed direction. We're not selling to those types anymore."

"Who you selling to then?"

"To you. To ladies like you. We're going to have a shop. You'll be able to come in, see the dresses already made up in your size, try them on, buy them, and wear them that same day." She pointed to the new dresses. "Special dresses that are functional yet make a woman feel pretty. Easy-to-wear dresses. Fashion for the unruffled, unveiled, unstoppable woman."

Mrs. Tuttle laughed. "Sounds like a description of you, Annie. And a store. How about calling it Unruffled?"

The word hung in the air between them, as though waiting for her approval. "It's unusual, but I quite fancy it. Very much."

"You open your shop and we'll be loyal customers, and bring others with us," Jane said.

❧

Annie rushed back to the workshop, driven by her desire to share the name of their store.

Edna looked up from pinning a seam. "How's the baby?"

"She's beautiful."

Maude stood on a chair, installing pegs in the walls to hold spools of thread. "What's her name?"

"Danielle Ann Tuttle."

She stepped off the chair and hugged her. "After you and Danny."

"That's sweet of them," Edna said.

"You and Sean need to be thinking of names too," Vesta said.

"For your baby and for the store," Maude said.

"I don't have a baby name yet, but. . . ." Annie said, ". . .I do have a name for the store."

"You do?"

"When did this happen?"

"What is it?"

The name was so unusual that Annie hedged. "First, let me tell you a description of our designs and of the shop: fashion for the unruffled, unveiled, unstoppable woman."

Maude clapped. "Un-believable," she said. "It's perfect!"

"It is!" Edna said. "Who wouldn't want to shop in such a store?"

"We're offering our customers more than just a dress," Annie said. "We're offering them the chance to embrace their choice to be a modern woman."

Vesta touched her arm. "I just got shivers."

Maude raised her hand. "But what of the name? I still like Annie's Dresses."

Annie shook her head. To name it after herself when all her friends were involved seemed the epitome of being prideful. "I thought—"

"Most of the other stores are someone's name," Edna said. "Macy's, Tiffany's, Lord & Taylor, even Lane Bryant. That's what most stores do."

"Bergdorf Goodman," Vesta added. "Gimbels."

"All men's names," Maude said. "Except for Lane Bryant."

Did they forget she'd told them she *had* a name in mind?

Edna must have read her thoughts for she pressed her hands in the air, quieting the discussion. "Annie? What is the name of the store?"

"We're not like most stores. We want to be different," she said.

"Annie!" Maude said. "Tell us."

She fueled herself with a fresh breath. "Unruffled."

No one responded at first, as though they needed a moment to let it settle.

Or, they hated it and weren't sure how to tell her.

Edna repeated the tag line. "Unruffled: Fashion for the Unruffled, Unveiled, Unstoppable Woman."

Maude raised her hand. "I vote yes to Unruffled, for we four are the epitome of the unruffled woman."

"I vote yes too," Edna said.

"Me three," Vesta said.

"Us four and five," came from their two sewers, Ginny and Gert, who stood in the doorway of the sewing room.

"Not that you asked us," Ginny said.

"But we should have asked you," Annie said. "For you are our customer."

The girls raised their chins higher. "I like the idea of being unruffled—in fashion and in just being who we are," Gert said. "We'd buy in a shop like that. So would our friends, eh, Ginny?"

"They would. I knows it."

Annie's throat grew tight. It was all coming together, like so many roads converging. "This is it," she whispered. "This is what we are supposed to do."

There were hugs all around. And praise to God who had supplied the answers.

❧

"I will not allow you to sleep on the sofa, Sean," his mother said. "Now give me that sheet and help me tuck it in."

Sean reluctantly handed it over, and together they created a bed for Vesta on the sofa in their small parlor. Annie brought a pillow and blanket.

"There," Vesta said when they were finished. "I'll be snug as a bug in a rug." *I'll have to be, as the sofa is short.*

Annie closed the window just a tad. "Let me know if it's too warm or cool."

"The October air is quite refreshing. And I am quite capable of adjusting the window, my dear."

"Of course you are," Sean said. "We just want you to be comfortable."

"And happy," Annie added.

They both studied her, and Vesta knew she had to say something about her extraordinary day. "I did the right thing, leaving."

"I'm surprised Father hasn't shown up here. Surely he knows where you went."

Which proves how little he cares. She put on a brave face. "I rebelled against him. I either expected him to come here and order me home, or. . ."

"Or?" Annie prodded.

"Or he'd be glad that I'm gone and proceed with his dinner and his after-dinner cognac and cigar with little notice of my absence."

"He has to be worried," Annie said.

"I'm sure he's pried at least part of the truth from Baines and Lola," Vesta said. "If they told him you came. . ." She fluffed the pillow and returned it to its place. "I just hope he doesn't take his anger out on them." *Or any of us.*

They bid each other good night, and Vesta settled onto the sofa—which wasn't *that* uncomfortable if she lay on her side. The moonlight cast a swath across the room. The evening breeze was too warm and she cast off the covers.

As Richard has cast me off?

Why hadn't he come? All day she'd looked toward the door of the workshop at any sound upon the stairs, expecting him to burst through the door and demand she come home where she belonged. But mostly she'd wallowed in the busyness of the work, letting it—and the voices of her friends—weave a cocoon of safety around her, or at least diverting her thoughts from the repercussions that would surely come.

Only they hadn't come. She wasn't sure whether to be relieved or sad.

Either way, tears accompanied her to sleep.

⸎

Vesta was awakened by knocking on the door.

"Vesta?" His voice was a sharp whisper.

Richard? She got up to answer it so as not to awaken Annie and Sean. But too late, for Sean came out of their bedroom, and Annie appeared in the doorway.

"It's your father," Vesta said.

"Vesta, you open the door this minute!"

Sean did the honors. "May we help you?"

Richard looked past him. "I want to see my wife."

"It's after midnight. She doesn't want to see you."

He pointed over Sean's shoulder. "Don't be silly. She's right there."

Vesta didn't want to create a scene or wake the neighbors. "Let him in, Sean."

Richard entered like a storm cloud. He wasn't wearing a tie but wore a coat over trousers that had his nightshirt tucked into the waistband. His hair was tousled instead of smooth. His appearance spoke volumes. And gave her courage.

"What do you want, Richard?" she asked.

"You know very well what I want." He pointed outside. "Baines has the car waiting."

She sat upon the sofa. Her bed. "I wish to stay here."

"Don't be ridiculous. You belong at home. With me."

"To do what?"

His head pulled back. "To be my wife."

"To be your prisoner?"

"You exaggerate."

"Did you not lock me in my room and forbid Lola and Baines from letting me out?"

He scoffed. "Some good that did."

Sean intervened. "Her escape is my doing, Father. Do not blame them."

Annie added her two cents. "You should not have locked her in, Richard."

Suddenly his demeanor changed. His forehead ruffled and he pressed his fingers against it. "I regret that. But you were so agitated I had no recourse."

"Did you ever consider I might have been right? That perhaps I *should* have access to my inheritance? Especially when it could be used to help our son and his wife?"

He removed his hand from his forehead, and Vesta could see him trying to regain his usual control.

Quick! Before he fully finds himself! "I want to help them here at the workshop—continue to help them. If not monetarily, by working with them."

"But you have nothing to offer. No skills."

His words stabbed.

"That's rude and untrue, Father," Sean said. "Mother is an enormous help."

"She has a good eye for design," Annie added.

"You humor her."

"We do not." Annie sat beside Vesta and put an arm around her shoulders. "She has talent. She'd hoped to design fashion before you two were married. This is her chance to reignite that talent."

Richard cocked his head. "I remember no such interest."

For him not to remember who she was before they were wed, for him to discount those talents and dreams. . . "Do you remember me designing dresses for myself, Mother, Grandmother, and my friends? Designs that our dressmaker sewed up?"

He waved a hand at her, discounting the notion in its entirety. "A female matter. It was of no concern to me."

Vesta rose to face him. "No, I suppose it wasn't. For all you cared about was opening your store."

"That store has sustained us for twenty-six years. You were a part of that store."

Now it was her turn to scoff. "So you admit I had a hand in it? That I was there? Working *with* you to achieve your dream?"

He realized his error. "Don't goad me, Vesta."

"And don't insult me." She walked to the door and opened it. "Go home, Richard. Leave me here to attend to this female matter called fashion."

He hesitated and looked to Sean for support. But Sean said, "I think it's best you go, Father. She is fine here."

Vesta was surprised when he walked through the door. And not surprised when he turned and offered a final word. "This cannot be sustained, Vesta. You *will* come home."

"Good night, Richard."

When she closed the door, she held on to the doorknob for support and leaned her forehead against the wood. Her heart beat in her ears. Her chest felt heavy.

Sean came to her side. "Are you all right?"

"I'm not sure." She stood upright and drew in a fresh breath, let it out, then repeated the process twice more. With each breath she felt strength return. And something more than that. . .

Gumption.

"I am fine," she told them. "And actually, though I abhor confrontation, I am glad he came so I can stop worrying about his coming."

"There is truth to that," Annie said. "For I expected him long before now."

"As did I," Sean said.

"Will you go back to him?" Annie asked.

No. Yes. Maybe. "Probably. But until then, I have a new world to explore." She glanced at the clock. "A world that expects me to function six hours from now. Off to bed now. All of us."

This time when Vesta lay down on the sofa, she did not let tears have their way.

Instead, she smiled.

CHAPTER TEN

Maude draped her shawl over her shoulders, ready to leave for work. Edna looked up from her morning cup of coffee. "It's not yet seven."

"I need to talk to Annie before the day begins."

Edna eyed her like the mother she'd come to be. "What's wrong?"

Maude shook her head, began to open the door, then closed it again. "I couldn't sleep last night."

"What are you worried about? We ended yesterday on a positive note. Vesta has been rescued from harm. We're opening a store, and it has a name: Unruffled."

"We still need money."

Edna set her cup down. "Oh."

"Oh? That's all you can say?"

"We've been praying, Maude. I assume God will take care of it."

Maude scoffed. "He's going to make it rain money?"

"He could."

"Your faith is different than mine." Which faith was the better faith was yet to be determined.

"Don't you believe He answers prayer?"

"I do. I trust Him because I know everything depends on Him, yet I also feel the need to do my part as if everything depends on me. Us."

"That's contradictory."

"No, it's not. We can't pray for success then sit in the kitchen all day, drinking coffee. We have to do the work *while* we wait to see how He answers our prayers."

"What if we do the wrong work?"

Maude pulled her shawl tighter. "I guess we have to trust Him to stop us."

Edna sipped her coffee. "I like the idea of that."

"I count on the idea of that," Maude said. "I have to go."

"To speak to Annie about. . . ?"

Maude didn't want to go into it unless she had to. "I'll let you know."

She crossed the street to Annie and Sean's apartment, saying "Good morning" to the street vendors who were setting up their wares. The smell of freshly baked bread almost caused a detour.

Almost.

As she climbed the stairs and stood outside their apartment door, she realized she didn't know how she wanted Annie to respond to what she was about to say. Her uncertainty added to her uncertainty.

Sean answered the door, adjusting his suspenders on his shoulders. "Maude? Are we late?"

"I'm early." She saw Annie sitting at the table, spreading butter on a roll. Vesta sat beside her. "How was your night, Vesta?"

"Very good," she said.

Maude hesitated. "I'm sorry, but I need to talk to Annie. Alone, if I may?"

"Of course," Vesta said. "I'll head up to the workshop."

"And I'm off to Butterick," Sean said, drinking the last of his coffee. He kissed Annie, grabbed his jacket, and was gone.

"Sorry," Maude said, as she entered the flat. "You and I could have gone to the workshop. . ."

"It all worked out," Annie said. "Have a roll."

Maude shook her head. Although she was not one to miss a meal, she knew it would not settle well upon her nervous stomach.

"My, my," Annie said. "What's wrong?"

"We need money."

"This is not a new concern."

"I know someone with money."

Annie's face brightened. "Who?"

You can still stop this. Don't say it, Maude. Don't say. . . "My mother."

"Your. . . ?" Annie's words trailed off, and Maude could tell she was remembering what Maude had told her about her mother. "You've talked to her recently?"

"Not for six years."

"*Will* she talk to you?"

"I don't know."

"Your father was a British diplomat, correct?"

"He was. That's why I think Mother has money. I assume she inherited a goodly amount when he died. I was only twelve then, and she and I moved to America and lived well enough with my maiden-aunt—who absolutely, positively deserved to be a spinster. Beastly woman."

"Beastly?"

"She only cared about herself, about 'me, myself, and I.' Since Mother and I held none of those titles. . ." She shrugged.

"Didn't her selfishness bring you two closer?"

"Could have. Should have. But didn't." Maude remembered too many hours spent alone—even if all three females were in the same room.

"If life was so miserable for both of you, why didn't you and your mother move to your own place? Could it be she *didn't* receive much of an inheritance?"

"I think she had money, I never had any indication otherwise. And I asked her to move out. Begged her. But she couldn't bring herself to deal with the decisions involved. It was easier to stay and suffer than take a risk and be happy. I don't think she wanted to be happy. There was a hint of sick satisfaction in her grief."

"That's harsh."

Maude shrugged again. "Truth often is."

"You were the one who cut ties with her, yes?"

Maude remembered the day when she decided to leave and never return. She hadn't been brave enough to tell her mother in person but had left a note. The memory shamed her.

"Maude? You cut the ties?"

"I did. Though my leaving should not have come as a surprise to her. While Auntie focused on her own needs, Mother focused on *hers*. She mourned my father's death long and hard, and became a bitter recluse, living among her relics of days gone by. She didn't want anyone around, much less me."

"I'm sure she did the best she could."

Had she? Maude ignored the inner question and continued her explanation. "She wasn't the only reason I left. You know that. I left because of what happened to me. And its consequences."

Annie lowered her voice. "The rape."

Maude nodded once. It had been hard for Maude to tell Annie and Edna about it, but she was glad someone knew the truth. "I left because of the rape, and the fact I can't bear children because of it. It was quite the occasion to lose my virginity and all hopes of motherhood in just a few frantic minutes."

"You joke but. . ."

"Joke or cry. Those are my options."

"I still don't understand why you had to leave home. Maybe your mother could have comforted you. Eventually. Wouldn't that have been better than to remove yourself from her life so completely?"

"She and Auntie would have blamed me."

"For being assaulted?"

Maude wasn't sure if this would have come to pass, but the very threat of it had added to her decision to leave.

Her throat was dry as she remembered what she'd said in the note she'd left behind. *Dear Mother, I am sorry for leaving but I have my reasons. Please do not worry about me. You'll be better off without me in your life.*

Maude cringed at the memory of the final line. It was a phrase begging to be argued, yet Maude hadn't given her mother the chance.

Coward.

"Have you had any contact? Does she know you're all right?"

"I send flowers on her birthday—though I wouldn't be surprised if Auntie commandeers them for herself. And last year, they were returned."

"So she's moved?"

"Apparently." The truth of it caused a bite of stabbing pain.

"Have you ever had second thoughts?"

Third, fourth, fifth. . . "Of course. Repeatedly. But. . ." She remembered standing on the street corner across from the luxurious flat she had shared with her mother and aunt. She'd stood there until dusk fell and the rooms lit up with light. She imagined her mother sitting in her favorite chair, needlepointing a dining room seat cushion that never seemed to get finished. When a police officer accosted Maude and asked if she needed anything, she had assured him she was fine and moved on.

Maude felt defensiveness rise in her breast. "I really had no choice. The real reason I pulled away is that I couldn't live the life she wanted me to live. I couldn't marry."

"You *could* marry, but you've chosen not to."

"I dare not fall in love with a man who expects to marry and have children. The pain of telling him what happened to me. . . I can't do that to a man. That's why I pulled away, moved away, stayed away. I couldn't bear to witness any more of Mother's pain."

"You do realize you caused her pain by leaving."

Maude sighed. "I tried to save her from the pain of *my* pain, and my unusual choice of a future. At the time there seemed no alternative."

Annie sat back and studied her, making Maude grip her shawl tighter. "But now you want to ask her for money."

"I don't *want* to, but I think I need to. What other choice do we have? Sean's parents have said no. Edna has no money to spare, and your parents are in England."

"And don't have a farthing to their names. Not that they would help me even if they could."

"It's down to me. It's said that pride goest before a fall. Goes where, I'm not sure. I know I've been prideful staying away and have suffered my own bout of bitterness. But I'll swallow that pride if it will help the business."

Annie reached across the table and touched her arm. "I appreciate your offer."

Finally it was settled, though being so made Maude's stomach *un*settled. "Would you come with me to see her?"

"Of course. But do you know where she lives?"

Maude nodded. "I think so. I saw her the day we went to Lane Bryant's. She was walking down the street and went into a brownstone."

Annie's forehead crinkled in thought. "The woman with the blue hat?"

"That was her."

"I noticed your interest, but why didn't you tell me she was your mother?"

Maude shrugged. "Seeing her confused me. That's definitely not where she lived last. And there is the chance she doesn't live there now. Perhaps she was only visiting a friend."

"When would you like to go?"

"Today. I'll sleep better if I know we have funding." *And it's done with.*

❧

Maude looked up at the brownstone. It was a far cry from the houses where she and her parents lived when her father had been a diplomat. The steps were chipped and stained with someone's wash water—or worse. The front door was in need of painting. She remembered hearing her father ordering the butler to see to it that scuffs on the baseboard were painted over. *He'd have a conniption if this door had been his door.*

Suddenly, she realized the full magnitude of her mother living here, especially when she was a woman who did not suffer change easily. Something had happened to alter her status.

Maybe she didn't have money anymore.

Annie must have sensed a change in Maude's thinking, for she took hold of her arm, holding her steady on the sidewalk.

"We've come this far," Annie said.

Indeed they had. *God, be with us.*

They went into the vestibule but had no idea where to go beyond that. The stairs stood before them, with two doors on either side. They had no recourse but to knock on one and make inquiries.

Maude's heart beat doubly as she knocked. An elderly man answered, gave them both a good once-over, smiled, then said, "Well, hello ladies."

"Sorry to disturb," Maude said. "But I'm looking for my mother, Mrs. Nascato?"

He shook his head. "No Nascato here."

Maude's hope drained. "Amelia Nascato? Are you sure?"

His eyes brightened. "Amelia? Why didn't you say so? 2B right above me."

"Thank you."

But as he began to close the door, he said, "It's not that Nas-name though. It's Brunner."

She looked back at him. "Brunner?"

"They're newlyweds," the man said.

"Married? Mother has remarried?"

"If she's the one you're looking for. A nice couple, they is."

Annie took her arm. "Thank you for your help."

He tipped an imaginary hat. "Good day to ya."

Somehow Maude made it up the stairs. Her mother was married? In Maude's absence she had left her grief behind, fallen in love, and started a new life? Maude didn't know whether to be upset *at* her or happy *for* her. And how would she react to seeing Maude? She'd clearly moved on. Would she resent Maude's sudden return? Her intrusion?

Annie knocked on the door to 2B.

Maude's mother opened the door, took one look at her daughter, and pulled her into a tight embrace. "Maudey! My dear girl!"

Maude let herself relax in the affection, resting her head against her mother's, basking in the familiar scent of honeysuckle. Tears threatened, so when her mother pulled back, she had to quickly swipe at her eyes to stop their descent.

"Oh, dear girl. Don't cry. Come in." She looked to Annie. "And you are?"

"Annie Culver."

"My best friend," Maude added.

They went inside the apartment. It was smaller than Edna and Maude's, with the parlor, eating table, ice box, and stove seen in a single glance. It had an odd look to it, being furnished with too many exquisite pieces of furniture that had graced their diplomat-mansion combined with far simpler pieces. A familiar painting of the Seine held the place of honor above a fireplace, its intricate gilt frame standing out like a woman dressed for a ball visiting a fish market.

"You remember that painting, don't you, Maudey? Do you remember when we bought it from the artist, who painted it right there, on the river-bank in Paris?"

She did remember the moment vaguely, but remembered with more clarity the glistening strawberry tart Father had bought for her from a *patisserie* nearby. She could have eaten a dozen.

A man stepped out of the bedroom and smiled. "Did I hear correctly? This is your Maude?"

Her mother went to him, linking her arm through his. "Hans, this is my daughter, Maude. Maude, this is my husband, Hans Brunner."

They greeted each other, and Maude was immediately taken with his kind eyes and ready smile. He had tawny hair, streaked with gray. He looked like someone who would see the bright side of life rather than the dark.

"Do sit," he said. "Let me get some coffee. It's still hot."

"No," Maude said. "That won't be necessary."

"Thank you," Annie added.

"Don't you need to be getting to work?" Maude's mother asked her husband.

"I can be late. This is too important to miss." He flicked the tip of his wife's nose and leaned close. "I'm so happy for you, *liebchen*. Your prayers have been answered."

Maude felt convicted. *She* had never prayed to be reconciled with her mother. To know that her mother had prayed to find her? To be shown as a coward *and* selfish?

"Well then," Mother said.

Maude and Annie sat on the one settee, while Mother sat in a familiar chair, the chair she always used when she worked on her needlework. Hans stood behind his wife.

Maude spotted a satchel with yarn peeking out. "Are you still working on your seat covers?"

Mother laughed—in itself a jarring experience because Maude had heard laughter far too seldom. "I finally finished two," she said, pointing to the kitchen table. "We have no need for more. I'm working on a pillow now."

Maude remembered their vast dining room with eighteen chairs and dinner parties manned by footmen in full livery serving bejeweled guests—many who spoke in languages unknown. Maude would often be permitted to make an entrance before dinner, and the guests would ooh and ahh over how pretty she was and how her mother and father must be so proud. Maude always thought it odd to receive gushing praise for an attribute she'd had no control over and liked it better when she was given the chance to sing "Barbara Allen"—all eight verses. Women would cry and grown men would clear their throats and huff about needing a drink. Being able to make people *feel* was something to be proud of.

"Now then," Annie said.

With Maude's memories properly visited, it was time to get down to business.

Mother must have felt it too, for she asked. "I am pleased you are here, Maudey, but why now? Tell us what's been going on in your life to bring you back to me on this happy day."

To ask for money without preamble seemed wrong. Her mother's graciousness deserved something more. "I'm very sorry I left home like I did."

For the first time, her mother's face grew serious. "I didn't understand. I still don't."

"I. . ." Maude looked to Annie, who encouraged her with a nod. "My leaving had little to do with you."

Mother put a hand to her chest and let out a breath. "I'm glad to hear that. I worried that I had caused it. I know how it was to live with Auntie. And I too was being difficult and wasn't the mother I should have been, but—"

"I was raped."

Her unexpected words had the expected effect. Shock and silence. And then. . .

"You were what?" Mother asked. She put her hand to her right shoulder, and Hans took it, offering comfort.

Maude felt stronger for saying the words. The barrier had been broken. She could finish the story. She would finish it.

"It was six years ago. I'd taken a walk after dark." She didn't mention that it was due to an argument between them. "A man jumped out of an alley, pulled me in, and—and assaulted me."

Her mother's forehead furrowed. "I knew nothing of it. Why didn't I know anything about it?"

"I was ashamed."

Hans interjected. "You are not the one to be ashamed. Did they catch the man?"

She shrugged. "I never reported it. I went home and—and I just wanted to forget it ever happened."

Mother rose from her chair and drew Maude to standing so she could give her a proper hug. "I'm so, so sorry that happened to you. And appalled that I didn't know. Didn't even suspect."

Maude wanted to wallow in her comfort but needed to finish the story. "There's more," she said.

Her mother returned to her chair and found her husband's hand once again.

Maude hesitated saying the rest with a man present—a man she did not know—but found she could not stop with anything less than a full confession. "I began to have. . .female problems. I went to Dr. Coskins."

"He never said anything to me."

"I asked him not to."

Hans patted her shoulder. "Let her finish, liebchen."

Maude took solace in fingering the carving on the arm of the settee. "The doctor said I was damaged and that I would never have children." She risked a glance to her mother's face and found it, as she expected, pulled and distraught with sorrow.

And then anger. "He ruined your life! I wish they'd caught him and made him suffer for—"

"He didn't ruin my life, Mother. But he did change it. For because I cannot have children, I have chosen not to marry. It wouldn't be fair to let a man fall in love with me, only to have him discover his dreams of a family are impossible."

Mother took a breath then let it out slowly.

Maude needed to finish it. "I left because I knew you wanted me to marry. My entire growing up was focused on becoming a wife. You'd already lost Father. I didn't want to confront you with the loss of your dreams for me, and for grandchildren. I know it was the cowardly thing to do, but. . ." She shrugged. "At the time, it seemed the only thing I *could* do."

Her mother relinquished her husband's hand and clasped her own in her lap. "My dear girl. I don't blame you. Though I *could* have comforted you." But then she hesitated. "At least I hope I could have comforted you. I was different then."

Maude was moved by her honesty. "We both were." This time it was Maude who went to her mother, drawing her to her feet and into her arms. Together they rocked gently. Each to-and-fro seemed to remove a year that had separated them, until they were finally together, in the moment, in each other's company.

Annie stood, allowing mother and daughter to sit side-by-side on the settee.

"I'm so glad you came today. I'm so glad you—" Her mother stopped the sentence. "Did you come with the purpose of finally telling me all this? Somehow I think you didn't."

"There is more," Maude said. "But I. . ." She looked to Annie. Somehow, talking about money was like discussing sickness at a celebration.

Annie shook her head. Maude agreed. There would be no talk of money. It was obvious her mother had lost what wealth she had. There would be none to spare for their risky venture.

But Maude *could* tell her happy news. "Annie and I are starting our own fashion company. Opening a shop."

"How marvelous," Mother said. "Do you sew the dresses? You always loved to sew."

"We do. And we have hired others to help. Annie is a talented designer."

"What's the name of your shop? Where is it, for I will surely go there."

"The name is Unruffled."

Her mother cocked her head. "How unusual."

"It's fashion that is comfortable, functional, and accessible for the working woman."

Hans nodded. "Unruffled. . .I like the connotation. Well done."

"Thank you," Annie said. "You asked about the location. We aren't that far in the planning yet, though that is the next step. We do need to find a storefront to rent. One that rents at a reasonable cost."

Hans raised a finger. "I may be able to help you. I am a bookkeeper and work in a building where there is a real estate office. The man who works there is a friend, a good man named Antonio Ricci. Surely he can show you some spaces to rent."

He wrote down the address and the man's name. *Ricci.* A fellow Italian.

It was time to leave. Maude gave her mother a parting embrace and a promise. "I will not disappear again."

"No, you will not. God has brought us back together and neither of us will do anything to disgrace that blessing. You will come to dinner next Sunday?"

It was too soon. "Another time." Someday.

⬬

Once on the street Annie linked her arm with Maude's. "Are you all right?"

Maude drew in a breath, let it out, then repeated the process. "I believe I am just fine—which surprises me."

"Your mother is much changed?"

"Very much."

"Her husband seems quite amiable."

"Which makes me happy for her."

Annie's grip tightened. "Are you glad for telling her. . .everything?"

Maude let a pause fall between them, wanting to answer with full honesty. "*Glad* implies levity. Let's say I am relieved." She patted Annie's hand. "And yet I believe I am ten pounds lighter for the telling."

Annie chuckled. "Only ten pounds?"

"Make it twenty." Maude noticed they were near Lane Bryant's. "Let's stop in and see Lena. It will be a good transition between the injurious past and the vexatious present."

"And the glorious future."

"That's my Annie. Always the optimist."

Hardly that. Unfortunately.

Lena welcomed them with open arms. "My fellow designers! How nice to see you. Come and tell me how you are. How did your fashion event go?"

As before, they were led to the back of the store. Though offered tea, they declined.

"Tell me everything," Lena said once they were settled. She sat forward in anticipation.

Annie wasn't sure how much to share.

At her reluctance, Lena sat back. "Oh."

Annie had to clarify. "Actually, the event went smoothly, and all in all, the ladies in attendance enjoyed it."

"But. . . ?"

"But they did not place any orders. They appreciated the designs but thought them too simple for their own use."

Maude interjected. "Those froufrou ladies were not—are not—our customer."

Lena nodded, knowingly. "As I found my customer, so you must find yours. And she is. . .?"

"A working woman, a mother, the women you see everywhere," Maude said.

"We provide fashion for the unruffled, unveiled, unstoppable woman."

Lena clapped. "Bravo! What an inspiring slogan."

"We are opening a shop called Unruffled. With sized, ready-to-wear clothing."

Lena spread her arms. "A shop like this one."

"A much smaller shop," Annie said.

"At first, perhaps," Lena said. "But it will grow. I know it."

"From your lips to God's ears," Annie said.

Lena nodded. "Actually, I have to thank you."

"For what?"

"One of the ladies at your soiree came in the store needing maternity wear. A Mrs. Campbell?"

Annie remembered the woman. "I never knew her name, but did she have copper-colored hair?"

"That's her. She spent a lot of money here with the promise of sending her friends." Lena held up a finger to make a point. "Word of mouth is priceless. The key is to get people talking—in a positive way."

"We will do our best," Annie said. "Once we have something for them to talk about."

"First, we need to find a storefront," Maude said.

Actually, first we need the money to pay for a storefront. Annie thought about asking Lena the name of her banker but decided against it. She was wary of banks, mostly because she'd never been in one nor had need of their services.

She remembered an old saying: *Neither a borrower nor a lender be.* She didn't want to borrow money from a bank who would lend it. She wanted an investor.

Suddenly a thought came to mind, but it was so audacious, so pushy, so. . .

"Annie?" Lena asked. "You look like a thunderbolt struck you, and you're not sure about the experience."

You won't know until you ask.

Before she could talk herself out of it, she voiced the question. "We need an investor."

"I thought the Sampsons were your patrons."

"They were. Until we deviated from her 'Eleanor's Couture' vision."

"Eleanor's Couture?"

"She wanted our clothes to be suitable for her society friends."

"Who already have favorite dressmakers and designers."

"So we found out."

Lena sat forward again. "It sounds as though Mrs. Sampson became a little too. . ."

"Vain," Maude said. "Sorry, but that's the truth of it."

Annie had a disturbing thought. "So are we vain for wanting to create *our* own line of clothes? Are we no better than Mrs. Sampson in that regard?"

Lena put a hand on her knee. "We are artists of the cloth. As with any artist, we create because we must but also with hope of affirmation."

"And profit," Maude added.

Lena smiled. "A necessity. There is no sin in profit if it is the result of hard work."

"Hard work is not an issue," Annie said.

Lena sat back again. "Money is."

She was glad Lena had been the one to bring it up. "Money is. Would you. . .perhaps. . .would you be willing. . . ?"

"Willing yes," Lena said. "But not able, I'm afraid. We have recently expanded to this store and must put all our profit back into the business."

Annie felt herself redden. "I'm sorry to bring it up, I never should have said anything."

"It was *not* the reason we stopped by to see you," Maude added.

"Not at all," Annie said.

Lena waved their concerns away. "I do not question your motives and am happy with the visit. Please come again." She stood. "Let me know when Unruffled opens. I would love to see it."

They exited the store before Annie felt the full weight of what she had done. "I should never have asked her for money! I cannot believe I did that!"

"She did not take offense."

"Because she is a gracious woman. But I overstepped our acquaintance."

When Maude didn't answer, Annie stopped on the sidewalk and faced her. "I did, didn't I?"

"She was very kind."

"She was, but—" Annie pressed a hand to her forehead. "What are we going to do?"

Maude put her arm around Annie's shoulder. "I'll say something Sean or Edna would say."

"We don't know, but God does?"

Maude laughed. "Exactly."

"I wish He'd show us."

"Exactly."

CHAPTER ELEVEN

The patterns were created. Fabric was cut. Being Saturday, even Sean was there to help, cutting out two dresses with great concentration. Ginny and Gert pedaled so fast that the sounds of the sewing machines whirring and the shuttlecock clicking mixed with the sound of the busy street below, often making conversation difficult.

Annie oversaw the work, in awe of it. She was also in awe of the optimistic attitude of her friends and colleagues. After meeting with Maude's mother and Lena, Annie had once again been forced to gather them close and tell them the bad news about their continual lack of funds—which they took with amazing grace.

And faith.

"God will provide."

"He'll send us the money we need."

"Keep praying."

Even Gert had chimed in. "My mama always said when things look the bleakest, that's when God sends a ray of sunshine—if we believe He will."

Did Annie believe He would? Such hopes sounded naive and simplistic.

The facts were this: they had enough money left from the two hundred dollars the Sampsons had given them to buy supplies to sew the dresses. But that left a meager bit to pay the workers. Gert and Ginny must be paid first. But the rest of them needed a salary too. They all had to pay rent and buy food—Sean and Annie even more so with Vesta living with them.

Just this morning, Sean had asked Annie where their favorite scones were—the ones they liked to buy from the bakery down the street. Annie had told him they would have to forgo the special scones for a while. They needed to economize.

"But surely a scone or two will not break us," he'd said.

"Not today, but we have to look ahead. What if we don't get an investor before the money runs out? Maybe your father was right. Perhaps God is telling us no."

Sean and Vesta had responded with all the right words, and they'd prayed together, asking for God's help and favor.

For a few hours, Annie anticipated a miracle. Every time the door of the workshop opened she looked up, hoping someone with deep pockets was coming to their rescue.

But as one hour moved into the next—with no savior coming to their aid—Annie had to fight back despair. The fact that the rest of them seemed cheery and worked as if worry were a stranger, shamed her. Why couldn't she share their faith?

The disparity between their confidence that everything would work out fine and Annie's doubt that it would, became too much for her. So much so, that she sent everyone home an hour early. She put on a smile and told them how proud she was of the work they had accomplished, giving them encouragement she didn't feel.

Edna invited the core group to dinner that night, and everyone went to help her with the preparations. Everyone but Annie.

She needed solitude, if only for an hour. Once everyone had left, worry fell upon her shoulders with such weight that she gave way upon the window seat, unsure for a fleeting moment whether it would be strong enough to hold her.

She fell on her side, cradling her head in her arms, letting the sobs come. "Help us, Lord. Please, help us."

Although her tears did not last long, she did not sit up but turned on her back, using an arm as her pillow. Despite her mood, she enjoyed the mesmerizing ripple of the lace curtains as the autumn breeze washed over her. She took a calming breath, in and out, in and out. Her heartbeat slowed. The baby fluttered inside her. She smiled. How could she not smile at the reminder that she was carrying a new life?

"Thank You, God. Forgive my worry. You tell us to 'fear not,' and I have trouble with that. Please give me the faith I need to believe Your promises."

As peace flowed over her, she closed her eyes. She drifted. . .

Annie was drawn awake by distinct voices in front of the building, on the sidewalk below. One voice was familiar. . .

"Thank you for taking the time to talk to me," said the woman with an

English accent. "I'm looking for Annie Wood? Do you know her?"

"There ain't no Annie Wood here, but there is. . ."

No! It can't be! Annie bolted upright. She looked out the window and saw that it was true. "Miss Henrietta?" she called out.

The mistress from her past life as a maid stood below her. She held her hat in place as she looked up, then smiled and waved.

"I found you!" Miss Henrietta said.

Found me? "I'll come down," Annie said.

"No, I'll come up." She counted the stories. "Two up?"

"I'll meet you on the landing."

Annie smoothed her dress and hair, her thoughts swirling with questions. She went out to the hall.

Miss Henrietta turned to climb the last set of stairs and spotted her. "These stairs are testing my mettle." As she reached the top, she pressed a hand to her midsection. "I'm quite knackered."

Annie laughed at the term she hadn't heard since leaving England. "I've gotten used to the climb."

Then Annie was faced with a delicate dilemma. Should she bob a curtsy like she used to do when she was a housemaid? Or shake Henrietta's hand? Or—

Henrietta took her hands then kissed Annie's cheeks. "It is ever so good to see you, Annie Wood. You were not an easy woman to find."

"Why were you looking for me?"

Henrietta peered into the workshop. "You were in here? May I sit?"

"Of course. I've forgotten my manners. This is our workshop." She pulled out two chairs and set them near the window to catch the breeze.

Henrietta lingered at the cutting table and picked up a pair of shears. "So. . .it appears you are a full-fledged seamstress now?"

"I am."

"Your colleagues at Butterick said you had left to start a design business."

"So that's how you found me."

"I knew about Butterick after seeing you in Paris last April, at Paquin, yes?"

"Yes. At the House of Paquin."

"You were working for Butterick, adapting Paris couture designs for home sewers."

"You remembered."

"How could I forget? To see you there was quite the surprise."

"A pleasant one," Annie said. "To see you and your mother was awkward at first, for it was the first time we'd seen each other since I. . ."

"Ran away from service?"

"Yes," Annie said. "I did run away from your relative's house. There is no kinder way to say it. I apologized then, and I apologize now."

"You left a note, which Mother and I took to heart. Discovering that our lady's maids were taking credit for your sewing work was good reason for you to leave."

"But I still regret hurting both of you. Your family was always good to me, letting me come to work at Crompton Hall when I was only fourteen. It was hard work but a good living, and a much better situation than I had at home."

She nodded and fingered a ruby earring that Annie recognized. "By the by, Annie, your parents still live in the same place in Summerfield."

Annie felt guilty for having little thought of them. "Is my father still. . . ?" She could think of no delicate way to say it. "Is he still a drunk?"

"I've heard talk. They do not strive for anonymity."

"Though they should."

Henrietta shrugged. "Beyond the drunkenness of your father, your mother got in a spat of trouble for pinching something from the mercantile."

"It's about time she got caught."

Her eyebrows rose. "So she's stolen things before?"

"You don't wish to know."

"Well then." Henrietta took a deep breath, clearly enjoying the breeze. "I'm sorry there's not better news on that front."

Annie needed to change the subject. "Did you come over on the White Star line?"

"Cunard. Why do you ask?"

"My friends and I were supposed to sail back from Europe on the White Star's *Titanic*, but we missed the sailing."

Henrietta put a hand to her chest. "Oh my. So close. Thank God you did."

Annie nodded. "We do thank Him." She shook the memory of the close call away, replacing it with memories of Paris, seeing Henrietta when she was ordering a trousseau for her wedding. "When does your return trip sail?"

"It doesn't."

Annie was taken aback. "Did your husband come with you?"

"I have no husband."

"But you were betrothed."

"We were. But Hank didn't love me. Not really. And more importantly, I didn't love him."

"Well then," Annie said.

They both laughed at having shared the phrase.

"Actually, Annie, you are the reason I broke our engagement, and the reason I booked a one-way passage."

"How did I do that?"

"You inspired me."

"Again, I ask, how did I do that?"

Henrietta's face glowed with excitement. "When I saw you in Paris and witnessed how you'd risen from housemaid to pattern artist, I took a long look at my own life. I decided I deserved better than to marry a man I didn't love because he deemed me good enough."

Annie was stunned. "But you seemed so happy."

Henrietta shrugged. "I *was* happy to have lost some weight, but I was *un*happy because I lost it to please him." She put her hands on her hips. "I have gained back a little but not all of it. For I do enjoy eating."

"Clotted cream and scones is a favorite, if I remember."

"It is and always will be. Now I believe I have found a weight that suits me *and* allows me to eat most things. In moderation."

"That sounds very wise."

"It does, doesn't it? No more ordering dresses with extra-wide seam allowances to allow for my ups and downs. Or should I say my ins and outs." Her smile was testament to her good nature.

Annie remembered taking out the seams in many a dress, as Henrietta's weight had previously tended toward the up more than the down. "I think you look quite excellent," she said. "Just right."

"I feel just right. In all ways. For just as you would not settle for your lot, I will not settle for mine. I want my life to mean something. I want to be like you, Annie. I want to find my purpose."

Annie felt like an impostor, for her purpose seemed tenuous. "How long are you staying in New York?"

"Indefinitely."

"You're not simply visiting your relatives?"

She shook her head adamantly. "They do not even know I am here."

"Do your parents know?"

"I left a note. But they won't understand what I'm doing."

"I can't imagine they would. They had a plan for you, and—"

"I've turned that plan upside down."

Annie's memories of Lady Newley were of a kind and stately woman for whom family was all-important.

"They have my brother at home. Adam is the heir. *He* has married and his wife has produced an heir for yet another generation. He is the one who matters."

"That's not true." Or was it? English aristocracy had many rungs to its ladder that had to be climbed until the next generation took over the title. Those not in line were deemed less. . .vital.

"I truly believe my purpose can be better played out in New York City rather than living in some country estate in tiny Summerfield."

Summerfield, with its one mercantile, one bakery, one smithy, one sewing. . . "Does the Summerfield Sewing Workshop still exist?"

Henrietta beamed. "My cousin Pin still runs it."

"Miss Pin taught me how to sew!"

"I remember. Many a village woman has learned how to sew in that room." She paused. "Including me."

"You?"

"Again, Annie, you are my inspiration. I even bought a Butterick pattern in their London store and made it from scratch. It didn't fit well, but I learned much in the process." She swept a hand across the room. "As we speak of sewing, tell me what all this is about."

Annie told her everything, from working at Butterick, quitting to design with Mrs. Sampson, the change of heart and break-up with her patrons, and her current dreams of opening a shop. "Yet all this may amount to nothing."

"Why? Unruffled sounds delightful. If anyone can appreciate the word *unruffled* it is I."

"As I said, the Sampsons are no longer backing us."

Henrietta bit her lip, looked out the window, then back at Annie. "I have money. Father has given me a hefty allowance. I can fund your company."

Annie's first reaction was to say, *You can't do that*. But then she remembered all the prayers that had been offered up. Was this God's answer?

"You'd do that?"

"With much joy." She got out of her chair, knelt before Annie, and took her hands. "Please, Annie. Let me do this. Let me give back to you the hope you gave to me."

Annie realized how absurd it was, that the daughter of a viscount—a woman who used to be her mistress—now knelt before her as Annie had often knelt to help Henrietta with her shoes. That one act revealed how much Henrietta had changed.

To relieve the incongruity of the scene, Annie stood, drawing Henrietta to standing with her. "Thank you. I accept your offer. We accept it. Yet a thank you doesn't seem enough."

Henrietta cupped her chin in her hand and peered into Annie's eyes. "It is I who thank you." She let go. "But who are these 'we' people? Let me meet them."

❧

Upon Annie entering Edna's flat and announcing that her companion was Miss Henrietta Kidd, Edna, Vesta, and Maude took a step back and looked unsure of the proper protocol.

"Are we supposed to curtsy?" Edna whispered.

Henrietta laughed. "There will be none of that." She held out her hand for them to shake. "It's nice to meet you. . . ?"

"Edna. Edna Holmquist."

"And I'm Maude Nascato."

Henrietta looked at Sean, and he stepped forward to offer a greeting.

Henrietta smiled. "I remember seeing you in Paris. Congratulations for marrying such an amazing woman."

He winked at his wife. "She *is* a prize."

Having enough of the flattery, Annie moved toward the final person. She drew Vesta forward. "This is my mother-in-law Vesta Culver."

"Miss Kidd," Vesta said with a nod.

"Please. I am Miss Kidd in England. But this is America. Here I am Henrietta."

Annie shook her head. "I'm not sure I can do that. Without the 'miss.'"

"Please try. I don't wish to stand out; I wish to fit in."

Edna asked a question. "To be clear. . .are you the same woman Annie served at Crompton Hall?"

"She served my mother and me."

"Your mother is a viscountess?"

Henrietta corrected Edna's pronunciation. "It's pronounced vy-countess. And yes, you're right. Mother is a viscountess, which makes my father a viscount. Lord and Lady Newley."

"But your surname is Kidd," Sean said. "So shouldn't it be Lord and Lady Kidd?"

Henrietta hesitated, as if she'd never been asked the question. "No. Newley is the title."

"So Viscount Newley is your father."

She shook her head. "You never use the word 'viscount' in speech."

"Why not?" Vesta asked.

She laughed. "I don't honestly know. But my parents are called Lord and Lady Newley."

"Which makes you. . . ?"

"Their daughter. I have no title." She put a hand to her mouth. "I may be called 'honorable,' but I'm not sure."

"Why not?"

"Because *that* term is never said aloud either."

Annie stifled a laugh. Maude also looked on the verge.

"Do you have a brother?" Edna asked.

"Adam."

"What is his title?"

"The Honorable Adam Kidd."

"Shame on you," Maude said.

"For what?"

"You said 'honorable' aloud."

Henrietta chuckled. "I did. And the honorable in regard to Adam is stretching it. He struggles with the honorable part on occasion. He can be quite a card."

"But *he* gets to use your last name." Annie grinned. "Or is that also never spoken?"

Henrietta put her hands on her hips. "Now you're getting cheeky."

They all laughed. It was odd for Annie to see Miss Henrietta laugh—*Henrietta* laugh. To see her as a person and not a mistress tapped into some long-hidden insecurities from when Annie's status was that of a lower servant, not a businesswoman.

Speaking of business. . .

"Let's sit," Annie said. "Henrietta has something to talk to us about."

As they moved into the parlor, Edna rushed to fluff a Niagara Falls pillow and pick up a stack of books that was topsy-turvy on the end table.

"We meant no disrespect with all our teasing," Maude said, as Henrietta sat on the sofa.

"I know you didn't. Actually, I rather enjoy a good go of it, back and forth."

"It's all done in fun," Sean added.

"I've been on my own for nearly two weeks, traveling here from Summerfield, so I appreciate the camaraderie."

"If I may be bold, why did you come here?" Vesta asked. "And how did you find our Annie?"

Henrietta told her story of a chance meeting in Paris, second thoughts about a wedding, and finding courage enough to travel across the ocean to start anew. "Annie inspired all of it. That's why I am here. To be a part of whatever Annie is undertaking in her amazing life."

"I told her about Unruffled."

"What an exciting enterprise that is." Henrietta looked at each face. "You are all a part of it?"

"One and all," Maude said.

"For better or worse," Edna added.

At the wedding vow terminology Annie smiled. "It does seem a bit like a marriage."

"And as such, we have high hopes," Sean said.

"Perhaps too high," Edna said.

"No!" Henrietta said with a sudden ferocity. "I will not allow you to have doubts. Annie has told me what you need, and I am here to provide it."

Sean looked at Annie, his face asking questions. "Meaning?"

"Money," Annie said. "Henrietta has offered to fund our business."

Mouths dropped open, making the lot of them look like fish in a bowl.

Henrietta laughed. "Close your mouths, ladies and gentleman. Money is the least I can provide for dear Annie, the woman who changed my life in so many ways."

The silence was ended by cheers and happy chatter. Everyone came to thank Henrietta with handshakes and hugs. Annie stepped back, enjoying the scene. Marveling at it.

Sean stepped beside her. "It's hard to believe."

"No, it's not," she said with a grin. "Don't you know that God always provides?"

In abundance.

⬧

Annie helped Vesta tuck a sheet and blanket on the sofa. Having her mother-in-law stay with them the past three days had been a challenge, not due to Vesta herself, but due to having any third person in the small space.

Vesta set a pillow into place. "I like Henrietta. She's not at all what I would expect from someone of her status."

"Yes indeed," Sean said, folding up the day's newspaper to stack near the stove. "She is quite honorable."

"Very funny," Annie said.

"I feel badly you had no sofa to offer her since I am here. Though even with her humble nature, I'm not sure her sleeping on a mere sofa would be proper."

"Don't worry about any of that," Annie said. "She told me she already has a room at the Hotel Astor."

Sean laughed. "Fancy. Maybe we should go stay with her."

Vesta ignored him. "Her offer of funding should ease the situation greatly. I still wish I could have helped financially, but it was not to be."

Annie adjusted the opened window to allow a breeze suitable for sleeping. "Do you realize when you spoke with Richard about it, Henrietta was already on her way to New York?"

Vesta held a second pillow to her chest. "God was sending an answer to our prayers in an extraordinary, unexpected way. Meaning my money was *not* the answer." Her face brightened. "God knew Richard would say no."

"And Maude's mother would have no money to offer," Annie said.

"*And* He knew the Sampsons would pull their money to start off this mess," Sean added.

The notion that God had a plan set in place long before they even knew they had a problem, overwhelmed her. "He knew," Annie whispered.

"He knew all about *that* detail," Sean said, "which means He knows what we need in the future too."

"How marvelous," Vesta said, getting under the covers. "We should all be able to sleep well knowing the Almighty has it covered."

She was right. That night, for the first time in a long time, Annie enjoyed the sleep of the faithful.

CHAPTER TWELVE

Henrietta stood in front of the mirror in her suite at the Hotel Astor. A maid—provided by the hotel—buttoned her dress in the back. It was a simpler dress than she had worn the day before, for today she was going to work.

Imagine that.

She studied the end results of the maid's attempt to fix her hair. The girl had misshaped the hair rat, with the result that the upsweep tipped a bit on the left side. Once again she regretted not bringing a maid from home on the trip, yet to do so would have shown her hand too soon. Her family knew nothing of her scheme to board the ship in Southampton. They knew now, only because of the note she had left. As far as the money she'd offered to fund Unruffled? There was enough of it, for she had secretly stashed away her allowance for months. When that ran out? She'd worry about that later.

On the ship over, she'd accepted the offer of sharing the maid of a new shipboard friend, for to change clothes multiple times a day for the First Class events was undoable on her own. Yet the fact she had found someone to help each time gave her some semblance of satisfaction. God provided. Again and again.

"There now, miss," the maid said with a pat to Henrietta's buttoned back. "Would you like me to get your hat?"

Anything to cover my hair. "The smaller one I think. The workshop is not in a posh neighborhood. I don't wish to stand out."

The maid retrieved a straw hat with a small brim. And no ostrich feather. It was placed, just so, and secured by a hatpin.

"Your gloves, miss."

There was a knock on the door. The maid answered it.

"Your car is ready, Miss Kidd," said a bellhop.

She was off and away to her first day of work.

❦

Henrietta was early. No one was at the workshop. The door was locked.

"Overeager, are we?" she said to herself. Only then did she check the time on her watch pin. It was ten minutes before seven.

She weighed her alternatives. She could sit on the stairs and wait—yet the dustiness of the top step was uninviting. As was the thought of not being able to get up gracefully once she'd sat down.

Alternative two: since she didn't know what time people would arrive, the idea of standing in the hall to wait made her feet hurt just thinking about it.

The only recourse was to go to Annie and Sean's flat. Annie *used* to be an early riser. When she was a maid.

Henrietta sighed. She would have to risk it.

She went down one flight and softly rapped on their door. To her surprise Vesta answered. "Why. . .good morning."

"Good morning to you, Vesta. I seem to have misgauged the hour. I'm quite early."

"Come in. We are just making coffee."

Henrietta stepped inside. The flat was smaller than Edna's. There appeared to only be one bedroom instead of two. A stack of blankets and a pillow were on the end of the sofa. Was Vesta sleeping there?

Vesta must have noticed the direction of her gaze. "I am a houseguest for a time."

"I guess I knew that from yesterday's gathering at Edna's. But. . ." *I thought you had your own bedroom.* Suddenly, she got an idea. "Vesta, I have a lovely room at the Astor. Would you like to come stay with me?"

Annie stepped out of the bedroom, with Sean right behind her. "The Astor. How glamorous."

Vesta cocked her head, clearly thinking about it. Finally, she said, "Thank you for the offer, but I am glad to be here with Sean and Annie. I'm close to the workshop, and. . ."

Annie finished the sentence for her. "Are you worried what Richard might think if you move there?"

Vesta nodded. "Our situation is fragile. To look as if I am enjoying my independence to such a lavish degree seems wrong." She looked to Henrietta. "But I greatly appreciate the kind offer."

Henrietta was glad she'd made it but was a bit disappointed Vesta had said no. It would have been nice to have the company. Although New York City was full of people—too many people compared to what she was used to in tiny Summerfield—Henrietta felt quite alone.

"Do sit down," Sean said, pouring four cups of coffee. "We've fresh morning rolls and blackberry preserves."

Don't mind if I do.

❧

Work.

As Henrietta took lessons from Gert, Edna, and Ginny about sewing construction, the knowledge threatened to overwhelm her. Although she possessed basic sewing skills, the act of sewing for others—with the intent of selling to others—created an added pressure to make it perfect.

The needle on her machine broke, startling her. "Drat! That's the second one today." She turned to Gert. "What am I doing wrong?"

Gert got up from her machine, and Henrietta vacated her seat so the girl could have full access. Gert pulled out the upper half of the needle and examined it. "You're putting it in backward. Flat side goes to the back."

"Uh. Now I remember you said that. Sorry. I'll pay for the wasted needles."

Gert smiled up at her. "Don't be so hard on yourself. You're doing fine, miss."

Henrietta took a deep breath, appreciating the encouragement, but still felt overwhelmed.

Edna must have been watching because she appeared in the doorway. "You've done well for your first day."

"I have much to learn."

"You show wisdom by admitting that."

Henrietta chuckled. "I have no trouble admitting what I lack, for the list is long."

"Don't be so hard on yourself."

"That's what Gert said."

"Twice heard makes it gospel," Edna said. "But take heart. It's near quitting time." She led Henrietta out of the sewing room and added. "My son is coming for dinner, so I've invited Sean, Annie, and Vesta to join us. And now you."

"You are too kind."

"We have to eat, don't we? We might as well do it together for the good company of it." Then she seemed to have another thought. "Unless you'd rather eat at the Astor. I'm sure their meals are far more tasty than mine."

"Rubbish," Henrietta said. "I do not need fine ambiance and finicky presentation. The food is secondary to the company."

"Company you shall have. Why don't you help straighten things up? I'm leaving now to get the food started."

Edna left, and Henrietta helped by picking up scraps, sorting them into toss-away and keep piles. She took up a broom and got the strays hiding under the cutting table.

Annie held the dustpan for her. "I can honestly say I never once expected to see you with a broom in hand."

"Nor did I." She would add it to her résumé of "firsts."

❧

"And this is my son, Steven. Steven, Miss Henrietta Kidd."

He smiled but quickly looked away as though he was shy. "Very nice to meet you, Miss Kidd."

"Henrietta. Please," she said. "And it's nice to meet you. . ." she was going to say, Mr. Holmquist but added, "Steven." She liked the American way of using first names more quickly than they did in England.

He looked Scandinavian—as befit his surname—with dark blond hair that was neatly parted on the left side. He was clean shaven, which was a style Henrietta preferred on younger men. Leave the mustaches and beards to those of middle age.

"Steven used to teach English in Pittsburgh," Edna said as she linked her arm through his. "But he has recently moved here and has taken a new position teaching upper grades. I am proud of him and am glad to have him close enough to visit me often."

"I enjoy reading," Henrietta said. "What is your favorite novel to share with your students?"

"*Robinson Crusoe,*" he said without reservation. "Young people enjoy survival stories."

"As do adults. I was fascinated with the situation of a lone man having to fend for himself, finding God in nature and by reading his only book, a Bible."

This new smile changed Steven's countenance from reserved to alive, as though a light had been switched on inside. "Well said."

"Well then," Vesta said.

Henrietta felt herself blush. In truth she had forgotten others were present.

❧

"You are staying at the Hotel Astor?" Steven asked.

Suddenly Henrietta felt foolish. What had seemed natural to her upbringing now seemed ostentatious to the point of embarrassment. The feeling was so disconcerting that she found herself saying, "I would like to get a small flat near here. Near all of you."

"That would be quite a change," Annie said. "Are you sure?"

No, she wasn't. But then she realized an important point in favor of the move. She had funds, and yet. . .

"I'm sure it would be far less expensive," Edna said, as if reading her mind.

Sean chuckled. "Far less. Though I'm sure that's not an issue."

Could be. Eventually will be.

"And you wouldn't need to hire a car to get you here and back," Maude said. "Though I *could* help you find the right streetcar from the hotel."

Streetcar. Traveling alone in public made her remember the train ride from Summerfield to Southampton and then the voyage on the ship. She was proud of how she had accomplished these two adventures on her own, but if there was a way to simplify her life and bring her closer to her new friends, she was willing to do it.

"How do I go about finding a flat to let?" She looked to Steven, but he offered no ideas. In fact, since their camaraderie over *Robinson Crusoe* he had grown quiet, saying little during the dinner of roast beef and potatoes. He answered his mother's questions but avoided Henrietta's gaze. Had she said something to offend him?

"I believe I saw a FOR RENT sign in the next block south," Maude said. She stood from the table. "Would you like to see it?"

"Now?" Edna said. "It's evening."

"Landlords are eager to fill their buildings. They don't care what time of day their rent is assured. And often they have a building super whose job it is to help with such things."

"Steven, go with them," Edna said.

"I'm sorry, Mother, but I can't. I have essays to grade."

"I'll go," Sean said.

"As will I," Annie said.

"I'll help with dishes," Vesta said.

Everyone thanked Edna for the fine meal and were shooed away on their mission to find Henrietta a place to live.

Outside the building, Steven donned his hat and looked at her for the first time since dinner. "It was fine meeting you, Henrietta. Best of luck finding an apartment."

He walked in the opposite direction as the group.

"Steven recently rented a place. Why didn't he offer to help?" Annie asked.

"I don't think he likes me," Henrietta said.

"You had the novel in common," Sean said.

"But only that. Is he. . .is he usually so silent?"

"I have met him more than the rest of you," Maude said. "When he comes to visit his mother, he keeps conversation going well enough. I'm not sure what was bothering him this evening."

Me. I am the new fish in the pot. Henrietta remembered how all but Steven had faded from her interest. Apparently he had felt none of it.

◈

The flat was the same size as Sean and Annie's, but it faced the alley in back—an alley that was dark due to another building being built so close. As they stood in the parlor area they could look into the bedroom of another flat in that building. A woman was changing her baby's diaper on a bed. She looked up and waved.

How disconcerting.

"We could sew you some curtains beyond these sheer ones," Annie said.

Back in the parlor, the building superintendent said, "There's the fireplace for heating and cooking." He pulled a metal arm that swung out and then back over a fire. A black pot hung from it. There was no sink. No ice box. No kitchen area at all but for a wall shelf and a small square table set with two chairs.

"Shades of the last century," Maude said with a grimace. "Though you're not going to be doing much fancy cooking, are you?"

"I don't know how to cook at all."

"As I said."

"It's good enough to make a stew or soup," Annie said. "And you can eat meals with us."

"Or us," Maude said.

"So, miss. You interested? I got others looking."

"Excuse us, please?"

With a shrug, the man stepped into the hall.

"Is this a good place?" she asked her friends.

"Good, no," Maude said. "Adequate, maybe."

"It's not posh like you're used to," Annie said. "But we've seen no other options close by."

The "posh" comment was an understatement. There were only two rooms and six pieces of furniture in the entire place: a bed, a dresser, a short sofa with a hole in the seat, a table and two chairs. There were gas wall sconces, meaning there was no electricity. The bathtub and loo were shared—down the hall. She was used to sharing such facilities—with family. Not strangers.

"We could help make it nice," Sean said.

"The location is good. It's fairly clean," Annie said.

"And the rent is reasonable," Sean said. "Four dollars a week."

"I'm glad you negotiated it down," Annie said. "It is not worth the six dollars the super asked for."

When Henrietta had heard the price—be it six or four dollars—she'd made a decision to take the place. She was currently paying more than that amount each *night* at the Astor. Plus paying a driver and paying exorbitantly for meals. Despite what she'd implied to Annie, her funds were not limitless. This was the prudent thing to do.

She opened the door to find the superintendent. "I'll have a go of it."

❦

Henrietta adjusted the four pillows that were on her bed at the Hotel Astor. Then she smoothed the covers over herself and sank into the soft luxury.

As of tomorrow there would be no more luxury. The bed in her flat was far smaller than this one. And the linens provided. . .they would be other people's linens.

She shuddered at the thought. She was used to fresh linens every Monday, washed and ironed, smelling of starch. Who knew what the sheets at her flat would smell like. Or when they'd last been washed.

In spite of her reservations, she marveled at one large fact: it would be *her* flat. She'd never lived alone. She found the thought heady and frightening.

So until then. . .she wallowed in comfort one last time.

CHAPTER THIRTEEN

Henrietta hired two men from the hotel to bring her luggage to her new flat. They set her trunks in the bedroom, which made getting from the doorway to the bed a bit like walking through a maze.

"You want us to push them up against the wall, miss?"

She shook her head. "I need space behind to open them properly. Thank you."

They stood before her, caps in hand. "Will there be anything else, miss?"

She reached into her reticule and pulled out two quarters. "No. Thank you for your help."

She wasn't sure about the amount of the gratuity but they seemed pleased enough.

She let them out and closed the door. That simple sound—heard thousands of times—sounded different this time. For today it represented a distinct demarcation between the rest of the world and a world that was hers. A world she had chosen and was paying for with her own hard-saved money. She leaned against the door and peered at her flat. She could see the bulk of it in a single glance: fireplace, table and chairs, the sofa with a hole, trunks in front of her bed, and the hint of a dresser along a bedroom wall. There was no direct sunlight but light enough to spot a littering of mouse droppings on the ragged rug.

"Easily taken care of," she said to herself.

If she had a broom. If she had some towels. The missing items caused her to take an inventory of other needs: a cup, bowl, plate, spoon, fork, knife, bowl to stir in, sharper knife to cut with, soap, bathing towel, necessary paper for the water closet in case it was without. . .

She had no paper or pencil to write with—and added those two items to her mental list. The ladies would know where she could obtain these things. She would take a short time away from work today to procure them.

Work!

Henrietta saw the time on her pendant watch. She was already late.

She exited her flat, closed the door, and once again reveled in the sound of the satisfying click. It was a sound she would never take for granted again.

❧

The workshop was aflutter when Henrietta came in, and at first she feared it was because of her tardiness.

But then Annie showed her a newspaper. "Theodore Roosevelt was shot last night while campaigning. He's all right, but it was quite a scare."

Henrietta had heard of him. "He's the president, yes?"

"He was," Edna said. "Though only because McKinley, the previous president, was shot and killed eleven years ago."

Maude explained. "Roosevelt was the vice president and took over, but then he ran on his own account in '04 and won. But during the '08 election, he supported his friend Taft as a candidate. Taft is our president now."

Henrietta was confused. "You say he's running again?"

"He is, through a third party. He now thinks Taft is too conservative, so he formed the Progressive party."

"They call it the Bull Moose party," Maude said.

What a silly name. She'd never paid much attention to elections back home. Summerfield was so small, there wasn't even a mayor. And of course, royalty like King George V dealt with succession, not election. But she *did* know the Prime Minister was H. H. Asquith, mostly because her family complained about his liberal ways. "Will all of you vote for Roosevelt?" she asked.

They all looked at each other. What was she missing?

"Only Sean can vote. Women don't have that right."

Henrietta was shocked. "I know that is the way in England, but I thought America was the land of opportunity for all."

"Opportunity, yes," Edna said. "But men and women are not treated equally—in many areas."

"Like inheritance." Vesta told Henrietta about inheriting money from her grandparents but having it transfer to her husband. "Is it like that in England?"

"I'm not sure," Henrietta said. "I must admit I never had cause to think about it."

"Women are thinking about it now," Maude said. "The suffragettes often march through the streets demanding the vote."

"Many are put in jail for it," Edna added.

"Many suffer hunger strikes," Annie said.

"How horrible," Henrietta said.

"Yet perhaps it's necessary in order to elicit change," Maude said.

Henrietta's life was all about change. She was becoming an independent woman herself. To know that others were fighting for such freedom filled her with hope.

"Back to Roosevelt. . .as I said, he did survive." Annie picked up a newspaper and pointed at a headline: *Maniac in Milwaukee Shoots Col. Roosevelt.* "He was shot in the chest, but his heavy overcoat, steel-reinforced glasses case, and fifty pages of notes for his speech slowed the bullet."

"God took care of him," Edna said.

"He even gave a ninety-minute speech afterward, showing people his blood-soaked shirt."

"Before he was treated?" Henrietta asked.

Vesta nodded. "That's Teddy. He's a tough one."

"He gets things done," Annie said. "Speaking of. . ." She gave them a pointed look. "With private prayers for his recovery, let's leave Mr. Roosevelt to his doctor's care. Now is the time for *us* to work."

Now was *not* the appropriate time to ask for special time away to buy cups and bowls.

⌒∞⌒

At lunch all the women ate sandwiches and fruit they'd brought from home. Henrietta had already scrounged from her friends yesterday on her first day of work and chastised herself for not remembering to provide her own today.

Maude handed her half a sandwich.

"I'm so sorry. I should have remembered. Tomorrow I'll bring my own, I promise."

"When are you moving?" Annie asked.

Finally, something she could be proud of. "I've already moved. This morning."

"Before work?"

"That's why I was late. I had two men from the hotel bring my trunks over."

"Good for you," Vesta said.

"But. . .I do need a few basic items. A cup, a bowl, some towels. . .that sort."

"I have extra," Edna said. "I'll make sure you are supplied."

Henrietta was moved. "You are all so accommodating."

"We're friends," Maude said.

"Forever friends," Annie said with a smile.

Edna put on a mischievous grin meant for Henrietta. "I'm so glad you got to meet my Steven last night."

"He seems like a nice man."

"He likes you."

Henrietta felt her eyebrows rise. "He does?"

Maude stepped into the conversation. "Are you matchmaking, Edna Holmquist?"

"Heavens no. Henrietta just arrived here. I wouldn't think of it."

Her grin said otherwise.

Henrietta wasn't sure what to think of the idea. She *was* attracted to Steven—the air between them *had* trembled. But then he'd ignored her. Yet now his mother said he liked her?

Henrietta felt like a girl at her coming-out, whispering with her friends about some handsome lad who refused to acknowledge her. She wanted to ask more and encourage the situation. But she was in a new country, away from home, having spurned her fiancé. It had taken all her courage to be here, with these new friends, in this new life. And now she had a flat to contend with. There was no time for romance.

Yet she was twenty-nine years old. If not now, when?

Annie touched her arm. "Don't let our talk overwhelm you. We're just teasing."

After work, Henrietta declined dinner invitations with Edna and Maude, and with Annie, Sean, and Vesta. She needed to learn to fend for herself.

But she did let Edna put together a bag of supplies: every item on her mental "need" list.

Walking home—home, her very own home—she passed a bakery that was just closing for the day. She rushed inside. A ruddy-faced man was wrapping the leftover goods in white towels.

"Pardon, but I'd like to buy some bread please?"

He pointed to three loaves. "Only ones left. I'll have fresh tomorrow morning."

"I'd appreciate one now please." She looked around. "Do you happen to have any cheese or butter?"

"I'm a baker, miss, but. . ." He sized her up in a glance. "You new around here?"

"I just moved in down the block. I'm afraid I didn't think about eating."

He chuckled. "A body won't let you forget about that for long. Hold on." He went to the back of the shop to an ice box and brought back some slices of beef and cheese.

"I don't want to take your personal—"

"Hunger is very personal. Here."

She opened her reticule. "How much?"

He waved a hand. "Call it a welcome meal."

Henrietta felt tears threaten. "Thank you, Mister. . . ?"

"Cody. And you are?"

"Henrietta Kidd."

He extended a hand for her to shake. "Nice to meet you. Come back tomorrow morning and I'll have something fresh for you."

"Thank you. You are so kind." She carried the food close to her chest like a treasure.

⁂

Henrietta sat on her very own chair at her very own table. Using the stash of utensils and dishes from Edna—she'd given Henrietta two of each in case she had guests, which was a laugh—Henrietta sliced two pieces of bread and painstakingly laid the beef and cheese upon them as though she were a chef at a fine restaurant creating a meal for the king. Then she raised the sandwich and said, "Bon appetit!"

It tasted as good as any meal she'd ever had. Was that because it was seasoned with the satisfaction of her independence?

Her memories returned to her journey from Crompton Hall to this flat. She'd had a wonderful life there. Her mother and father loved her; her brother annoyed her—as was the job of all younger brothers. The village of Summerfield was populated with lifelong friends, and the Kidds had extended family at Summerfield Manor. Her uncle Morgan was the earl. His children were her cousins. Henrietta lived in peace, wallowed in harmony, and wanted for nothing.

Except for a long-hidden desire to discover some special meaning for her life—her purpose, if she could be so bold. She'd been correct in telling Annie that *she* was the reason Henrietta had come here, for Annie discovering *her* purpose had inspired Henrietta to do the same.

On the surface it seemed odd to think that a servant could change her life, especially a servant who had caused all sorts of drama and commotion when she'd run away.

Annie had left a note for Henrietta. Remembering it now spurred her to find it and read it again, fresh. She went into the bedroom and opened the smaller trunk. There, in a small pocket along the side of the lid, was the note. She sat on the bed and read it aloud, needing to hear the words.

Dear Miss Henrietta,

Please share this with your mother. I am leaving your family's employ and am venturing out into New York City to find my new path. I am sorry to do this in such an abrupt fashion, but I have realized that as a housemaid there is no place to go, no ladder to climb. I have a stirring within me that forces me to take this drastic step. I know it is a risk, but it is a risk I must take. Please forgive the trouble this causes, and know that I truly appreciate your family's past kindness. Also know that I have greatly enjoyed serving you. Especially you. I wish you all the happiness in the world, Miss Henrietta, for you deserve it.

Sincerely,
Annie Wood

Henrietta carefully folded the note and let it sit upon her lap. Although she had been peeved for her own loss—because it was Annie who always made her feel good about herself, despite her weight fluctuations—Annie's blatant show of courage moved her. And this was not Annie's first escape from a life that didn't suit her. Five years before fleeing in New York, Henrietta's mother had given Annie a job at Crompton Hall, when she was only fourteen. It wasn't because Annie possessed any great promise as a housemaid except for a willingness to do the work.

Any work was better than staying with her despicable family—two loathsome parents who were lazy, mean, and abusive, and who contributed to her brother's death from a burst appendix. They'd been good at hiding their abuse, but when it had become common knowledge, many in Summerfield took Annie under their wings. That she'd been eager to learn skills such as basic sewing with gratitude and a willing heart made their largesse increase, causing Henrietta's mother to hire her, successfully giving her a safe place to live and work. And thrive.

One escape had been handed *to* her, but Annie's second escape had been *her* choice.

Henrietta's mother had been incensed when Annie had disappeared with two other young servants of a relative's household while visiting New York. But when they eventually found out what had been going on the previous year—that Annie had been doing all the sewing and needlework on their dresses, work that the two lady's maids took credit for—her mother's anger had cooled to understanding and even admiration.

The clincher was seeing Annie at the House of Paquin in Paris when Henrietta and her mother were there to order Henrietta's trousseau and wedding gown. Annie was representing the Butterick Pattern Company, getting ideas to transform couture into fashion for the home seamstress. Annie, a girl to be pitied, had turned into a woman of great potential. She'd found a life far better than any she—or anyone else who knew her—could have imagined.

Annie's courage to grab hold of her destiny and try to make it better had spurred Henrietta into wanting to do the same. It was after that Paris trip, when she and her mother had returned to Crompton Hall and continued the plans for the wedding, that Henrietta began to have doubts there should even be a marriage. It wasn't that Hank wasn't a loving man. He was. He'd been supportive when Henrietta had tried—and succeeded—to lose weight. He usually said all the right things, including that he loved her no matter how plump she was. But instead of embracing his words, she distrusted them, finding them variable, like the nap of velvet that felt smooth when stroked in one direction and rough when stroked the other way.

Why did he have to mention her weight at all? Actually, he had been instrumental in making her lose the weight in the first place—by adding a thorny caveat. They had just enjoyed a fabulous feast of trout, mutton, wild duck, and a savarin of peaches for dessert. Although it was highly unladylike,

Henrietta had followed her father's lead and had leaned back in her chair with a satiated moan. They'd laughed about it. It was later than evening when she and Hank were walking through the garden to admire the stars, that he'd made the comment about loving each other through their weaknesses. In retrospect she could see how he'd wisely turned the issue to himself first, stating that he knew he enjoyed cigars a bit too much. She'd agreed, for she hated the foul things.

But then he'd said, "What weakness plagues you, my dear?" She'd of course mentioned her love of food, laughing again at the communal moan she had shared with her father. Which had led to his comment about loving her no matter how plump she was. It sounded akin to saying, "I'll love you no matter how ugly you are," but she'd tossed that interpretation aside and had thanked him for it.

And then she'd started to lose weight. This was not a new phenomenon but a pattern. Yet once again in hindsight, it could be found interesting that Hank had finally proposed after she'd lost a goodly amount. She'd been so happy to finally be engaged—at age twenty-eight—that she'd enjoyed the moment for that fact alone. And of course she'd said yes.

Only after witnessing Annie's success did she rethink her choice. Annie's courage had been a beacon that had lit her path and made her see its shadows. The fact her trousseau had been ordered and her wedding dress designed pressed the timing of her decision, for she did not want her father to waste his money. It was only two days after her return to Summerfield from Paris that she'd sat down with Hank and told him she appreciated his proposal, but no thank you. He'd been understandably confused, and Henrietta had trouble explaining it because she knew he would never comprehend how his word choice in one sentence had been instrumental in making her change her mind. So she'd used vague words, blaming herself, building up his ego, wanting what was best for him. All excuses were valid. But none helped ease his pain.

And yet. . .once he'd left their home she felt as though she could breathe freely for the first time in years. Part of this freedom was due to her broken betrothal, but there was more involved. For the first time in her life, Henrietta was free from the expectations of others. Not that her parents were pleased at her action, not that they wouldn't expect her to find another man to marry so she could live out the customary life of a young woman of society. The change involved her realization that she wanted none of it. She wanted *more*.

"That's why I'm here," she said aloud. "I'm finding my *more*." The thought of it made her smile as she finished her simple dinner.

That accomplished, she realized it was chilly in the room and looked at the fireplace. Only then did she realize she had no wood. No paper. Nothing to burn. And no matches. And more than that, she had no practical knowledge of how to build a fire.

She shook her head in shame. "Snap to it, Henrietta. You chose this."

She decided the night wasn't so chilly that she couldn't tolerate it, and put wood and matches on a mental list. She would gain her warmth by movement. She had two trunks of clothes to put away. But where? At Crompton Hall she had a dressing room attached to her bedroom. Here she didn't even have an armoire. Just some nails and hooks on the wall. And a small dresser with four drawers. After hanging up the dresses that would be most affected by wrinkles, and putting her undergarments, stockings, and nightclothes in the drawers, she rearranged the trunks to hold her other dresses with as few folds as possible.

Then she placed a trio of porcelain vanity boxes on top of the dresser. One contained hairpins, one face powder, and one was a stoppered bottle of perfume that Great-Grandmother Addie had given her on her twenty-first birthday. She removed the top and dabbed some on her neck and wrists. The aroma of lavender—though a little pungent because of its age—transported her back to Summerfield. She closed her eyes and enjoyed the trip. But the cry of a child next door broke the spell. Lastly she put her comb, brush, and mirror on top of the dresser. Their gilt, filigreed handles seemed incongruous on the battered dresser top, yet they were an apt illustration of her current life.

To continue her unpacking, she removed a stuffed stocking from the trunk and emptied it onto the bed. These coins and bank notes were the extent of her wealth, and but for a few American coins she'd obtained on the ship before disembarking, they were in pounds and shillings. It had been a wise choice to move from the pricey hotel to this flat, especially since she wasn't yet familiar with American prices. But would this amount be enough to help her friends?

It was distinctly odd to compare her past when she never concerned herself with prices, to this present life where each cent and dollar was precious. From riches to rags. Or nearly so.

The lie she'd told Annie and the others weighed on her. Yes, she *could* fund them—to the level of her own savings. The lie lay in the fact there would be no money coming from her parents.

"Why did I imply otherwise?"

The room held no good answer other than the obvious one, that she'd wanted to help, wanted to fit in, and wanted them to like her.

Thinking of her parents made her remember the letter she'd sent them from the hotel the day before—the letter asking their forgiveness and telling them she was all right.

But was she all right?

She sighed. Being in a pensive mood, she tried to think about what she would be doing this evening if she were at home.

She'd take a bath. She'd ring for her maid, who would draw the steaming water, scented with rosemary and thyme. Henrietta would soak neck high, closing her eyes, letting her thoughts float away.

A bath would do her well right now. Unfortunately, the room was shared by three other flats on her floor. From what she'd seen, the porcelain was chipped in many places and held testament to the last user, who'd left a distinct ring.

The idea of a bath in such a tub was too unappealing. But at least with her newly procured towel and a bar of soap she could wash her face and arms.

She removed one last item from her trunk, her beauty bible, *Health and Beauty Hints,* by Margaret Mixter. Henrietta's mother had given it to her two years ago when it had first come out, telling her that to follow Mrs. Mixter's regime would keep her complexion young and her body fit. One line from the book had stuck with her and had made her frenetic in her loyalty to the tome. She turned to it now—for it was underlined: *By the time a woman is twenty-five years old, she should devote at least ten minutes, night and morning, to massaging her throat under the chin. If she does this religiously, by the time she is forty, she will not have the hanging "dewlap," which, more than anything else, proclaims a woman no longer young!*

Once Henrietta had a chance to wash her face—for the prescribed five minutes—she would proceed with the book's seven-step program, massaging her skin with a mixture of almond oil, white wax, lanoline, elderflower water, witch hazel, and spermaceti. Her face, eyelids, neck, and arms. . .nothing would escape Mrs. Mixter's diligence.

Before she proceeded, Henrietta did the ordered exercises of her body, balling her hands into fists at her shoulders and thrusting them outward, then touching her toes. Mrs. Mixter assured that a mere five minutes a night would keep one's waist small. Although she'd seen no results—as yet—Henrietta dared not stop. She had trouble enough with her waist, best not make things worse by ignoring solid advice.

Since it had been less than three weeks since she'd washed her hair, she was safe from that chore. For Mrs. Mixter declared washing more often was detrimental, as was washing hair when it was cool or cloudy. Yet looking in the mirror, Henrietta could see her hair was oily. So she took out her jar of fine corn meal. A little sprinkle and a good brush would keep it another week.

The jars in hand, she took some clean undergarments from the dresser, her nightgown, and her dressing gown to give some sense of modesty while walking down the hallway after her wash. Her comb, toothbrush, and tooth powder came too.

Henrietta walked to the bathroom and was relieved to find it unoccupied. Once inside she perused the room with disdain. She was right to forgo the bath and noted she would also need to buy some sort of scouring agent before she could indulge in a good soak. The sink could use its own scrub. And the loo. . .all she could say was that it was better than using a chamber pot.

There were plenty of hooks for her clean garments, and she hung them up. She turned on the sink faucets and held her hand under the water until it was hot. Then she began to get undressed. Only she couldn't.

Her dress unbuttoned in the back!

On shipboard there had been a stewardess to help and then a maid at the hotel. Now that she was alone. . .she tried to contort her arms to free herself but could not.

She shut off the water and began to cry. It's not like she could knock on the door of a stranger's flat and ask for assistance. That would make a grand impression.

And so Henrietta used the loo, washed her face—soaking her sleeves and neckline—brushed her teeth, and went back to her flat. Exhausted by the act of surviving, she ignored Mrs. Mixter's list of beauty to-dos for the first time in two years.

She removed her shoes, fell upon the bed, and began to cry again, missing her mother and father. Missing home. She'd risked everything to come here. "Lord, thank You for getting me this far and for the amazing friends You've given me, but I need help!"

With the request made, she had no choice but to trust that the Almighty had heard her and would answer her prayers. He would forgive her faults and frailties.

But would Mrs. Mixter?

CHAPTER FOURTEEN

Annie took a second look when Henrietta came into the workshop. Her hair was disheveled, but it was more than that. Her clothes—which were usually impeccable—were horribly wrinkled *and* she was wearing the same dress she'd worn the day before. Neither point was the norm for her former mistress.

She didn't have time to ask her about it, as Gert had not shown up to work at all and a new shipment of fabric was delivered just in time for the third dress in their line to be constructed in all sizes. Annie was especially proud of this dress. It would be a perfect dress for work: the fabric a steel blue rayon chambray. The sleeve length was three-fourths—the length of choice for most of Annie's designs. The neckline had no collar, but a facing that was squared off six inches below the neck, with two strips on either side of the square continuing down the front of the bodice halfway, ending in two points. Within the center squared-off area the bodice sported tucks to provide ease over the bust, with matching tucks at the shoulders. Top stitching added ornament to the facing and the edge of the comfortable sleeves. The skirt was made in six straight panels that opened into six pleats at knee level providing ease of movement. The top of each pleat was adorned with a column of three silver buttons that matched the silver buckle on the matching belt. The dress had a side zipper and a small opening at the back of the neck.

"I appreciate all your designs, Annie," Henrietta said as she helped Maude pin the pattern pieces to the fabric, "but the detail of this one is a favorite."

What an odd choice of words. "Appreciate?"

"I appreciate that they don't have buttons down the back." She turned around to reveal her current dress.

"So that's why you're wearing your yesterday dress today," Annie said.

Henrietta nodded sheepishly. "I couldn't get out of it."

Maude swiped a hand across the air. "Headline: Woman Held Prisoner by Dress!"

"It's not funny," Henrietta said. "Actually it is very funny, and rather pitiful."

"Men designed those dresses," Maude said. "I'd bet a hundred dollars on it."

"If you had a hundred dollars," Edna said.

Henrietta moved to a dress on a mannequin and pulled the ample sleeves outward. "My mother and grandmother used to talk about narrow sleeves that were designed so tight they couldn't raise their arms above shoulder height. It was almost a sign of wealth to be unable to do work."

"How silly," Annie said.

"I agree," Maude said. "Think of the absurd styles over the years. Side hoops, circle hoops, bustles, hobble skirts. . .none of which allowed a woman any comfort or ease of movement."

"From what I've heard, the styles a hundred years ago *were* comfortable," Edna said. "High waistlines right under the bust, flowy fabrics, no hoops at all."

"Why did fashion revert back to hoops?" Maude asked. "If women were free of them, why go back?"

"It's a mystery," Annie said. She thought of something she'd always wondered about. "Did they have corsets in that era?"

"I believe fashion has always constrained women with corsets," Edna said.

"There are brassieres now," Maude said. "I saw some in France."

"I'm not aware of any woman actually wearing one," Edna said. "Are you?"

They all shook their heads.

"How hypocritical are we to complain about corsets yet continue to wear them," Maude said.

"We have no alternative," Vesta said, "but to go. . .naked."

"We shan't have that now, shall we?" Maude laughed. She pointed to Annie's midsection. "How are you faring with your maternity corset?"

Their interest spurred her to make an adjustment for more comfort. "Better than a regular corset to be sure, but life would be much easier if we didn't have to cinch everything in."

"I can't imagine that will ever happen," Henrietta said. "To wear no structure. . .it would seem scandalous."

"It would be such a relief," Vesta said.

As if on cue, each woman made corset adjustments—which brought about laughter.

"Back to work, corseted ladies," Annie said.

❦

While the women began to discuss some detail of dress construction, Annie asked Henrietta out to the hall.

"Yes?" Henrietta said, once they were alone.

"This is awkward, but since you offered. . ."

Henrietta nodded, anticipating the subject of the conversation. "Money. You need money?"

"We will shortly. I used the last of the funds from the Sampsons to purchase the fabric that was delivered today and to pay some wages." Annie looked so hopeful.

"I suppose the wisest action would be to go to a bank and deposit it there. But I'm not sure how to do that," Henrietta said.

"Sean could go with you."

"Doesn't he have to work the same hours as the banks are open?"

"He could come home on his lunch hour and take you. Or perhaps Steven could help. His school is not far from here. Perhaps he could come over during their lunchtime."

She liked the idea of Steven's help. The only way she would be able to truly find out if he had any interest in her was to spend some time with him. "Whoever is willing and available. I would appreciate the support."

"I'll call the school presently and leave a message." She smiled, as if remembering something. "Make sure they spell your name right."

"What?"

Annie shared a story about Lena Bryant Malsin going into a bank and her first name being misspelled to Lane.

"That one mistake changed everything," Henrietta said.

"Mistakes often do."

Henrietta cocked her head, curious. "You have a personal example?"

Annie hesitated then said, "None that come to mind. None that I can share."

"You tease me with a good story."

Annie shrugged away her secrecy. "Actually we are living the story. I hope my business choices do not turn out to be mistakes."

Henrietta felt compelled to offer encouragement. "We need to remember that God can use anything for His purposes."

"I count on it."

&

Steven came into the workshop, bringing with him the spicy smell of autumn. "Afternoon, ladies."

Henrietta found herself touching her hair. She tucked in a stray wisp.

Edna looked up from her lunch. "Steven. What are you doing here?" She handed him half a sandwich, which he declined.

He looked directly at Henrietta, and she felt herself blush. "I've come to help Henrietta with some banking."

"Really."

"Annie left me a message."

Edna turned her gaze to Annie and flashed a mischievous smile. "Really."

Henrietta didn't want the conversation to continue, so she wrapped up the last portion of her bread and cheese, retrieved her jacket and reticule, and addressed the others. "I will be back as quickly as I can."

"No hurry," Edna said.

Henrietta heard their giggles from out in the hall even after they closed the door. She was mortified. "Forgive them," she told Steven. "They like to tease."

She had hoped he would say he didn't mind, but instead he said nothing and followed her down the stairs. Obviously he wasn't happy about his assigned task.

Only when they reached the street did he speak. "Do you have the money with you?"

"I do not," she said. "I didn't know I would be doing this today. We will have to stop at my flat and get it."

They walked in silence. Why did she always find herself without words around him? She was thankful the walk was brief. She assumed he would wait for her at the street, but he held the door and followed her inside.

"You can wait here."

"I would like to see how you're faring."

She was glad she'd unpacked. At least to the casual guest she would appear moved in. She opened her door. "See? All settled—thanks in part to your mother's additions of dishes and towels."

His eyes scanned the room. "It's chilly in here."

"Yes. Well, I decided not to start the fire."

He stepped to the grate. "You have no wood."

She sighed, beaten. "A good point. And I also have no kindling or matches."

"Why not?"

A plausible story surfaced, but she pressed it down. "Because I don't know where to get them. And honestly, I also don't know how to make a fire."

"You've never made a fire?"

"I have not done many things."

His forehead furrowed as if her words annoyed him. So much for ever thinking he would find her amiable.

She tried to think of a defense. "I had never crossed an ocean to a foreign continent on my own either, or found my way through a city, or checked into a hotel, or lived on my own. My everyday skills may be lacking, but I do believe I have shown some measure of gumption and courage, Mr. Holmquist." She hoped he caught her formal mode of address.

"I apologize. I do not mean to disparage you. But if you need help, *Miss Kidd*, please ask."

She didn't like their banter and backed down. "Thank you, *Steven*. I did ask. And now you are helping me with my banking."

"Actually, Annie asked." His face looked hopeful. "Though at your request?"

His need for affirmation made her soften. "I am very glad for it."

"As am I, Henrietta."

They exchanged a smile, creating a truce. Of sorts.

❧

"Nice to see you again, Mr. Holmquist," said the bank officer.

Steven turned to Henrietta. "I recently opened my own account here." He looked back to the man. "Which is exactly what Miss Kidd wishes to do today. Will you help her, Mr. Stein?"

The man's right eyebrow rose and Henrietta was reminded of their morning discussion regarding the rights of women. She gained strength from it. "I assume you *will* take my money, or do I need to go elsewhere?"

There were no more raised eyebrows.

"Of course, Miss Kidd. We are happy to serve you."

She put her stuffed reticule on the table. "My funds are in British currency."

"That is not a problem."

She pulled the bills and coins from the purse, the clatter making another bank employee look in their direction. Apparently it was fine to deal with money, just not to let others hear the process.

Mr. Stein expertly divided the money into denominations and counted each stack, noting the total in a neatly written column. He added them together twice, to check his work, consulted another page, did some more math, and then said, "After charging a small transaction fee, you have the equivalent of $125.34."

She smiled. It sounded like a lot. She glanced at Steven, but his face was noncommittal. "I would like to keep out a sum for daily expenses but deposit the rest."

"Perhaps fifteen dollars so you have rent money and a little more for food and such?"

"That will do." Again, she looked at Steven. "Yes?"

"That should suffice."

"Very good then." Mr. Stein took out a form and asked her questions. She made sure she spelled her name for him. Telling him her address made her American life seem real and permanent. When he was through, he gave her a small notebook. "This is your passbook where you write transactions." He showed her where to note the date and which column to use for deposits and withdrawals, and then on the far right, a column with a running balance. Although Henrietta had never had a bank account, she *had* seen such a ledger when she helped out at the family's mercantile where she assisted customers, made change, and took inventory on occasion. Money transactions were not completely foreign to her.

She smiled at the thought. Now they were not foreign at all.

Mr. Stein left for a moment, taking her money with him, saying he would return with her fifteen dollars.

Henrietta let out a breath she'd been saving. "I did it. It's done. Thank you for helping me, Steven."

"It's my pleasure."

She looked at the noted total in her passbook. "It feels very satisfying to have done this. My money is much safer here than in a stocking."

"You sailed across the ocean with your money in a stocking?"

"I—I didn't have time to make arrangements before I left."

His brow furrowed. "You make it sound as though your journey was on impulse, unplanned."

She chose her words carefully. "It was very much planned." *But there were limitations because of its secret nature.*

"I didn't mean to cause offense or be nosy," he said. "And it's good your parents are available for more funds."

"Really? I mean, I thought this was a goodly sum."

"It's quite respectable—if it only needed to cover your expenses. But as you've offered to help fund Unruffled. . ."

"It's not enough for that?"

"It will certainly help. But it is good you have other resources."

A swell of panic rose within her. Why had she offered to pay when she had no idea how much fabric, supplies, and wages cost?

Mr. Stein returned with her fifteen dollars. "Here you are, Miss Kidd. Thank you for your business. Please let me know if there is anything I can do to help you."

If only he could.

⟨⟨✦⟩⟩

"How did you fare at the bank?" Annie asked when Henrietta returned to the workshop.

"Quite well." She hung her jacket and hat on a hook.

"Steven's gone back to work?" Edna asked.

"He has. Your son was very helpful. He is a kind man." Henrietta didn't want to talk about it anymore. "Do you have some seams for me to sew?"

It was best to keep busy. Though "busy" wouldn't solve her problem. Nothing would.

⟨⟨✦⟩⟩

Annie was pressing the seams of the latest dress when she heard a communal gasp. She turned around to see the reason for it. Gert stood in the doorway of the workshop. Her face was puffy, and one eye was nearly swollen shut.

The ladies ran to her.

"Oh, dear girl."

"What happened?"

"Sit down."

Gert eased herself into a chair. Her winces proclaimed unseen sources of pain. Memories of Annie's family flooded back. Her bruises. Her groans. Her excuses for her father.

Annie got to the point. "Who did this to you?"

"Frankie. Who else?"

Vesta put a comforting hand on her shoulders. "No husband has a right to beat his wife."

"Right or no right, he gives me a go once in a while."

"Were you arguing?" Edna asked.

Maude scoffed. "Of course they were arguing. A man doesn't haul off and hit his woman out of the blue."

Gert adjusted herself on the chair, favoring her right hip. "He drank up all me wages, and I called 'im on it. Shouldn'a done that, but it ain't the first time."

"You worked hard for those wages."

"Aye, I did. I work harder 'n him any day of the week. *If* he works."

Again, Annie remembered her family. A drunkard of a father who couldn't keep a job. A mother, hardened by her own abuse, who didn't have enough left in her to love her children. "You're not going back there," she said.

Gert nodded toward the doorway where a small satchel stood. "No, I'm not—at least not right away. I wanted to ask if I could sleep in the sewing room a few nights."

"There's no bed."

"I don't much care. The floor's fine enough."

Annie wanted to offer her a place at their flat, but with Vesta there. . . Edna and Maude's flat was a possibility, but—

Henrietta raised a hand. "You could come stay with me. My flat's not fancy, but I do have an empty sofa—such as it is."

Annie was surprised at the offer. Although Henrietta was a nice woman, by her station she wasn't used to sharing a room with anyone, much less a simple working woman—who was being abused. Henrietta's life had been sheltered.

Until now.

Gert looked to Annie, clearly wanting guidance. Annie could think of no reason to object.

"That's very generous of you, Henrietta. Are you sure?"

A flash of doubt passed over Henrietta's face, but she nodded. "I want to help in whatever way I can help. You are very welcome, Gert."

Gert's face relaxed. "Thank you, Miss Henrietta. I am ever so grateful." She looked to Annie. "I'm ready to work."

"Are you sure?"

Gert nodded adamantly. "It'll get me mind off me troubles."

⁂

It was awkward walking back to her flat after work with Gert in tow, but it felt good to think of someone else for a while. At least Gert was physically safe. And Gert would not ask Henrietta about her adventure at the bank or the amount she had deposited there.

"I really appreciate you doing this for me, Miss Henrietta. I would have been fine sleeping in the sewing room."

"Nonsense. I have the room and am glad to share it." As they passed street vendors, she thought about dinner. Now she had a guest. All she had at home were remnants of bread and cheese, the roast beef already eaten. She would have to splurge.

She bought two cones of roasted chestnuts, four apples, and a large pail of some lovely smelling stew. She even remembered to buy matches and a few pieces of firewood.

"Here, let me pay half."

"No need," Henrietta said. "You are my guest."

"Then let me help in another way." She walked into the bakery where Henrietta had been given the bread. Henrietta *was* down to the last part of the loaf. She followed Gert inside.

"Hello again." Henrietta smiled at Mr. Cody.

But he only had eyes for Gert. "Did Frankie do that to you?" He came around the counter and lifted Gert's face for a better look.

"Of course he did, Da."

Da?

"I shoulda killed 'im when he came looking for ya."

"He was here?"

"Said you'd had a row and he was sorry. I shoulda known he'd gone too far and hurt you."

"You didn't tell him where I work, did you? Cuz I's never told 'im the where of it."

"I didn't say a word. You'd told me not to."

So this has happened before. "Should you be contacting the police about him?" Henrietta asked. "Is he dangerous?"

"More stupid than dangerous," Gert said.

"But he hit you, and since it isn't the first time. . ."

Gert pointed at a roll in a case, and her father handed it to her—and gave one to Henrietta too.

Gert took a bite before answering. "Here's the deal of it. I love 'im, and he loves me. He's a good man most a the time. But when he drinks with his mates, he forgets that. I'll go back to 'im. I always do."

"Not too fast on that," her father said.

"Not too fast." She nodded toward Henrietta. "Da, this is my friend, Miss Henrietta Kidd."

He smiled. "Miss Kidd and I had the pleasure last evening. Did you enjoy your dinner?"

"Very much so." She looked to Gert. "Your father took pity on me and gave me the gift of some food. He saved me."

His face grew stern. "I want to save *you*, Gert. I'd like it better if you just left the louse. You can't let him beat on you—"

Gert raised a hand, stopping his words. "Trust me, Da. Please."

He shrugged as though they'd had this conversation before. "Where you staying?" Before she could answer, he pointed to the floor above the shop. "We could find a place for ya on the floor somewhere, or John-John could give up his portion of the bed."

"Thank you, Da, but no." She explained to Henrietta. "I have six brothers and sisters, all younger than me."

Seven children in the family? "You have been mightily blessed," she told Mr. Cody.

"I agree with you—depending on the day." He wrapped up some bread and rolls for them. "So where *are* ya staying?"

"With Miss Henrietta," Gert said. "Just down the street."

"How nice for both of you."

Henrietta hoped he was right.

They accepted a gift of another loaf and some cheese, said their goodbyes, and then reached the flat. Suddenly Henrietta saw it for what it was: a rather pitiful place with run-down furniture. The sofa with the hole was smallish. It would not allow Gert to stretch out. Maybe Henrietta shouldn't have offered.

But Gert was gracious. "This is nice," she said. "Very cozy."

"I'm sorry it's so small."

"It's not much smaller than the place I have with Frankie." She gave Henrietta a sincere smile. "Your generosity and kindness have made it a palace."

Henrietta's throat tightened. "Thank you for saying that." She swept a hand toward the food. "Shall we dine?"

Gert giggled. "We shall."

But when they took the cloth off the top of the stew tin, they saw that a thin layer of fat had congealed on the top.

"Ew," Henrietta said.

"No worries. It just needs heating up." After checking the cleanliness of the pot that hung over the wood and finding it acceptable, Gert poured the stew into it. Then she knelt and made a fire.

Henrietta watched intently so she could repeat the process on her own. It wasn't that hard. Just a bit of small pieces, with larger ones on top. Once the flame was steady, Gert swung the arm holding the pot over the heat.

"There now," she said, getting to her feet with a groan, "dinner will be ready soon. Show me around."

There wasn't much to show. Just the bedroom and the mention that the communal bath was down the hall. Henrietta took one of the two pillows from the bed and the coverlet. "I hope these will suffice."

"It will be dandy." Gert stirred the stew.

Henrietta got out bowls and spoons and sliced the last of the bread, saving the new loaf for tomorrow. She wanted to know what had happened with Gert's husband but didn't want to be blatant about it. She settled for asking, "Tell me about yourself, Gert."

"I never shoulda married 'im."

The subject was officially open. "Because he beats you."

Surprisingly, Gert shrugged. "That's but the half of it."

"There's something worse than beating?"

Gert put a fist to her chest as though needing it in such a position to accompany her answer. "He makes me feel wee small. In here."

Henrietta wasn't sure what she meant.

Gert continued. "I always thought love would make a heart grow, I mean not really. I knows that. But love should make a person feel like they's more than they were before. Doncha think?"

I do think. I very much think. Unexpected tears threatened.

"You all right, miss?"

She forced the tears away. "I agree with you completely."

Gert studied her a moment. "You've had occasion where the love weren't enough?"

"I have."

"Tell me about it—if you wants to."

Henrietta would have loved to, but this wasn't about her. "We were talking about you."

Gert flipped a hand. "We're talking about all women, if you asks me. All people. Tell me about your man."

It *might* be good to talk about him. "Hank and I were betrothed. The trousseau had been ordered, the wedding dress designed."

"Trousseau," Gert said with a laugh. "I did buy meself a new nightie before we tied the knot."

"I'm sorry," Henrietta said. "I shouldn't have—"

"Think nothing of it," Gert said. "You's the daughter of a nobleman, and I's the daughter of a baker. You're English, and I'm American by way of Ireland. But we both want the same things, don't we?"

Henrietta was impressed with her thinking. "We do."

"We want love, a family, a roof over our heads, food in our bellies, and—"

"And purpose."

"Purpose?"

Henrietta took a stir of the stew then sat beside Gert on the sofa. "I'd never thought about it much until I met Annie. Did you know she used to be a housemaid in my family's house?"

"I knew she knew you, but no. . . . She's come so far. And now, she's yer boss."

"Exactly," Henrietta said. "She rose above her circumstances because she felt there was more she was supposed to do with her life, something important. She had a purpose. Her journey made me question my own."

"So you didn't feel a purpose with yer man?"

"Not really. I'm sure we would have had a nice marriage and perhaps a lovely family, but I couldn't see any reason to it. Perhaps if I'd been deeply in love we would have found our purpose together, but just like you, my heart felt small inside, and I realized if I didn't stop the direction of my life, I might just shrivel and die."

Gert touched a finger to her nose. "That's it, miss. That's why I left Frankie today. Sure, the beatings are part of that decision to leave, but it was the inkling that my heart would shrivel and die that was the true reason for me leaving."

"We are the same."

"The same but different," Gert said.

"Not that different."

Gert smiled. "Yer right." She got up and swung the pot off the fire. "A good rule of cooking is to cook it till it smells. Smells done to me."

Together they took up dinner and sat at the small table. "Bon appetit," Henrietta said.

Gert nodded but then bowed her head. "Father, thank You for this food and a place for me to stay. But above all, thank You for Miss Henrietta. Help us both find our purpose, whatever it may be."

Amen.

⧉

Henrietta felt foolish, but there was no way around it. "Gert? Could you help me, please?"

Gert was already dressed in her nightgown, her makeshift bed created on the sofa. She stepped into the bedroom doorway. "Whatcha need, miss?"

Henrietta turned her back to the girl. "Buttons. I haven't changed clothes in two days because I can't get out of my dress."

They laughed about it, two women with more in common than not.

Two friends.

CHAPTER FIFTEEN

Annie turned over for the umpteenth time. She faced Sean and watched him sleep. The moonlight made his fair skin glow like an angelic being. He *was* an angel to her, always there to help, always reminding her of how God worked in their life. Yesterday he'd pointed out how remarkable it was that God had brought Gert and Henrietta together. How God had turned Gert's deplorable situation into something good.

"In just over two weeks they've become fast friends."

Annie agreed, and yet. . .she suffered a twinge of jealousy about their special bond. Henrietta was *her* friend. It was a silly and selfish reaction, and she'd said her own set of private prayers to combat it. And yet, this was not the only duo who sparked envy.

Edna and Maude were a tightly bound pair. Annie had known each one separately. If not for her, they would never have met.

Vesta and Sean had become close since Vesta had moved in—again, Annie's doing. Last evening she'd stopped hemming a sleeve and had watched them playing Whist, laughing and joking with each other.

She'd helped all her friends and family find new bonds but in the process felt left out. She was friends with all but close to none.

That wasn't true. She returned her attention to Sean. She gently brushed back some hair that had swept over his brow, threatening his eyelids.

He opened his eyes and they lay there looking at each other. "I love you," he whispered.

She kissed his nose. Then kissed some more. And more.

~⟡~

Vesta awakened to the soft sounds of intimacy behind the bedroom door. She smiled, happy that Sean and Annie loved each other so much.

Richard and I used to be like that.

She turned her back to the door and snuggled under the blanket. In spite of everything, she missed him. Yes, Richard was controlling; yes, she had felt stifled and trapped. And yes, leaving had been the right thing to do.

But why hadn't he come after her? She'd been gone over three weeks. Twenty-three days to be exact. Other than showing up that first night—with his nightshirt tucked into his pants—he had not called, visited, or accepted *her* calls. Baines always promised to give Mr. Culver her messages, and she assumed he had. Which meant Richard had chosen to ignore her.

Did he want her back? Did she want to go back?

She opened her eyes and looked at the tufted back of the sofa. She couldn't live the rest of her life here. Annie and Sean needed privacy. And soon there would be a baby. Yes, Vesta could help with its care—she ached to hold the baby in her arms—but. . .

What about Richard? He would be a grandfather. Although he'd never shown much interest in Sean and Sybil as children, he did love them. But how would he love his grandchild when he was estranged?

She clasped her hands beneath her chin. *Father, heal our family. If I need to change, so be it. If Richard needs to change, show him the way. But bring us back together, whole again. And better for it.*

There was silence in the next room, and Vesta could imagine Annie and Sean, falling asleep in each other's arms.

And so she did the same in the arms of the Father.

∾❧∾

Annie awakened earlier than usual—five fifteen. Her mind swirled with to-dos and worries about the business. She knew that the only solution was to get up and go to the workshop. She needed time alone to sort it out.

She quickly used the facilities and washed her face. Her hair was accomplished in a swirl and twist and pinned in a chignon at the nape of her neck. She paused when the baby also awakened, placing a hand upon her growing belly. "Good morning, sweet one," she whispered.

Suddenly she remembered last night, when she'd mourned the notion that she didn't have anyone except Sean. That was not true. She had the baby. For nine months *they* were a pair. No one had what they had. Once the baby was born, Annie would have to share the child with others—would gladly do so—but for now. . . "Let's go to work, little one."

She got dressed but didn't put on shoes—the benefit of having the workshop in the same building. She tiptoed through the parlor.

Vesta opened her eyes. "Morning?"

"Not yet. Go back to sleep."

Her eyes closed. If only Annie could close her eyes and let others take charge. The weight of their success fell upon her shoulders as she walked upstairs. Once inside, the first thing she did was take out some paper and a pen. She was a list person and always felt better after she'd transferred thought to paper. She made a list of the twelve styles but found her notation for them clumsy: the green serge, the blue stripe, the rust-colored side drape. She looked at the list and found it functional but uninspiring. "I need to name the designs."

Suddenly the door of the workshop opened and Vesta came in, wearing a wrapper.

"What are you doing here?" Annie asked.

"I ask you the same question. You need your sleep. The baby needs you to be rested."

"If only I could." She looked at the list.

Vesta looked too. "The dresses?"

"I just realized we need to name them, something we could call them in public, in advertising. Names that will raise them to an elevated, appealing level."

Vesta sat on a stool beside her. "What about. . .flowers?"

"Flowers?"

"Call them the Magnolia, the Rose, the Aster, etcetera."

"I love that idea!" Annie started a new column. "Name some flowers. We need twelve."

"The three I already mentioned, then. . .the Daisy, the Forget-me-not, the Lily. . ."

Annie could barely keep up with Vesta's listing. She counted them. "One more."

They sat in silence a moment then Vesta said, "The Bluebell for that blue chambray."

Annie added it to the list then set her pencil down. "This is marvelous, Vesta. You've eased my mind tremendously."

"I'm glad to be of help." Her voice grew soft. "I feel I do far too little to earn my keep."

"Don't be silly. You are invaluable. You do whatever needs to be done, and that's extremely important."

Her shrug made Annie wonder if there was something else on her mind. "Do you miss Richard?"

"Of course I do."

"Do you want to go home?"

She shrugged again. "Why hasn't he come to fetch me? To check on me?"

So that was it. "He knows you're safe. He did come that first night."

"That was all I was worth? One attempt, then let me go?"

It did seem rather pitiful. "He's a proud man."

"Too proud to check on his wife?"

"Who's gone off to pursue her own aspirations?"

Vesta moved to the window, crossed her arms, and looked out over the raw beginning of the new day. "Can't I live out my aspirations *and* be his wife? I know I could do both. I worked here at the workshop and lived at home with him for over a month before our row. Why did he force me into making it all or nothing?"

"You took the control away from him."

"So he locked me in my room?"

It wasn't surprising the incident haunted her. Yet Vesta had given no indication of still being upset. She worked with a smile and was usually cheerful.

Wasn't she?

Or had Annie been too preoccupied with her own troubles to notice?

Annie put a hand upon her arm. "I'm sorry I've been so focused on the business that I haven't seen your pain."

Vesta faced her. "Do not apologize. You are the one who gave me the courage to fight for myself."

"But if you'd rather be home. . ."

Vesta bit her lip. "I want to be home *and* help with the business. But until Richard comes around, I choose to stay here and work."

"Do you. . .do you think he *will* come around?"

Vesta's eyes grew sad and a bit panicked. "I hope he will. I hope one of these days he will miss me enough to come see me."

"He could come see you and insist you go home and abandon all this."

She sighed deeply. "I hope it doesn't come to that."

"Which life would you choose?"

She hesitated. "I have no idea."

The door opened behind them. Maude came in. "I saw the light on. What's got you two up so early?"

Annie looked at Vesta, wondering if she wanted to share, but Vesta shook her head no. So Annie picked up the list and gave it to Maude. "We've named the dresses."

Maude perused the list. "Well done. I'd been wondering if we should name them. Now when we have an advertisement we can put a caption on the dresses instead of having women come in and say 'I want the dress with the large collar.'"

"Exactly," Annie said. She moved to the next item of her to-do list. "Let's make an inventory of how many we have completed in which size."

Vesta and Maude counted, and Annie made the list. "We only have a dozen more to make and we'll be ready."

"Ready for what exactly?" Vesta asked. "You've never really said."

"We need to have a fashion show," Annie said. "Right here, on the street."

"On the street?" Vesta asked.

Maude scoffed. "That will certainly be different than the one we had at the Sampsons'."

"Which is the point." Annie moved to the window and looked out at the lightening day. "I can imagine women lining the street like they do for a parade. Our models—their neighbors—will walk down the middle of the street, showing off the dresses."

"That sounds glorious," Vesta said.

Maude raised a finger to make a point. "But before we do that, we need a place where the women can buy the dresses. We need a storefront. I said as much weeks ago, and we haven't pursued the idea."

"I know," Annie said.

"What's stopping you?"

"The expense."

"But Henrietta said—"

"I know," Annie repeated. "She's made a generous offer, but the expense will be great. Rent, counters, racks. . . . I want to make sure the dresses are ready before I commit to such a thing."

Maude pointed to the inventory list. "We are nearly through. It's time."

"Are you sure we can't just sell out of this space?"

Maude shook her head. "If we are a success and have high demand, do you really want women coming to the workshop, interrupting our work in order to buy? There's barely room for all of us when we're here working."

Annie knew she was right. "Nothing big. Nothing fancy. Even Lane Bryant started small. We need to do the same."

"I agree."

"How do we find a space?" Vesta asked.

"I'll be in charge of that," Maude said. "My mother's husband gave me the name of a man who could help us. I'll go see him today."

Annie pressed a hand to her heart. "Things are moving so fast."

"No, they're not," Maude said with a laugh. "We've been working toward this for months. It's just that now we are close to our goal. Close to offering our dresses to the world."

"It's frightening."

"It's exciting," Maude said. "But we'll need money for the rent. Can I ask Henrietta for it?"

"I've already asked her for money twice. Two draws of twenty-five dollars each."

"Then make it three times." Maude put an arm of comfort around Annie's shoulders. "Worry no more. I will find us a home for Unruffled."

⚮

Maude stopped in front of the building, checked her note, then went in. She found the offices of Ricci & Company on the left, the name etched into the glass of the door in a manly block lettering.

She went inside and found a secretary at a desk and two seats nearby for waiting. There were two offices. Inside one, she spotted an Italian Adonis. He had chiseled features, an Italian nose—like her own—and black wavy hair that refused to be tamed. She had the fleeting thought that she much preferred this tousled look to hair that was oiled down.

"May I help you, miss?" the secretary asked.

She stepped forward. "My name is Miss Nascato. I am here to see Mr. Ricci. My stepfather, Hans Brunner, recommended that I—"

Then he was in the doorway and stepped forward to offer his hand. "Welcome, Miss Nascato. How is Hans?"

"Very well." *I think.*

"I am glad for his recommendation. How may I help you?"

"I am here to rent a retail space."

He swept a hand toward his office. "Come in and tell me your needs."

I need you to not be so handsome. And charming.

He held a chair for her, and she had a whiff of him. Musk and spice. Quite delicious.

He sat behind an oak desk and moved the papers he had been working on to the side, giving her his full attention. At the moment, she almost would have preferred him to be less attentive. His gaze made her look away.

"I…my partners and I are seamstresses, fashion designers actually, and—"

"I admire creativity. Beauty begets beauty."

She felt herself blush. "Yes, well, thank you, I guess."

"You're welcome."

Maude had the impulse to go into the reception area, close the door, and speak through it. Anything to remove herself from his heady presence. *You do not get heady about men, Maude. You care nothing for any man. So just say what you came to say and be done with it.*

She took a breath to fuel her courage. "We need a retail space to sell our dresses."

"Where?"

"We're not sure. We'd like it to be near other retail spaces, not isolated, but not in an exclusive area either, as our customers are working women."

He took up a pen and made some notes. "How many square feet?"

"I don't know."

"Do you have a large inventory?"

That she could answer. "Twelve designs made in eight sizes, two of each size. So racks for 192 dresses."

"And accessories?"

"We haven't thought of that, but yes. Perhaps."

"You'll need a back room for stock, a counter out front, a sitting area, fitting rooms."

She found she could smile. "It appears you know what I need better than I do."

He returned her smile. "It's my job."

She thought of a point that might help. "Are you familiar with the new Lane Bryant store?"

"On Fifth?"

"That's the one."

"I found that space for them."

How encouraging. "We need less space than they have. One floor. I was never in their first store, but I expect its size is more appropriate."

"I understand." He set his pen in its holder. "What is your budget?"

She had no idea. "Next to nothing. We haven't sold a dress yet. We assume they will sell but have no guarantee."

"You are proceeding on faith."

His words pleased her. "We are. God-willing, our store will be a success."

"God-willing. What is its name?"

"Unruffled."

He thought about this a moment then laughed. "A name that has numerous implications." He leaned forward a bit, his eyes gleaming. "Are you an unruffled woman, Miss Nascato?"

She used to be.

⸙

Where did the day go?

Maude and Mr. Ricci stood outside the last property on their list while he found the right key. She perused the neighborhood. The street was still a side street, but wider than many, allowing some sunlight to linger, even at the end of the day. She spotted a millinery shop, a tailor's, a tobacconist, a grocer, and a shoe store. All had bay windows for their displays, with jaunty signs above, marking their establishments. A worker at the shoe store was outside, sweeping the sidewalk, and nodded toward her. There was pride of ownership here, a sense of respect and common purpose.

And there were customers. Although it was late afternoon—nearly four o'clock—men and women strolled the street, stopped at the windows to discuss some offering on the other side, and entered the stores. And more importantly, a good many came out with a package and a smile that indicated the transaction inside had been successful to both parties.

That was the essence of it. Satisfaction. Maude felt it herself, just standing there, observing. It was a feeling of inevitability, of rightness, of peace.

"We'll take it," she said as he found the right key.

"But you haven't seen inside yet."

She shook her head at his caveat. "It's the right place. I know it." She swept an arm as though presenting the neighborhood to him. "Just look at all this."

172

He took a moment and did as she asked. "I told you it was a bustling area. In fact, it's rare for a space to open up. I saved this best space for last."

"If you'd shown me this first, we would have been done long ago."

He grinned. "But then I would have missed spending an afternoon in your presence."

Although his words were the essence of flattery, she felt the same. She had enjoyed every minute of their excursion around Manhattan. Although the topics of their conversation had centered on business, she felt she'd grown to know him at a level that would not have been possible without the time spent by his side.

"Shall we?" he said, opening the door for her.

Is this the place, Lord? As she entered, she felt a wave of assurance wash over her. This *was* the place.

There was one large room with white wainscoting. The upper walls were painted a soft green, and the floors were oak and shone with a layer of shellac. There was a long display case as often seen in department stores and another raised counter that held a cash register. She touched its keys. "Does this come with the space?"

"It does." He moved to the three doors on the back wall. "These are the dressing rooms." He opened one door to reveal a tufted chair and a full-length mirror.

Maude could imagine customers trying on their clothes, preening in the mirrors, saying the words she had uttered just minutes before: "I'll take it."

"And back here. . ." He moved to the final door, off to the right. "Here is the back room." He found a light switch.

The room was long and narrow, and would be clean with a good sweeping. There were built-in shelves at the far end, a door leading to an alley that would be perfect for deliveries, and even a small water closet that was a step above the other such necessary rooms they'd seen in storerooms. It had a gilt oval mirror above a small sink that was actually clean. There was even a painting of roses on the wall.

Mr. Ricci nodded at the space. "The previous renter sold fur coats, so they created a nice room for their guests' needs."

"It *will* allow ladies to linger longer," Maude said. She returned to the main room, stood in the middle of it, and swirled in a circle, her arms outstretched. "It's perfect!"

"Do you want to know how much?"

She felt silly for not asking. "I suppose I do, though I'm not sure I'd know whether it was a good price."

"You can trust me on that. The price is fifty dollars a month."

His smile suggested the price was a good one. And yet. . . . "It's much more than an apartment."

"It's much larger than an apartment. It has a presence on the street. A display window. You don't live here, you make money here. Money to pay the rent."

It was all true. And they *would* sell dresses. Wouldn't they? Plus, Henrietta had said she would pay for it.

"Do the others need to see it?"

She hesitated but only for a moment. "I don't think so. I know them well enough—I know our business well enough—to know this place *is* Unruffled. We'll take it."

"You will not be disappointed. Let's go back to my office and sign the papers."

As he locked up, she looked into the store through its display window. She could visualize a mannequin inside, some hats on stands, some shoes, a floral arrangement. . .

"How did you know this was the place?" he asked.

There had been nothing concrete, no ray of light shining down from heaven, no booming voice saying, "Rent me!" It was more subtle but no less certain.

"I felt peace. A knowing."

"That sounds too simple."

"I've heard that's how God often works."

He offered her his arm and they walked toward the streetcar stop. "I admire your certainty, and I'm sure He appreciates the credit."

It was an odd way to put it. "He deserves the credit on this, and so much more."

His eyebrows rose.

Although she rarely spoke of it, his question elicited a memory. "I should have been on the *Titanic*."

"The—?"

"My friends and I were in Paris, getting ideas from the fashion houses to take back to our employer, the Butterick Pattern Company. We were coming home and had tickets on the *Titanic*."

"What stopped you?"

"God."

"Again, I'm sure He appreciates the credit."

She stopped walking, forcing him to stop with her. "Do not disparage my faith, Mr. Ricci. It may not be perfect, but it has brought me through many hard times."

His face grew troubled, and he nodded his acquiescence. "I apologize. I did not mean to do so."

"You weren't there," she said.

"No, I wasn't. Tell me what happened."

She forced her ire away and took his arm again. She wanted him to know, to understand this enormous milestone. "We were in the train station in Paris, catching the train to Cherbourg. The *Titanic* was stopping there before heading to America. But then we heard a little boy crying, calling for his mother. We went to help and learned that he couldn't find her, and she was expecting a baby."

"How frightening for him."

"We could not abandon him though the train was leaving. We stayed behind, found the mother, and Annie even helped with the birth. They named the little girl after her."

"How dramatic."

Maude was disappointed that was all he saw in the moment. "We missed the train and there was none other leaving in time for us to catch the *Titanic* before it sailed. Madame Le Fleur, a woman we all worked for at Butterick, did not stay behind. She perished."

"Oh."

"That could have been us. Yet God made us cross paths with that little boy. His need saved us."

"You could have ignored him. I'm sure many people did."

"I've thought of that. God gave us a choice, and we made the right one. *That* is why I look to Him to offer me choices. That is why I depend on Him to lead me rightly."

"Like He did today when we found this property?"

"Like He did today."

In more ways than one.

❧

Maude paused at the top of the stairs, out of breath. She'd rushed back from Mr. Ricci's, wanting to catch everyone at the workshop before they left for the day. She straightened, needing extra space to breathe beneath her corset.

She heard voices inside, the rumblings of work being wrapped up for the day. She went inside, raised her arms in the air, and declared, "Unruffled has a home!"

But instead of applause or words of joy and acclamation, she was greeted with blank stares.

"Did you hear what I said?"

Annie broke the silence. "You signed papers? You agreed to it without us seeing it first?"

Maude dug her fists into her hips. "That's what you sent me to do, isn't it?"

"To look, not to sign."

A wave of panic swirled inside her. Had she gone too far? The deed was done. The papers were a legal document. Money had been promised.

Edna stepped forward, her hands pressing downward. "Calm now, ladies. We did send her out on this task. We do need a space quickly. Give her a chance to tell us about it."

"I'd love to hear," Vesta said.

Maude struggled against wanting to storm away and leave them hanging. But her excitement took over. She told them all the details. As she did, their eyes lit up, their heads nodded, and their smiles won out.

"It sounds marvelous," Henrietta said.

Henrietta. The source of their funding. "I did have to promise Mr. Ricci some money up-front. Fifty dollars for a month's rent and fifty more for a deposit. It's Friday, so could you give me a money order or bank check on Monday? Or go with me to see him?"

An odd flash passed over Henrietta's eyes before she said, "Of course."

"When can we see it?" Annie asked.

"Antonio said—"

"Antonio?"

She felt herself blush. "As we were going over the papers, we exchanged first names."

"Is he young and handsome?" Vesta asked.

"I gave you no indication of his looks or age."

Henrietta laughed. "The flush of your cheeks gave it away."

Maude needed to nip this in the bud. "Yes, he is handsome. And young. And charming. But he means nothing to me beyond the business we have together."

"Ha!" Gert said. "I's heard that before."

Vesta joined in. "His name sounds Italian. I've heard Italian men are often charming, romantic, and—"

"I care nothing for him!" Maude realized her outburst was melodramatic, and also realized it was directed at herself as much as her friends. She calmed herself with a breath. "I'm sorry. But you know I am not interested in finding a beau or courting or any such matter."

"Why not?" Henrietta said.

Annie and Edna were the only friends who knew about her past and the violence done against her. She didn't want the others to know, so she simply said, "I cannot bear children. And so I have decided it would be unfair to lead a man on with the normal expectation of having a family."

"But maybe Antonio doesn't want children," Gert said.

Maude had to laugh. "Now you have us marrying? He might even *be* married. I just met him." *Listen to your own words, Maude. You've let yourself get swept up in the moment. You had a lovely afternoon with a pleasant and entertaining man. That's all there is to it. All there can be to it.*

Annie came to her rescue. "Spare Maude your romantic imaginings. It appears we now have a storefront. When can we see it?"

Maude dangled the key in front of her.

⟨≈⟩

"That's it, up ahead," Maude said. "The store with the striped awning."

Annie loved it already. The awning brought back memories of many quaint shops in Paris.

Maude got out the key as the rest of them peered in the window, their hands cupped against the glass.

"This front is a good display area," Edna said. "We could get two, maybe three mannequins set up."

Maude used the key, went inside, switched on the lights, and swept an arm, welcoming them. "Voila! I present to you, Unruffled."

The seven women—including Gert and Ginny—fanned out over the store. They touched the wainscoting and the counter, explored the fitting rooms and the back storage area. Annie let the others exclaim and chatter. She let them move ahead of her. She needed time to process everything she saw, and as she did so, her mind moved beyond the here and now into a future time. She could see racks of dresses, pretty chairs set in small groupings, displays of accessories. And the customers…they milled about the store, their eyes bright with anticipation that these gorgeous dresses could be theirs. The store was heady with joy and satisfaction, and something many women didn't have in their busy lives: fun.

"I want them giddy with it!" she said loudly.

The other ladies stopped their explorations and looked at her.

"What did you say?" Henrietta asked.

I didn't mean to say it aloud! "I want our customers to be giddy with their experience here. I want Unruffled to be a place where they leave all their troubles and to-dos outside. They look through our dresses, try them on, and ooh and ahh over their reflections. I want them to swirl and feel pretty, smile and laugh."

"And buy," Maude added.

"Of course. And they *will* buy because the experience here will be fun."

"Fun?" Edna asked.

Annie laughed. "You say the word as if it is foreign."

"To most women, it may be. They go through each day with survival in mind, not fun."

"Yet when we both worked at Macy's, we saw that women had fun shopping."

"They did."

"When a woman came into the dress goods department wanting to sew herself an outfit, *I* had fun waiting on her, helping her choose the pattern, the fabric, and the trims. When she left she was full of satisfaction and excitement about how she would look in her new garment. I want that to happen here."

"But 'giddy,' Annie?" Vesta asked. "How do we make them giddy?"

"I don't know yet. But I want that to be our goal. Understood?"

"Giddy is as giddy does." With those words, Maude took Annie and Edna's hands and formed the beginning of a circle. Vesta pulled a reluctant Henrietta into the fray, along with the two seamstresses. At Maude's prompting, the women skipped around in a circle, laughing at the childlike feeling of abandon—until they were giddy with it.

CHAPTER SIXTEEN

Although it was Saturday, Henrietta and Gert were readying themselves to go in to work. Now that they had a storefront, the pressure was on to finish the dresses.

Now that we have a storefront, the pressure is on me to pay for it. In two days.

Henrietta closed the door of the bedroom. "I'll be out in a minute," she told Gert.

She opened her trunk, and from a secret pocket in the side of the lid, she removed a velvet bag. She emptied the contents onto the bed. As a young woman Henrietta often emptied her jewelry box onto the bed when the sun was bright, just to admire the dazzle of the stones and the settings. Now, in her tiny bedroom with its dark alley window there was no sunlight. No sparkling.

She indulged in the memory of putting on her favorite necklaces, bracelets, and earrings, and admiring her reflection in the mirror, practicing her curtsy for the next ball, holding out her hand for some invisible beau to kiss.

Today, Henrietta did not try on the jewelry. There was no time to admire, no need to practice her curtsy, and no man to kiss her hand. Today the jewelry held a different promise: the assurance that her lie would stay hidden.

The rent on the store was fifty dollars a month, with the first month's rent and a month's rent as a deposit promised to Mr. Ricci on Monday. Henrietta only had $45.34 in her account, as she'd made another withdrawal for rent and expenses in addition to giving Annie fifty dollars to pay for wages and supplies. It was time for drastic action.

She picked up a pearl necklace that had been a present from her parents for her sixteenth birthday. She smiled at the memory of opening the purple velvet box, exclaiming with delight, and wrapping her arms around her parents' necks, kissing them, thanking them.

Annie spoke of women feeling giddy. That's how she had felt at her first ball, wearing the pearls. She'd tried to stop smiling but had been unable to do so. Especially when her dance card was quickly filled. She knew she was pretty, and she danced every dance, immersed in the joy of dancing.

She set the pearls aside, for the memories were too dear. And it was probably not worth enough to help the business.

She took up a lapis blue necklace. She'd never worn it because the setting was intricate and heavy. But it was precious to her because it was given to her by her father. The necklace had been his mother's, his mother who had died soon after he was born. A previous Lady Newley— whose portrait hung over the mantel in Crompton Hall's drawing room, a beautiful young woman, eternally twenty-one. She wore the necklace in the painting. That it was so strongly tied to family history made Henrietta set it aside.

Last was an emerald bracelet and matching drop earrings that had been her great-grandmother's. Adelaide Weston, the Dowager Countess of Summerfield, had passed these on to Henrietta when she'd become betrothed to Hank. "Wear them on your honeymoon as you tour the Continent, my dear Etta."

But there had been no honeymoon, no tour.

Although she hated to give up something that reminded her of Great-Grandmother, it was the best choice. She put the other pieces safely away, wrapped the bracelet and earrings in a handkerchief, and stuffed them into her crocheted purse.

Gert knocked on the door of her room. "There's someone here to see you."

Henrietta had been so immersed in her memories that she hadn't heard a knock. Who would be visiting? The ladies were all meeting at work.

She opened the door of her bedroom and found Steven Holmquist standing in the parlor, hat in hand. They'd seen each other often during the past few weeks, but always at Edna's for a meal or at church. Henrietta had been relieved when their awkward start had evolved into a comfortable camaraderie. She had high hopes that her initial feeling of connection had been on the mark.

"Good morning," he said.

"Good morning." Her confusion fed her next question. "What are you doing here?" She immediately couched her bluntness. "That was rude. It's nice to see you."

"My coming without warning was rude. But if you're willing, I've come to take you on a Saturday outing. Since New York City is new to both of us, I thought we could explore it together."

"We're working today," she said with true regret. "We were just leaving."

His smile faded. "As a teacher I don't work on Saturdays. I just assumed..."

Gert intervened. "I'm sure it would be all right if you didn't come in today, Miss Henrietta. At least not for a few hours."

"But Annie said she needed all hands."

Gert grinned at Steven then said, "I'll work hard enough for both of us. Go on now. See the city."

Henrietta longed to do just that. "Are you sure?"

"I am." Gert slipped past Steven and was out the door before Henrietta could change her mind.

"Well then," Steven said. "It appears you are free."

"It appears I am."

He held her coat for her, and she secured a straw hat with a pin. As she picked up her gloves and purse, she realized it held the jewels inside. She should put them back where they belonged in their safe hideaway. Yet she didn't want to delay their outing. She would just have to be extra vigilant.

"Where are we going?"

"We could go to the Statue of Liberty, the Metropolitan Museum of Art, or Central Park."

Henrietta had seen the Statue on the way into the harbor. And art held little interest to her at the moment. "What I crave most is the outdoors: trees and sky and green expanses. I miss the English countryside around Crompton Hall."

"Being November now, there is little green, but the Park offers two out of three."

"Then Central Park it is."

They took a streetcar north. It was new territory for Henrietta. Other than staying at the Hotel Astor in Times Square, she had been in Greenwich Village, where she and her friends lived and worked.

At the beginning of their outing, she spotted a reputable-looking jewelry store: Cohen & Cohen. She noted its location. She would return later and conduct her business.

A few blocks beyond that... "Look! There's Macy's!" she said. "That's where Edna and Annie worked."

Steven smiled. "I know."

She felt herself blush. "Sorry. Of course…*your* mother. And Annie. I was too exuberant."

"I appreciate exuberance. And we *are* exploring."

"I admit I have done little of it. Every year my parents would take my brother and me to London for the social season, and occasionally we would travel to Brighton by the sea, but they were homebodies and preferred the pastoral life."

"I'm surprised," he said. "I assumed you'd seen all the great sights of Europe."

"I have been to Paris. That's where Mother and I saw Annie, at the House of Paquin." Suddenly, she pointed. "There's Lane Bryant. Annie and Maude told me about Lena."

"An American success story, to be sure."

"I expect there are thousands of those stories about the American Dream and streets paved with gold."

"You didn't believe the latter, did you?"

"Of course not, but I do believe in the dream." She needed to risk saying one thing more. "I'm living it."

He laughed. "In your tiny apartment that must be the size of a pantry back at Crompton Hall?"

She took offense. "It is *my* apartment as I live out *my* American dream."

He touched her hand. "I didn't mean to make light of it." He pointed to the left. "See there? That's St. Patrick's cathedral. And across the street live the Sampsons."

"Who are they again?"

"The ladies didn't tell you about them?"

"Annie mentioned them in regard to the business. What should I know?"

"Perhaps nothing. They were the couple who initially supplied funds. But they pulled out."

"Wasn't it Annie who pulled out?"

"Annie and the others decided Mrs. Sampson's fancy preferences did not suit their customer."

"That took a lot of courage."

"It did. But then the money ran out and they began to panic." He smiled at her. "Until you came along and saved them."

That her rescue might soon come to an end made her stomach clench.

"Are you all right?"

She had to brush it off. She had jewelry to sell. Hopefully that income would be enough to fund the move into the store until the dresses began to sell.

❦

Henrietta drew in a deep breath, relishing the fresh air and the smell of fallen leaves. Yet half of the trees were still wearing their autumn colors—her favorite colors. "This is exactly what I needed. Some leisure. I'm glad Gert made it possible for me to go with you."

"*I* am glad."

His frequent compliments made her feel warm inside. "You said this is called the Mall. There is also a Mall in London, near Buckingham Palace, though as you hear, we pronounce it 'mal.'"

He laughed. "Of course you do. I've noticed we pronounce many words differently."

"Such as?"

"You said 'lezsure,' we say it 'leesure.' And your 'shed-yule' is 'sked-ule.'"

It felt wonderful to laugh.

He held up a finger. "We do laugh the same."

"A common language."

He bent down to retrieve a lovely red maple leaf. "For you."

"Thank you, dear sir." She spun it in her fingers.

"Tell me about your home, though I suppose being called Crompton Hall makes it a bit more than a home."

"It is. The residence sits on a country estate that's been in my family for centuries. But in truth, some parts are a bit run down."

"Centuries of use will do that."

"It partially burned in 1884 when I was a baby. When it was rebuilt, my grandfather had it wired for electricity and indoor plumbing. It was the first in the county to have such luxuries."

"Here we are twenty-eight years later and such perks are still absent in many homes, even in a progressive place like New York City."

"Progress can be slow." She thought of her shared bathroom down the hall from her flat. "Our estate is near the village of Summerfield."

"Which is where Annie lived."

"She lived in the village until Mother took her in."

"Was she an orphan?"

"It would have been better if she was. Her parents were horrible people."

"Are they gone now?"

"I misspoke, for they are very much alive."

"What's so horrible about them?"

"Mr. Wood is a ne'er do well. The sort who makes people nervous by his very presence. I remember my father saying that no one could count on Mr. Wood—except to cause trouble. And Mrs. Wood is a nasty woman, acting entitled."

"To what?"

"To whatever anyone else has, what anyone else has worked hard for and earned."

"They are moochers."

"I'm not familiar—"

"They are leeches."

Now she understood. "Indeed. They sponge off anyone and everyone. When people see them coming, they hurry inside. The two of them argue over the color of sky. They stir up dissension as easily as stirring up dust with their footfalls."

"Why not put a stop to their mooching? Just tell them no?"

"Because they are also mean." She remembered a young Annie, her face bruised. "Although it was not known for a long time, it turns out they hit Annie frequently. And it was said that a blow by the father contributed to her brother's appendix bursting—and his death. That's why Mother gave her a position as an under housemaid."

"She probably saved her."

"I believe she did. Though Annie's father was arrested, he spent little time in jail. If Annie had continued to live at home, I fear she would have also died from their blows and kicks."

A bench opened up, and Henrietta led Steven toward it. Once seated, she wished she had a parasol as the November sun was warm. Steven traded places with her, giving her the shade.

"Annie has come far," Steven said. "In distance and self-betterment."

"Her courage inspired my own." She spread her hands. "Hence, Henrietta is here, sitting beside you."

"For that, I am utterly thankful." He took her hand, resting it on her knee. "I am very glad we both moved here. So very, very glad."

She squeezed his hand.

His smile was infectious. "It's as though God brought us together, you from England and me from Pittsburgh. Two people converging in one place. Perhaps with one purpose?"

Her stomach flipped. "Which is?"

He pointed to the blue sky overhead. "Limitless."

Henrietta relished his joy, for she felt it too. She had never met a man like Steven. Though reticent at first, he continued to show himself to be open and enthusiastic about life. In his presence she felt appreciated. Their amiable connection *did* seem God-sent.

They watched as a family walked by, the mother pushing a pram. *That is the life I long for.*

The scene seemed to spur him to speak. "My mother wants me to ask you to dinner tomorrow evening. Will you come?"

The invitation fed into her thoughts. Although she'd eaten at Edna's table often, she had never been invited by Steven. "I would love to."

Suddenly he stood and pointed past the family to a man who was taking photographs. "Let's go!"

He pulled her to the man, and they stood in a short line, waiting for their turn.

"I wish you'd warned me. I would have taken more time on my hair." She removed her hat and pushed some stray strands into her updo.

He also removed his hat and ran a hand through his thick hair. "You are beautiful. Always." Then he kissed her cheek.

The other couple waiting in line took their cue and also exchanged a kiss.

Henrietta blushed. She couldn't imagine being happier.

When it was their turn, the photographer had them stand side by side, but at the moment he said, "Hold!" Henrietta glanced away.

"Oh dear," she said afterward. "I'm afraid I wasn't looking."

The man paid no attention to her objection then took partial payment for the picture—Steven asked for two copies—and gave Steven a card of where to pick it up in the studio on Monday.

"Next!" the man said.

Henrietta and Steven walked away. "I'm sorry to ruin the picture," she said. "Don't pay him the rest if it isn't any good."

"Nonsense," Steven said. "Would you like to see some elephants?"

"What?"

"The zoo. Would you like to go?"

She laughed. "Elephants in New York. What will they think of next?"

⚬⚬⚬

As soon as Steven saw Henrietta home, she rushed out on her mission. She knew she should go directly to the workshop but decided it was more important to procure rent money.

She walked to Cohen & Cohen, the jewelry store she'd seen that morning, and paused at the door to compose herself. But then a man came to the front and turned over the OPEN sign to say CLOSED.

"No!" She knocked on the glass door and called out. "Please, sir. I need to speak with you immediately."

He peered through the glass. "We're closed."

"But I need. . .I have business." She decided to lure him into staying open. "I would like to sell you my family heirlooms. Jewels."

His eyebrows rose and he opened the door. He shut it behind her, keeping the CLOSED sign intact. "So we won't be disturbed," he said. "Come show me what you have to offer."

They moved to a display case that was mostly empty. Apparently, it *was* closing time and they'd already put their wares in a safe for the night. She would make this quick.

The man took a place on the back side of the case. "Show me."

She noticed he was dressed oddly for the proprietor of such a lovely store. She'd expected a dark suit and fine tailoring. Instead he wore a brown wool jacket that had frayed edges at the cuffs.

He must have seen the direction of her gaze. "Forgive my casual attire. I am closing early to do a good cleaning of the place." He extended his arms. "This was my first suit that I bought after I was hired to my first job. I keep it for sentimental reasons."

She looked around the fine store. "You have come far. You should be proud."

"I have. And thank you, I am proud." He pulled a swath of blue velvet close. "Now then, what do you have for me?"

She removed the emerald bracelet and matching drop earrings. "They are emeralds and were my great-grandmother's." She thought about telling him exactly who her grandmother was, but wasn't sure she wanted him to know so much.

He took up the bracelet and then the earrings, studying the settings.

Henrietta wanted to ask if he found them to be fine pieces, but by doing so she might cast doubt on their value. "I believe they are from the 1820s."

"I concur," he said. "The filigree work dates them so." He set the pieces on the velvet. "May I ask why you wish to sell them?"

Her resolve began to crumble. "I *don't* really wish to sell them. My great-grandmother gave the set to me as a gift when I became engaged. She told me to wear them on the Continent on our honeymoon."

"But you are not on the Continent. And I see no wedding ring upon your finger."

Out of nowhere tears flowed and she used the handkerchief she'd wrapped around the jewelry.

"Sit down, my dear," the man said as he led her to a chair behind the counter. He sat beside her, a hand upon her shoulder. "I'm sorry you are so distraught."

She felt an utter fool. "I'm sorry to have put you in the position of comforting me. I should be stronger. They are just *things.*"

"Things that have meaning to you and your family." He waved a hand across the store. "All of these baubles are just things. They become precious in the giving and receiving, in the memories they make."

She nodded and tried to blow her nose discreetly, though the latter was difficult. "Even if I sell them, I will still retain the memory."

"Here is what I will do. I will give you five hundred dollars."

It was a considerable sum that would pay the rent for nearly a year. Surely by then, Unruffled would be making its own money. "I agree to the amount. Thank you, Mr. . . . ."

"Cohen. Abel Cohen. And your name?"

"Henrietta Kidd." His name was Jewish but his accent otherwise. Irish perhaps? Yet she suspected that accents changed when in America. She stood and held out her hand. "Thank you for your assistance, Mr. Cohen."

He shook her hand then walked toward the cash register. "Drat. I have already emptied the register for the day and my partner has the combination and key to the safe. Could you come back Monday?"

The lack of cash made sense, considering the nearly empty display cases. But Monday was difficult, for Mr. Ricci needed the payment Monday morning. "Would there be any way I could come by tomorrow? I know it's the Sabbath, and you're not officially open, but—"

He hesitated then said, "We could do that. Actually, Saturday is our Sabbath."

She'd never heard that. "Tomorrow afternoon then?"

"Agreed."

She extended her hand for the jewelry. "I will bring these back."

He did not relinquish them. "My brother is coming in later to help me clean. I would like to show these to him and get his much-more-expert opinion regarding their value. May I keep them overnight? I wouldn't want to give you five hundred when they are worth much more."

More? "Of course. I would appreciate the extra opinion."

"Perfect," he said, showing her the door. "After he sees them, we will lock them away in the safe. Have a pleasant evening, Miss Kidd. We shall see you tomorrow. Noon?"

"That would be perfect."

He closed the door behind her, and she paused to smile and give him a wave.

Now, she was ready to go to work.

⁂

Edna pulled Annie aside. "A word?"

Annie didn't want to interrupt the work. They were accomplishing much on this Saturday. But knowing tomorrow was Sunday—a day off—and they wouldn't be back to it until Monday..."I suppose." She nodded to the hallway, which had become everyone's standard place for private conversations.

"What is it, Edna?" She heard the annoyance in her voice, but it could not be helped.

"Oh dear. Perhaps this is not the time or place..."

"You've got my attention. Talk."

"But it has nothing to do with the business."

Annie felt her annoyance spike. "Talk, so we can get *back* to business." Edna looked uneasy, yet Annie knew they would never get done with this until she was cajoled into speaking. "Please. I'm sorry to snap at you.

What is on your mind?"

Edna's face softened with relief. "Steven and Henrietta are courting, or if not courting on the verge of it."

"I knew there was interest but didn't know it had gone that far until she didn't come in today."

"I do not know her heart, but I know my son's. He is smitten."

"I am glad for both of them." *Henrietta could use a good man in her life.*

"The trouble resides in the fact that we are not familiar with the protocol of a romance between the daughter of a viscount and an American. A normal, everyday American. A teacher."

Annie hadn't thought much about that. Had she been in America so long that the propriety of Lord and Lady, and the correctness of British society faded from her thoughts?

"I didn't know it was that serious."

"I believe it could be." Edna turned her back to the closed door as if wanting even more privacy. "Steven requested that I ask you about this. He doesn't want to completely fall in love if marriage isn't a possibility."

Annie put her hands on her hips, hoping her thoughts would settle into a logical answer. "I know—if they had their choice—the Kidd family would choose a gentrified man for their only daughter."

"Oh."

"Yet Henrietta is nearly thirty years old. And I know her mother's cousin married the town carpenter back in Summerfield, and *she* was the niece of the earl."

"An earl is of higher rank than a viscount?"

"It is."

"The family allowed that marriage."

"With reluctance, I believe. But Lady Clarissa had always been a rebel, even having a foray on the stage in London. And Henrietta's uncle is the earl and *he* married an American heiress. . ." Annie sighed. "It gets complicated."

"Apparently," Edna said. "So you don't know whether it would be allowed?"

"I don't. But Henrietta coming all the way to America by herself and breaking off with a man who suited her parents' wishes *does* indicate she is a strong woman who is capable of living out her own choices."

Edna released a breath. "I hope so. I do not want my son to suffer a broken heart."

"So you'd like Henrietta as a daughter-in-law?"

"Of course. I like her very much."

"Perhaps we should just let things play out as they will then?" *And not push too hard?*

Edna nodded. "If God wants them together, then they will be together."

"That is a good way to think of it." Let God figure it out. Annie had enough on her mind.

They heard footfalls on the stairs below and paused their conversation. Henrietta appeared on the lower landing.

"Hello, ladies," she called up, out of breath. "Thank you for giving me the freedom to be late."

"Did you have a fine time with my Steven?" Edna asked.

"We did. We walked in Central Park."

"How lovely." Edna gave Annie a pointed look.

Henrietta joined them on the upper landing. "Did I interrupt something?"

"Not a thing," Annie said. "Come in. I'd like ask your opinion about a skirt length."

CHAPTER SEVENTEEN

Henrietta and her friends exited church, shaking the hand of the pastor. Henrietta had enjoyed the service, needing the special time to thank God for providing the five hundred dollars—or more—from the sale of her jewelry.

Upon reaching the sidewalk, Steven asked, "Would you enjoy another walk in Central Park this fine afternoon? I'm afraid winter will come upon us sooner rather than later."

"I'm afraid I have a few tasks at home." Upon seeing his disappointment, she squeezed his hand. "I will see you at your mother's this evening for dinner."

"I look forward to it. The least I can do is walk you home."

She would have objected—for going home first would make her trek to the Cohen store a lengthier one—but she longed for his company. Her plan was to present the five hundred dollars to Annie and the others at dinner. Their gratitude would make up for the loss of the jewelry. The knowledge that her sacrifice would enable them to open Unruffled was butter upon bread.

Steven accompanied her to the steps of her building and she bid him goodbye until dinner. She walked into the vestibule, waited a reasonable time for him to be gone, then came out again. She hurried to Cohen & Cohen.

But as she neared the store, she saw something was wrong. The area was abuzz with police. A crowd of onlookers created a second ring of interest.

"What's going on?" she asked an elderly man.

"The store's been robbed."

"Which store?"

"Cohen & Cohen." The man pointed with his cane.

"What?" Henrietta nearly shouted the word.

"Calm it down, missy. It's just a bunch of high-falutin' jewelry gone. I don't think anyone was hurt."

The man on Henrietta's other side begged to differ. "I heard tell the Cohens were tied up in the back all night. They took old Abel away on a stretcher. Both brothers are in their late seventies, you know."

"They're not that old," Henrietta said. "Or at least Abel isn't. I spoke to him last evening. He was not even fifty."

"Then you didn't talk to Abel," the man said.

"Then who did. . . ?" Henrietta gasped and rushed forward to one of the bobbies. "Officer, officer!"

"You need to stand back, miss. Let us do our job."

"But I was here last evening just as they were closing. I gave some family jewelry to Mr. Cohen, but apparently it wasn't Mr. Cohen at all, and—"

She'd gained his attention. "You were here? You saw the thief?"

"I had a long conversation with him." *He comforted me when I cried.*

The officer motioned another bobby over. "This woman was here last night. Talked to the thief."

The new officer took out a pad and a pencil. "Tell me about him. His looks, what he said. . .everything."

Henrietta did her best. Yet her story was full of red flags that *should* have warned her things were not right.

"When you noticed the empty cases and him wearing a worn coat, didn't you sense that things weren't on the up and up?"

"What?" She'd never heard that term.

"They weren't. . ." He smiled. "Kosher?"

"He was a nice man."

"He was a con man."

Again, she looked to him to explain.

"A confidence man. He gained your confidence in order to steal from you."

Her insides grabbed. "He certainly did that," she said. "My grandmother's jewelry. . .did you find an emerald bracelet and earrings inside?"

He gave her the look she deserved. "You expected him to take pity and *not* steal from you?"

"I hoped." *A ridiculous hope.*

"They are gone, miss, as is everything else of value."

The first officer added. "You're lucky he didn't take you in the back room and tie you up with the Cohens."

Henrietta shuddered. "Will they be all right?"

"They've gone through a lot, but they will be fine. We wouldn't even have found them this soon if not for the fact that some friends went to check on them this morning. Neither brother ever married, and they live together. Apparently they didn't show up at synagogue last night, but people got busy with their own Sabbath matters and forgot about it until today."

She said a quick prayer for them. She had lost a little. They had lost a lot and had physically endured more.

The officers asked for her name and address and said they would contact her if they needed more information.

On the walk home, all Henrietta could think about was what *might* have happened. *And* her utter and total failure to provide for Unruffled as she'd promised.

⁓

Gert knocked on the bedroom door. "Miss Henrietta? Are you all right?"

Henrietta sat up on the bed and wiped her eyes. She hadn't realized she'd been crying that loudly. She cleared her throat before speaking. "I'm fine. Thank you."

"When you came in you were all upset. Is there anything I can do to help?"

"I'm fine now. Really. It was just a silly thing."

There was a pause. "All right then. I trust what you say is true. As I'd told you, I'm going to visit Frankie this afternoon."

Henrietta remembered. "Are you sure about going?"

" 'Tis just a visit. He'll be on his best."

"So you're not going back to him?"

"We'll see. At any rate, I probably won't be to home till after dinner."

"Have a good visit. And be careful."

Henrietta heard the door of the flat open and close. But Gert's words lingered: *I trust what you say is true.*

"I'm a liar. You can't trust me. Not a bit."

Maude needed to pay Mr. Ricci the rent money tomorrow.

There was no money.

Her grandmother's jewelry was gone.

She thought of the only other items of value she possessed. The pearls and the lapis piece. Both were family heirlooms. Both were taken from

193

Crompton Hall without her parents' knowledge. If she sold them she would be breaking a family trust.

"I need to bring them back where they belong."

The idea of going home took root. That was the answer. Go home to Summerfield. Endure their reprimands and disappointment, and be accepted back into their loving, forgiving arms.

She'd sent her family a few letters, telling them she was well. They were not fearful for her safety. Yet she'd kept other details of her American life secret.

She looked around the shabby flat. They would cringe at the sight of it with its thin walls that shared sounds she would rather never hear, water-stained ceilings, and a communal bathroom. The furniture came with the rent and the other accoutrements of living were borrowed from Edna. Henrietta had nothing of her own but what she'd brought with her from England.

Would her parents be proud of the fact she knew how to pay rent, heat a pot of tea, buy food for herself, and work at a real job?

The clothes she'd brought from home hung on nails around the room. Clothes she couldn't remove or put on without Gert's help with the buttons up the back. Undergarments, washed in the sink down the hall, hung over a rope they'd found discarded in an alley. A thick layer of dust had settled on the top of the dresser, and dirt from her shoes—which needed a good shining—littered the floor.

"I don't even own a broom."

It was a silly statement, a minimal "don't have" compared to more striking needs, and yet it filled the room, demanding attention.

She was used to having others do things *for* her, take care *of* her, watch *over* her. Although she had survived in New York, she had not thrived.

Except where people were concerned.

She moved to the main room and sat on the window seat, peering out at the bustling street below. On her outing with Steven yesterday she'd mentioned being a country girl, needing to see trees and open spaces. He'd complied. Their stroll through Central Park was an afternoon she would never forget.

He is a man I will never forget.

Her own word choice suggested a separation, a parting. Distance. All would be true if she left New York and returned to Summerfield. She would never see Steven again.

She paused a moment, letting her feelings catch up with this possibility. Tears formed. "I will never see him again. Whatever we have will be cut short. Losing him is my punishment for lying."

The idea of hurting him propelled her to standing. "I can't stay. I can't face any of them with my lie and my failure to do as I promised. I *have* to leave!"

The force of the decision made her spring into action. She rushed to the bedroom and quickly packed all her clothes and toiletries into her two trunks.

Then she spotted the red maple leaf on the table. She reopened the smaller trunk and placed it between the pages of her Bible.

Henrietta had one more thing to do. She took out a paper and pencil and wrote a note:

To my dear, lovely friends,
    Forgive me for this quick departure. I have no other choice.
    I have deceived you. I did not come to America with my parents'
blessing. As such, I do not have access to their fortune.
    I made promises to all of you and to Unruffled that I cannot keep.
My humiliation and deception force me to return home in shame.
    Please forgive me. I wish you the greatest success and happiness.
    I love you all.

                                 Henrietta

She read it over one more time then reverently laid it on the table. She quickly wrote a smaller note to Gert, thanking her for her help. She folded it in half and inserted rent money for another two weeks that she'd recently drawn from her account.

Then she put on her traveling coat, her hat, and her gloves, and took up her purse. She still had enough cash to pay a hack to take her to the pier and would need to depend on the ticket agent accepting a bank draft to buy a passage home.

Once in Summerfield she would be a typical woman of society and never worry about money again.

❧

"Annie, would you set the table please?"

Annie was happy to oblige. These frequent dinners ala Edna were always welcome. Annie's cooking talents were minimal, and poor Sean—though uncomplaining—suffered for her lack. At Edna's he always had second helpings and ate to the point of a contented moan. After the baby was born she hoped to improve her skills. Yet with the store opening. . .all she could promise was that their child would not starve.

She spotted Edna and Steven at the stove, whispering over the stirring. Edna's previous questions about whether Henrietta could marry an American teacher had obviously led to some conspiring toward that end. Did Henrietta feel the same affection? Although they had spent time together yesterday at the workshop and had sat next to each other at church that morning, Annie had not had a chance to speak with her privately. Yet the couple's loving glances and soft touches spoke without words.

Edna turned away from the stove. "Dinner is ready. Where is Henrietta?"

"She's coming," Steven said. "We mentioned it again when we parted after church."

The mantel clock struck the half hour. "It's not like her to be late," Annie said.

"I'm famished," Sean said.

"I'm sure she's fine," Maude said, sneaking a carrot from the serving tray and handing one to Sean.

Vesta adjusted folded napkins under the forks. "Why don't you go check on her, Steven?" It was said with a wink.

"I'll go with you," Annie said. It would give her some private time to talk to him.

Steven took up his hat and they were out the door.

"We'll keep dinner warm," Edna called after them.

❧

"So it's that serious between you?" Annie asked Steven as they neared Henrietta's flat.

"On my side, yes."

Annie was glad he'd been open about his feelings.

"What does she feel?"

"I don't know for certain. But I believe she feels the same. I am in love, Annie. I've never felt like this before."

"Maybe you're just hungry, like Sean."

"Stop teasing. It's real. From the first time I met her, I knew it was different from any other meeting I'd ever had. It was not just a 'nice to meet you' moment, but an instant connection, as if I didn't care if I met any other woman after her."

"That's quite romantic," Annie said.

"Too much time teaching Byron and Browning I guess. Or Shakespeare. 'Did my heart love till now? Forswear it, sight, for I ne'er saw true beauty till this night.' That night."

Annie stifled a laugh. "My, my. You are wholly smitten."

"Wholly."

They reached Henrietta's building and went in, taking the stairs to her flat.

Steven knocked. "Henrietta? Are you home?"

There was no answer. Annie took a turn, though it was silly to think Henrietta would respond to her voice and not Steven's. "Please come to the door. You're late for dinner at Edna's."

A woman came out from the room across the hall. "If you's lookin' for Henrietta, she left. Took two trunks with her too."

"Left?"

"Just an hour ago. Had two chaps come up and carry down her things."

"Where was she going?"

"Didn't say. But somewhere far considering all the luggage."

This didn't make sense. Henrietta didn't know anyone else in New York—or in America beyond their small group. Which meant. . .

"She's going home."

Steven blinked, unbelieving. "But why? And why so suddenly?"

Annie's stomach clenched with nervous knots. "Did she leave a note?"

"I have a key," the woman said. "She left it with me to give to Gert."

"Let us in, please," Annie said.

They were let inside, and Annie immediately saw two notes. She took up the larger one and read it aloud to Steven.

"She doesn't have any money to invest in your business?" he asked.

"Apparently not." The full implications had to be set aside. It wasn't about money now. It was about Henrietta. "We need to stop her. We need to go to the pier."

"Which pier?"

Annie remembered their discussion about the White Star and Cunard lines. "Cunard."

"Let's go."

⚬⚬⚬

Henrietta was exhausted before she began. She'd had a hack pick her up, along with her luggage, and the driver had taken her to an agent who sold her a ticket to Southampton. Then he'd taken her to the Cunard pier, number 54. Although the ship would not leave until the next morning at noon, she had no choice but to wait.

The hack driver balked. "I'm not sure about leaving you in the waiting room with your trunks. There ain't no place to sleep here, miss."

"I don't need a place to sleep."

"I could take you to a nearby hotel like the Chelsea."

She didn't have money for a hotel. In fact, she'd paid for a second-class ticket home. At least they'd taken her bank note. Her father would know how to withdraw the rest of her money—what little there was of it.

The driver followed her into the terminal building. There were few people inside—for who would arrive a day early? She instructed the man to place her trunks along a wall, paid him, and thanked him for his help.

"Mind yourself, miss," he said with a tip of his hat. "And good journey."

As soon as he left, she sank upon the larger trunk. This would be her home for the next eighteen hours.

She nodded at a man who was sweeping the floor. And at a family with two children who were huddled near their belongings. It was clear they were curious about a woman traveling alone.

She scooted back on the trunk, using the wall for support. She supposed, if need be, she could use her carpetbag as a pillow and curl up to sleep.

Sleep was exactly what she craved. It was hard to fathom that just yesterday she had spent a lovely morning in Central Park with Steven and last evening she had been conned into giving up her grandmother's jewelry. Church, the police, and the decision to leave had consumed this day, leaving her here, alone, in a stale-smelling terminal awaiting a ship that would remove her from this failure and bring her home to suffer the consequences of her recklessness.

She sighed and closed her eyes, finally able to take a full breath for the first time all day. In this first moment of peace, her thoughts sped to the Lord.

Her eyes shot open. *I haven't prayed! Not once! Father, I'm so sorry. I went through all of this alone, without consulting You!*

She wondered if things would have been different if she *had* prayed. Would God have stopped her? Would she be having dinner at Edna's right now? Or. . .would she still be in Summerfield, married to Hank? Her on-again, off-again prayers created a long trail. Although she *had* offered up a few quick appeals, she rarely waited for God's reply but sped along on her own course, mindful only of what *she* wanted.

The realization made her snicker. No good had come out of those choices. She'd enjoyed an adventure to America and had experienced the pleasure of reuniting with Annie. But she had caused much harm by offering empty promises and winning a man's heart only to break it.

Henrietta bowed her head. *I am so sorry, Father. I mucked up everything. My impulsive nature got the best of me, as has my delusion that I am in control. I give You control. I need and want You to guide me from this moment on. Please direct me according to Your will.*

She opened her eyes and let out a sigh. *It is what it is. I cannot go back. I can only go—*

"Henrietta!"

She looked to her left and saw Steven rushing toward her. And Annie!

She slid off the trunk to standing. She was thrilled to see them, yet wanted to flee to avoid facing her hard truths.

Steven pulled her into his arms. "I'm so glad you're still here."

He's not mad?

Annie touched her hand. "Your neighbor let us in your flat. We saw your note. She said you had left with your luggage so we took a chance. . ." She smiled. "I am also glad we found you."

Henrietta pulled away from Steven's embrace and stepped back to create a space between them. "I lied to all of you. I have no money."

"I wish you would have told us," Annie said.

"I—I just wanted to help. The business was so exciting. I had never been involved in anything like that with everyone giving of themselves." She took a ragged breath. "Out of a desire to belong, I misspoke. And when I found out how much the rent was going to be and it was due tomorrow. . . I'm so sorry. I never should have come here."

"I'm glad you came," Annie said, taking her hands. "Forget the money. I am glad for your friendship."

"But we can't forget the money."

They had no response to that.

"I tried selling my grandmother's jewelry last night, but apparently I am too stupid to know a jeweler from a robber posing as a jeweler."

"What are you talking about?" Steven asked.

She told them the story of Cohen & Cohen. "So you see, I am not only a liar, I am a fool."

"You made a mistake. Your intentions were good."

"Such as they were."

Steven's eyes were full of compassion. And pity? She didn't want him to pity her.

"It's best I go home where I belong. Unruffled can get along without me."

"Probably," Steven said.

"What?" she said.

"Steven!" Annie said.

"She's right," he said. "Unruffled can get along without her." He stepped closer and put his hands upon her cheeks. "But I cannot."

At his touch, she felt lightheaded and totally under his influence.

He peered into her eyes, his own gaze intent. "Henrietta Kidd, would you stay here in America for my sake? We only met three weeks ago, and yet. . . I feel my heart would break if you left."

Her emotions took over, threatening happy tears. For she had feelings for him too. Although all logic told her it was right to leave, all emotions told her it was right to stay. Looking into his gentle eyes, she chose the latter. "I do not wish to be responsible for such breakage, for either of us."

He beamed. Then Steven gently lifted her chin and they shared their first real kiss. It was gentle yet firm, and full of promises. She wanted more, but a long embrace had to suffice. For now.

Henrietta heard a smattering of applause and saw the family and the others in the terminal sharing her joy.

Which was complete.

Annie opened the door of Edna's, swept in, and made a pronouncement. "Look who we found."

Edna rushed toward Henrietta. "Are you all right? We were worried."

"I was. . .delayed." She looked at Annie and Steven. Steven had told her she didn't need to share the details, and Henrietta had agreed.

At first.

But in the ride from the pier to her flat to drop off her trunks, and then to Edna's, Henrietta knew he was just trying to make her feel better. She *had* to tell. How else would she explain that she couldn't provide the money for the rent?

"And the truth shall make you free."

Free to face the consequences but also free to not have to worry about her friends finding out on their own. Her parents had always taught her it was best to own up to mistakes. Plus, amid the bad, they had good news to share. She smiled at Steven. His faced glowed with a joy that surely matched her own. Good with the bad. Such was life.

"We've kept dinner warm," Vesta said.

"Though the carrots look horribly wilted for the waiting," Maude said.

It was time. "Let's not delay Edna's delicious meal any longer."

Amid a flurry of culinary activity, everyone was seated. They held hands while Edna said the blessing. "Dear Father, thank You for bringing us together for this meal. Bless our relationships and this food. Amen."

Edna winked at Henrietta and smiled at her son. She must have sensed something had happened between them—been nurtured. Yet her confidence and support made Henrietta suffer a twinge of guilt. She hated to disappoint them on any level. But it was time.

"I feel privileged to once again share a delicious meal with all of you, but there is something I need to tell you."

Steven shook his head. "You don't have to."

"But I do."

They all looked at her with worry creasing their brows.

"I am thrilled to have found the friendship of such astonishing people." Her gaze lingered on Steven. "Honorable people."

"We like you too, dear," Edna said. "Very much."

Henrietta held up a hand. "But I have not been so honorable."

"You're too hard on yourself," Annie said softly.

Sean gave his wife a questioning look, confirming to Henrietta that it was best to get to the point.

She shook her head vehemently. "The degree of my sin can be judged by our Maker. But I must confess it to all."

"'Lantic Ocean, Henrietta," Maude said. "You certainly know how to get our attention."

She looked to Steven and gained strength by his reassuring expression. "Go on, dear lady," he said. "You've come too far to stop now."

Henrietta took a deep breath and let it out, along with the necessary confession. "I have no more money to give you. I left Summerfield without telling my parents. I've sent them letters, but I'm sure they don't approve of my exodus. They will not give me any funds. My money is gone. There is no more."

After the initial silent shock, there were questions, and the full truth was revealed in all its awful entirety—including her stupidity in trying to sell her jewelry to a thief. Finally spent, Henrietta sat back in her chair. "There it is. I apologize profusely." She hated the silence that settled over their uneaten dinner. "Say something. Please."

"We need the rent money tomorrow," Maude said.

That was the bulk of it. "I know. And I'm very sorry for it. Please forgive me."

"Of course we forgive you," Edna said. "And we are sorry for the loss of your great-grandmother's jewelry. How horrible for you. Plus, to think of what could have been. . .The man could have tied you up in the back with the Cohens and—"

"But he didn't," Maude said.

Though maybe he should have.

As was her nature, Annie was practical. "Maude, maybe you can talk to Mr. Ricci and postpone the payment a few days."

"Use your charm," Vesta said.

"You presume too much."

"To be blunt, delay will not solve the problem," Sean said.

Henrietta wished there was something she could do to help. "Could I speak with him? Tell him it's my fault, that you expected the money to be there, and I am to blame?"

"I see no benefit in that," Maude said. "He's a businessman. I made a promise to pay him tomorrow. *That* he respects."

Which means he wouldn't respect a liar like me.

The mood darkened as though the electric lights had dimmed. Had the light of their friendship dimmed?

Edna came around the table to hug Henrietta from behind. "Don't worry, dear girl. The circumstances are unfortunate but not insurmountable."

Maude huffed. "You have a stash of cash we don't know about?"

"No," Edna said, standing tall. "But God does. He knows our needs—He has provided for us at every turn. He will continue to do so. Our job is to—"

"Have faith," Sean said.

"Exactly." Edna waved her hands over them. "Come now. Bow your heads. Let's pray for His provision."

"And," Steven said, "thank Him for bringing Henrietta into my life."

"Into all our lives," Vesta said.

Henrietta heard Edna's heartfelt prayers, was humbled by them, and fervently added her own.

⌘

Henrietta returned home and found her trunks where they'd been placed after returning from the dock. Gert was not home yet from visiting her husband, the note and cash for rent still on the table.

She made a decision. If she worked quickly she could get all her clothes unpacked and back where they belonged. Gert had enough personal troubles without knowing about Henrietta's folly with the jewelry and nearly sailing back to England.

She'd just hung the last dress on a hook when the door opened.

"I'm back," Gert called out.

Henrietta tidied her hair then walked into the front room. "How did it go with Frankie?"

"Well enough." Gert placed her hat on a hook. "The devil can be quite the charmer when he tries."

"You didn't stay."

Gert fell onto a chair, clearly done in. "I did not—though he begged me to."

"Will you go back?"

"I's not sure. Going back home is the easy thing, but I's not sure it's the right thing."

Henrietta applied the sentiment to her own situation. "I agree."

"Do ye?"

"Sometimes we need to be brave."

Gert shrugged. "I donna feel brave."

Henrietta laughed. "Me either."

"But I am hungry. Do we have any of those apples left?"

CHAPTER EIGHTEEN

As expected, Cohen & Cohen was closed when Henrietta arrived the day after the theft. Actually, the brothers' absence reinforced her decision to come. She'd been told they lived above the store. She stood before the outer door and inhaled the fragrance of the flowers she'd purchased from a street vendor. The spicy autumn scent ignited her courage.

Yet she was unsure of protocol. She turned to Steven. "Do I knock here?"

He tried the door and found it unlocked. "As I expected, there are stairs inside. Let's go up and knock at the inner door."

They entered the narrow foyer and took the stairs that were dimly lit by a single bulb.

Henrietta hesitated. Although she'd often gone with her mother to visit people who were ill or injured in Summerfield, she'd known those people. To do the same with strangers she'd never even seen was odd. Yet she had to do it. For the three of them had shared an awful experience.

Upon knocking, an older woman answered, her gray hair pulled severely into a bun. "Yah?"

"My name is Henrietta Kidd. The thief who tied up the Cohens also stole some of my jewelry."

Her eyes cleared with recognition. "The girl."

"Yes. And this is my friend, Mr. Holmquist."

"Good morning, ma'am."

The woman studied them.

Not knowing what else to say, Henrietta held out the flowers. "Will you give the brothers these flowers for me? And tell them I am sorry for their—"

"Berta, let the girl in," came a voice from inside the flat.

Henrietta and Steven were led inside. Though the curtains were open, the flat was dark with drapings of heavy fabric over furniture and mantel.

From out of the dim came the voice again. "*Shalom*, Miss Kidd. It is good of you to come."

Once Henrietta's eyes adjusted she could make out two men, sitting with their backs to the windows, their feet propped on footstools, blankets covering their legs. They had long gray beards and wore spectacles.

"I wanted to see how you were," she said.

"Feh," said the older man.

The younger man—though still old—raised a hand to his brother's response. "Forgive Aaron, for he likes to *kvetsh*." He pointed at the woman. "And Berta has no manners. Offer them a chair, sister."

As the woman moved to do so, Henrietta declined. "We cannot stay. We have to get to work."

"Oy vey!" the older one said. "*Mishegoss*. Work with nothing. It's all gone."

"Shush, Aaron. Behave yourself. We have lived through worse than this. We will recover."

"I hope you do," Henrietta said. "In body and business." She gave the man the flowers.

"You are indeed a *mentsh*, Miss Kidd."

"Pardon?"

"An honorable person."

She began to shake her head but simply said, "Thank you."

"We are sorry you suffered too."

"I pray the police catch the man."

"As do we." He nodded to his brother, who managed a nod too.

"I'll leave you then," she said.

"*Kol tuv*," the man said. "Be well. And *hashem imachem*. May God be with you."

"And with you," she said.

Upon exiting the building the sunlight of the new day held extra warmth.

❦

I'm sorry, Mr. Ricci, but we have no money to pay the rent.

Maude rode the streetcar to meet him, the jostling of the vehicle worsening the condition of her knotted stomach. Vesta had told her to use her charm. It was the last thing she wanted to do. For there was too much of a spark between them to begin with. How was it possible to keep her distance yet use her charm at the same time?

When she entered the building that held his office, she was glad it was on the ground level. She wasn't sure she could find enough breath to climb stairs with her insides ajumble.

She was just about to go inside when he entered the building after her.

"My, my. The early bird catches the worm, Maude?" he said.

"I thought it best to come first thing." She stepped aside so he could unlock the door.

He swung it open for her. "The shop space is worth being eager about." He motioned to a chair near his desk. "Shall we proceed?"

She sat—because her legs required it—and immediately regretted the decision. She should have given him the bad news in the doorway so she could flee.

He studied her face. "What's wrong?"

Best to just state it plain. "We can't rent the space right now. We don't have the money."

He cocked his head as though uncertain he had heard her correctly. "You *had* the money on Friday."

"We had promise of the money. The one who promised has been forced to rescind her offer."

He sat back in his chair with a *huff.* "You have no other alternatives for funding?"

"None."

"I see."

She hastened to couch her directness with explanation. "We *will* be good for it but will not be receiving any income until after the store has opened."

"I see."

"We are nearly through creating the inventory. We hoped to be open in time for Christmas buying, perhaps soon after Thanksgiving."

"I—"

"Please don't say 'I see.'"

"What would you wish for me to say?"

She stood and began to pace the length of his desk. "I wish you didn't see. I wish it were not about dollars and cents. I wish I could say we'll find the money elsewhere, but we are all spent—physically, mentally, emotionally, and monetarily."

He smiled. "All that."

"The full of it."

He rested his elbows on the arms of his leather chair and tented his fingers, touching them to his lips. "Hmm."

She turned toward the door. "I am truly sorry for wasting your time. Perhaps this is God's way of delaying the opening of our store."

His eyebrows rose. "You believe that?"

"I don't. But some of the others do."

"You have no such certainty?"

"Who has certainty about the will of the Lord? I *certainly* have no such knowledge."

"If only we did. . ." His words seemed to apply to something else. He snapped out of his short reverie. "Let me see what I can do."

"Do?"

"Let me contact the landlord and see if the first payment can be delayed."

She couldn't believe her ears. "He would hold the property for us?"

"I will ask." He stood. "I will see you soon."

"Soon?"

He blinked then added, "I will contact you when I get a response."

She wanted to rush into his arms and embrace him for his kindness, but stood her ground near the door. "Thank you, Mr. Ricci."

"Antonio, remember?"

Ah yes. Antonio.

Stop it, Maude.

❧

Annie looked at her reflection in the full-length mirror, turning sideways. She smoothed her dress over her midsection, cupping her hands below. Baby was showing itself and could not be ignored. And it wasn't just her midsection that had changed. Her bosoms had grown large and her face puffy.

"Only a few more months, sweet baby."

The words gave her comfort but also filled her with panic. In only a few months she would be a mother—in addition to her other roles as wife, friend, and business partner. Her days were already overly full. How much more so would they be with a baby to attend to?

Sean came into the bedroom, adjusting his tie. "You look glorious."

"Chubby."

"Radiant."

She let him have the last say, for she knew he would never let her win an argument against herself—a trait she found endearing, though often exasperating. Sometimes a woman needed to wallow in pity, if only for a bit.

He stood behind, wrapping his arms around her. They looked at each other in the mirror. He kissed her ear then put a finger on the crease between her eyebrows. "What's this for?"

"You know very well what it's for."

"You shouldn't worry. We prayed about it."

She sighed and pulled his arms tighter around her waist. "Sometimes my faith is as weak as a second brew of tea. The rest of you are so strong, so sure He will come through for us."

"Name a time when He hasn't."

Her mind went blank.

"Exactly." He spun her around to face him. "He protected you when you left the employ of Henrietta's family. He led you to the Tuttles. He allowed you to get a job at Macy's and then Butterick. He brought you to me." He grinned. "And, He saved you from the *Titanic*—try to dispute that one."

"I can't."

"You can't dispute any of them, and I'm only naming the highlights." He took a fresh breath, gazing into her eyes, reaching her core as no one else could. "He loves you and has led you to this moment. He will not suddenly say, 'I think I am done with Annie Culver. Goodbye.'"

Sean was completely right. "Why do I waver? God has done so much for me, and yet I doubt."

Sean thought a moment, moving his gaze from her eyes to the air. "To have faith, have faith."

She scoffed. "It's that simple?"

He cocked his head, considering her question. "Yes."

"I want to believe as you do."

"Then do it. Believe."

"How?"

"Tell Him you trust Him. Then let Him do the rest. The more you say it, the more your words will become reality. God is not going to ignore you."

Annie loved the sound of that but still had her reservations. She thought of another flaw in her faith. "I thought He sent Henrietta to save us, to fund us."

"Maybe she's here for other reasons."

Annie remembered her friend's glowing face when Steven stopped her from sailing home to England. "She found Steven."

"And he, her." Sean pulled her into his arms. "Life is a grand puzzle, with pieces interlocking, pieces elusive, pieces missing. But in the end, God puts it all together and we see the full picture."

She lovingly touched his cheek. "God made you incredibly wise."

"Occasionally."

"Always."

"You may be right. Thank you."

She smacked his arm, her worries forgotten.

For now.

❧

Everyone stopped working when Maude returned from Mr. Ricci's. They looked at her with expectancy and hope. She wished she had more concrete news for them.

"What did he say about us not having the rent money?" Edna asked.

"He was quite understanding."

"Meaning?"

"He will talk to the landlord and see if the rent and deposit can be delayed."

The women hugged each other. But Maude raised a hand. "He will ask. Nothing is certain as yet."

Annie put a hand on her chest, as though calming the beating of her heart. "It is a reprieve. Since your meeting could have gone differently, I will accept the 'ask' as a blessing."

Maude hung up her coat and unpinned her hat. But then her hat hung in midair between head and hook.

"Is there something else?" Annie asked.

Vesta grinned. "Did the subject of your meeting veer from business issues to those of a more personal nature?"

"Not like you think." *Although they could have.* Maude placed her hat on the hook. "We talked about God."

"Making it *not* your usual business meeting," Henrietta said.

Maude shrugged. "His name was mentioned. That's all." *And His will. Whatever that is.*

"Mr. Ricci's ability to look beyond the numbers to the divine makes me like him even more," Edna said.

She should never have brought it up. "All of you must stop this. If I said he was wearing a purple plume in his hat, you would find reason for liking him more."

"Not purple," Vesta said. "Perhaps blue. . ."

Annie seemed to remember something then retrieved a note. "From your mother."

Maude broke the seal.

Come to dinner Wednesday night at seven. Hans and I look forward to seeing you.

Love, Mother

"What's she say?"

"She's invited me to dinner."

"How nice of—"

She tossed the note into the trash bin. "I'm not going."

"Why not?" Edna asked.

It was hard to explain. They had reconciled. There was no reason she shouldn't go, and yet. . .

"You're not upset with her for being unable to fund us, are you?" Annie asked.

"No, of course not. You know I never asked. It was clear she had no money."

"She was kind to you," Annie said. "All that was between you was repaired, was it not?"

If you mean that I told her about the rape, yes. "I suppose."

"Then why not fully rekindle your relationship?" Edna asked. "As a mother I can't imagine the pain I would endure if Steven pulled away from me."

"She *is* making an effort," Vesta said. "That's worth effort on your part."

"She's remarried." As soon as Maude said the words she realized how petty they sounded.

"So you want her to grieve your father all her life?"

"No, of course not." *Though I do.*

"Meaning, you want her to be happy," Henrietta said.

"It's just a dinner. You owe it to her to try and—"

"Enough!" Maude said. "Between matching me up with Mr. Ricci and repairing my family life, you all have far too many opinions."

"That's what friends are for," Annie said with a smile.

"Interfering?"

"Only if necessary." Edna gave her a motherly look. "So…are you going?"

"As if I have a choice?"

The women clapped. Unfortunately, Maude did not feel like celebrating.

⁓

Annie stood back and gazed at the rack of newly made dresses. "We're nearly finished."

Edna plucked a string from the sleeve of a blue serge jacket. "Gert and Ginny will finish up the last of this design by evening. Then we will have two of each size."

"But is that enough?" Vesta asked. "What if three women, who are the same size, want the same dress? What do we do then?"

"We make them one," Annie said, though she knew this *was* an issue. "We will have to keep a tight inventory list so we know which dresses need to be in production."

Henrietta called to the seamstresses, hard at work in the other room. "You two are going to be extremely busy. Continually busy."

"We don't mind," Gert said.

"We don't," Ginny said. "My son needs new boots for the winter. I needs the wages."

The mention of the workers' needs added to Annie's constant burden, but she remembered Sean's simple formula: to have faith, have faith. She said a quick prayer, *Provide, Lord. Provide for us all.*

There was a knock on the door to the workshop. "Come in," Annie said.

Mrs. Sampson swept into the room with a rush of exuberance that unsettled the air itself. "Hello, my dear ladies!"

It took Annie a moment to acknowledge her presence. "Eleanor. Hello."

Eleanor kissed Annie's cheeks. "Hello? That's all the greeting I get?"

Annie forced herself fully into the moment. "How nice to see you."

"That's better. For it is very nice to see all of you."

Annie noticed a sash strung diagonally across her chest: VOTES FOR WOMEN. "You are a suffragette?"

She flung her fist into the air and called out, "Votes for women!"

The others were taken aback.

"Come, ladies. Don't look so appalled. Tomorrow is Election Day. Don't you wish you could vote?"

"I'm not a citizen," Annie said.

"Then become one!" Mrs. Sampson turned to the others. "But you ladies, you should be champing at the bit to make your voice heard."

"I do like Teddy Roosevelt," Maude said. "He's feisty."

"But he's been president twice already and didn't win the Republican nomination from President Taft," Vesta said. "He's a rabble-rouser. He didn't get what he wanted so he started his own party—which has little chance."

"He's better than Eugene Debs," Edna said. "He's a socialist."

"I'm a Woodrow Wilson fan myself," Eleanor said. "I know it took forty-six ballots at the convention to choose him as our candidate, but let me assure you, if women had been allowed to participate, we would have wrapped it up in the first ballot." She shook her head in tiny bursts. "Men seem to like brouhaha and drama."

And you don't? Annie kept the opinion to herself. "I'm impressed you ladies know so much, especially when you can't vote."

"It's our duty to be in-the-know," Eleanor said. "What leg do we have to stand on, asking to vote, if we show ourselves ignorant?"

Henrietta looked at Eleanor, rapt. Annie realized they had never been introduced. "Eleanor, I would like you to meet Henrietta Kidd. Henrietta, this is Mrs. Sampson."

Eleanor studied her a short moment then her face became animated. "I saw you before! At the House of Paquin in Paris!" She looked at Annie then back to Henrietta. "Annie used to be your maid, yes?"

"That is correct."

Mrs. Sampson made herself at home on a stool. "Did you come all the way to New York to lure her back into your employ? For I don't think that is ever going to happen. We won't let it happen."

"I came to America to celebrate Annie's new life, and be a part of it."

Annie knew Henrietta's wounds of humiliation were still raw, so she wrapped an arm around her shoulders. "We are partners."

Eleanor blinked. "Partners?"

Annie immediately regretted using that term, but there was no delicate way to back out of it. Instead she changed the conversation to Eleanor's favorite subject—herself. "How is Eleanor's Couture doing?"

"What?"

"Your design house?"

Eleanor brushed the words away with a hand. "I've moved on. Women's rights is my new passion."

"But you adore fashion. You were the one who inspired me. . .us. . ."

"I still adore fashion but will leave the designing to those who have the talent for it. Harold helped me see that my efforts could be more beneficial to women in regard to rights rather than ruffles. Or no ruffles."

Edna spoke up. "We are opening a shop called Unruffled."

"Really."

She nodded and added the tagline, "Fashion for the Unruffled, Unveiled, Unstoppable Woman."

Eleanor clapped, her gloves creating muted sounds of affirmation. "Very nice, ladies. I approve."

Annie was surprised at the compliment and the fact she felt relief at hearing it. She'd thought she was past needing such a thing. She and Mrs. Sampson had parted ways, and none too amicably.

Eleanor fingered a remnant of narrow corded trim. "Not as fancy as I brought you."

Was that why she'd come back? Annie rushed into the second bedroom and returned with a box of fancy trims. "You may have them back," Annie said. "I should have returned them to you immediately. I apologize."

Eleanor picked up a hank of fringe. "These were purchased on a lark. I see now that they do not suit your aesthetic."

My aesthetic. So she was truly letting go of her own design ideas?

Eleanor shoved the box an inch away and sighed. "Where is Sean?"

"At work."

"I would like to see him. Perhaps another time."

There would be another time?

"When does the store open?"

The partners exchanged glances. "We'd hoped to open in a month, to take advantage of the Christmas season."

"You seem uncertain."

An idea shot into Annie's thoughts. *Really, Father? This is Your doing?* Her heartbeat quickened. "We have a lovely space to rent but ran out of funding. We are delayed until that is remedied." *Come now, Eleanor. . .reveal your generous nature.*

"Funding, you say?" She examined a spot on her glove. "Why didn't you come to us? You know we would be happy to help."

Annie nearly laughed at her friends' communal expulsion of air.

"You'd do that?" Edna asked.

"I don't see why not."

Annie clapped a hand over her mouth. She was torn as to whether or not she should point out that it was Eleanor who had withdrawn their monetary support after the fashion show or ignore that salient fact because *she* seemed to be ignoring it.

As if reading her mind, Eleanor said, "Yes, it is true that I revoked our interest in your venture, Annie—when you ignored my suggestions." She shoved the box of trim another inch. "When my friends didn't place any orders, my pride was sorely wounded." She looked Annie directly in the eye. "I took it out on you, my dear. Wrongly on you."

The burden that had sat heavily on Annie's shoulders slipped off, leaving her able to breathe.

"Do you forgive me?" Eleanor asked.

The timeline since Eleanor's withdrawal sped through Annie's mind: the initial panic, seeking money with Sean's father, Maude's mother, and finally Henrietta's sudden appearance outside the workshop window. That Henrietta's funds had proved not enough just a few days ago. . .that they had prayed for God's providence and provision just last evening. . .

Annie's legs gave out, and Vesta helped her onto a stool. "Are you all right? Is the baby all right?"

She assured them she was fine. "I'm just overwhelmed by your offer. It comes at a time when it is sorely needed."

Maude was more clear. "We need funds today to secure the shop space."

Eleanor nodded, as though unsurprised. But then she shook her head. "I will not proceed until you answer my question. Do you forgive me?"

"Of course I do." Annie rose and the two women embraced, the tension of their past parting evaporating.

Eleanor pulled back first and touched Annie's cheek. "I've missed you."

"I've missed you too. If not for your belief in me, I would still be at Butterick."

She returned the compliment with a nod. Then, in usual Eleanor fashion she said, "How much do you need?"

⸎

Maude stood before the telephone in the hall. *Should I or shouldn't I?*

After hearing the good news from Mrs. Sampson, Maude struggled with wanting to race to Antonio's office to tell him in person versus calling him on the telephone. Both would be satisfying, but the former would be more pleasant.

And yet not so, because whenever she was with him she found herself in a battle against herself, wanting to fully indulge in the nearness of him while trying to heed warnings to retreat lest their hearts be broken when their parting proved inevitable. For he did act as though he wished to see her beyond business.

Maude didn't have that much experience with good men—and one horrible experience with a very bad one—so she didn't know if he was simply being charming or showing true interest. Or was he just being Italian? Being of Italian descent herself, she knew that men of that upbringing were taught to make women feel more pretty, more delightful, and more desirable than they actually were. Some used this skill for foul ends, but most were pleasant to be around. For who didn't like to feel better about themselves?

Her father had used this aptitude to earn himself a position on the diplomatic corps where he made those in power feel more able, strong, and yes, even more desirable than they were. When he and Maude's mother would have soirees in their foreign homes, Maude would be banished upstairs with the nanny, but through her own ability to charm, would be allowed to watch the festivities from the upstairs hallway, peeking through the railings. If Mother saw her, she would send a stern glare her way, and with a subtle flick of her hand, Nanny would be instructed to take Maude back to her bedroom. But if Father saw her. . .he would smile or twirl his mustache or wink at her—or all three, which let them enjoy the shared moment. And occasionally he would invite her down to meet the guests, and rarer still, ask her to sing for them.

Although the pain of losing him had eased, occasionally she suffered an ache that threatened to eat her from the inside out. When she'd been assaulted she'd been glad he wasn't there to witness her humiliation and shame. She knew the assault hadn't been her fault, she knew she shouldn't feel those emotions, but they were real, and it had taken a long time to bury them. She was doubly glad he hadn't been around to witness the doctor's prognosis that she could never have children. For her father had often spoken of the joy he would feel pampering her children, as he had pampered her. Perhaps God had taken him before his time to save him from the anger, pain, and consequences of her experience.

"What do I do, Papa?"

She felt a sudden need to simplify, to avoid anything that would complicate her already complicated life.

She picked up the phone.

Annie adjusted the fork next to the plate, just so. Then she moved the vase of flowers an inch to the right. Dinner was ready to be served as soon as Sean got—

She heard him at the door before he opened it. She did the honors herself, startling him. The hug and the kiss added to the surprise.

"My, my, Annie-girl. If I didn't know better I'd think you were about to tell me you were expecting."

She drew him into the room and showed him the kitchen table. "I made chicken, potatoes, and green beans, and bought some bread and boysenberry preserves."

"Now I am doubly curious. What are we celebrating?"

She'd thought about how to tell him. One word seemed to sum it up best. "Freedom."

"From...?"

"Financial worries."

His eyes widened. "Henrietta got her jewelry back?"

"No, I mean, I don't think so."

"Did you rob a bank?"

She scoffed. "Stop it. Let me talk!"

He sat on a kitchen chair and pulled her onto his lap. "There," he said, kissing her again. "Now I'm ready to hear your news."

Finally! "We had a visitor in the workshop today."

"If you're waiting for me to guess, you need to give me some clues."

"It was a she."

He considered this a moment. "Most of the 'shes' I know already work there."

"She lives across from a cathedral."

"Mrs. Sampson?"

"In the flesh."

She could see by the flash in his eyes that he was putting it together, but she wanted the moment to linger a bit. "She's a suffragette now."

"One of those marching ladies with the signs?"

"She didn't have a sign with her, but she *was* wearing a sash that said, 'Votes for Women.'"

"With the election tomorrow, she's probably very busy."

The subject of voting caused Annie to allow a detour to the conversation. "What do you think about that? About women voting?"

"I'd be excited if you could vote."

"But I know nothing about the candidates other than what I've heard the ladies say."

He nuzzled her cheek. "But if you had the right to vote, you would learn. I know you, Annie; you would not vote just to vote."

"I wouldn't. I would take the right seriously."

"As you should."

"Who are you going to vote for?"

"Wilson."

"Why?"

"Taft is too timid. A good-enough president is not good enough anymore. Times are changing, and I fear he will not change with them."

"Roosevelt seems strong. He was shot yet still gave a speech."

"A definite show of strength—physical strength."

"And determination."

"Agreed. But that doesn't necessarily translate into making good, presidential decisions."

"But—"

He nodded toward the neatly set table. "You did not make this delicious— what I hope is a delicious—dinner to talk of politics. You said Mrs. Sampson stopped by?"

Annie stood, needing to fully see his reaction when she told him the good news. "She will fund our shop!"

He blinked, clearly surprised. "What happened to Eleanor's Couture?"

"She bodged it."

"Without you to help."

Annie shook her head vehemently. "We never sang the same song."

"And now you're singing a duet?"

Annie shrugged, unable to say yes with full honesty. "She has forgiven and forgotten. As have I."

"And she's found a new passion in the vote."

"That too."

"So how much is she going to give us?"

Annie grinned. "Whatever we need."

"Oof, Annie-girl. I am impressed. That *is* a good reason to celebrate."

Annie needed to get even more serious. "We prayed about it, Sean. Just last night. And today God sent her back to us."

"With a full purse."

"With a full and willing purse." She sat on his lap again. "Why would He do that for us?"

"Because He is very generous."

"But I'm sure other people prayed for help, prayed for bills to be paid, prayed for His intervention, and He told them no. Why are we receiving His blessings? Why *have* we received His blessings, time after time?"

"That is the question of the ages. God's ways cannot be fully explained, for He sees the big picture while we only see a small slice."

"But some people suffer so badly. Why does He let them suffer when He could release them from pain in the blink of an eye?"

He stroked her cheek with the back of his hand. "I don't know."

"Who does?"

He laughed gently. "No one. But even in the dark times, He is there. And in the good times we need to be good stewards of the blessings."

"I've tried not to be extravagant with the expenses and—"

"Being good stewards goes beyond money. You've given people employment, a sense of purpose, a goal, and a sense of family. You should be proud of yourself."

She was proud. But she also felt very humbled. "Thank you."

He flicked the tip of her nose. "We need to thank *Him* for what He's done for us and trust Him for the rest. We need to have faith that His way is the best way."

"Because. . . ?"

"He is God and we are not." He gently pushed her to her feet. "Now let's eat. Your good news has made me famished."

⊗

Vesta had invited herself over to Edna and Maude's for dinner, wanting to give Annie and Sean some time alone. As the ladies ate and chatted—Edna and Maude chatted—Vesta felt oddly removed. As though she were there, but not.

It was noticed.

"Vesta?" Edna waved a hand in front of her face. "Are you in there?"

"Sorry."

"Surely we aren't boring you." Maude shook her head vigorously. "No, that's not possible. Maude Nascato is never boring."

"No, you're not. Neither of you."

"Then what's wrong?"

After feeling melancholy most of the afternoon, Vesta *had* determined the cause of her mood. "Everyone has someone to share with. We had great news today with the Sampsons funding us again. And I have no one to share it with."

"When was the last time you called Richard?" Edna asked.

"A better question is, when was the last time he took my call?"

"And?"

"Two weeks ago. He had a question about whether he should order ornamental hair combs for the store anymore—were they still in style? I said he should. Until women cut their hair—which they never will do—women will like the pretty combs."

"At least he asked your opinion," Maude said.

"He didn't need my opinion. He buys what he wants to buy."

"Then he used it as an excuse to talk with you."

She shrugged and moved a potato from left to right on her plate. "He didn't ask anything about me, about how I was."

"Did you ask how he was?"

She hesitated. "Well, no."

Maude took Vesta's fork and laid it down on the table. "You need to speak to one another. Absence does not always make the heart grow fonder." She cocked her head. "Or does it?"

"I do miss him. Our marriage was far from perfect, but it was ours."

"Then go home to him," Edna said. "A marriage is nothing to be dallied with. You made your point; you took your stand. Surely he's accepted that you're involved in our business by now."

"There is no *surely* about anything regarding Richard. He is not easily swayed."

Edna reached across the table and took her hand. "You are a great help to this company, Vesta, but no business should cause the loss of a marriage."

"Why don't you call him again?" Maude suggested. "Maybe he'll surprise you."

"I'm not sure I'm up to being rejected again. One time, two times, twelve times. . .each time the pain begins anew."

"I'm so sorry," Edna said. "I don't know what else to say."

There was nothing more anyone could say.

⸎

After sharing an evening walk, Henrietta and Steven reached her building. "Would you like to come up for a bit?" she asked.

"You don't have to ask. Besides, I have something to show you."

Inside the vestibule, Henrietta checked her mail. "I never get anything, but I can always hope." Yet there was a letter inside. "It's from my mother!"

She began to open it right there, but Steven suggested they go upstairs. "You've received a letter from them before now, haven't you?"

"I haven't. I've sent them more than one, but they've never responded."

Once they were settled inside she hesitated opening it. "What if they're angry? What if they want nothing more to do with me?"

Steven did not give her the easy answer. "Then you concentrate on the family you have here."

It was large compensation, but was it enough?

He touched her arm. "Open it. No matter what they say, I am here."

Henrietta nodded and said a silent prayer, wishing God could change their angry words to words of understanding. She stood, needing privacy. "Excuse me a moment."

She opened the letter and read silently.

Dear Etta,

We are glad to hear you are well, but we are angry that you put us through so much worry. We try to understand your reasons for going. You say that ending your relationship with Hank was not the cause of your departure, and after speaking with your grandmother, I can see the truth that he was not for you. But that does not mean there isn't some other fine man in your future.

She paused to look across the room at the man sitting patiently before her. He was definitely a fine man. But not a man of her family's social standing. What would her parents think of Steven Holmquist, a schoolteacher? Would they accuse him of showing interest because of her family's money or title? What would they think of her dilapidated flat? What would they think knowing she had used up most of her money to survive and had wanted to give more of it to Annie—who used to be their housemaid?

"Are you all right?" Steven asked quietly, as he put something in his pocket.

She nodded and continued to read.

Although Annie Wood left our family's service unceremoniously—taking advantage of our trip to New York — I do admire what she has accomplished. I also understand how her drive and gumption could inspire someone who is searching for their own special place in the world.

So we understand, Etta. Reluctantly. But we also worry. I have contacted our New York cousins to tell them you might be contacting them. I have not given them your address, for I know their penchant for interference and do not want them to interrupt your journey of discovery unless you choose to involve them.

Be safe, my darling. Be happy. And know that we are here for you in all ways, for always.

Your loving Mother and Father

She let tears flow freely and went to Steven's side, letting him take her into his arms.

"Oh, dear lady. Don't cry. I'm sure they'll come around."

She spoke into his shoulder. "They have come around. It's a wonderful letter."

He pushed back to look at her. "So these are happy tears?"

She nodded and added a laugh. "All my worries were for nothing."

He gave her his handkerchief, and she wiped her eyes. "I have another bit of happiness for you." He pulled out the photograph from the park. "It turned out quite nicely, I think."

Her fear about looking away as the photo was taken was unfounded. Steven was looking directly at the camera, with Henrietta looking aside. But it was still a fine picture. "We look quite smashing."

"We do. And we are."

CHAPTER NINETEEN

Although they all would have liked to immediately cement the deal on their shop space after the Sampsons' offer, they had to delay a day. Election Day demanded Mrs. Sampson's attendance at key polling places. Annie wondered if the Votes for Women protests did any good, but she did admire Eleanor for trying, for making her voice heard. She was told it was the American way and a right that was not to be discarded easily. Or abused.

Sean was happy with the election, for Woodrow Wilson was declared the winner by a landslide. It was the first time in history that a seated president—Taft—had come in third place. Bull Moose Teddy Roosevelt had claimed second.

With the election and its protests behind them, the ladies—including Gert and Ginny—stood before the building that would become Unruffled. Sean had taken off work to be there for the occasion.

Mr. Sampson held the keys he had procured from Mr. Ricci that morning after paying the necessary rent and deposit. "Shall we?"

His wife plucked the keys from his hand. "No, Harold. *We* shall not unlock the door." She gave the keys to Annie. "It is yours to open, my dear."

Annie took the keys, her emotions full with the immensity of this moment. If she'd been alone she might have lingered in order to revisit the steps along her journey, but the others were waiting, their excitement palpable.

She unlocked the door, and they streamed in like sheep through an opened gate. Although they'd seen the shop before, to see it now, after they had lost it. . .such victory over hardship created a new enthusiasm. She reveled with them, for their excitement matched her own. She immediately began to see beyond what was there, into what the shop could be and would be in just a few short weeks. "It's beautiful," she whispered.

"As are you," Sean whispered back.

She took his arm, leaning her cheek against his shoulder. "Did you ever imagine this would really happen?"

"Absolutely," he said. "And so did you."

"Perhaps. But to actually walk in the space, touch its walls, look through its window. . ." She glanced at said window. "I'd like the name to be painted on the glass, so people can see it as they walk by on the sidewalk."

"I like that idea. I'm sure Mr. Ricci knows of someone who has that talent."

Maude interrupted to make a pronouncement. "With the cash register here, this will be the counter to take payment."

"Maybe we should use the glass display case for accessories?" Vesta said.

The thought of coming up with accessories seemed too much. And yet. . .

Annie stepped outside to confirm her memory. She came back in. "In this immediate vicinity there is a milliner; a shoe store; and a store with jewelry, gloves, and other accessories. What if we speak with these shop owners and see if they would like to display their wares in Unruffled?"

"If a customer was interested we could send business their way," Maude said.

"Perhaps they could display a few of our dresses with *their* products?" Edna asked.

"And send people to Unruffled to purchase them," Mrs. Sampson said. "What a marvelous idea!"

Just then, Annie looked out the window and saw a man peer inside then step away as though not wanting to be seen. *No. It couldn't be.* She went outside to confirm her sighting. "Richard?"

He stopped walking and turned around, his face red. "Hello, Annie."

"What are you doing here?" She couched her question. "I mean, you are very welcome but. . .would you like to see our new store?"

He nodded and followed her inside.

"Look who I found."

Vesta gasped and ran to him. Annie could tell she wanted to draw him into an embrace, but Vesta stopped short. Instead, she merely put a hand upon his arm. "Richard. I'm so glad to see you."

Oddly, Mr. Sampson was the next to greet him. "Glad you could make it, Richard."

"You two know each other?" Vesta asked.

"Of course we do," Mr. Sampson said. "We both belong to the same business club."

"I didn't know that," Vesta said.

"We ran into each other at the last meeting a few weeks ago," Richard said. He kept turning his hat in his hands like a nervous beau.

Mr. Sampson slapped Richard on the back. "He told me about your business, and your dire need." He looked at Annie. "This was before we stepped back into your life."

Richard interjected. "I'd been told the Sampsons were funding you, but then they withdrew." He looked at Annie and Vesta. "You said as much when you came to our house and asked. . ." He didn't mention Vesta's inheritance or his refusal to give her the money.

"Richard and I got to talking, which made me realize that our recusal had been the cause of your financial difficulties, and so—"

Mrs. Sampson took over. "Harold came to me and suggested we get back in the fashion business."

So that's why you suddenly showed up at the workshop?

Vesta's eyes were full of happy tears. "You did that for us, Richard?"

He cleared his throat, obviously uncomfortable with the attention. "Despite what you all think, I do not want your venture to fail."

You could have fooled me.

Sean shook his father's hand. "Thank you for intervening. It is much appreciated." He looked at his mother. "We all appreciate it."

Vesta ignored her previous restraint and wrapped her arms around him. He blushed at the public display of affection.

"Why don't you show Richard the neighborhood, Vesta?" Annie suggested.

Her face lit up. "Thank you. I will."

As the couple left, Mr. Sampson nodded in their direction. "I didn't know there was any dissension between them."

"Hopefully what was, is no more," Annie said.

Mrs. Sampson reached into the bag she had been carrying and pulled out a box. She handed it to Annie. "For you."

Annie removed the lid and found stacks of cloth labels embroidered with *Unruffled*.

"They're to sew into the neckline of each dress," Eleanor explained.

Annie was genuinely moved and embraced them both. "I'd thought about getting labels but had deemed it a luxury since we had more basic needs. Though we *have* sewn a hand-printed tag into each side seam, marking its size."

"Very wise," Eleanor said. "As for the Unruffled tag? It's advertising. Women need to remember where they bought their favorite dress, don't they?"

Annie set aside the labels and took the hand of each Sampson. "This gift is so thoughtful, and yet my gratitude extends to so much more. To not have to worry about money...it is such a relief."

Mr. Sampson squeezed her hand and gave her a wink. "Do it up right, Annie."

❦

Vesta walked beside Richard, pointing out the different shops. "Annie thinks the merchants could promote each other's stores by displaying their wares—"

"It's a good idea," he said. "You can complement each other."

Like we *can complement each other?* Vesta wished she could say it, but it seemed presumptuous.

But then Richard said the words. "*We* complement each other. Or we did."

"We could again."

He offered her his arm, and her stomach danced happily.

"I've missed you," he said.

For him to say it first was memorable. His admission deserved her own. "I've missed you too. So much."

"I apologize for avoiding your calls. Your leaving upset the balance of my life, a balance I never thought *could* be upset. After nearly three decades..."

"Things change. Circumstances change. We change."

"I don't take change well."

"I know." He seemed a bit taken aback by her honesty, but she had come too far to speak placating words just to make him feel better. "You should never have locked me in my room. That was unconscionable."

"I know. It is a large regret. But again, my balance was tipping too far to one side. I panicked."

"Your admission means a lot to me. But...do you understand why I had to leave?"

"I've tried to."

"If you would have talked *with* me, not *at* me. . ."

She felt his arm tighten. She'd gone too far.

"You are here now," Vesta said. "And I am glad for it. And thankful that you chose to help us as you did."

"All I did was speak to Mr. Sampson. It's his money. If I were a really good person I would have paid the money myself. I would have let you have access to your inheritance." He stopped walking and faced her. "I know that the law says your money is mine, that you have none of your own, but that doesn't make it right." He let out a breath. "I was wrong, Vesta. And I'm sorry for it. I want you to come home."

She blinked a moment, startled at his words. Then she threw her arms around his neck and kissed him.

Embarrassed, he pushed her back. "Vesta, really."

"I can't help that I'm happy."

He smiled for the first time and touched her cheek. "I am happy too."

They began to walk again, but this time Vesta was the one to stop their progress. "One more thing. A condition, if you will."

"What is it?"

"I want to continue to be a part of this business. The shop. I *am* helping. The work fills me in a way that I can't give up. I enjoy being a part of something special, something new. And I especially enjoy being near Annie and Sean every day. With the baby coming. . ."

"She looks well."

"She is. But it will get harder for her in the coming months, and then afterward, with the baby born. . .our grandchild, Richard. I want to be a part of the baby's life, every day."

"But we live in Brooklyn."

"Baines can drive me and bring me home every night. Or you could take me and visit the baby too."

"And leave the store?"

He was so single-minded. "For a few hours, my dear. After all these years if it cannot function without you for that length of time, then you have not trained your employees well."

"It can run well enough."

"Well then." She couldn't help but beam. The world was right again.

And balance was returned.

❦

Richard strolled through the empty shell that was Unruffled. "I agree with your idea of the counter to use for payment, but you also need ancillary display cases, perhaps smaller, to get people to move throughout the store, into every corner."

"That's a fabulous idea," Vesta said, even though they'd already thought of it.

Annie loved how Vesta had returned from their private talk on Richard's arm. She hadn't had time to speak with her alone yet, but by the glow in her mother-in-law's cheeks she expected good news.

Richard stepped off the width of the store. "Twenty-four, give or take. Not a bad size. How many different dresses do you have?"

"Twelve different dress. Each in eight sizes. Two of each. One hundred ninety-two, all told," Annie said.

"Twelve is a good start. You'll need racks."

"I know," Sean said. "Where do you get your store fixtures made?"

"I haven't had cause for new ones in years, but I used Wilson & Company. I will give you their information. Tell them I sent you. They will treat you fairly."

From naysayer to encourager. How extraordinary.

❦

Sean and Richard climbed the stairs to Annie and Sean's flat. Annie purposely lagged behind with Vesta. "Are you sure you are ready to move back home?"

"I am. Richard has changed."

Annie was doubtful. "Are you sure?"

"No."

Annie stopped her on a stair. "Then don't go. Wait until you're sure."

Vesta shook her head. "One thing I've learned after nearly thirty years is that marriage involves give and take. And it's rarely equal. But when the balance tips too far, changes must be made."

"Are you glad you left?"

"I am. For I believe it forced a change for the better."

"But will it hold fast?"

"We will have to find a new balance. I'm ready to work on that. Neither one of us is without flaw. The point is, we love each other. What God has joined together let no man put asunder."

Annie pulled her into an awkward embrace, balancing on the stairs.

Life was all about keeping one's balance.

⸺⸙⸺

Vesta carefully folded a white blouse and placed it in her carpetbag. She snapped the clasp shut. "There it is. I am ready to go now."

Richard nodded toward the bag. "That's all the luggage you have?"

"It is."

"When we travel, you pack trunks full of clothes."

"I didn't have time to pack trunks. I made do with two outfits, a nightgown, and other necessities." Vesta stood straighter. "I'm rather proud of myself for surviving on so little."

Richard eyed the sofa. "You slept there, all this time?"

"I was quite comfortable."

She would have been more comfortable at home if you would have been nice to her. Annie handed Vesta her straw hat. "We will miss you."

"I'm coming back every day."

"I know. It's just. . ." Annie couldn't find the right words and was about to say, *let us know if you need us* but realized the words might do more harm than good. "See you tomorrow then."

Vesta hugged her and then her son, adding a kiss to his cheek. "Thank you for being there for me, Sean. I will never forget it."

And then they were gone.

Annie leaned against the door, spent. "I knew she wasn't staying forever, but. . ."

"I know." Sean sat on the sofa and patted the space beside him. "Her departure came unexpectedly."

Annie snuggled under his arm. "I find it hard to believe your father was the one who got the Sampsons to fund us again."

"His bark is worse than his bite."

"But he was adamantly against us from the beginning."

"I do think Mother leaving was the impetus for his change of heart. If she had stayed with him, I doubt any of this would have happened."

"We would be without Vesta working for us."

"We would be without the Sampsons' money."

"Which means we wouldn't be renting the storefront."

"Or ordering new fixtures from Wilson & Company."

"God works in very mysterious ways."

"He does," Sean said. "He took something bad and brought good out of it. He amazes me."

"Me too." Annie sat upright. "You do like the store, don't you?"

"I think it will be everything you hoped it would be."

"You too," she said. "You had hopes for it too."

He pressed a finger to her forehead. "But you're the one who had the vision for it."

She found her snuggle place again. "We are so lucky."

"Blessed, Annie. God does not deal with luck but with blessings."

❧

Maude's thoughts jostled with the movement of the streetcar. She was not looking forward to this evening. When she'd first contacted her mother, wanting to ask her for money, they had made a tenuous reconnection. Her mother had said, "We shall have to have you over for dinner." But when Maude had received the recent invitation, she'd wanted to decline.

But why?

One dinner won't hurt.

She knew her attitude was unbecoming and mostly illogical. She reminded herself that it had been she—Maude—who had pulled away from their bond.

That her mother had so kindly accepted and forgiven Maude only heightened her turmoil. Her confusion made little sense, but she couldn't seem to shake it away.

She was just stepping off the streetcar when she heard—felt?—some inner words, not of herself: *Me. Ask Me for help.*

"Miss? Excuse me?"

She'd stopped on the last step, barring other people's exit. She moved out of the way, the words lingering. Was "me" God?

Don't be silly, Maude. Why would God speak to you—about this?

She shoved aside the inner promptings, walking with her head down until she entered her mother's building.

Her mother greeted her with open arms and a warm embrace. "It's so good to see you, Maudey. Come in, come in."

Hans also drew Maude into an embrace. "*Velkommin*, Maude." His German accent was thick, yet rather charming. "Come. Sit."

But as she entered the parlor, there was another guest present.

"Antonio!"

"Good evening, Maude."

Maude looked to her mother, needing an explanation. As soon as they were seated she received one.

"Hans ran into Antonio the other day, and he said you had chosen a property to rent for your store."

"Yes, but—"

Antonio smiled. "I am so pleased you found someone to help with the rent discrepancy. When Mr. Sampson came to my office yesterday to pay. . .I would have liked to have seen *you*."

His smile was so infectious, Maude had to look away.

"I am glad everything turned out as it did," he said.

"So are we." Although there was so much more she could say, Maude didn't say it. There was only one reason her mother invited Antonio tonight. Had she not heard anything Maude told when she'd last visited? That she didn't wish to marry, could *not* marry?

Silence settled over the room like a heavy cloud.

Maude's mother tried to lift it. "How long have you been in the business of real estate, Antonio?"

"Ten years."

"It makes you a good living?"

"Mother!"

"It was just a question, dear. Nothing behind it."

Everything behind it.

Antonio ignored the exchange and smiled in Maude's direction. "I was involved in the deal when Butterick purchased the land where they built their current building."

"You know I worked at Butterick?" Maude cast a glare at her mother, who had obviously shared personal details with him.

"I may have mentioned it," her mother said.

"It's not a secret," Hans said. "Is it?"

"No, of course not," Maude said. "I just don't like my business discussed behind my back."

Her mother frowned and lowered her voice. "I assure you, Maudey, I did no such thing."

So she didn't tell Antonio *about* the rape and its repercussions, yet by having him here she completely *ignored* the rape and its repercussions.

Her mother moved on without her. "Are you married, Antonio?"

You try to push us together yet you don't know whether or not he's married?

"I am widowed."

"Oh my," Mother said. "If I may ask, how did she—?"

"You may not ask!" Maude sprang to her feet. "This has gone too far already." She turned toward Antonio. "My mother is trying to be a matchmaker, but I need to nip this in the bud right now. I am never going to marry, Antonio. Mr. Ricci. Not that you had any such intentions toward me, but I need to stop this before Mother embarrasses all of us any more than she already has."

"I did not mean to embarrass—"

Maude swung toward her. "But you did. You know very well I will never marry and have children. Yet you ignore my wishes and bring us together at this dinner, push us together."

"I didn't intend—"

Maude plucked her hat and coat from the rack near the door. "You did mean, and you did intend." She turned to Antonio one last time. "Please forgive her blatant intentions, and please forgive this outburst, but I find I cannot sit here and let Mother try to maneuver you toward something that will never happen."

He rose from his chair, his cheeks ruddy, his jaw set, all charm gone. "I am sorry that any possibility of a friendship with me is so appalling. You will not have to worry about any acquaintance between us again, Miss Nascato. Take comfort in that."

Her heart skipped a beat. *What have I done?*

Unfortunately, she had gone too far to undo her actions. All hopes of a nice dinner were irretrievable, all possibility of normal conversation crushed.

There was only one thing she could say, one thing she could do.

"I'm sorry" was immediately followed by her departure.

She rushed down the steps and out to the sidewalk, the dark clouds that had hung over their meeting turning into a storm with foul winds that blew her out and away.

"Maude!"

She turned around to see her mother hurrying down the steps after her.

233

Maude wanted to flee and suffered an image of herself as a child doing just that to avoid a scolding. With difficulty, she stopped walking and waited for her mother to catch up.

She was out of breath. "What was all that about? Why were you so rude?"

Maude saw Antonio exit the building. He spotted her but did not tip his hat or acknowledge her. He walked away in the opposite direction.

Maude eyed the pedestrians strolling by. She led her mother to the top of a stoop to attain a modicum of privacy. "It was rude to bring him here. I told you I'm never going to marry."

"Well, now you're never going to marry *him*, that's for sure."

"So you *were* setting us up?"

"Of course I was. Hans said Antonio sang your praises—though I don't know why. He'll never want to even speak to you now."

Good.

"I'm disappointed in you, Maudey. We raised you to be polite and kind. I don't recognize this offensive person who so purposefully inflicts pain."

I don't either.

Once again Maude felt like she was ten years old, getting scolded. She'd learned then what she applied now: nothing good came from trying to explain herself. It was best to apologize and move on. "I'm sorry, Mother. I don't know what else to say."

Her mother's face softened. "Say you'll not be so stringent in the 'will nevers' of your life. You're young. You shouldn't close off the possibility of great joy, of great love." She glanced back toward her apartment. "After your father died, I never thought I would love again. I was resigned to my role as the widow of a diplomat. But Hans changed all that. It's like a light was turned on and I could look forward to a bright future. I have never been happier—I say that without taking anything from your father."

"I'm happy *for* you, Mother. I truly am. Hans seems like a very agreeable man."

"He is a God-sent man. I didn't *think* I would ever marry, but I didn't cut off the idea like you have. I prayed that God would do whatever *He* wanted to do with the rest of my life. And then He sent me Hans." Her smile was completely genuine and made her look ten years younger.

Suddenly Maude realized why she had been hesitant to fully rekindle their relationship. Her mother was content living a new life. Her mother had endured pain by losing her husband and her social station, yet had been able to move on and find happiness.

Maude could pretend she had moved on from *her* pain. But in truth, she hadn't. She'd lost her father and then had violently lost her virginity and her chance to be a mother. She'd been unable to move past the pain and find happiness. In fact, her decision to never marry kept happiness hidden away in its own room, with the door locked.

"Saying no to marriage is *your* decision, Maudey."

It was unnerving to hear her mother's words at the same moment of her revelation. "I know. But I think it's a good—"

"It's your decision, not God's."

And there it was. The full truth of it. *She* had shut happiness away and locked the door.

And she was in possession of the key.

Though her logical mind accepted this truth, Maude still couldn't take that key and. . . She fought tears, turning her back to the street. "Where was God when I was raped?"

"Right by your side. As He is now."

"But He let me get raped!"

A man walking by looked up and gave her a horrified look. She lowered her voice. "I'm dealing with the hand *He* dealt me."

"I am sorry for your pain," Mother said. "I don't know why God allowed it, but I do know He will take that darkness and turn it into light."

Her mother was gullible and naive. This wasn't faith, it was fantasy. Maude mentally stepped away from the room that held the possibility of a happy life. "I'm glad Hans is your light. But I don't have a light like that in my future."

"How do you know?"

Argh! Maude took a breath to calm herself. "No children are possible, so I am being kind and thoughtful by accepting my fate and not becoming a burden to a man—no matter how handsome and charming he is."

Mother drew Maude into an embrace and whispered in her ear. "Open the door, Maudey. That's all I ask."

Maude closed her eyes and lingered in her mother's care a bit longer.

Even though she was totally wrong.

❧

"You're back early," Edna said when Maude came home.

"I'm not feeling well." It was not a lie.

"Is that it?"

"Why do you say that?"

"I know you weren't thrilled about going to your mother's for dinner. I don't understand why, but—"

"Let's just say it lived up to my expectations."

"You weren't gone long enough to have eaten."

"Yes. Well." She hung up her coat and hat. "I'm going to lie down for a while."

"I have dinner ready. Since you weren't here I didn't make much, but—"

"I'm not hungry."

"Maude. . .talk to me. What happened?"

Although she knew that Edna would probably have great wisdom to share, she also knew it would be God-wisdom, and right now she didn't want to hear any more about God or open doors or trusting Him. She just wanted to pout and wallow.

"Maybe tomorrow. Leave me be, Edna. All right?"

Edna's faced revealed a growing concern. "You know I'm here if you want to talk."

"I know that."

Maude went into her bedroom and fell upon the bed. Through the door she could hear Edna praying for her. She took a breath to call out, "Stop that!" but let the words die.

Let her pray. It wouldn't help, but it wouldn't hurt.

❧

Vesta sat at her dressing table in her bedroom and brushed her hair. She wore her favorite nightgown and wrapper—or rather, Richard's favorite. She remembered what he'd said the first time she'd worn it: *The pink color brings out the blush in your cheeks, Vessie.*

She embraced the compliment but also the memory of his nickname for her. When they'd first been married he'd always been Richie to her and she Vessie to him. When had they transitioned into the more formal Richard and Vesta? It had not been a conscious choice but had sprung from a newborn emotional formality. She'd recognized it during its evolution but had not known how to stop its steady progression and, honestly, had told herself that the change in their relationship was natural. Fifty-something couples did not pepper their conversations with sweet talk. Did they?

Vesta's decision to test this premise came on the ride home from Sean and Annie's. She had already tested the status quo by standing up to Richard and moving out. Tonight she planned on testing it in another way, a more affirmative way.

She smiled at her reflection, took up her favorite perfume bottle, removed the stopper, took a deep whiff, smiled all the more, and then dabbed it on her wrists, behind her ears, and at her breastbone. With a final encouraging look, she whispered, "Ready or not, Richie, here I come."

She opened her bedroom door with great care, not wanting to announce her movements to the household—though Baines and Lola were surely downstairs for the night. She knew her desire for discretion was silly, for it was natural that a wife and husband would occasionally seek each other out.

The husband is supposed to seek the wife, not the other way around. At least that was how it had always played out before.

The act of bucking convention ignited Vesta's nerves, and only with conscious will did she tiptoe down the hall to her husband's bedroom.

Then she hesitated. Should she knock? Or just slip in? She imagined the knock and him saying, "Come in," her entering, and the possibility of him telling her to stop this nonsense and go back to her room. Rejection would devastate her.

So she chose surprise.

She put an ear to the door and heard no movement. She hoped he was already in bed. To slide in behind him seemed the best way to avoid rejection.

Vesta took in a quiet breath and let it out. *Please God. Let it all work out.*

Then she turned the knob and opened the door.

There was a light on.

"Vesta?"

He sat in his favorite chair by the fireplace, reading. She had no choice but to alter her plan.

"Is there something wrong?"

It seemed best not to say a word. Instead she walked to his side, took the book from his hands, then removed his glasses, setting both on a nearby table.

"What are you—?"

She crawled up on his lap, curling herself against his body, leaning her head against his shoulder. He responded immediately, wrapping his arms around her.

"I love you, Richie."

There was a choking sound in his voice as he said, "I love you too, Vessie."

Chapter Twenty

Annie was at work early, but this time it had nothing to do with sewing. Not directly.

Spread on the worktable were bills. All were due or past due. Her neglect in paying them had nothing to do with having the money. Her delay was due to her ignorance in knowing exactly how to go about it.

Her previous experience with money was minimal and involved earning a wage and buying necessities. When the Sampsons had initially deposited two hundred dollars in a bank account for them, Annie had sent Sean for the withdrawals, and he had paid Gert and Ginny cash, and some suppliers too. Henrietta had also given her cash that Sean had dispersed.

But Sean had a full-time job. Annie wanted to deal with the money like a true businesswoman. She wanted to understand the process.

Yesterday Mr. Sampson had given her an envelope full of dollars. To have so much cash on hand made Annie nervous. Surely there was a better way. A more professional way.

Now that Unruffled had some payment history, the suppliers delivered the goods and handed her a bill. Should she bring around cash? Or send a check? But from where? The account the Sampsons had set up for them was long closed. Unruffled didn't have an account of its own. At least not yet.

And shouldn't she be writing all this down in some sort of organized listing? She'd considered asking Sean about it, but lately she'd been too needy. She wanted him to think she was capable.

When she heard footsteps on the stairs, her first instinct was to gather up the bills until tomorrow. But she didn't have the energy to be discreet.

Vesta entered. "Good morning, Annie. A fine morning, isn't it?"

Her mother-in-law's cheeks were glowing. "My, my, you seem chipper."

"I am. Very much so."

Annie wondered but could not ask directly. . . . "How was your homecoming?"

"Very good, thank you." She gave Annie a mischievous grin. "Very good."

Annie chuckled. "I am glad to hear it."

"I'm thinking you are also glad to have your parlor back."

She was. And yet, "You are always welcome."

Vesta removed her hat and stuck the pins in its brim. "That won't be necessary."

"You're sure?"

"As sure as I can be."

Annie hugged her. "I'm so happy for both of you."

Henrietta came in. "Hugging is not allowed first thing in the morning."

"Sometimes it can't be helped," Vesta said.

Henrietta studied her. "All is well?"

"Very well."

She hugged Vesta. "I guess hugging is very necessary some mornings."

Their celebration complete, the ladies noticed the bills on the table. "Bookkeeping?" Henrietta asked.

"It should be but isn't." Annie pointed at the different piles on the table. "I have the bills, and the Sampsons gave us money, but I have little idea how a business should deal with or make note of it all."

"I do."

"You do?"

Henrietta scanned the papers. "I believe I can make a good go of it. You know my family has run the Summerfield mercantile for three generations. I often helped." She looked at a few bills. "These need to be paid soon."

"I know," Annie said. "And we have cash. But how. . . ?"

"Businesses like ours shouldn't deal with cash. Do you have a business account at the bank?"

"No."

"These bills should be paid out of an Unruffled account."

I thought so. "How do I get that?"

"I'll do it," Henrietta said. "I recently opened my own account, so I can go back to the same banker and open one for the business."

Relief took over. "That would be marvelous."

"You also need a ledger," Henrietta said.

So that's what it's called. "Where do I get one of those?"

"I'll find out and purchase one."

"Do you know what to write in it?" Vesta asked.

"Money in, money out. It's quite simple really."

Annie laughed. "Then I simply declare that you are the official bookkeeper of Unruffled."

"I accept."

Annie remembered another money matter on her mind. "You two deserve to be paid wages."

"I am glad to volunteer," Vesta said.

Annie shook her head. "That's kind of you but unacceptable. You are both working women. Working for us."

"I've never received wages," Henrietta said.

"Then I'm happy to be the first to pay you." She felt compelled to add, "Edna, Maude, and I are partners in Unruffled, so we will be sharing the profits, but you two are also a large part of the venture, so I insist on compensating you. As generously as I can."

"That's very kind." Vesta's eyes sparkled. "Goodness sakes. I'll have my own spending money."

"And I'll be able to pay the rent without dipping into my last reserves."

"Then it's agreed. You'll have to wait a wee bit longer until the shop opens and there's money coming in, but I promise you will get paid."

"Yes, ma'am. Boss-lady," Vesta said.

Boss? Add another label to her mantle.

⁓⊛⁓

"Good morning, Maude," Edna said with a smile. "I made scrambled eggs."

Maude wanted to say, "I don't want any," but in truth her stomach rumbled with hunger. She hadn't had dinner last night, and today her body demanded sustenance.

Plus, apologies were best tackled on a full stomach.

"Thank you," she said, sitting at the table.

Edna brought her a cup of coffee and then a plate of eggs, setting the salt and pepper close by. She did the same for herself and sat down. "Did you sleep well?"

Horrible. Barely at all. "Well enough."

"Good. Good."

It was Maude's fault there was tension between them. Best to rid the room of that encumbrance. "I'm sorry about last night. You wanted to help and I wouldn't let you."

"I still want to help."

And I still won't let you. Maude shook her head. "I'll be fine. It's a new day."

"I take comfort in knowing each day is a chance to start over."

Maude was depending on it.

❦

Maude did not allow second thoughts. She took the streetcar to Antonio's office, strode to the door, opened it, and presented herself to the secretary. "I'm here to see Mr. Ricci." She hastened to add, "If you please."

"Miss Nascato, is it?" the woman said.

For a moment, Maude feared that Antonio had issued a particular ban in case she showed up. It would serve her right.

"Yes, that's right," Maude said. "I know I don't have any appointment, but I was hoping he would see me."

The woman rose from her desk. "Let me check." She knocked on his office door, slipped inside, moved the door nearly closed in order to speak, then opened it again. Fully. "He will see you now."

He stood behind his desk when Maude entered but made no move to shake her hand or show her a seat. So she stood near the door.

"Good morning, Mr. Ricci."

"Good morning, Miss Nascato." There was no smile. "Is there an issue with the rental space?"

She was taken aback. "No. I mean not that I know of."

"And so. . . ?"

This was going to be harder than she expected but no easier than she deserved. "I came to apologize for my rudeness last night. There is no excuse for such behavior."

"No, there isn't."

Her heart beat doubly hard. "My life is rather complicated right now. And I did not expect you to be there, and when you were. . ."

"I assure you I will not be so again."

He was so harsh. "Don't ostracize yourself from my mother and Hans on my account."

"I was there on your account. Willingly."

So he was in on the matchmaking. Shame squeezed Maude's heart to the point of bursting. "I know it's hard to understand everything I said, and I meant nothing against you personally because I find you to be a kind and charming man, but—"

His eyebrows raised. "It was an odd way to treat such a man."

She adjusted her purse in her hands, wishing it were a shield to hide behind. "Again, I can only offer my sincerest apologies. Do you accept them?"

"I suppose I do."

She could finally breathe. "Perhaps we can see each other on occasion? As friends?"

"I doubt it. I'm overly busy and my life is quite. . .complicated."

Touché. "I understand."

They exchanged an awkward goodbye. Maude closed the door of his office for the last time.

Open the door, Maudey. . .

Too late now.

◈

Maude could barely make it up the stairs to the workshop. Her emotions weighed her down, a burden too much to bear.

She paused on the landing, willing herself to smile, or if that wasn't possible, at least feign some semblance of normal. Above everything, she did not want her friends to know what a fool she'd been.

She entered and was glad everyone was busy with this or that. It gave her a few extra moments to hang up her coat and hat, a few extra moments to collect herself.

But when she turned around, everyone was looking at her.

"What?"

Edna took a step forward. "Where have you been?"

"I had some personal business to attend to."

Edna's head shook back and forth. "That's not an acceptable answer. Not after you came home early from your mother's, wouldn't talk to me, and barely said two words this morning."

"What happened at your mother's?" Annie asked.

"Nothing. My mother is fine." Maude draped a dress across her lap and threaded a needle to sew on buttons.

"We didn't ask about your mother," Vesta said. "*You* aren't fine."

Henrietta took the dress from her, removing its shield of busyness. "Tell us."

And then it happened, something that had not happened in years.

Maude burst into tears. Not just tears, but sobs that made it hard for her to breathe.

Her friends fluttered around her, bringing her a handkerchief, a glass of water, and a calming hand to her back. She appreciated their efforts but hated the attention.

"I'm sorry. This is ridiculous. I don't ever cry."

"It's true. I've never seen you cry," Annie said. "Not even when the *Titanic* went down and we realized how close we'd come to death."

Maude forced herself to take deeper breaths. "Long ago I realized crying does little good."

"I disagree with that," Vesta said. "Sometimes crying is very good and is exactly what's needed."

Maude remembered that Vesta had gone home with Richard last night. Was she referring to herself? Last night? "How are you? Did everything go well at home?"

"Very well, thank you." But Vesta would not be deterred. "My point is that you are allowed to cry. We simply want to know why."

"Something happened at your mother's," Edna said. "You didn't stay for dinner."

"No dinner? Why not?" Annie asked.

Maude knew they would not give her peace until she told them. "Antonio was there."

"How nice," Henrietta said. "I didn't know your mother knew him."

"Hans does. Their paths crossed, and Antonio told him we'd found a place to rent. Mother took it upon herself to play matchmaker, even though—"

Edna chuckled. "It worked with Steven and Henrietta."

"But did not work for me and Antonio."

"Why not?"

It was best to spell it out. "Because I was totally and absolutely rude to him. Before dinner even started I stood up and made a grand pronouncement against marriage, defaming my mother for trying to find me a husband when I have vowed never to marry."

"Oh," Edna said.

"How did he react?"

"He was suitably appalled and embarrassed."

"I know we are guilty of teasing you, shoving you two together romantically," Edna said. "But perhaps you can be friends."

Maude shook her head, the morning's memories raw. "I am late for work because I went to his office to apologize."

"Did he accept?"

"Technically, yes. But he has no desire to be my friend."

"Oh dear," Edna said.

"You've hurt each other's feelings," Annie said. "That happens."

"Well then," Henrietta said. "The space is rented. Your connection with him is over. You don't have to see him again."

Maude shook her head. "You don't understand. I *want* to see him again."

"But you said—"

"I know what I said. But that doesn't change the fact that I've fallen in love with him."

Silence.

"Oh, Maude," Annie said. "What are you going to do?"

"There's nothing I can do. I've insulted him horribly."

"You said he forgave you."

She blew her nose. "It doesn't matter. I still can't marry anyone, so my love can have no happy ending."

"It could. . ." Henrietta said.

Maude shook her head adamantly. "It can't. I ruined everything. On the way to the dinner God spurred me to ask for His help, but I ignored it. I took matters into my own hands and spoiled everything that was good. God had opened a door for me with Antonio—a door that had never been opened before with any other man. But I didn't walk through it. I slammed it shut."

"And now you wish it was open?"

"I do."

"Then open it."

"I tried, but Antonio locked it for good." She sighed with her entire body, her shoulders rising and falling in despair. "I had come to terms with never loving, never marrying. I was given a chance but now am back where I started. I deserve to be alone."

Although the ladies tried to cheer her, Maude gave the sobs free rein.

Perhaps it was fitting. Lost love deserved a proper show of grief.

Annie and Edna exited the streetcar near their new shop, each holding a dress draped over their arms—a dress that had an Unruffled label sewn inside.

"I hope this works," Edna said for the umpteenth time.

"Why would they refuse?" Annie replied. She pointed to the store closest to Unruffled, a milliner's shop called Helen's Hats.

A bell rang on the door when they came in—a nice touch that Annie wanted to remember for their own shop. The store was lovely, with hats displayed on numerous counters. Plumes, flowers, and ribbons galore.

"Hello, ladies," said a woman behind the counter. "May I interest you in our newest chapeau?" She pointed to a head-hugging hat made of velveteen.

"Actually," Annie said, extending her hand. "We'd like to introduce ourselves. I am Annie Culver, and this is Edna Holmquist. We are opening a shop down the street. Our stores are going to be neighbors." She pointed to the north.

"I'm Helen Dobbins. Nice to meet you." She shook their hands. "I heard the space was rented. What sort of shop?"

"A dress shop."

"Unruffled," Edna said. "Fashion for the Unruffled, Unveiled, Unstoppable Woman."

Helen giggled. "How delightful. I thought of naming my shop something creative like Hats Off, but my husband told me I needed to use my name like most of the other shops do."

"We discussed that too," Annie said.

"And decided to be bold and do something different," Edna added.

"I commend your choice." Helen pointed at the dresses. "Are these some of your wares?"

"They are."

Annie and Edna showed off the two dresses, heralding their comfort and fashionable lines.

"The price point?" Helen asked.

"Five to ten dollars." Annie was interested in her reaction.

"I think that's very reasonable. How long will it take once a dress is ordered?"

Annie beamed. "We will have dresses offered in most sizes, on the rack, ready to purchase and wear the same day."

Helen clapped gleefully. "How marvelous!" She moved to a counter and brought back a blue straw hat with orange flowers on the sweeping rim. "Look how this hat complements this dress."

Annie could not have orchestrated the moment any better. "Your point is a good one. Which is why we are here. What if we display some of your hats in our store and give you a dress or two to display here?"

"Oooh," Helen said, her eyes wide. "Both our businesses would surely benefit."

"That is the intent."

"I would be happy to participate," Helen said. "When do you plan to open?"

"We are hoping for Saturday, November 30th."

"Just in time for Christmas."

"Again, that is the intent."

Helen chose another hat to go with the second dress. "Lovely, just lovely." She held a finger in the air, as if announcing an idea. "What if I did something special on the day of your opening? Perhaps we could coordinate an event."

Annie remembered a past idea. "I was thinking about having a fashion show, right here on the street."

Helen beamed. "Outside where everyone can see. What a unique idea. Of course, only if the weather allows."

"We could put up posters," Edna said. "Draw a crowd."

Annie hugged Edna, and Helen joined in.

Annie and Edna waited for the streetcar, exhausted but happy with their afternoon's work.

"Stabler's will show their jewelry; Meindorff's their shoes; O'Hanna's will show their parasols, purses, and hosiery; and Helen her hats."

"And they all agreed to a Fashion Parade," Edna said. She sat on a bench, laying both dresses across its back. "I should have purchased a fan at O'Hanna's. All this exertion has me glowing."

Annie laughed. "We should have bought two. You may be glowing, but I'm sweating." She spotted a man walking close and hoped he hadn't heard her crude terminology. He must be waiting for the streetcar too.

But then...

He grabbed the dresses from the bench, wadded them under his arm, and raced off.

"Stop! He stole our dresses! Thief!"

Passersby looked alarmed but simply stepped out of his way, though one did shout out, "Police!"

Annie began to run after him but was quickly reminded of the baby when she felt a stitch in her side. She stopped.

Edna caught up with her and helped her back to the bench. Moments later a police officer appeared.

"Are you all right, miss?"

"No, I'm not all right. A man stole our dresses."

He looked confused, for of course, both of them were wearing dresses.

"Two dresses we had on hangers. We'd draped them over the back of the bench."

He wrote down their names and addresses, and a brief description of the clothes and the man, but the latter description was minimal. Dark hair, medium height, thirty. Plus, he was a fast runner.

The officer closed his notepad. "If we find the dresses, I will contact you."

"What are the chances of that?" Edna asked.

He shrugged. "Slim to none. He'll probably be selling them on Mulberry Street by evening. Is there anything else I can do for you ladies?"

As opposed to doing nothing?

The streetcar arrived, taking them home.

❧

Henrietta tucked Annie into bed. "Sean will be back from Edna's with some dinner for you momentarily." She sat on the edge. "It's just two dresses, Annie. They can be replaced."

She'd heard the same from everyone, yet Annie had questions. "Why do we encounter one problem after another? First, the Sampsons bow out, then we have no money, then we get money from you, then you have no more money and we almost lose our shop space, and then—"

"Stop it. Listen to yourself. Every issue was resolved, one by one."

"Stolen dresses can't be resolved. Even the bobby said the dresses would be sold on the street. They're gone. We'll never get them back."

"No, we won't. But we *will* go on. God hasn't failed us yet."

Annie let her head sink deeper into the pillows. She stroked her abdomen, a new habit and her way of comforting the baby. And herself.

"You should never have run after him."

"I didn't think. And no one else was running. Where was my hero?"

"Busy elsewhere, I guess. We'll remake the dresses tomorrow."

Annie closed her eyes. It wasn't just the dresses. Her exhaustion was due to much more than that. "Sometimes. . .sometimes I just wish I could be by myself, only responsible for me."

"You wish to be alone?"

"Sometimes."

"Sorry, my dear, but that's not possible." Henrietta pointed to Annie's midsection.

"Oh. Yes."

"Oh. Yes. That. A baby. There is no greater responsibility than a child."

Annie sighed. "You're not helping."

"Making you see reason *is* helping."

She was right. Annie loved the baby so much her heart physically ached from it. "I didn't mean what I said. About being alone."

"I know you didn't."

"But the business. . .it overwhelms me sometimes."

"I know that too. But we have much to be thankful for. The other businesses agreed to your idea, and we're having a Fashion Parade. How marvelous."

It was. But Annie was in no mood to think of the positive.

"You're not smiling," Henrietta said.

Annie sighed. "This is going to sound totally ungrateful, and terribly cowardly, but sometimes I wish I was still a housemaid."

"You wish to make the beds, scrub the bathtub, and polish the furniture from dawn to dusk?"

"Not that part of it."

"Then what part is better than the life you have now?"

"The part where I had little responsibility. The part where I was told what to do each morning and didn't have to think beyond making the beds and polishing the silver. The part where I wasn't in charge of making decisions. The part where I didn't mentally take my work home with me at the end of the day."

"But that wasn't enough for you. You've always gone above and beyond what was asked. You set your sights on being my lady's maid, not just a housemaid. You did skilled sewing work, altered my clothes, and beaded Mother's gowns. To just do 'enough' is not in you, Annie Wood Culver. You are not satisfied with enough. You want more."

Annie huffed at her own faulty memories. "You're right. I want more. I want it all."

"Then you will have it."

Annie scoffed. "You say it with such assurance."

"If it is what God wants for you, you will have it, and nothing *you* do or anyone else does can stop it." Henrietta grew pensive. "God has given both of us something very precious: choices. Neither one of us had many choices in our before-lives. Our futures were set. Now, we are free to choose…choose so many things."

Annie sat up in bed. Henrietta adjusted the pillows behind her.

"Why can't it be easy?"

"It can be." Henrietta thought a moment. "Actually it was for you."

"Easy? Surely you jest."

"How many housemaids get the chance to work at Macy's?"

"A few, I suspect."

"How many discover they have a hidden talent and get a chance to use it at a great company like Butterick?"

"Fewer."

"And how many get the chance to design their own fashion and open up their very own store?"

"I see your point."

Henrietta held up a hand. "How many housemaids get to marry a man who adores them and get to be the mother of a child who will be brought up surrounded by people who love them?"

Annie let her frustration fall into puddles of foolishness on the floor.

"How many people get to live their lives knowing that God has them where He wants them?"

Annie put a hand on her forehead, hiding her shame. *Forgive me, Lord.* "You're right. One hundred percent right." She held out her hand and Henrietta clasped it. "I would not want to go back to being a maid. I am where I am supposed to be. It's just that sometimes I feel He's trusting me too much."

"He will not give us more than we can handle."

"Are you sure?"

"Positive."

Annie felt better. But then she had a thought. "I do believe God also has *you* where He wants you. Yes?"

Henrietta smoothed Annie's covers. "Steven is remarkable."

"He is, but he's just part of the plan."

Henrietta stood then paced in front of the bedroom door. "I lived a life of no responsibility."

"You did not have to work. You were the daughter of a viscount."

"Although I occasionally helped in the mercantile, listened when my mother tried to teach me how to be a good wife, and reluctantly learned how to play the piano enough to impress guests, I had no true purpose. Each day I awakened without enthusiasm, for one day was like the last, which was like the next." She stopped pacing and shook her head. "That is no way to live—or live fully. Beyond the parties and pretty dresses I drowned in complete and utter boredom."

Annie was surprised to hear it. She'd always thought Henrietta's life was free of stress, and free of need and longing. "You are not bored now."

"Not at all. In fact, I'm rather proud of myself. I came here on my own—a frightening but satisfying experience. I've let my own flat and can now make my own fire and deal with my own personal needs—though I still need Gert to unbutton me. I vow I will never buy a dress with back buttons again."

Annie had to laugh. "And now you are doing the books for us."

"You discovered you had an aptitude for design? I guess I have one for math." Henrietta sat on the bed again. "Neither one of us could have guessed what our lives would become, but I dare say neither one of us would change anything, would we?"

"We would not."

"God is good."

"And He knows best."

CHAPTER TWENTY-ONE

Henrietta sat at the small table in her flat in front of the newly created ledger for Unruffled. It had been two weeks since she had taken over the financial accounting from Annie, and she felt satisfied with the system she had created. But there was work to be done this Saturday morning. New bills lay before her for counters, racks, hangers, shelves, mannequins, and various accessory stands for the front window.

"I wish I could help." Gert stood at the door, putting on her coat. "But I'm lucky to add two plus two right."

"I can add, but I'm not highly skilled at sewing," Henrietta said. "And Annie has made her preference known. I am not to help sew right now as the final finishes of the dresses need finesse. So off with you. I will check in at the store later on."

As soon as Gert left, Henrietta heard a familiar voice in the hall. With a single knock, Steven came in, his smile wide. "Best of the morning to you, dear Etta. How would you like to spend our Saturday?"

She enjoyed his pet name for her—the same name her family used. "What I'd like is not the same as what I must do. I really must get these bills paid."

He kissed her cheek before sitting at the table. He perused a few bills. "There are so many."

"I hope not too many," Henrietta said.

"The Sampsons have promised perpetual funding."

"They have, and they have been generous. Which is why I hope there's enough to cover the expenses. I don't wish to ask for more."

Steven rotated the ledger so he could see it better.

"How does it look?"

He turned it back. "Very neatly done. You have beautiful penmanship."

She laughed. "Spoken like a schoolteacher. My question was in regard to the accounting, not the neatness of the entries."

"I teach English. I know very little about debits and credits, and. . ."

"And?"

"I am impressed that you do."

Was there an insult in his words? "I may be a woman, but I *am* educated."

"I mean no offense, dear lady. It's just that you, being from the aristocracy. . ."

"So we have no reason to learn?"

The look on his face was pathetic, as if he wished he could take back all he had said. She took pity on him and put her hand on his. "Take ease. I know you do not mean to offend."

He let out a breath of relief. "Did you attend school or were you taught at home?"

"Both. When I was small, a school was started in Summerfield by two family members. Miss Tilda and Miss Beth were my first teachers. As I grew older my parents hired a tutor for me. My brother was sent away to school."

Steven shook his head. "I know it was the norm not to let girls go to formal school beyond the basics, but I am against it."

"Do you have girls in your school?"

"I do. But alas, the number of girls going into secondary and upper grades still lags behind the boys."

"So in your opinion, the gentler sex has equal capacity to learn?" She grinned.

"You are goading me, but yes, of course." He pointed to the ledger. "Your tutor taught you bookkeeping?"

"My nana did, and my mother. Helping at the family mercantile gave me the knowledge I need to do this work."

"Did you ever think you would use it like this?"

"Never," she said, getting ready to write a check for the mannequins. "I came to America to find Annie and hoped she would sweep me up into a whirlwind of purpose."

"It appears she's done just that."

"Indeed she has, and as such I am eternally grateful."

"I'm sure your family would be pleased to see how you are applying what they taught."

The thought of family caused a wave of melancholy to swirl around her.

"You miss them, don't you?" he asked.

"Very much."

"Perhaps they will come for a visit?"

"Why would they? I disappointed them by not living the life they'd planned for me."

"But it's your life to live, not theirs."

It was complicated. "Because of my father's title there are expectations and responsibilities. I disregarded all of that to do what I wanted to do." The melancholy grew heavier. "I was selfish."

"Do you regret coming here?"

She heard his unspoken *Meeting me?* and gave him a reassuring smile. "Of course not. Although I *have* been surprised and upturned by many of the details of my life here, I feel fuller for it. Does that make sense?"

He drew her close across the table so he could kiss her. "Completely."

The love she felt for Steven validated her choice more than any sense of purpose brought about through Unruffled. She wanted to tell him that *he* was her purpose—because her feelings were that strong—but didn't dare just yet. Although she had shown a streak of rebellion in her nature by leaving home, she still believed that a man should be the first to declare his love.

"Wouldn't it be marvelous if they did come and visit you here?"

"They wouldn't."

"Why not?"

"Because they have duties at home. Because I've told them I am well and have assured them there is no reason for worry."

"They'll accept that?"

"They *have* accepted it. I have been here nearly six weeks, with a week of travel before that. They have accepted my absence." Her voice caught in her throat.

His face showed his compassion. "As I said, they would be proud of you."

Perhaps. Henrietta needed to change the subject. "Enough about me. How are your students faring?"

"Since we are reading *The Last of the Mohicans* they are faring quite well. Fighting and soldiers, damsels in distress. . ."

"I have not read that one."

"It's very American, set in the 1750s during the French and Indian War."

"I believe we call it the Seven Years' War."

"Really?"

"Surely you knew that."

He grinned. "I believe I did."

"So. . .the story is set before you fought *us*." It felt good to push the melancholy fully away with teasing.

"Us? Yes. You. The British."

"Considering where I am right now, who I'm with right now, I am glad you won that skirmish."

He laughed. "How revolutionary of you, Miss Kidd."

There was a knock on the door and Steven answered it.

The sight of the younger Mr. Cohen caused Henrietta to rise. "Mr. Cohen?"

"Good day, Miss Kidd."

"Come in, please. Have a seat."

"I can't stay long," he said. "Nice to see you again, Mr. Holmquist."

"And you, sir."

"How are you feeling?" Henrietta asked. "And your brother?"

"We are well recovered." His smile hid behind his beard, and his dark eyes sparkled. "Very well recovered."

"I am glad to hear it."

He removed a drawstring bag from his coat pocket. "I believe these are yours."

She opened the bag, saw inside, then dropped the contents on the table. "My bracelet? The earrings." She examined them. They appeared in perfect condition.

"So the thief has been caught?" Steven asked.

"He has. He had a satchel of jewelry and was trying to pawn them. He'll be in jail a long time, not only for the theft but also for the injuries he inflicted on my brother and me."

"So your inventory was recovered too?"

"Each piece." He grinned again. "*Adoni tov v'salach.* God is good and forgiving."

"Indeed He is." Henrietta had a disconcerting thought. "Will I have to speak against the man?"

"I don't think so. There is enough against him without your testimony."

It was a relief. "Thank you for bringing these back to me. They were my great-grandmother's."

"As you said during your visit."

"She was the Countess of Summerfield. She still lives on the estate."

He glanced around the shabby flat. "A countess, you say?"

She nodded, embarrassed for trying to impress him. Americans did love nobility.

"Which makes you...?"

She put a stop to what she had started. "Very grateful." She shook his hand. "Thank you for bringing them back to me, Mr. Cohen. Please greet your brother."

"Feel free to come and visit at any time. And if you ever do wish to sell..."

She shook her head. "I will keep my heirlooms heirlooms." She gave him her best smile, which he returned.

"Good day to you, Miss Kidd."

She closed the door and returned to her work at the table. "It's good to see him and a relief to have the jewelry returned, but I'm angry at myself."

"Why?"

"For bringing up the countess title. Since I'm in America I should try to fit in, not set myself apart."

Steven took a seat and eyed the jewelry. Something seemed to be bothering him.

"If I offended you by the mention, I apologize."

"Offend? Never."

"Then what's wrong?"

He pointed at the jewelry, though seemed to make a point of *not* touching the stones. "I could never give you jewels like that."

He implies a future together! "I don't want jewels like that."

"But you've grown up with such beautiful things. I am but a teacher. I..."

She touched his cheek and forced him to look into her eyes. "I am but a woman. You give me something that is more precious than jewels."

She let her kiss speak for her.

❧

Annie checked the fit on a model. "I do believe this size fits you better, Jane."

"I do too. It's lovely, Annie."

"You look lovely in it."

The workshop was abuzz with activity as the twelve models who had shown fashion at the Sampsons had all eagerly returned to be a part of the street fashion show.

"My turn in front of the mirror."

Annie's friend Mildred from Macy's stood behind Dora from Butterick. Behind her was Mrs. Tuttle. Each wanted a turn to admire their fashionable selves.

It was time to unveil her new idea. She unrolled a three-yard length of fabric that matched Mrs. Tuttle's dress. "Voila."

"What's that for?" Mildred asked.

"It's for warmth in case the weather is cold. We can't have you wearing coats over your dresses, but you could drape this"—she draped it around Mrs. Tuttle's shoulders—"like a shawl."

"Pretty," Mrs. Tuttle said. Then she let it drop off her shoulders, grasped the edges, extended her arms, and twirled with flourish. "Feast your eyes!"

They all laughed at her dramatics. Yet it was perfect. Annie pointed to the sewing room. "I'm having Gert and Ginny hem all the edges, and you each will get one. Just in case."

"Very innovative," Maude said. "I was wondering what we'd do about bad weather."

"What if it snows?" Mildred asked.

"We pray it doesn't."

"But if it does?"

"We'll have a fashion show in the shop. We'll adapt." It was the story of her life. That detail accomplished, and the models chatting among themselves as they tested out the shawl, Annie stepped back, taking it all in. The women of her American life were in one room, working together toward one goal.

Edna grasped her shoulders from behind. "Excited?"

" 'Tis too small a word."

"Satisfied?"

"Awed."

Edna laughed. "That *is* a good word, and an apt one."

"I never thought it would really happen."

"Ye of little faith."

She was right. "I wanted to believe, but it was so far-fetched to think that we could actually do it."

"Yet it will be done. In ten days Unruffled will be opened."

"Speaking of. . . I really need to go over there. Sean and Steven are papering the walls."

"You don't trust them?"

"Of course I do."

Edna pointed to Henrietta. "Go on then. And take Henrietta with you. I'm sure the lovebirds are dying from being apart so long. We'll finish up here."

⬥

"Annie, don't walk so fast!"

Annie held back, waiting for Henrietta and her much shorter legs to catch up. "I'm sorry. But I'm eager to see what our men's work has wrought. And the sign painters are supposed to get done today."

Henrietta took up beside Annie in the final block. "We could have hired the interior work done."

"We could have. And I suggested it. But Sean and Steven wanted to contribute, so how could I refuse?"

"They *are* hard to refuse."

There seemed to be more to Henrietta's words than wallpaper. "How *are* you and Steven?"

"We are wonderful, glorious, very fine indeed."

Annie laughed and took her arm. "Perhaps you should add 'stupendous' and 'magnificent' to your list?"

"I would have—could have—if I would have thought of them."

"Gracious, Henrietta. Is a betrothal imminent?"

"If I had my way, yes."

"He's not as smitten?"

"Oh, he is. He definitely is."

Annie noticed a healthy blush on her friend's cheeks. "But you're not certain he will ask?"

"I hope for it. But he seems overly concerned about my family's status compared to his."

"I know."

"You know?"

"He talked with his mother about it, and Edna spoke with me."

"What did you say?"

"I said that your parents probably preferred you marry someone of their own set but that I didn't think you cared."

Henrietta stopped walking. "I don't care! I want Steven and only Steven!"

They received the smiles of many passersby. Annie got her walking again. "Does he know this?"

"Yes."

"So you've told him you love him?"

"Well. . .no. Shouldn't the man say it first?"

It was Annie's turn to stop their progress. "This is America. You are a modern woman, are you not?"

"Well. . .I don't know. Perhaps."

"Then tell him."

She bit her lip. "Oh dear. I don't know."

Annie threw her hands in the air. "Did you ever consider that he might be wondering how you feel about him? Added to his uncertainty about your family. . . Perhaps these issues hold him back from declaring his love."

"Surely he knows how I feel."

"He will if you tell him."

❦

Henrietta and Annie gasped when they walked up to Unruffled. The sign painters were packing up their brushes and paint.

One of them looked up. "You like it, Mrs. Culver?"

Annie put a hand to her chest, hoping words would eke their way through the tightness there. "It's perfect."

"Nice of you to say so. It was a bit of a challenge getting 'Fashion for the Unruffled, Unveiled, Unstoppable Woman' spaced right, but we got it done."

"Indeed you did," Henrietta said. "You're both very talented."

The younger man nodded at the elder and said, "Pa taught me everything I know."

"Come, boy. Let's leave the ladies to their business."

Annie took Henrietta's arm and lingered in front of the store where Unruffled was painted in the center near the top of the window in block letters that had a bit of frill to them, making them slightly feminine. The words of the store's motto were curved around the main word, like a cursive smile. "To see it in writing, up there on the glass. . .it makes it real."

"That it does."

"We did it, Henrietta," Annie whispered.

"That we did."

There was a crash from inside, ending their sentimental moment. They rushed in and found Sean righting a chair.

"All's well," he assured them. "What do you think?"

The men had finished wallpapering two walls above the white wainscoting, transforming the space from ordinary to exceptional.

"It's absolutely elegant," Henrietta said.

"I hope not too much so," Annie said. "Our customer is the working woman who wants function and fashion. Not fancy."

Henrietta studied the paper. It was embossed, creating a three-dimensional effect. Its background was gold metallic, with a raised floral pattern colored in a rich leaf-green. "It's not too fancy. Just enough so. Aren't we espousing the fact that function does not have to be boring? If we want women to shop here we need to give them an experience that ignites all their senses and makes them feel pampered. It's perfect. You and Vesta chose well."

Steven came over and kissed her cheek. "I'm glad you approve."

"Very much so," she said. "Where did you learn to hang wallpaper?"

"At home. In case you didn't notice, Mother has a penchant for roses on her walls."

Henrietta had noticed. Every room in Edna's flat was adorned with a different rose-covered wallpaper. "You did that?"

"I did." He brandished a pasting brush like a sword. "Holmquist Papering, at your service."

Sean called over from his place on a ladder. "Culver and Holmquist, you mean."

"I suppose I'll give you first billing. But only because your father gave us a discount on the supplies."

"Speaking of your father," Annie said. "I expected him to be here already. And Vesta too. The display cases are due to arrive. Since he oversaw the order, he said he'd be here."

"Then he will be." Sean stepped off the ladder and flicked the tip of her nose. "You worry too much, Annie-girl."

Henrietta spotted activity out front. "Ask and it shall be given. . ."

They rushed toward the door and held it open as Richard directed the shipment of counters, cases, and racks for hanging. The store became a flurry of activity as instructions were given for their placement. To their credit, they had already decided on the proper arrangement.

As Annie and Sean saw to the final tweaks, Henrietta stepped back and admired the work. Steven came by her side. "It's good, isn't it?"

"More than good," she whispered. "It's like a dream being made real. Annie's dream."

Vesta hurried to the door, letting more men inside carrying a parade of tufted armchairs, upholstered in gold velvet.

"We didn't order those," Annie said, stopping the men. "The chairs we ordered were far plainer."

"Don't you like them?" Vesta asked.

"Of course I do. They're lovely. But—"

Vesta put a hand on her arm. "They are a gift from Richard and me. You've come this far; we thought you needed this extra dose of elegance for the fitting rooms and out here on the floor."

Annie hugged her tight. "You are so kind."

Vesta laughed. "And I have extremely good taste."

"You do."

The color of the chairs highlighted the gold of the wallpaper perfectly— Henrietta knew it was not by chance. She sat in one and ran a hand along the depth of the velvet nap.

Touch, sight. . .

"Annie? Remember I just spoke of igniting the senses of our customer? I think we should have fresh flowers in the store at all times. Their scent will be very pleasing and special for women who don't have money to purchase flowers for their homes."

"As long as it's not too costly," Annie said.

Henrietta respected that Annie's mind was always on the bottom line, but she knew small details could make all the difference in a purchase. Back at her family mercantile, they were in the habit of offering a sample of fresh berries, preserves, or the latest skin balm to entice their customers to buy.

Sean sat in a chair, testing it out. "Add a plate of sweets and I'll shop here."

"So will I," Steven said.

Henrietta noted the four senses that had been accounted for. "That leaves hearing. . .perhaps we could have a harpist here, providing lovely background music."

Annie shook her head. "Perhaps during the opening, but it would be too costly to employ one every day."

She was probably right.

"I could stand in the corner and sing," Steven said.

"You're a singer?" Henrietta asked.

"Not really. But I wouldn't charge much."

"Good thing you're busy teaching," Henrietta said.

Steven put his hands to his heart dramatically. "You wound me!"

The front door opened and a thirtysomething woman entered. "We're not open yet, ma'am," Henrietta said.

The woman shook her head, her eyes scanning the room. When they fell upon Annie she smiled. "There you are."

Annie's eyes lit up. "Lena! How good to see you." The two women embraced.

"I heard through the business grapevine you'd rented a place. I had to come see for myself." She looked around. "Very nice. The fabric on the chairs brings out the gold in the wallpaper."

Vesta beamed.

Annie made introductions. The woman was Lena Malsin, the owner of Lane Bryant. Henrietta had heard Annie's stories about the store and its maternity wear, plus stories about the amazing entrepreneurial talent of Mrs. Malsin.

Lena stepped toward her, offering her hand. "Miss Kidd. So former mistress becomes collaborator?"

"I help where I can."

"It's good of you to come and support Annie's dreams." Lena looked around the store. "So many of us New Yorkers share a rags-to-riches story."

Annie joined them. "There are no riches yet. Just a lot of faith, hope, and hard work."

Lena raised a finger. "Three essential elements of business." She glanced at Annie's midsection. "How are you doing?"

"Very well. The baby moves often."

"Always a good sign." Lena smiled and touched her own abdomen. "Mine is active too."

"You're expecting?" Henrietta asked.

"My fourth." She returned her attention to Annie. "I see you're wearing one of my dresses."

"Lane Bryant is my first—and only—choice in maternity wear."

"I thought you were going to make some maternity dresses for your line?"

"Really?" Henrietta said. "I didn't know that."

"It was a thought. And I did make one. But I decided since you've been so kind and supportive of my venture, that I would not create competition between us."

Lena shook her head. "Piddle. Competition is the American way."

Annie shrugged. "I will send all expectant mothers to your store."

"And I will send them to yours once their confinement is complete."

The two women shook on it. Henrietta was impressed at their businesslike camaraderie. Annie and Lena were definitely the epitome of the modern American woman.

The front door opened again and Maude came in, carrying a stack of flyers over her arm. She spotted Lena, smiled broadly, and greeted her. Only then did she look around the store.

"My, my. I leave to put up advertising flyers and come back to a finished store."

"Not finished yet," Annie said.

"Very nearly."

While the women discussed the store and business issues, Henrietta spotted Steven pulling a new piece of wallpaper over the makeshift sawhorse table in order to cut it. Since entering the store she had been dogged by Annie's directive that she should declare her love. More than anything, she wanted to do it. Right now.

But it was far from a romantic setting. Everyone was busy in body and mind. Yet if she didn't say something now, she felt she would burst for the waiting of it.

She'd already waited too long.

She watched Steven make his mark on the back of the wallpaper and take a yardstick to draw a straight line for cutting. If she waited until the paper was slathered with paste, who knew how long it would be?

"Steven? May I speak with you a minute?"

He looked surprised but nodded. She motioned him into the back room where it was quiet. And private.

He snuck a kiss, but when she didn't smile. . . "You look so serious. Is everything all right?"

Not a good start. She smiled through her nervousness. "Everything is very right. I just wanted to tell you something."

"What?"

"I . . ." It was difficult to say in a cluttered back room, with people talking just a few yards away.

He took her hands and spoke softly. "Etta. You can tell me anything. Anything at all."

She took him at his word. "I love you. I wanted to tell you I love you." She took a breath to replenish herself. "I love you."

He laughed—which was not her first choice of reactions. But he quickly stopped himself and ran a hand along her cheek. "What brought this on?"

It was notable that he had not said "I love you" in return. "I'm sorry. I shouldn't have blurted it out like that, here, without warning. The time wasn't right, I'm being presumptuous, and—"

He pulled her close, peering down at her. "I love you too, dear lady. More than words can say."

The room and all other voices faded away. There was only Henrietta and her Steven.

Until. . .she heard a rustling and saw Annie and Vesta standing in the doorway, grinning at them. She began to pull away from Steven, but he wouldn't let her go. Instead he wrapped his arms around her waist.

"Excuse me, ladies? May we help you?"

"I'd say you're doing a good job of helping yourselves," Vesta said.

He looked down at Henrietta. "She loves me."

Henrietta glanced at Annie, who winked. "I know."

"You know?"

She pointed at Henrietta's eyes. "It's quite evident."

Vesta nodded.

"I'd hoped but. . ."

"Did you say something to her in return for her declaration?" Annie asked.

"I did."

"And?"

"We love each other."

The two women applauded as Steven kissed her yet again.

❦

Maude heard a commotion from the back room. Was that applause? By the time she looked in its direction she spotted Steven and Henrietta coming out, arm in arm. They were glowing. Were they engaged?

When they didn't say anything, she assumed not but wouldn't have been surprised. It was clear they shared strong feelings.

She watched as Vesta sought out her husband and they exchanged a sweet moment. Annie found Sean, and they traded private words.

Which left Maude standing alone. She had no one to share with. No one to turn to or express her feelings with, to make this experience larger through closeness and a common goal.

A wave of regret swept over her, threatening to drown her. What would this moment be like with Antonio by her side?

You've ruined all chances of that, Maude. Get on with it.

Although she knew it was rude and self-serving, Maude needed to break up the couples' *tête-à-têtes* or expire from regret and envy. "Excuse me? I came back to elicit some help in getting these flyers distributed. Any volunteers?"

❦

Everyone was gone for the day except Sean and Annie. While Sean cleaned up the wallpaper supplies—for he and Steven had finished their work to marvelous results—Annie wiped off the last display case. Tomorrow they would bring over the dresses—which were currently taking up every square inch of the workshop. She let her hand pause on top of the counter and closed her eyes. *Thank You for taking us this far, Lord. Help Unruffled be a success. Help us be a blessing to many women.*

The bell on the door interrupted her prayer. A twentysomething woman with white-blond hair came in. She had something wrapped in a shawl draped over her arms.

"I'm sorry, miss. We aren't open yet."

She nodded, but her eyes were furtive. Why was she so nervous?

She stepped forward. "I need to give you something." She removed the shawl to reveal two dresses.

The dresses that were stolen.

She handed them to Annie. "My husband took these. He just wanted to give me something pretty—and they are that—but I don't want such gifts. I saw the tag, and so I bring them back to you with sincerest apologies."

Sean came over to join them. "That's very good of you."

She shook her head and avoided their gazes. "No, no. Not good. Not good at all."

Annie felt empathy for her and draped the dresses over a rack—their first dresses in the shop. "I know it must have been difficult to come here."

"Johnny said I was daft to do it. I already had the dresses. Let it be." She glanced at Annie then cast down her gaze. "But I couldn't do that. Even though times are hard. . .thou shalt not steal." She took a new breath. "I'm sorry. And I know Johnny is sorry too. Or should be."

Annie had to smile at the final words.

"He should be," Sean said. "And perhaps through your right action, he will be."

On impulse, Annie removed the dresses from the rack and held them toward the girl. "Here. Take them."

She took a step back, as if not wanting to touch them. "No, I can't."

"It's a gift."

"No," she said, shaking her head adamantly. "It wouldn't be right."

Annie draped the dresses back over the rack. She admired the girl's sense of right and wrong.

"Actually," the girl said, her voice cracking, "there is one way I would take those dresses."

"And what's that?" Sean asked.

"If I earned money enough to buy them." She straightened her shoulders. "If you need help in the store, I would love to work here. I could wrap purchases or sweep up or go on errands. Whatever you need." She glanced at Annie's stomach. "I have a three-month old boy. I worked in a factory before having him, but Johnny says he doesn't want me back there again."

"Who would take care of the boy while you work?" Sean asked.

"My mother lives in the same building as we. So I *am* available to work. I want to work. We need me to work." She looked at Sean, then Annie. "May I work for you?"

Even though paying another employee would be a risk, Annie couldn't say no. "You're hired."

The girl beamed. "Thank you, Mrs. . . . ."

"Culver." Annie looked to Sean. "And this is my husband."

"Nice to meet you." She bobbed once, in the way Annie used to do as a maid.

"And you are?" Sean asked.

"Birdie Doyle."

"Nice to meet *you*, Mrs. Doyle."

Birdie's face flushed with pleasure and excitement. "When do you want me to start?"

"Monday," Annie said. "Come here around nine. We will be bringing all the dresses over then."

Birdie bounced twice on her toes, her blue eyes gleaming. "I will be here. Thank you so much. I promise I won't let you down."

Once outside, Birdie waved through the window.

"With that kind of character and enthusiasm, I predict she will be a very good employee," Sean said.

⊰⊱

Sean and Annie sat at either end of the window seat in their flat. Sean rubbed her feet, the massage painful yet blissful. "I've never had anyone massage my feet before," she said. "When I was a housemaid my feet always throbbed at the end of the day."

"I'm sure you weren't alone. The Kidds should have provided a foot masseuse for their staff."

She thought of their newest employee. "Birdie worked in the factory while she was pregnant with her son. I'm guessing her feet hurt something awful at the end of her days."

"They probably did."

"I hope her husband rubbed them."

"I doubt it." Sean took up her other foot and the pain-pleasure began anew. "The world is full of sore feet."

She closed her eyes to better enjoy the massage, but in doing so found her thoughts drifting to the necessity of work. Without work, people didn't eat. Or pay rent. Or buy dresses.

She opened her eyes. "Maybe we should lower our prices."

"What brought this on?"

"Birdie. We need to make sure our customers can afford them."

"I think we've done that. You asked the models about the prices and they think them fair."

Annie stroked her tummy.

Sean nodded at her action. "Have you thought about whether the baby is a boy or girl?"

"Yes." *She's a girl.* Annie didn't want to say more, because she assumed

Sean wanted a boy.

"I hope the baby is a girl," he said.

She could not have been more surprised if he'd hoped for purple hair. "A girl? I thought all men wanted sons."

He shrugged. "I do. Someday. But right now, I think a little girl would be a perfect addition to our family. Besides. . ." He shook his head. "Never mind."

She put her feet on the floor. "No, you don't. There is no never mind. Tell me."

"This will sound silly."

"Tell me."

"I. . .when I refer to my family I want to be able to say 'my girls.'"

"That's very sweet." She took his hand and pulled him close enough to kiss him. "I think you'll have your chance."

"You do?"

"I think we're having a daughter."

"Why?"

"I just always think of the baby as a girl. And with Unruffled opening. . . I can imagine her growing up in the shop among Edna, Maude, Henrietta, and your mother, playing in the dressing rooms, trying on hats, and even helping us choose fabrics for new dresses. She will have exquisite fashion sense."

"She'll learn to sew, of course."

"Better than me. For she will have many teachers."

His face relaxed with the vision of it. "I can see it too."

Annie changed position so she could nestle under his arm. He kissed her hair. "I pray Unruffled is a success. So many people depend on it being so."

She felt him take a breath to speak, but when he didn't say anything, she drew back to look at him. "What?"

He grinned. "I have a surprise coming."

"Tell me!"

"Not yet."

"A good surprise?"

He pointed to his smile. "What do you think?"

"I think I want you to tell me."

He pulled her back under his arm. "Be patient, Annie-girl."

Patience was not one of her virtues.

CHAPTER TWENTY-TWO

It was the Saturday after Thanksgiving, November 30. Annie and her friends had spent the holiday counting their blessings and enjoying a feast at Edna's. Yet beyond the blessings were prayers for what was to come: the fashion show and the opening of Unruffled.

Thank God it's a sunny day.

That bit of gratitude held the place of honor in Annie's mind as she helped the models ready for the show. What would they have done if it had been raining? Or snowing?

Those worries didn't matter, because God had provided them with a bright sky and temperatures in the fifties. Although warm enough to go without, the ladies opted to use their shawls as a fashion accessory.

The Sampsons had offered to have the fashion show in their home if need be, but the entire purpose of this street show was to display their fashion among the women who would wear it—not merely a few invited guests in a Fifth Avenue mansion.

Besides, letting Mrs. Sampson take possession of the show would have been a large step back in their relationship. Be it pride or some other vice, Annie was glad the show could go on as planned in front of the shop.

Sean and Steven came into the store with a report. "There are people lining the street. I see four new street vendors selling sandwiches, roasted nuts, bakery items, and hot coffee."

"Are the other stores ready?"

"They are. Some even have tables outside, displaying a sampling of their wares."

Edna linked her arm through Annie's. "It's working. Just as you envisioned."

Next, Vesta came inside and proclaimed, "They're asking when it's going to start."

Annie took a deep breath and let it out. "I suppose we are as ready as we'll ever be."

Mrs. Sampson raised her arm in victory. "I've been ready for this all my life. Ladies, follow me!" She nodded to her husband, and the couple exited first. Eleanor carried a rolled-up sign she shared with Mr. Sampson, who walked to the other side of the street, unfurling it: Now OPEN! UNRUFFLED: FASHION FOR THE UNRUFFLED, UNVEILED, UNSTOPPABLE WOMAN!

"You next, gentlemen," Annie told the musicians who waited nearby, wearing beautiful plaid kilts. They'd discovered the group after hearing them practicing in a room above the shoe store.

Mr. Stuart filled his bagpipes, like breathing life into an animal. His son took up his drum, and together they stepped out behind the Sampsons. Annie spotted two pieces of paper pinned to the back of their jackets: STUART MUSIC FOR HIRE. She admired their pluck. Perhaps they'd get some new business out of the day.

"Just keep playing!" Annie called after them.

In mere moments, she heard the first haunting wail of the pipe. It soon filled the street side to side, careening off the roofs and into the sky. The younger Stuart marked the beat.

Maude laughed. "If that doesn't get everyone's attention, I don't know what will."

"Go now, ladies," Annie said. "Strut, walk, dance down the street. Stop to talk to people. Show off your dresses. Have a glorious time!"

One by one the models left the store, walking in time to the music, their shawls a prop that gave them wings.

"They're doing it!" Edna said. "Look at Mrs. Tuttle dance with Jane!"

Annie laughed at her exuberant friend and her usually shy daughter. "This is what I want our fashion to do. Set women free."

Sean pushed her out the door. "Go on now. Walk after them, all of you. Enjoy your moment. Steven, Richard, and I will stay here."

"And me," Birdie said.

"Get our first sale, Birdie." That said, Annie, Maude, Henrietta, Edna, and Vesta formed a line and took up the rear of the parade, waving wildly.

Surprisingly, many of the people on the sidewalks applauded at seeing them and called out "Congratulations!" and "Job well done!"

Annie felt her entire being overflow with a goal accomplished, a victory won.

But the true test would come afterward. Would anyone buy the dresses?

As she passed Helen's Hats, she saw Helen speaking with two women about her own hat and others in the shop window. One woman pointed at Mildred's hat, and Mildred stepped over to join the conversation.

Mr. Stabler was pointing out a necklace worn by young Betsy.

Mrs. O'Hanna had a small table of gloves and fans outside her store and was showing a beautiful plaid parasol to a customer.

And Mr. Meindorff was doing a hefty business, tempting a woman with the shoes that Mrs. Trainer was wearing.

"It's working," Maude said to her. "Just as you planned."

Annie heard an inner voice. *Just as I planned.*

She shivered with joyful gratitude. "Thank You, Lord," she whispered.

"Look." Edna pointed to Maybelle, Gloria, and Mrs. Dietrich, all chatting with three other women. The sleeves must have been the subject of discussion, for they were being studied.

Her friends from Butterick were speaking with another group, with Dora turning in a full circle while a woman felt the fabric in Suzanne's dress.

A few steps later, Annie saw that Mrs. Tuttle and Jane had expanded their dance to include a passel of neighborhood children. She spotted her friend Iris marking the beat with her baby strapped in a sling across her chest. Iris, a fellow maid who had run away with Annie. Iris, who had found happiness marrying the Tuttles' son. It was all such a marvel.

Iris saw her and hurried over. They embraced around baby Danielle Ann. Annie peeked at the child. "She's such a darling. And getting big."

"She's nearly two months old." Iris checked out Annie's midsection. "And you are due when?"

"February." Annie put a hand on her own child. "I'm excited. And more than a wee bit scared."

Iris gave Danielle her little finger to suckle. "I was too, and now look at me. There is nothing like motherhood. I promise."

"So people say."

Iris nodded toward Unruffled at the far end of the street. "You're not just a shop girl anymore, Annie. You have your own shop. You achieved what you set out to do."

Annie remembered how Iris had wanted to work in a shop too. Yet her life had taken a far different turn. "Are you happy with the Tuttles and the bakery?"

"It's where I'm meant to be."

Annie nodded, understanding completely.

Iris squeezed her hand. "We did well leaving as we did."

The Stuarts stopped their walking and turned toward the revelers. Mr. and Mrs. Sampson turned their sign too, and soon the entire street was full of people gleefully dancing together, linking arms, waving shawls, clapping to the music. There was much hooting and laughing.

Sean slipped beside her. "Are you happy?"

"More than that. I am blessed."

❦

Annie watched as Birdie carried a neatly wrapped parcel to the front counter. It was tied with twine, including a handle she'd created. "Here you are, Miss Steel."

The customer took the package. "Thank you, Birdie. And thank you for helping me find the right size."

The girl beamed then remembered something. "Did you put your name in the box? There will be a drawing for a free dress."

"I did."

"I hope you win," Birdie said confidentially.

"Me too," the woman whispered.

"Come again soon."

"I most certainly will." Miss Steel left the store, perusing one last rack of dresses on the way.

"You're doing well," Annie told the girl.

"I'm enjoying it so much. I never thought a moment about fashion until seeing those dresses Johnny stole for me. And now, helping women find their own dresses..." She sighed and looked down at the dress Annie had supplied as a uniform. "I'm so thankful for the two working dresses you gave me."

"You're very welcome. I believe we are our own best advertisement."

Birdie smoothed the dress against her hips. "It makes me feel pretty."

"Pale blue is a good color for you. It matches your eyes."

"That's what I told Miss Steel about *her* dress. It really did bring out her eye color."

"Good for you." Annie saw a woman looking at the Magnolia dress. "Go see if she needs assistance."

Annie moved behind the counter and adjusted a rose in the huge bouquet Lena had sent for their opening. She leaned close to take in the heady scent, which reminded her of the gardens back at Crompton Hall. When it had been nice outside, she would often take her assigned mending out among the flowers where she could enjoy the sunshine and their heady scent.

It was a lifetime ago.

She spotted a little boy taking a piece of shortbread from a plate near the door. He moved to take a second one but saw Annie watching him. She held up one finger. He smiled and let the second one lie. The Tuttles had been generous, supplying ten dozen biscuits. The day had been full of music, food, fashion, and frivolity.

And sales.

Annie moved to check with Henrietta, who was in charge of keeping track of inventory. She stood back from the counter, a clipboard and pencil in hand.

"How are we doing?" Annie asked.

"We've sold twenty-two dresses already."

Unbelieving, Annie took the clipboard. Henrietta had made a list of all the dresses and sizes in neat rows and columns. The blue chambray dress—the Bluebell—and size thirty-two bust were the biggest sellers. And though they had sewn two in each of the eight sizes, two styles had only sold one each. Adjustments would be made to supply the demand.

Annie found great delight in seeing Maude help her mother choose a dress. Hans stood nearby, giving his opinion.

Then she spotted Mr. and Mrs. Sampson come in from holding court outside. They brought with them two men holding notepads and pencils.

"Annie, come talk to these fine journalists. They wish to write an article about Unruffled."

"Each, an article," said the tallest man. "Joe there works for the Herald, and I work for the Tribune."

Annie called Maude over and introduced her. "Maude, will you take care of these gentlemen, please?"

Maude would not be rattled by such men. She would provide them with a fine story for their articles.

Edna, Vesta, Gert, and Birdie were all helping customers. The fitting rooms were full. Annie spotted Steven peeking out from the back room where he was wrapping purchases.

Where was Sean? She'd lost track of him during the last hour. But then she saw him through the front window. He was talking with a woman. . .

They both turned to come inside and Annie recognized her old boss at Butterick. She rushed to greet her. "Mrs. Downs! How nice of you to come."

The woman kissed Annie's cheeks. "I wouldn't miss it." She drew Sean close. "Sean has been talking of nothing else for months."

"He is our biggest supporter."

"He's more than that," Mrs. Downs said.

"What?"

"He is your biggest promoter."

Annie wasn't certain what she meant. "Promoter?"

Mrs. Downs looked to Sean. "Would you like to tell her, or should I?"

Sean offered her a bow. "I give you the honor."

What *were* they talking about?

Mrs. Downs took Annie's hands in hers. "Some weeks ago your dear husband came to me with a revolutionary idea. I pooh-poohed it at first, but he was quite insistent that Unruffled would be a success, and even more than that, that your designs, dear Annie, would be a success. After seeing your sketches, I agreed and went to the higher-ups at Butterick. And"—she took a new breath for effect—"and they have finally agreed that we would like to create sewing patterns from your designs."

Annie didn't know what to say. "Patterns?"

Sean explained. "We'd still have the ready-made dresses sold in the store, but we could also provide patterns to the home sewer who may want to create her own version."

"You'd be expanding your customer base, Annie," Mrs. Downs said.

Annie put a hand to her forehead, trying to take it all in. "Patterns. Of our designs."

"We'll give you credit, printing the Unruffled logo on the pattern envelope."

She looked to Sean, who nodded. "It could be huge, Annie-girl."

Tears threatened, a full welling up of joy, surprise, and awe.

He saw her turmoil and put an arm around her. "Happy tears?"

"Flabbergasted, happy tears." She took a cleansing breath. "Thank you,

Mrs. Downs. I don't know what else to say."

"Thank your husband. It was his idea."

Oh, she would thank him. Very definitely.

◦◦◦

Annie stood before her friends in Edna's parlor where they had gathered to rehash the day.

She'd just told them about the partnership with Butterick.

They stared at her.

She was not surprised.

Edna was the first to speak. "Do you realize this means our designs will be worn all over the country, as women sew up creations by Unruffled?"

"All over the world," Maude said. "Remember that Butterick has storefronts in London, Paris, and Vienna."

"Oh my." Vesta put a hand to her chest. "Europe?"

Sean nodded. "It is part of my job to call on them each spring. Next year I will have a special incentive."

"Next year you'll have a new baby." Annie wondered how the timing would work out.

He gave her one of his looks that said, *Don't worry.*

"We'll have to get some bins to hold the patterns," Edna said. "And a display rack."

"Or two," Steven said. "You have twelve dresses this season, but each season you'll add more."

"Oh my," Vesta repeated.

Everyone started talking at once, bringing up every detail, every challenge.

Henrietta stood amid the chatter, interrupting. "Excuse me, but we need to set aside this splendid news to take care of immediate business. Our stock is depleted. We need dresses made as soon as possible." She pointed at her clipboard. "We had a successful opening, and word will—"

"How successful?" Sean asked.

She consulted her statistics. "We sold sixty-three dresses."

"That's nearly a third of our stock," Annie said.

"And some sizes are completely sold out," Henrietta noted.

"Gert, Ginny, and Edna can't sew that fast," Vesta said.

"We'll have to hire more girls immediately," Maude said.

"Perhaps we need a factory," Sean said.

275

Annie was taken aback by the immensity of the idea. Her shock must have shown on her face, for Sean added, "Someday."

They needed to get through next week first.

Henrietta held up the list. "Also, some women were interested in the shawls."

"But those were only for the show," Annie said.

Henrietta shrugged. "Perhaps we should make some to sell."

Gracious sakes.

Henrietta continued. "I know which sizes and styles have sold out, and all the details. We need to make those first, before any shawls are made."

Annie sighed with the task of it. "Henrietta, thank you for your careful records. Without them we would be flying blind."

"We can work tomorrow," Vesta said.

"But it's Sunday," Edna said. "It's the Sabbath."

Although there was work to be done, Annie made a decision. "We will not work tomorrow. We will go to church together, thank God together—"

"And ask Him for extra skill and fortitude," Maude said.

Annie nodded and shared an idea. "And then we'll go to Central Park and—if the weather holds—have a picnic to relax, rejuvenate, and celebrate."

Steven looked suddenly pensive. "What time tomorrow? Where should we meet?"

"Meet? We'll all go together."

"I—I have something to do in the morning," he said. "I will meet you there."

"All right then," Annie said. "One o'clock at the Bethesda Fountain."

Maude perused the list. "A picnic sounds lovely, but maybe I should cut out some dresses tomorrow afternoon. To be ready to sew on Monday."

Annie shook her head adamantly. "No. God has granted us great favor today *and* has given us hope for a promising future through our partnership with Butterick. In appreciation we can grant Him a day of rest, as He commanded."

No one argued, and Annie felt stronger for the decision. Surely God approved.

CHAPTER TWENTY-THREE

Annie awakened to find that Sean wasn't in bed—or anywhere in their flat. It was still early morning, so she had no idea where he could have gone. And then she remembered.

The newspaper! They'd been told by the newspaper reporters there would be articles today. She felt an inner twinge. What if they said something negative? What if they disparaged the shop, or worse than that, the designs?

She thought of the Sampsons and the fact that *they* had arranged for the men to be there. Eleanor had clout. And in his days as the founder of Sampson Fine Shoes, Mr. Sampson had supplied a plethora of advertising dollars to the papers. Surely the reporters wouldn't do anything to offend them.

Annie got dressed for church, made coffee, and began boiling some eggs for breakfast.

She stopped when she heard footsteps in the hall. Sean entered, holding a stack of newspapers draped over his arm. Which could only mean. . .

"They were good articles?"

"We will need a larger workshop sooner rather than later. I got copies for everyone."

He spread one of each newspaper on the table for her to read.

The descriptive words in the articles made her spirit soar. The words describing the fashion were *delightful, flowing, comfortable, unfettered,* and a comparatively mundane *pretty.* But the reporters didn't stop there. They described the Unruffled shop as *charming, welcoming,* and the staff *helpful* and *friendly.* The prices were declared *reasonable for all budgets.*

"They mentioned the accessories too."

Sean pointed to a specific line and read aloud. " 'Unruffled helps its customers create a complete ensemble by providing hats, shoes, and accessories in cooperation with nearby merchants. Upon visiting those other establishments, this reporter found examples of the dresses from Unruffled. This brilliant marketing move—to assist each other in helping the customer fulfill every fashion wish—is entirely commendable. When asked about the idea, Mrs. Harold Sampson (of Sampson Fine Shoes) stated that the idea originated with Annie Culver, the dress designer. We commend Mrs. Culver on her insight and progressive initiative.'"

Annie's throat grew tight. "Gracious."

Sean laughed. "Yes, they were." He took her by the shoulders. "It's working, Annie-girl. Everything you ever hoped for is coming to pass."

She drew him close, needing the beat of his heart to meld with her own—which was racing.

Thank You, God!

❦

Although it was December the first, the weather spoke of autumn. The temperature was crisp, but the sun shone brightly, and the wind took a day off. It was a perfect day for an outing.

Annie left church on Sean's arm, feeling revitalized, refreshed, and very, very grateful. Her feelings were not simply attached to the business but to life in general. She had so much to be thankful for: friends, family, faith, and the growing baby inside her. When hymns had been sung the baby moved. Did the child hear what she heard? Did it feel her happiness? Her sadness? Her stress? If so, she owed the baby a calmer version of herself. God was with them all. Fear not.

The couple walked down the Mall in Central Park alongside Henrietta, Maude, Edna, Vesta, and Richard. Steven was going to meet them at the fountain at one. They'd all found this unusual, yet no amount of prodding would get Steven to tell them the reason for his delay. It must be something important for him to miss going to church with them.

"Why am I nervous?" Henrietta said as they walked. She put a hand to her stomach. "Steven's insistence we meet him...I hope everything is all right."

"Did he hint it wasn't?" Annie asked.

"He assured me all was well."

"Perhaps it is," Maude said. "But it is odd."

"I agree," Edna added.

Sean chuckled. "You women, always finding schemes in every action."

"Not schemes," Henrietta said. "For that would imply something devious.

Steven is not devious."

Edna nodded fervently. "He certainly is not. But he can be inventive. I remember he once surprised me for my birthday by having a neighbor play the guitar while Steven sang for me."

"He's sentimental," Vesta said. "I like that in a man." She glanced at Richard.

He patted her hand. "I'm trying, Vessie."

It warmed Annie's heart to see them so close and hear their nicknames for one another. Obviously Richard had needed a little push to realize how much he loved his wife—and how much he needed to pay her some attention. She saw Sean looking in their direction too. He was smiling. It was comforting to see one's parents love each other.

"What song did he sing for your birthday?" Vesta asked Edna.

" 'Beautiful Dreamer.'" She sighed. "He has a lovely tenor voice."

"He lied to me," Henrietta said. "At the shop he implied he had an awful voice."

"We'll have to ask him to sing for us one evening," Maude said.

They neared the Bethesda Fountain. Obviously their decision to have an outing was a popular choice. Dozens of people milled around the fountain and the area between the terrace steps and the edge of the lake.

"If only the fountain wasn't turned off for winter. . ." Annie said.

"The angel is still beautiful," Sean whispered. "But not as beautiful as—"

"Ah!" Henrietta shouted.

She'd stopped walking and was staring toward the far side of the fountain.

"What's wrong?" Annie asked.

Henrietta didn't answer but put her hands to her mouth.

Then Annie saw a woman and man extend their arms in welcome.

She recognized them.

❧

Henrietta's mind stopped working. What she was seeing didn't jibe with what was possible.

But then her mother and father smiled and stretched out their arms to her.

Her mind worked quickly to catch up. *They're here in New York. They're not in England. They're smiling. They're not mad at me. They want me to run to them.*

And so she did.

She ran into her mother's arms first, clinging to her embrace, needing the solidity of her arms, her hands, and the familiar floral of her perfume to confirm this was real.

"My turn," her father said.

His embrace was stronger still, his arms encircling her with their protective warmth.

She closed her eyes, leaning her head against his shoulder. "Father," she whispered.

He released her, put a finger beneath her chin, and tilted it upward. "We were worried about you. We missed you."

Considering the way she had left, the reunion *could* have been filled with tension and anger. That it wasn't, that they greeted her with love, was testament to their character. "I missed you too. So much."

Her mother studied her a moment. "You are slimmer. Are you eating well enough?"

Henrietta smiled. "Enough yes, but differently. I've had to learn to fend for myself."

"You cook?" The surprise in her mother's question implied such a task was commensurate with learning to do something truly astounding, like driving a motor car.

Henrietta laughed. "Not well at all. But I manage. And I eat many meals with my friends." She spotted them a few steps away, watching. She motioned them close. "Annie. . ."

Annie came over, looking a bit anxious. She bobbed a curtsy. "My lord. My lady. How nice to see you."

"As it is nice to see you, Annie Wood," Lord Newley said.

Annie drew Sean close. "It's Annie Culver now. This is my husband, Sean, and his parents, Mr. and Mrs. Culver." She swept a hand toward each in turn then said, "This is Lord and Lady Newley of Crompton Hall."

"Nice to meet you," Vesta said with a nod. Her husband said the same.

Henrietta drew Edna and Maude close and introduced them.

While accomplishing this, she kept looking for Steven. Where was he? For above all the others, she wanted him to meet her parents.

Suddenly, she saw people in the crowd look toward the top of the terrace where a man stood with a guitar. And there, next to him, stood Steven.

"There he is!" she said. "There's Steven!" She waved.

He waved back then nodded to the guitarist, who started playing. And then, Steven began to sing. " 'Let me call you sweetheart, I'm in love with you.' "

Everyone stopped where they were and listened.

Steven walked down the steps toward her.

" 'Let me hear you whisper that you love me too. Keep the love light glowing in your eyes so true. Let me call you sweetheart, I'm in love with you.' "

He began another verse, and all the people on the steps and in his path to the fountain parted, letting the duo pass.

Henrietta didn't know whether to laugh or cry. She pressed her hands to her chest, her heart overflowing. By the last chorus, he stood directly in front of her, taking her hands in his.

" 'Let me call you sweetheart,' " his voice cracked, but he finished the sentiment by speaking the words. "I'm in love with you." Then he dropped to one knee. "My dearest Henrietta, would you do me the honor of being my wife?"

Although she knew she was surrounded by a complement of friends, family, and strangers, when Henrietta said yes to her beloved Steven, all others faded away. She drew him into her arms and they kissed, sealing their vow.

The applause and cheers shocked her out of her reverie, and she giggled and blushed, kissed him again, and giggled some more.

Her friends surged forward to congratulate them while the guitarist took up a position by the fountain to entertain for the sake of entertaining—and earning a few cents, as he set his hat on the ground nearby.

During the well-wishes Henrietta got separated from Steven but found him talking with her parents. She hadn't even introduced them!

She hurried to rectify the fact. "Steven, meet my father and mother and—"

"We've already met Steven," Mother said.

"It's because of him, we are here," Father said.

Henrietta didn't understand.

Mother linked her arm with Steven. "He wrote to us, introducing himself."

"How did you do that?" she asked. "I mean, how did you know where to send a letter?"

"I looked at the address on a letter they'd sent *you*."

Henrietta remembered an odd moment when he'd fiddled with one of her letters from home. "I told everyone you weren't a schemer, but you are."

He returned to her side. "I can scheme with the best of them for a good cause."

Father took over his wife's arm. "He asked me for your hand."

Henrietta was moved. "You did?"

"I wanted to do this properly. And I asked them to come here to see you, for I knew how much you missed them."

The logistics of his plan overwhelmed. To think he had managed it all without her knowledge.

"We've been staying at my cousin's," her father said. "We arrived two days ago."

Steven continued the explanation. "Through many telegrams back and forth, we were hatching a way to surprise you." He nodded toward Annie. "Annie's idea of an outing today was perfect." He looked to his own mother. "I contacted Mr. Mueller to play the guitar and. . ." He shrugged. "I'm just relieved it all fell into place."

Henrietta leaned her head against his shoulder. "You are the most marvelous man."

"And I will do my best to be a marvelous husband."

"I wish I could marry you now."

Another kiss confirmed that he agreed.

Henrietta's father raised a hand, gathering their small group close. "We have planned a celebratory dinner at Delmonico's this evening. Eight sharp. We would like all of you to attend."

Sean raised a hand. "That sounds lovely, but. . .in such a posh restaurant, don't we need tuxedos?"

"And evening dresses?" Edna said.

Henrietta's parents exchanged a glance. "You are our guests. A suit or Sunday dress will be quite suitable," Father said. "We have dined there with my cousin on many occasions. All will be well."

Henrietta knew if anyone could overturn a point of etiquette, it would be Father.

"Please," he said to all. "Come and join us."

Her parents in town, an engagement, and an engagement party?

Henrietta's cup overfloweth.

❧

Maude backed away from the group at the fountain as they chattered happily about Henrietta and Steven's engagement and the reunion with her parents. And then Maude found herself walking away from the area, away from the Mall, away from. . .

Their happiness?

The heartlessness of her insight should have made her turn around and return to their celebration. But the brokenness of her own heart prevented such action. The struggle between how she *should* feel and how she *did* feel kept her walking away from them.

She had no destination in mind but wrapped her arms tightly around herself, not against the chill of a December day but against the chill of her mood. In truth, her attitude frightened her. She was a woman who knew her own mind, who handled every situation with aplomb, who set goals and reached them. She was not emotional in the stereotypical Italian female way. She had never giggled in her life—not even as a young girl. She had never plotted to get a boy's attention, worried overly about a new dress and whether it would attract male eyes, nor dreamt of a life as a wife and—

She stopped walking as a memory surfaced, actually more than one memory of times in her girlhood bedroom, sitting by the window, gazing out to the people below, thinking about a future that *did* include her own home, her own spouse, her own children to raise. And love. *I hoped for love once. I did.*

"Excuse me, miss. . ."

A man stepped around her, causing Maude to resume walking. She spotted the sailboat pond ahead. Although it was winter, she hoped the mild weather had spurred young sailors to come out for the day. The diversion of the calm sails sliding by on the blue of the pond would do her good.

Despite the distraction of choosing a destination, her memories returned. She *had* hoped for love and family and the usual goals of womanhood. But that had been in the before-time, before she had been violated and damaged forever physically. And mentally.

I recovered. I moved on. I took the hand that was dealt to me and made a logical choice to remain single. It's a magnanimous decision. Noble.

Another designation intruded.

Cowardly.

She shook her head against the intrusive word. She was not a coward. She had faced all of it head on, alone. She had displayed fortitude and courage.

You didn't have to be alone, Maude.

These inner words did not come from her own thoughts but in spite of them, like a shimmering thread weaving its way into homespun.

God. She could have turned to Him. Should have turned to Him. Yet she'd been ashamed of the situation, even though she'd been the victim. She had argued against herself more than once, yet she had not been able to share her pain with the Lord. In fact, she'd run from Him, like a child trying to hide from her father.

And then the full truth stepped forward. God was there for her then, and He was there for her now. She just needed to trust Him.

Maude's heart beat wildly in her chest, and her breathing grew heavy as her eyes stung with tears. Tears?

She couldn't break down in the middle of Central Park. She turned around to retreat, yet if she backtracked she would surely run into her friends. Friends who would help her.

Even though she knew this was true, she shook her head against it. They were celebrating Henrietta and Steven's engagement. Maude didn't want to ruin it by intruding with her crisis of. . .

Faith?

Maude turned yet again and continued to the sail pond. She'd find a vacant bench and collect herself.

She made a beeline for a long bench straight ahead and sat at the far end, turning her gaze to the right or left, in whichever way kept her face from being fully visible to those who strolled by.

"Papa, look! It's sailing!"

She looked toward the little boy's voice and saw him at the shore with an older girl who was clapping with delight as their sailboat caught a breeze and moved through the leaf-strewn water.

Their father rushed to see. "Well done, Matteo!"

Maude's heart stopped beating. Her tears forgot to fall. Her mind discarded all thoughts as she focused on one very important fact. The man was Antonio Ricci.

She stood, and by her action drew his glance. Then his gaze. Then his smile.

His smile? The last time they'd spoken he'd accepted her apology but he'd refused her offer of friendship.

He walked toward her, causing her heart to jump and restart its beating.

"Maude." He took her hands and kissed her cheeks. "How splendid to see you."

Somehow, she found her voice. "It's splendid to see you too."

The little girl, who appeared to be nine or ten, joined him and nuzzled against his side. "This is my daughter, Angela. Gela, this is Miss Nascato."

Daughter?

The girl smiled. "Are you that lady?"

"Gela. . ."

"What lady?"

"The lady I heard Papa talk about."

Interesting. "I don't know. What did he say about the lady?"

"He said he thought you were right for us, but then you said you didn't like children, and he was sad. Do you like children?"

Antonio's face had reddened. "I'm sorry. She speaks when she should remain silent."

"But it's true, Papa. Is she the one?"

"Well, yes, she is, but that doesn't mean you should tell her that."

The girl's face drooped.

Maude touched her chin, gaining her gaze. "It's all right. I am the lady he was talking about, but what he said about me isn't quite true."

"It isn't?"

"It isn't?" Antonio echoed.

"I like children very much, but. . ." She tried to think of a way to say what needed to be said, in words appropriate for a child's ears. "I was sad that I could never have my own children."

"You can't? Why?"

"Enough, Gela," her father said. "Go check on your brother."

She shrugged and ran off.

"I apologize for her bluntness. Most children speak their minds, but my Gela speaks far more than she should."

"I think *I* could have said less about what was on my mind," she said. "Can we sit? I need to talk to you. To explain. To apologize."

"You already apologized in my office. I forgave you. There is no need—"

"There is much need. Please."

They moved to the bench where they sat side by side. "Your son is handsome. What is his name?"

"Matteo. He's nine, and Gela is a very precocious ten."

"You mentioned that their mother passed away?"

"She died soon after Matteo was born."

The tragedy of it caused her chest to tighten. "I am so sorry."

"As are we. It was horribly difficult at first, but we have managed well enough." He looked to the ground and scuffed a shoe against an acorn. "Well enough but not full well," he said. "When I met you, a new hope ignited in me that what we lack as a family could be filled by. . ." He took a new breath and looked at her. "By someone like you. By you."

Everything that Maude was going to say scattered like pebbles on the path. "By me?"

His hand skimmed the side of her skirt. "By you." He looked toward the lake, at his children. "But when you so adamantly said you didn't like children, I—"

"As I told your daughter, I believe I actually said I will never marry and *have* children."

Silence slid between them.

He broached the delicate subject. "You can never have children?"

She sighed, relieved to have the truth in the open. "I cannot."

"I'm so sorry."

She could have left it as a simple statement but felt an inner nudge to share the entire truth of it. "A few years ago I was. . ." She hated to use the word, but there was no other. "I was raped."

Antonio gasped and said in Italian, under his breath. "*È orribile! Terribile. Mi dispiace tanto.*" He took her hand in his. "I'm so sorry. I wish I could wipe it away."

"As do I." She needed to finish this. "But due to my injuries. . .I cannot bear children."

He drew her hand to his lips and kissed it. "*Mia cara donna.*"

"That is the reason I so blatantly stopped the dinner at my mother's. She wanted us to be together and—"

"I wanted us to be together."

She looked into his dark, deep eyes. "*I* wanted us to be together, but because of the awful truth I had to stop the feelings before they went further. I didn't want my deficiency to be a burden to you."

He spoke softly, his words a caress. "You, and all you are, could never be a burden. And I see no deficiency. Only a delightful *suf*ficiency. A delightful abundance of all I hold dear."

Her throat tightened. "I didn't know you would feel this way." *I didn't know any man could feel this way.*

"You assumed too much." He smiled. "You didn't know that I am an extraordinary man. Quite remarkable really."

It felt good to laugh. But then Maude grew serious. "Actually, I did know you were extraordinary from the first time I met you." She slipped her arm through his and leaned toward him, feeling his warmth, finding strength in his strength. They watched the children sail. "I didn't know you had children."

"I was going to tell you—obviously—but I didn't want you to meet them until I felt certain you would consider us, as a whole."

She could understand that.

"At your mother's dinner, I was going to ask you to come on an outing with us, but then. . ."

"I ruined it."

"And then I was angry. At you, at myself for being drawn to you, and at God for teasing my emotions, giving me hope only to dash it."

"I'm so sorry. I thought my decision not to marry was what God wanted me to do. I thought. . ." This would sound silly. "That perhaps it was penance."

"For what?"

For being victimized? She hurried to explain. "I was taking a walk after dark and wasn't paying attention to my surroundings."

"That doesn't mean you deserved to be attacked."

She shook her head. "No, but I was usually smarter than that. My father was a foreign diplomat. I've lived all over the world. I was taught to be intuitive in strange situations. Wary and alert."

"But it wasn't a strange situation. You'd walked that way before?"

"Hundreds of times." *Whenever Mother and I had an argument.*

"But even if it was new, that doesn't mean you were in the wrong. It was not your fault."

His voice had risen, causing a couple who were strolling by to glance their way.

He lowered the volume of his words. "I never want to hear you say that again. Doing penance for someone else's sin? That's nonsense."

She felt a weight lifted. "I do wonder why God allowed it to happen."

"We may never know. As we may never know why He took my dear Sophia. All we do know is that He is with us, helping us through."

She scoffed.

"Why do you do that?"

"I've been rather mad at God."

"So was I."

"I don't think He likes anger."

Antonio raised a finger. "But He does understand it, and waits for us to see that He is right where we left Him. We move away; He doesn't."

Maude looked to her lap. She knew everything he said was true, and yet… "Knowing the truth and acting on it are very different."

"I've been where you are, yet I found my way back to Him."

Maude remembered her mother's words after Maude had humiliated herself. *"Saying no to marriage is your decision, not God's. . .open the door, Maudey."*

She began to laugh.

"What's funny?"

"God just opened a door for me today. Leading me away from my friends. Finding. . .you."

The way he smiled at her filled her in a way she never knew she needed to be filled.

Then he cocked his head as if thinking a new thought. He angled his body to face her. "This may sound *pazzesco*, but if I had not lost Sophia, and if you had not been attacked—which led you to spurn the idea of marriage. . ."

She grasped the direction of his words. "We would never have considered the other beyond a business relationship."

"I would still be happily married, and you too would probably be married."

"Our crises created a new need within us."

"They created us, new," he said.

"Changed."

"Which left us open to finding each other."

Maude took in a fresh breath, released it, then gasped with an additional thought. "I cannot have children, but you already have children."

He nodded, smiling wistfully at her. "You *can* be a mother, Maude."

Was he proposing?

He must have seen the look of shock on her face, for he backpedaled. "I am not asking you to marry me—yet. But remember when I went to dinner at your mother's, I said I was ready to tell you about my children and ask you to go on an outing with us?"

"I do."

"It appears we are already on an outing." He stood and drew her to standing beside him. "Shall we?"

Maude wanted to shout it for all the park to hear. "We shall!"

⚬⚬⚬

"I don't know where she went," Annie said, walking around the Bethesda fountain for the tenth time. Her feet hurt. Her back hurt. She wanted to go home and rest, for they had a big evening planned at Delmonico's.

"Go on home, Annie," Edna said. "I'll wait for her."

Sean shook his head. "We'll wait with you." He led his wife to a bench. "Sit."

It was up to the three of them. Vesta and Richard had left for home. Henrietta, Steven, and her parents had gone off to the Friesens' to spend the afternoon together.

They had to find Maude.

Annie was on the verge of letting her annoyance grow to anger when she spotted Maude walking toward them.

She was not alone. She had her arm linked with a handsome Italian-looking man who carried a toy sailboat. Skipping in front of them were two children holding hands.

Was this Antonio Ricci? If so, were those children. . . ?

Maude waved, and Annie waved back.

"Is that who I think it is?" Sean said.

"I expect so."

"He has children?" Edna said quietly.

"Apparently, he does."

"Maude is smiling."

Very much so. Something had happened in the last hour. Annie had never seen Maude's cheeks so rosy, her smile so broad, her eyes so bright.

"There you are," Annie said as they drew close. "We were worried about you."

"I'm sorry," Maude said. "I should have told you where I was going, but I didn't know myself."

"She didn't know she was finding me," Antonio said. "And I, her." He extended his hand to Annie. "I'm Antonio Ricci. Antonio. And you must be Annie."

"I am." She glanced at Maude who was blushing nicely. "We've heard so much about you."

When he looked at Maude her blush intensified. "I might have shared a few of your attributes with them."

"Attributes?"

"Good traits, one and all," Annie said. "Antonio, this is my husband, Sean."

They shook hands. It was quite a visual moment with Sean's blond handsomeness meeting Antonio's Mediterranean good looks.

Maude moved beside Edna and said, "This is my dear friend, Edna Holmquist. We share an apartment."

"*Very* nice to meet you, Antonio."

Annie knew they were all were sizing up this man who had stolen Maude's heart. He was charming and at ease, and attractive enough to turn any female's head.

But the children. . . Maude hadn't said anything about him having children. Annie pointed to the boy's sailboat. "Did it sail well today?"

"A little well. There's not much breeze. And there are leaves in the water, in the way."

"So you're Annie?" the little girl asked. She glanced at Maude. "Maude said we were going to find Annie."

"I am Annie. And you are?"

"Angela, but I like to be called Gela. And he's Matteo."

Annie shook their hands. Both children had eyes the color of rich chocolate. "Nice to meet you."

Annie wanted to take Maude aside and ask a thousand questions. Yet by her smile, she already knew the most important answers: Maude and Antonio were reconciled, and Maude had obviously changed her mind about letting romance enter her life.

"Where are the others?" Maude asked. "I want to introduce them."

"Gone home for the afternoon," Annie said. "We will meet at Delmonico's at eight." She hastened to take liberties with the invitation by addressing Antonio. "I'm sure Henrietta and her family would love for you and the children to come along."

"I don't wish to intrude."

"I assure you, you will be quite welcome."

"Then I accept," he said. "I am eager to know all of the important people in Maude's life."

They began to walk down the Mall, a happy gaggle, but soon Antonio and the children had to go home.

Which was fine with Annie, as it left Maude alone for some female interrogation. To fully embrace their chance, she whispered in Sean's ear, instructing him to walk ahead.

"I saw what you just did," Maude said to Annie. "And I thank you for it, because I really want to talk to you two alone."

"Tell us every detail," Edna said.

"Did you know he was going to be here?"

"Of course not. I had no plans to walk to the sailing pond either, but. . ."

"But what?"

Maude fiddled with her gloves. "God wanted me there. To see Antonio. To make things right between us." Her eyes glistened. "He gave me another chance."

"God or Antonio?" Edna asked.

"Both." Maude was so full of emotion she came to a stop, took their hands, and faced them. "You remember when I went to my mother's for dinner and Antonio was there, how I was rude to him?"

"You went to his office to apologize."

"He accepted my apology, but I'd hurt him so badly I thought I'd ruined everything." She looked over her shoulder toward the pond. "But then I saw him by the water. And he had two children. He saw me and smiled. He smiled at me."

"Of course he smiled at you."

She shook her head vehemently. "You don't understand how cold he'd been at his office. I thought he never wanted to see me again." She sighed. "But at the pond. . .the bad things in the past faded away."

"He'd forgiven you."

She nodded. "I got a second chance." She squeezed their hands. "God arranged for me to see him and softened his heart toward me. Even after all I did."

"God is merciful," Edna said. "He is the God of second chances."

"And third," Annie said. She remembered the many times she'd pushed Sean away before she'd come to her senses and married the man.

"Did you know he had children?" Edna asked.

"I didn't. He said his wife died soon after Matteo was born. He was going to tell me about the children the night of the dinner." She lifted her hands and let them drop. "I can't have children, yet I find a man who already has two—two children in need of a mother? It's incredible."

Annie felt a twinge of worry that Maude was jumping too fast.

Maude must have seen her wariness for she said, "We're not engaged. Yet."

Edna kept her voice low. "Does he know about the attack and your condition?"

"He does."

Annie was taken aback. "He does?"

"I just told him."

"My, my," Edna said. "You made quick work of many important issues."

Maude put a fist to her chest. "The need to tell him the truth and my change of heart that allowed the idea of loving someone have been stirring within me for nearly a month. When I saw him I was ready to lay the truth out between us. I'm so thankful I got the chance, for I truly believe if I hadn't, the could-have-beens would have haunted me the rest of my life." She linked arms with her friends and they began to walk.

Edna beat Annie to a question that was on her mind. "But two children... are you up for it?"

Annie was almost relieved Maude hesitated, for the pause made her words more credible.

"There is no way to know." She glanced at Annie. "Do you know if you will be a good mother?"

It was a good point. "There is no way to know."

"What I do know is that I am about ready to burst with happiness."

Her joy was Annie's joy. To have both Maude and Henrietta find good men who loved them...God was very, very good.

❧

The *maitre d'* at Delmonico's gave their attire a glance. He was dressed more formally than they were and led the group to a large table set for eleven—not thirteen, for Antonio had left the children with his parents.

As they walked past table after table where men and women were dressed in elegant formalwear, Annie was glad they were seated quickly to better hide her nice-but-not-fancy clothes.

Sean, Steven, and Antonio seemed oblivious to the disparity between their Sunday suits and the tuxedos around them. Only Sean's father, Richard, seemed embarrassed by it.

Lady Newley sat beside her and leaned close. "Don't be nervous. The other diners don't bite. They only take an occasional nip."

Annie let her worries pass. It was odd to be seated next to her mistress. Fifteen months ago Annie had been her housemaid. And now, to be seated next to Lord and Lady Newley, dining with them? It overwhelmed.

Once all were settled, Lord Newley rose. "I want to thank you for joining my wife and I for this celebration of our daughter's betrothal. I took the liberty of choosing a menu for us." He nodded to a waiter who brought over printed menus with the heading of *In Honor of the Betrothal of Steven Holmquist and Henrietta Kidd*. There were lovely illustrations of flowers and curlicues forming a frame. Annie scanned the exotic dishes: Oysters, *consommé souveraine*, green turtle, *timbales perigerdine*, filets of kingfish *meunière*, cucumbers, *persillade* potatoes, saddle of lamb Colbert, stuffed tomatoes, Baltimore terrapin, mushrooms on toast with cream, sherbet with kirsch, quail, red head duck, fried hominy and currant jelly, celery mayonnaise, and for dessert, fancy ice cream, assorted cakes, bonbons, and coffee.

Gracious. "I'm afraid I only comprehend every other dish."

Henrietta laughed with her. "I know *meunière* is a luscious butter sauce."

Sean raised a hand. "Butter always wins me over."

"Doesn't the word *timbales* mean drum in French?" Vesta asked.

"It does," Lady Newley said. "That is a truffle dish formed in a rectangular crust, like a drum."

"But drums are round," Steven said.

Lady Newley laughed. "That is what I always thought. But rectangular or round, it is delicious."

Lord Newley pointed to one of the dishes. "My wife and cousin chose the menu, and there is one dish *I* don't recognize. Hominy?"

"It's a kind of corn," Edna said. "They can make grits out of it."

"Grits?"

"Ground up hominy that's boiled. It's quite tasty, but you eat it more in the South than up here in New York."

"I will look forward to the ice cream," Antonio said. "My children ask for it far too often."

"I love it too," Maude said.

"Then we shall enjoy some together on our next outing."

The look exchanged between Maude and Antonio warmed Annie. Witnessing a courtship brought back happy memories of her own.

The service began, and Annie paced herself, wanting to try each and every dish—which were all delicious. And yes, Henrietta had been correct, the butter sauce on the fish was divine.

The conversation was lively, and stories were shared about the creation and opening of Unruffled. The Newleys were gracious and seemed genuinely interested in the details.

Annie thought she had absolutely no room to partake of the desserts, but when a tray of petits fours was offered, and then ice cream, she could not resist. She also chose one bonbon for good measure.

When all were satisfied and satiated, Lord Newley rose to offer a toast. "Our dear daughter Henrietta gave us a scare when she sailed to the United States on her own. Yet we have come to realize such an act took extraordinary courage."

Henrietta crossed her hands upon her heart. "Thank you, Father."

He continued. "Although we were distressed at first, we now see she made a wise choice in her journey, and in her choice of a spouse." He looked down at his wife and reached for her hand. "We wish for Henrietta and Steven to have what we have, a match grounded in love."

Lady Newley kissed his hand.

"What we didn't know at first is that she had been inspired to make her bold choice because of the bold choice of another. Of Annie." He smiled at her. "As our daughter is courageous, so is Annie."

He studied her a moment, and Annie felt ill at ease. Lord Newley had spoken few words to her and had never given her such scrutiny. Nor such a genuine smile.

"When we gave you a job at the age of fourteen, we never imagined the hidden talent you possessed. And honestly, it would never have been discovered if you had not been audacious enough to run away." He looked at Annie then at his daughter. "Two women who abandoned what was and chose to follow their dreams and discover their unique path."

"And love," Henrietta said, squeezing Steven's hand.

Her father smiled. "And love." He raised his glass. "And so I make a toast to Henrietta and Steven in honor of their betrothal. And to all their beloved friends who will stand behind them as they begin their lives together."

"Hear, hear!" Sean said as he rose from his chair.

Everyone stood.

"*Skål!*" Edna said.

"*Salute! Cent' anni,*" Antonio added.

The sounds of glass clinking against glass was a delightful complement to the moment.

Although Annie wasn't certain about protocol, she felt compelled to say something. "If I may add one more toast, please?"

"Of course," Lord Newley said with a nod.

Her mind raced to find the words, and then she remembered a moment with Sean, before they were married. "On the way to meet Vesta and Richard for the first time, Sean and I walked across the Brooklyn Bridge. We stopped halfway over and looked at the river, toward the Statue of Liberty in the distance. We spoke about our dreams." She looked at her dear husband. "And now my dreams have come true, for I have married a man I adore, I carry his child, and I am in the presence of friends who make my life complete."

Words of affirmation flittered around the table.

Annie lifted her hand, needing to finish. "On that bridge, in that moment, Sean said he dreamt of knowing he made a difference."

"I said that?" Sean asked.

Annie nodded, remembering his words as if they were spoken yesterday. "You said you dreamt of knowing there was a definite reason you were born, that you exist now—not a hundred years from now. You wanted to know God had a plan that would be fulfilled through you." She felt her eyes sting with happy tears and looked at all those gathered around her. "Together we have achieved that dream, not only through our store but through the bond and love we share. We are meant to live now. We are meant to be together now. We are meant to be a family now. God approves of us." She took a fresh breath and finished, "And so I thank Him and ask Him to bless us all and guide us toward our futures."

"To us!" Maude said.

Sean leaned close and kissed her. "To us, Annie-girl."

CHAPTER TWENTY-FOUR

Two Months Later
February 1913

Annie took the parcel from Birdie Doyle and handed it to a customer. "Thank you for your business, Mrs. Campbell. We look forward to seeing you again."

"You can count on that," the woman said. "I believe this is my third visit."

Three visits and three dress purchases.

The first time the copper-haired Mrs. Campbell had come in, Annie felt like they'd met before. Mrs. Campbell made the connection for her, telling her they'd met at Eleanor's soiree, when she'd been expecting. At that time, Annie had steered her to Lane Bryant's for maternity wear. That Mrs. Campbell remembered Annie and had sought her out for regular dresses was satisfying. Especially since she represented the posh set. Annie hoped she would start a trend.

As soon as Mrs. Campbell left, Birdie let out a long breath. "That's six sold this morning."

Annie marked the newest sale on a ledger so a replacement dress could be made as soon as possible.

"They seem to like the new designs you came up with for spring."

"Helen's gorgeous hats help. Speaking of, would you run down to her store and tell her we need three more to put on display?"

"Gladly. It's such a lovely day, I'm glad to get out."

Birdie had become quite the asset to Unruffled. She was always on time, had a good fashion eye in helping the customers, and was willing to do whatever needed to be done. It had been Birdie's idea to hire an alterations girl, Rachel Meindorff—whose father ran Meindorff's Shoes across the street. Rachel had been a customer early on but was very petite. All the dresses were too long for her. Rachel had bought one anyway, saying she was used to altering clothes. Since Rachel wasn't the only one whose fit needed a bit of altering here and there, Annie had hired her part time. Besides being a skilled girl, she was sweet, and Annie often shared stories of alterations she'd made for Lady Newley and Henrietta.

Rachel marked a hem of a dress that Edna had just sold as Vesta held out two pairs of gloves that could complete the ensemble. The banter between the women was a balm to Annie's soul. Often, during free moments, she looked across the store and marveled at all they had accomplished. Everyone had a skill that was necessary for the store to succeed, as if God had anticipated a need and brought someone to fill it. He was the ultimate Boss who masterminded His business, watching over it with loving care. Annie couldn't count the number of times she sent swift *thank Yous* heavenward each day. She could not have done it without Him.

She felt the baby turn over in her belly and put a calming hand on it. Any day now she would be holding a child in her arms. She was ready to enjoy motherhood, knowing that the shop was firmly planted and in good hands. Another God-sent provision.

Henrietta came into the store, her familiar clipboard in hand. That morning she'd stopped in at the new workshop space they'd rented—with Antonio's help—and was in charge of setting up the additional sewing machines and cutting spaces. They now kept ten seamstresses busy, yet they had not let their original workshop space go for it provided a good centrally located space to meet and discuss new designs, create the patterns, and sew the mockups until they were fully approved and ready to manufacture.

Annie wasn't sure she could ever let the workshop go, for it had been at the heart of their entire venture.

"How are things progressing?" Annie asked Henrietta.

"Very well, all in all, though I've already had to let one woman go."

"Who?"

"Mrs. Hiller."

Annie remembered the name. "You were worried about her skill level."

"It was that, but also her attitude. She was lazy, always late, full of excuses, and was a storm cloud hanging over the other girls. Even beyond all that, there was just something off about her that caused my hackles to rise."

"Then you did the right thing."

"I hate it."

"What?"

"Sacking people."

"No one enjoys it."

Henrietta held the clipboard to her chest. "I know Father has trouble with it. Although he is lord of the manor, he is always cognizant that people need work to survive. He usually attempts to put them in another position, trying to find a fit."

Annie thought of her own father, who'd flit from one job to another back in Summerfield. No one ever had trouble sacking Rufus Wood. By his theft, absence, bad attitude, and drunkenness, he gave them little choice. Yet in his eyes, it was always someone else's fault.

Setting her bad memories aside, Annie remembered a shipment that had come in, something that was sure to cheer Henrietta. "Look in the back. Something came for you."

Henrietta's eyes lit up. "It came?"

"It did."

She rushed to the storeroom, and Annie heard an exclamation of glee and paper ripping as Henrietta removed the outer wrapping. Soon after, she came out to the showroom, proudly lugging the heavy bolt of fabric.

Birdie rushed to help, taking one end.

"Over here," Annie said, clearing a place at the counter. "Let us all see it."

Henrietta untied the strings around the fabric, and unrolled enough to let it drape in her arms. A lush charmeuse satin created luxurious highlights and shadows.

All the women in the store gathered close—even the customers. Various renditions of "oooh" flit through the room.

"I want to see the dress design," Vesta said.

Henrietta motioned to Birdie. "Would you go in back and retrieve my other clipboard, please?"

A few moments later, Henrietta presented a sketch of her dress. It was a slim gown made of charmeuse, with long sleeves that had pearl buttons parading five inches up from the wrist. Over that dress was a fingertip-length sheer tunic with wider sleeves to the elbows. It was open in the middle, allowing for an outline of wide maline lace to extend around the neckline and the hem of the tunic. A draped charmeuse belt encircled the raised waistline, ornamented with a sprig of silk buds.

"It's beyond lovely," Edna said. "You did an excellent job, Annie."

"Thank you. Henrietta had good ideas to start with. I just put them together."

"It's as beautiful as any dress I ever could have ordered from the House of Paquin or Worth in Paris."

Annie felt herself blush but was pleased with the compliment.

Henrietta pointed at the sketch. "In honor of the store's name, you see I have no ruffles, and my veil covers my hair but not my face."

Annie laughed. "You are indeed an unruffled, unveiled, unstoppable woman."

Henrietta grinned proudly. "That I am."

"Maybe we should start a line of wedding dresses," Edna said.

Annie shook her head, adamantly. "Wedding dresses lend themselves to customization, which is not the Unruffled way."

Edna shrugged. "Never say never."

"That's true," Vesta said. "We never could have imagined having a second workshop, but now we do."

Actually, Annie liked the idea of having a few wedding dresses in their line. Simpler dresses than the gowns of the past with their ten-foot trains and hand-beading. There actually might be a market for it.

Luckily, Maude burst into the store and set such daydreaming—and challenges—aside.

"*Ciao*, ladies," she said.

Entering behind her were Antonio and the children. Their cheeks were rosy, their eyes bright.

"How was your visit to the zoo?" Edna asked.

Gela answered. "We saw an elephant that was taller than Papa."

"And a tiger," Matteo said. "He licked his chops."

Maude drew him close, tickling his stomach. "That's because you tossed him your sandwich, naughty boy."

Maude spotted the fabric and hurried to touch it. "Ooooh."

Annie laughed. "That's what we all said."

"Are you nearly done with the pattern for it?" Henrietta asked.

"I've started making it in muslin, just to be sure. I don't want to cut into this exquisite yardage until all the kinks are worked out of the design."

"Kinks? In my design?" Annie teased.

"The detail on the sleeves needs adjusting. Just a bit."

Annie waved away her comments. "Have a good go of it. If anyone can create a gorgeous gown for our dear Henrietta, it is you."

Maude shared an odd glance with Antonio. When he nodded, she said, "You will soon need to design another wedding gown, Annie." She held out her left hand to reveal an amethyst ring.

The women each took a turn to see. "When did this happen?"

"Somewhere between the elephants and the tigers," Maude said.

Antonio interjected. "I know it's not the most romantic of proposals, but I've had the ring for two weeks, and there never seemed the perfect time, so when we sat on a bench to rest, I knelt before her and asked."

Maude admired her ring. "It is a proposal I will never forget."

Antonio drew her close and kissed her—accompanied by the applause of the ladies and the children.

"When will you marry?" Vesta asked.

"The sooner the better," Antonio said.

Maude interjected. "We are content to let Steven and Henrietta have their day. And ours will be less formal. Just a few friends and family."

Henrietta's parents were planning a lavish wedding in New York, with many of the town's elite invited.

Matteo raised his hand. "I get to be a ring-bear." He turned to his father. "Do I have to growl?"

They all laughed and set him straight.

Just then Sean came in, carrying a wrapped parcel. "Well, well, what a jolly store this is."

Maude thrust her ring toward him. "Antonio and I are engaged."

He kissed her cheek and shook Antonio's hand. "Congratulations to you both." He moved to Annie's side. "I have my own surprise. Unwrap this."

Annie did the honors and saw a stack of Butterick patterns. But not just any patterns, Unruffled patterns.

"They're done!" Annie passed them around so everyone could see the designs come to life for the home sewer.

"Look at our name on the front," Edna said with awe in her voice.

Annie ran her fingers across the lettering that matched the font on the storefront: BROUGHT TO YOU BY *UNRUFFLED*.

Birdie studied the envelope. "To think that women across the entire country will know the name of our store." She looked up, catching her faux pas. "Your store."

"No, Birdie," Annie said. "You were right the first time. Our store. For we've all had a hand in—"

Suddenly, Annie doubled over with pain, as her belly tightened. "Ahhhh!"

They all stared at her, but only for a moment. "The baby?"

"Sit, sit," Sean said, bringing a chair close.

She fell into the seat, grimacing until the pain eased. "That was a hard one."

"You've been having others?" Edna asked.

"Off and on all day."

"You should have said something! We need to get the doctor," Vesta said.

Sean knelt beside her. "And we need to get you home."

She nodded. Although she'd tried to ignore the previous contractions, the intensity of the last one could not be denied. Its strength deemed the previous pain weak cramps.

The knowledge that the pain would intensify terrified her.

Antonio had rushed outside and returned, saying a cab was waiting to take her and Sean home. The men helped her inside and the cab pulled away.

"It's happening." Annie looked into Sean's eyes. "It's really happening."

He kissed her gently. "Everything will be all right."

She had to believe him.

⚬⚬⚬

For the next twelve hours, Annie's world grew very small even as it expanded beyond her comprehension. Sean, Dr. Grant, and Vesta hovered just outside Annie's realm of pain, a pain that teased her by its release then grabbed hold with new ferocity that consumed her.

During the breaks in the agony—breaks that grew shorter and shorter— Annie lived in a dream world where her thoughts had no firm footing but swirled around her with hazy edges that were yanked into sharp focus when another contraction took hold. The only cognizant thought that repeated itself was that she hadn't expected the pain to be so excruciating. Labor indeed. It was torture. And she wanted it to end.

Which it did in a frenzy of pushing. She could not have stopped the action had she tried, for the child demanded its freedom and would not be denied.

And then there was release. A sudden lack of pain followed by a baby's cry.

With an intake of breath, Annie realized it was over. She'd done it! The utterly focused world she had visited slipped away under the bedroom door. The new world that was born along with her child unfolded before her with limitless borders, a portal of time and life and air and joy.

"It's a girl, Annie. A healthy girl!" The doctor held up a wriggling, angry being who seemed to question her decision to be born into this too bright, too chilly world.

Annie's throat grew tight with awe, and she held out arms that ached to hold the baby. Needed to hold her or die.

Her. A girl. Just as she'd expected.

"Just a minute or two and you can have her," the doctor said.

She heard a knock on the bedroom door, and Sean asked, "Can I come in?" The doctor repeated his words to the father.

Annie was surprised to feel another contraction, but the doctor assured her it was normal. While he worked on Annie, she watched Vesta gently wash the baby nearby, speaking to it, smiling at it, loving her into the world.

Annie took the moments given her and closed her eyes in exhaustion but also in prayer. *Thank You for helping me through. Thank You for the baby's health. Help me be a good mother. Help—*

"Annie, would you like to hold your daughter now?"

It was a silly question.

Vesta lay the baby in the crook of her arm, her tiny body wrapped in a white blanket.

Annie gazed at her. "Oh. . .my darling child."

A wave of love beyond all love swept through Annie and over the babe, swaddling them together. Annie ran a finger along the baby's cheek and her mouth moved in that direction, responding to her mother's touch.

Then Sean was by her side, his face glowing in wonder. He touched the child as if needing to confirm she was real. Then he kissed Annie. "Well done, Annie-girl. So very well done."

"You got your girl."

Sean laughed with utter delight. "May I hold her?"

Vesta helped move the child from mother to father, and Annie marveled at Sean's ease, as if he was created for such a moment. He immediately began to rock and touched her head with reverence. The baby squirmed, and her hand appeared from beneath the blanket. Sean gave her his finger, and she wrapped her tiny fingers around it. His eyes lit up. "Look at this!"

"She likes you. It's the first of countless times she'll hold the hand of her papa."

Sean sat on the edge of the bed and leaned close to give Annie a proper kiss. "I love you more than I can say." He looked at their child. "I love the both of you. My girls."

"As I love you. And. . .Victoria."

They had discussed names but had not come to choose one. Until now. "Do you approve?" Annie asked. "She looks so regal, so strong. She is our victory."

He looked at Victoria as if weighing the name against the precious being in his arms. "Hello, Victoria. Welcome to the family."

And now these three remain: faith, hope and love.
But the greatest of these is love.
1 CORINTHIANS 13:13 NIV

Dear Reader,

I hope you have enjoyed the journey of the shop, Unruffled. Annie and the others worked so hard to make it happen! Actually. . .I would love to work there.

An entrepreneurial spirit is deeply embedded in my family. My husband, Mark, and I started a commercial flooring business in the eighties, and each of my siblings and my parents had (or still have) their own businesses. It's in our blood. Each of our immigrant ancestors did the same whether they came here in the 1640s or the 1800s. They grabbed hold of the American dream and made it their own.

As a seamstress I know there's a bit of fashion designer in me. I love to watch *Project Runway*, which challenges budding fashion designers to create on demand. I'm always thinking about what I would do to address each challenge. Just last week I bought a luscious piece of fabric for no reason other than it made me say, "Ooooh."

The era of *The Fashion Designer* was a time of enormous change in fashion. During 1912–13 the changes were just appearing, the focus turning to function and comfort more than frippery and frills. Coming next in history is World War I, which spurred designs offering additional ease of movement that led to perhaps the biggest change of all, the Roaring Twenties, with short skirts, boxy silhouettes, and bobbed hair. I'm glad Annie could be in business at the start of these monumental changes.

A few notes about the history in this book: I've mentioned this sort of thing before. . .but the inclusion of many of the historical moments came as a surprise.

I never planned on having Lane Bryant be a part of this story. While researching something else I came upon Lena Bryant Malsin's story and just had to include it. Lane Bryant was the first company to mass-produce maternity and plus-sized clothes. I read that between 1909 and 1923, their sales grew from $50,000 to $5 million! Truly, an American success story. (You can see an ad for their maternity corset in the back of this book.)

Pier 54, where Henrietta went to catch a ship home, was the pier where— just seven months earlier—the *Carpathia* docked, carrying home many of the survivors from the *Titanic*. It also was the pier from which the *Lusitania* departed in 1915. That ship was sunk by a German U-boat during World War I and 1,193 people were killed. The terminal had fire damage in the '30s and was finally torn down in 1991. But the iron arch at the entry remains.

The menu at Delmonico's in Chapter 23 was the menu for Mark Twain's seventieth birthday party held there in 1905. He invited 170 friends and peers. Half were women, with most guests having ties to writing or illustrating. Twain gave a long speech, proving himself to be a master wordsmith. He left his guests moaning with laughter but also brought them to tears. One particular bit of wisdom that impressed me was this: "We can't reach old age by another man's road." If you'd like to read an article about the dinner, written by a reporter who was there, go to: http://www.twainquotes.com/19051206.html. It will make you wish you could have been in attendance.

The Sampsons' home at 451 Madison Avenue still exists and is called the Villard House. In 1978 it was altered into Helmsley Palace. (Remember the notorious Leona Helmsley?) It is now the Lotte New York Palace hotel. I actually found floor plans and photos of the original structure, which interested me greatly since I have a college degree in architecture. The intricate marquetry and many of the intricate decoration still exists.

Mrs. Mixter's book: *Health and Beauty Hints* was another fun find. The quote Henrietta reads about exercising her face muscles is from the book. I bought a copy and found the suggestions for massage, exercise, and cleanliness logical, if not a bit overboard. But I cannot disparage Mrs. Mixter's directions too much—though I heartily reject going three weeks without washing my hair—because when I look in my cabinets and see all the miracle wrinkle creams, conditioners, shampoos, and lotions I realize the desire to look our best is timeless.

I also didn't plan on including the election of 1912. Most elections are rather ordinary—except this one, with Teddy Roosevelt being shot and creating a third party, and a sitting vice president dying before the election.

Beyond the history, the characters always surprise me. When Henrietta bowed out of funding the business, I had no idea where they would get the money. And then I realized it was Election Day (November 5, 1912) and Eleanor Sampson would probably be interested in the suffragette movement, and if she was interested in that, she wouldn't have time to pursue Eleanor's Couture. And Eleanor had money.... Voila! An answer to both our problems.

So if these points of history weren't planned, what was?

I wanted to talk about daily life. Yet that goal showed itself to be problematic, as nothing was standard. Since the country was going through so many revolutionary changes, some apartments had private bathrooms, stoves, iceboxes, and electricity. And some still did not. That's why Edna's and Annie's apartments were modern, while Henrietta's was behind the times.

I was surprised to find that almost all retail establishments bore someone's name. That's one reason I chose Unruffled for the ladies' shop. I wanted Annie to be ahead of the curve.

Women were filling up the workforce, from factories to offices. Male secretaries and bank tellers were being replaced by females—a change that has obviously endured. Rent was another detail that was hard to pin down. Hotel prices. And banking. And whether or not stores offered sized dresses "on the rack" to take home. I tried very hard to get it right.

I thank the internet for these details. The idea of going to a library to do this research one book at a time. . .the thought of that process overwhelms me. The internet let me take a rabbit trail to find a detail and still have time to return to writing where I could incorporate the detail into a scene. The hard point was staying on task. There's so much to learn!

On a personal note, when Sean tells Annie, "You got your girl," that's exactly what my husband told me when our oldest daughter, Emily, was born.

I also slipped in a reference to some characters from my Manor House Series. The love story of Lady Newley (Lila) is shown in *Love of the Summerfields* and *Bride of the Summerfields*, and Henrietta shows up in *Rise of the Summerfields*. I like to intertwine storylines when I can, as it makes the characters seem more real, as if life goes on after the last page. I hope you agree.

If you'd like to read about how Annie came to work as a maid at Crompton Hall, read my novella, "Pin's Promise" in the anthology *Christmas Stitches* (October 2018). There's a teaser excerpt of this story at the back of this book.

I hope you enjoyed getting to know the ladies and stepping into their world. I assume you are happy that Henrietta and Maude found love. You're all invited to the weddings. No gift required, but wear something that proves you are an unruffled, unveiled, unstoppable woman.

The Characters of *The Fashion Designer*

Annie Culver
(who happens to look like Coco Chanel)

Sean Culver

Richard & Vesta Culver's wedding photo 1885

Edna Holmquist

Maude Nascato

Eleanor Sampson

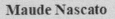

Steven Holmquist & Henrietta Kidd in Central Park

DISTINCTIVE STYLES FOR THE FALL SEASON

FOR DESCRIPTIONS SEE OPPOSITE PAGE

Chapter 14: "...the fabric a steel blue rayon chambray. The sleeve-length was three-fourths—the length of choice for most of Annie's designs. The neckline had no collar, but a facing that was squared off six-inches below the neck, with two strips on either side of the square continuing down the front of the bodice halfway, ending in two points. Within the center squared-off area the bodice sported tucks to provide ease over the bust, with matching tucks at the shoulders. Top stitching added ornament to the facing and the edge of the comfortable sleeves. The skirt was made in six, straight panels that opened into six pleats at knee level providing ease of movement. The top of each pleat was adorned with a column of three silver buttons that matched the silver buckle on the matching belt. The dress had a side-zipper, and a small opening at the back of the neck."

1913 "McCalls"

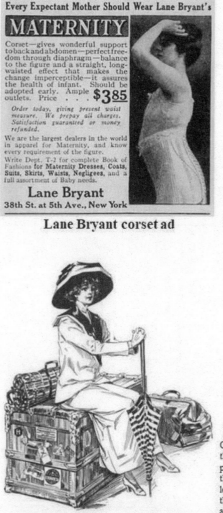

Lane Bryant corset ad

Henrietta's bridal gown

Chapter 24: "It was a slim gown made of the charmeuse, with long sleeves that had pearl buttons parading five inches up from the wrist. Over that dress was a fingertip-length sheer tunic with wider sleeves to the elbows. It was open in the middle, allowing for an outline of wide maline lace to extend around the neckline and the hem of the tunic. A draped charmeuse belt encircled the raised waistline, ornamented with a sprig of silk buds."

*Victorian and Edwardian Fashions
from "La Mode Illustree"*
Dover Publications, p. 211

Henrietta at the Cunard pier:

Chapter 17: "The hack driver followed her into the terminal building. There were very few people inside—for who would arrive a day early? She instructed the man to place her trunks along a wall, paid him, and thanked him for his help...As soon as he left, she sank upon the larger trunk. This would be her home for the next eighteen hours."

Discussion Questions for *The Fashion Designer*

*Note: I've provided a lot of questions to use for your book groups.
Feel free to choose the ones you like the best.*

1. In chapter 4, Annie is speaking with the owner of Lane Bryant, who shares her life story. They agree that every experience has a purpose and nothing is wasted. In Annie's path from maid to clerk to pattern artist to fashion designer, could she have achieved her current status without the other experiences?

2. In chapter 5, Annie falls down the stairs and is forced to stop overworking. Yet good comes out of the fall when she has time to embrace a new direction to the business. When has a God-stop in your own life brought about a change for the better?

3. In chapter 8, Vesta is crushed when Richard says her inheritance cannot be used to help Sean and Annie's business. It makes her reassess their marriage and their faith. She sees that, "With success had come spiritual apathy, or if not complete apathy, a passivity that bordered on taking God for granted. And—dare she say it—a certain level of expectedness and entitlement, as though they deserved their many blessings." Have you experienced this feeling of entitlement? How can it be countered?

4. In chapter 10, Edna and Maude discuss finding the balance of trusting God to do everything He can, while also doing our part. Name a time in your life when you applied this truth and trusted God *and* did the work while you waited for God's full answer.

5. In chapter 10, Maude visits her estranged mother and tells her about the rape, its physical consequences, and her choice to never marry. What do you think about Maude's choice?

6. In chapter 11, Annie is worried about money, yet everyone else seems to be in good spirits. "The disparity between their confidence that everything would work out fine, and Annie's doubt that it would, became too much for her." Name a time in your life when you were worried and others were not. How did you overcome your worry?

7. In chapter 11, Henrietta arrives in New York and offers to fund the business. God has met their need. Name a time God met a need, perhaps in unexpected ways.

8. In chapter 13, Henrietta is transported into memories of her great-grandmother when she smells a familiar lavender perfume. What scent reminds you of a specific person, event, or place?

9. In chapter 14, the women discuss corsets and comment that they can't imagine ever being without them. How do you think they would respond to today's fashions?

10. In chapter 14, the ladies discuss fashion through the ages. During the Regency Era (think Jane Austen), fashion was fairly comfortable with flowing fabrics, empire waists, and no hoops. But in the coming decades, huge sleeves, crinolines, hoops, and bustles made fashion fussy and impractical. If the fashion of 1800–1820 was relaxed, why do you think it reverted back to such constriction again—for another hundred years? Think of the fashion during the entire twentieth century. What constrictions did the fashion of that century place upon women?

11. In chapter 14, Henrietta and Gert discuss love. They've both had their hearts feel "small." Do you think small love can grow in a marriage? Do you think Henrietta should have married Hank? What do you think about her decision to come to America?

12. In chapter 15, Annie feels like everyone has someone special, a confidante. She has people around her but feels isolated. Name a time you have felt isolated—even in a crowd. How did you overcome the feeling?

13. In chapter 15, Maude tells Antonio that she will take the retail space before seeing it. When have you felt sure about something before knowing the details? How did you know it was right? *Was* it right?

14. In chapter 17, after being conned by the thief, Henrietta counts her choices and finds she has few. She chooses to flee rather than face the humiliation of her actions. What situation have you experienced where you fled? Was it the right decision? Or did it eventually lead back to facing the problem head-on?

15. In chapter 17, the partners have no funds coming in and need money by the next day. All they can do is pray that God will provide. Name a time

in your life when you were in dire need, you prayed, and God provided for you.

16. In chapter 18, Sean says, "Life is a grand puzzle, with pieces interlocking, pieces elusive, pieces missing. But in the end, God puts it all together and we see the full picture." How have you found this to be true in your own life?

17. In chapter 18, Annie and Sean discuss how God answered their prayer for money to fund the shop, yet He doesn't answer everyone's prayers so happily—or quickly. Why do you think God allows suffering? And why does He often make us wait?

18. In chapter 19, things are going well and Annie says they are lucky. Sean says, "God does not deal with luck but with blessings." Do you agree with that statement?

19. In chapter 19, after Maude is rude to Antonio, her mother wants her to keep the door open to love, saying that God has a plan for her. Maude thinks her mother is naive, that her optimistic faith is a fantasy. Who is right?

20. In chapter 20, Henrietta helps Annie see that although their lives are far different than they planned them to be, they are better because they've let God lead. How has God made your plans better?

21. In chapter 23, Maude finally tells Antonio about the rape and they discuss the crises they have each suffered, and their subsequent anger. Antonio says God understands our anger and waits for us to realize He is right where we left Him. "We move away, He doesn't." Name a time you were angry at God. How did you find Him again?

22. In chapter 23, Annie gives a toast at Delmonico's where she remembers Sean saying he wants to know why he was born, why he exists now—not a hundred years from now. Why do you think you live *now?* What is your unique purpose?

23. In chapter 24 Annie thinks about her father, who always blamed someone else for his problems. He was always the victim. Do you know someone like that? How do you deal with them?

About the Author

Nancy Moser is an award-winning author of thirty novels that share a common message: we each have a unique purpose—the trick is to find out what it is. Her genres include contemporary and historical novels including *Romantic Times* Reviewers' Choice finalist, *The Pattern Artist; Love of the Summerfields; Mozart's Sister; The Invitation; Booklist's* award-winning *An Unlikely Suitor; The Sister Circle;* and the Christy Award-winning *Time Lottery*. She is a fan of anything antique—humans included. www.nancymoser.com.

Here's an excerpt from "Pin's Promise" by Nancy Moser in the novella anthology *Christmas Stitches* releasing October 2018:

Annie Wood grabbed her little brother's arm and ducked behind the pile of cut logs.

And just in time too, as their mother stepped out of their shack in the Summerfield woods. "Annie! Alfred! If yer not back here in one-two-three yer in fer it!"

Alfie giggled. "I got out."

"Yes, you did," Annie whispered.

"Ma doesn't like me out."

"No, she doesn't."

Annie sat on the ground, using the logs as a backrest. This would not end well, yet grabbing these few moments of peace kept her sane.

Alfie picked up a stray stick and slapped it against his club foot. "Bad, Alfie. Bad. Bad."

Annie took it away from him. "Stop that."

He mimicked Ma's voice. "You no-good idgit!" He looked at Annie. "I got out. Ma's goin' to wail on us."

"She'll wail on us either way. When Pa's under-it, she takes it out on us. Remember the trickle-down."

He nodded. "Trickle down, trickle down. Slap, slap. Ouch, ouch." He touched his left arm that Ma had twisted because he'd stumbled against a chair, causing it to fall and wake their father.

Nobody wanted Rufus Wood awake more than necessary, though Annie had a hard time noting *any* time that was necessary for her father to be awake. He worked little, always finding some reason to quit a job or getting let-go for pilfering or laziness. Work and Pa sat together like a bottom on a sharp rock. Yet when he did venture out in public, he always smiled and bemoaned a sickly nature, often getting people to give him a coin or two. If it weren't for the money he made selling moonshine from his still in the woods, the family would totally depend on Annie's money, earned selling eggs. Actually, she *was* the main source of income as Pa usually drank more than he sold.

The only time there was peace in the house was when he passed out. Yet that was the calm before the storm. He was an angry bear when he drank and a crazed bear when he was awakened after sleeping it off, moaning about his head hurting and wanting the rest of them to shut it and leave him alone.

Leaving Pa alone was Annie's preference. And not just a preference but the best way to avoid getting hurt.

She glanced at ten-year-old Alfie as he stacked small pieces of bark into a tower. He took up a twig like a tiny sword. "Poke, poke, poke!"

"No poking right now. We must be quiet."

Suddenly Ma appeared from behind the woodpile and smacked each one on a leg. "There you are, you dossers! Get inside or I'll sic yer father on ya." She reached for Alfie's sore arm, but Annie stepped between them and took a slap to the side of her head for her trouble.

Alfie skipped back to the house, singing a fa-la-la song Annie had taught him. She rushed after him. If he annoyed Pa...

Long ago she'd taken on the role of his protector. Somehow saving one of them from extra hurt and harm made her own pain easier to bear.

CHECK OUT MORE HISTORICAL FICTION FROM BARBOUR!

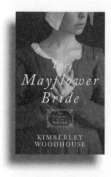

The Mayflower Bride
by Kimberley Woodhouse

Join the adventure through history, romance, and family legacy as the **Daughters of the Mayflower** series begins with *The Mayflower Bride* by Kimberley Woodhouse. Mary Elizabeth Chapman and William Lytton embark for the far shores of America on what seems to be a voyage doomed from the start. Can a religious separatist and an opportunistic spy make it in the New World?

Paperback / 978-1-68322-419-8 / $12.99

The Innkeeper's Daughter
by Michelle Griep

Officer Alexander Moore goes undercover as a gambling gentleman to expose a plot against the King—and he's a master of disguise, for Johanna Langley believes him to be quite the rogue. . .until she can no longer fight against his unrelenting charm.

Paperback / 978-1-68322-435-8 / $14.99